"Kim Law knows how to entertain you with scandals, emotion, and epic romance."

—*Jill Sanders NYT & USA Today Bestselling Author* on
Caught in the Act

"*Montana Cherries* is a heartwarming yet heart-wrenching story of the heroine's struggle to accept the truth about her mother's death —and life."

—*RT Book Reviews*, 4 stars

"A solid combination of sexy fun."

—*New York Times* bestselling author Carly Phillips on
Ex on the Beach

"*Sugar Springs* is a deeply emotional story about family ties and second chances. If you love heartwarming small towns, this is one place you'll definitely want to visit."

—*USA Today* bestselling author Hope Ramsay

"Filled with engaging characters, *Sugar Springs* is the typical everyone-knows-everyone's-business small town. Law skillfully portrays heroine Lee Ann's doubts and fears, as well as hero Cody's struggle to be a better person than he believes he can be. And Lee Ann's young nieces are a delight."

—*RT Book Reviews*, 4 stars

The Davenports Book One

CAUGHT

on

CAMERA

ALSO BY KIM LAW

The Wildes of Birch Bay

Montana Inspired

Montana Cherries

Montana Rescue

Montana Mornings

Montana Mistletoe

Montana Dreams

Montana Promises

Montana Homecoming

Montana Ever After

Sugar Springs Novels

Sugar Springs

Sweet Nothings

Sprinkles on Top

The Davenports

Caught on Camera

Caught in the Act

Caught off Guard

Turtle Island Novels

Ex on the Beach

Hot Buttered Yum Two

Turtle Island Doves (novella)

On the Rocks

Deep in the Heart

Hardheaded

Softhearted

Other novels

Marry Me, Cowboy

The Davenports Book One

CAUGHT
on
CAMERA

KIM LAW

This book is dedicated to my husband, Doug. I wouldn't want to do this without you. Thanks for the continuous love and support, and for always being my muse!

Also to my parents, Barry and Faye, the two people who believe in me the most. I love you. I hope I've made you proud.

CHAPTER ONE

$\mathcal{I}$t was a darn shame someone with that much raw sex appeal was a politician.

Vega Zaragoza readjusted the camera on her shoulder and zoomed in tight.

Yep. Disgustingly sexy.

Jackson Parker "JP" Davenport Jr., the governor's rumored choice to fill Georgia's empty senatorial seat, stood one hundred feet away, mixed among his expansive family and the elite of Atlanta, but Vega's body tingled as if he were breathing her same air.

She licked her lips.

"Hey." Fingers snapping in quick succession set her nerves on edge. The "request" for attention was directed at her.

Forcing a politeness she didn't come close to feeling, Vega lowered the camera and eyed the station reporter on assignment with her. Darrin Davis—overly slick and too in love with himself —was not her idea of a teammate. He was more a thorn in her side. And clearly, he thought of her simply as his subordinate. She was over it.

"You know my name, Darrin," she snapped. "Why don't you give it a try?"

She rolled her eyes at the perplexed look on his face. The jerk didn't even realize he spent more time referring to her as "hey" instead of by a legitimate name. He was likely equally shocked by her abrupt reply. She normally took everything he dished out, without comment, but she didn't have the patience for it today. Her job was riding on talking the man she'd just been ogling into giving her an in-depth interview, and she had no idea how to accomplish it.

She sighed. It was going to be a long weekend. "What is it?"

Confusion cleared from his eyes at the same time his usual smirk settled into place. "We're done until later, so I'm going to the hotel for a while." He jabbed a thumb over his shoulder to the ten-year-old stud mobile he'd driven to the golf course. They rarely got sent outside Savannah, but when they did, he always drove himself to location. He hated being tied to her schedule, and she hated leaving before securing enough footage to best showcase the event. The fact they'd be in Atlanta for several days hadn't changed his behavior.

"Fine," she said. "I'll see you back here this afternoon." She'd rather finish the next few days without him, but since he was the talent, she couldn't very well go it alone.

After he left, she scanned the surrounding area, taking in the scattered equipment tossed haphazardly around the bright-green grass. Each piece had been used throughout the morning as they'd interviewed both Cat and Emma Davenport, as well as a few of the muckity-mucks participating in the Davenport Foundation golf tournament.

The one interview she'd wanted—with JP Davenport himself—they'd yet to manage. Warmth bubbled in her lower belly at the thought of the man, and she didn't fight the slight smile trying to take hold. She'd drooled from afar for years, probably had what some would consider way too many nighttime fantasies featuring him, but today was her first opportunity at an in-person sighting.

And wow. Wow, wow, wow.

Magazines and newspapers didn't come close to doing him justice.

She mock-shivered at the thought of his broad, toned body and the power he exuded merely walking into the middle of a group of people, then got back to her task. The audio and video equipment wouldn't put itself away.

Reaching down for a cable, she peeked up through her lashes for one last glance but found only disappointment. While she'd been dealing with Darrin, the participants had loaded in their carts and disappeared. Dang. In all honesty, she'd wanted to capture a shot of everyone heading off to begin the first round. After all, the golf tournament was the official purpose for her being there today.

Her shoulders sagged as she straightened back to her full height, a cord dangling from her hand. And who was she kidding? She'd wanted one more glimpse of JP, too.

"Looking for someone?"

A sharp ripple shot down her spine at the words. She clenched her fingers around the cord as she fought the urge to whirl around and giggle like a giddy teenager. Because the fact was, she was pretty darn sure she knew who owned that low, vibrating rumble. And just as certain that she had to get over her infatuation of him.

Reminding herself she had a job to do, she whipped out an innocent expression and slowly turned, admonishing herself the entire time to keep her overblown fascination from becoming evident, and finally faced him.

And . . . *BAM!* Her heart stuttered as if exposed to live wire. He was even better close up.

Expensive cologne cocooned her, bringing instantly to mind a lush, deep forest with hot sun streaming through the trees, begging her to lift her face to the "sunlight" and simply drink it in.

Instead, with a polite nod and a small smile, she greeted JP. She casually glanced around until she located a waiting golf cart, two bags strapped to the back, but no one else in sight, and lifted a shoulder in a half shrug as if she couldn't care less who he was. "I was hoping to catch everyone as they drove off."

He studied her, the sunlight hitting his eyes in a way that turned them a shade identical to the aqua-colored polo stretched across his wide shoulders. "Too bad," his words were barely more than a murmur. "I was hoping you were turning your sights on me. *Again.*"

Humiliation rooted in her feet, then fired quickly up to her throat and threatened to stifle all oxygen to her brain. He had seen her watching him? Of course he had. She closed her eyes briefly, mentally kicking herself for being so obvious. But it wasn't like she'd flagged him down and waved him over, for Christ's sake. And anyway, a girl deserved to be given a break for staring the first time she saw him.

Plus, he should be used to that.

Then she realized what was going on. The man merely had to snap his fingers to get any woman he wanted, and for some reason, he'd decided to snap her way.

And *oh hell, yes*, she wanted to jump.

Instead, she ignored his words. She didn't get to take such chances, so no need pretending even for a second that the two of them and a fun afternoon was an option. Might as well use the moment to pitch her idea and see if she could turn the little white lie she'd told her boss into a reality.

"I appreciate you stopping by, Mr. Davenport," she began as if he'd come over at her request. "You're about to head out to the course so I won't keep you, but I have a work proposition I'd hoped to discuss with you later today."

A muscle twitched in his jaw. He tilted his head at an angle, roved his gaze up and down her less-than-flattering olive cargos and white pullover, then settled on her face. "I'm sure I can find time for you, Miss…?"

"Zaragoza." It was her mother's maiden name, but for the first time in eight years, she felt wrong using it. "Vega Zaragoza."

His lips quirked. "Nice."

Heat from his body seemed purer than the muggy late-summer morning and begged her to lean into him. She fought the urge. "If you could give me a few minutes at the end of the day, I'd like to discuss an opportunity with you."

It was more an opportunity for her, but she had no other way to sell it. She needed him to agree to a day-in-the-life exposé, or she didn't stand a chance of getting the promotion to the Atlanta office she was after. And, oh yeah…he'd spent his entire adult life making it clear he didn't allow the media behind his personal wall.

He looked her up and down once more. "You do know I didn't come over here to discuss work?"

Uh-huh. She knew that.

She nodded.

Then jerked, realizing what she'd done. She shook her head, hoping that negated her previous agreement, and once again pulled her shoulders back. "I—"

"JP," a man called out. "Time to head out."

She peered around him to find the governor now seated in the passenger seat of the golf cart. Governor Chandler tossed her a wave, which she returned. She and Darrin had interviewed him that morning, trying to get the goods out of him, but he'd been noncommittal on whom he planned to put into office. All he'd wanted to discuss had been the Davenport Foundation and the weekend activities surrounding the fundraiser, as well as Mrs. Emma Davenport herself. The governor was clearly Emma's fan.

Vega smiled up at JP, wondering why he seemed so large when she knew he had only a few inches on her five-ten frame. Man, he was good-looking. "Seems you have to go." Her voice came out more light and teasing than she liked. "May I have a few minutes of your time later?"

His square jaw broadened into a quick half-grin, and her heart once again went stupid. "Without a doubt."

LATER THAT AFTERNOON, JP stood at the back of the crowd, searching for the woman who'd distracted him the entire day. Every time his teammates had relied on his shot, he'd either caught sight of her—her camera aimed directly at him—or noticed her talking quietly, heads together, with one of the other male players.

And he'd promptly choked.

Clearly, he wasn't the only one captivated by her, but what he had yet to figure out was why. With the way she was dressed, she should more easily fade into the fairways than attract the interest of every man there.

Baggy clothes, bland colors, no makeup. Not to mention the hair pulled back in a ponytail so tight the only distinguishing characteristic he could make out was its long length.

But she did have that smooth, honey-colored skin. And the way she carried herself. Somewhat proud and elegant, yet at the same time as if she couldn't care less what others thought of her. Sort of like she was intentionally flashing a *stay back* sign with one hand while opening the door and beckoning people in with the other.

One thing was for certain. She must draw men to her all the time. And he was no exception.

He scrubbed a hand over his face, frustration and excitement warring inside him. Vega was the embodiment of what he didn't go for in a woman—downplaying her looks, few overt gestures for his attention—yet he'd not only been unable to ignore her presence all day, their conversation that morning had left him feeling like a foolish teen. She'd ignored every opening he'd lobbed, only to return them with an attempted discussion about work. Yet with the way she'd watched him throughout the day, there was no doubt she was the same as every other woman. It was merely her game to act as if she wasn't.

Yanking his sunglasses from where they were hooked into the front of his shirt, he shoved them over his eyes. Time for round two.

He gritted his teeth when he remembered where he was at the moment. He needed a swift kick in the head. Right now he stood in the middle of businessmen and politicians, all there for either the family foundation or to push him to enter politics, and he was thinking about the do-me shape of a near-stranger's mouth and what it could do to him. What he should be doing was talking up the cause or pretending he gave a shit about politics.

He closed his eyes and inhaled, picturing the roses along the walkway as their heady scent filled his senses. Thinking of something other than Vega would get his focus back under control.

"Tough luck out there today."

JP opened his eyes to find Evan Martens beside him, hands clasped behind his back as he scoured the area, obviously looking for someone in particular.

"Very unlike you," Martens said.

Tell me about it. JP fought the urge to punch the man in the face, instead digging around inside himself until he found the perfunctory smile a gracious loser might wear. "Can't win them all, I guess."

He couldn't stand Martens.

"You seen that camera woman around?" Martens cut his eyes to JP for a couple seconds. "Sure is a looker. I wouldn't mind getting some of that action."

And what a total tool the man was. No matter how many deep breaths JP took, words would not make their way past his windpipe. At least any words suitable of being spoken in public by someone about to become a politician.

"Of course, she could use some spicing up if you intended to use her as an accessory, but there're some *fine* raw materials there to work with." Martens trained his gaze back on JP and lifted one eyebrow.

"Come on, Martens." JP growled the words. He worried his hands would act of their own volition and strangle the man where he stood. "Women deserve better than that."

"Yeah? To their face at least, right? Least that's what I hear from the women you discard."

It was clear now he was simply trying to get a rise out of him. Like the women JP played games with—women who knew the rules and didn't object—he had some weird, ongoing match with Evan as well. The man antagonized, JP fought the urge to punch his lights out, then Martens went away until something else came up he felt the need to poke at.

What he was really after JP had yet to figure out, but he suspected it was along the lines of getting him to lose his cool in public so the governor might reconsider his choice to fill the seat left by JP's late cousin. It was no secret Martens had always wanted a political career himself. Getting the governor to slide him into the Senate would be a great start.

Setting his jaw so as not to rise to the bait, JP spoke tight and short. "The women I date know the score, so shut the hell up."

Laughter rang out beside him before the man clapped him on the back. "Always pretending to be the good guy, aren't you?"

Before he could figure out the best way to extricate himself, Martens let out a low whistle and headed off with the guttural words, "Ah, yes, come to Papa."

Husky laughter hit JP's ears, causing the hairs on the back of his neck to bristle with tension. Uncurling his fingers, he slid his gaze around behind the dark lenses until he found Vega laughing with a man who'd recently folded and sold his company to JP. The man was nothing. However, Martens was making a beeline straight for her, and like him or not, he did have a way with the ladies.

JP left his clubs where they stood and stalked along an identical path, ignoring everyone who tried to stop him, his goal one hundred percent focused on getting to the prize.

"JP, wait up." This time the voice came from his sister, and he made the mistake of glancing down at her. The pause allowing the man at her side to snag his attention.

"Great game today." Mayor Doty thumped him on the shoulder, clearly either a bald-faced liar or too uneducated to know what made a great game of golf. "I understand Governor Chandler intends to make his announcement next Saturday." He nodded as if his support in the subject mattered. "He couldn't do better than you, son. Your father would be proud."

Frustration ate at JP. He didn't want to talk politics. It had been the nonstop center of conversation for the last three weeks, practically since the moment his cousin's plane had gone down. And he certainly didn't want to discuss it with another person simply hoping to ride the Davenport coattails.

JP slipped on his politician's smile. "Thank you, sir. But I haven't yet actually been asked."

The mayor's eyes widened a fraction, then he smiled and nodded as if they were both in on a secret together. Though nothing had officially been stated, it was common knowledge the rumor of the upcoming announcement had come straight from the governor's office; the entire city had already heard about it.

"That's right." Doty pulled a straight face. "It's merely speculation at this point."

JP eyed his sister, attending dotingly to the mayor, and knew it was an act. As director of the foundation, Cat had to play to the egos of those with money, but he didn't appreciate her attempt to bring him in on the action just to relieve her own boredom.

As the mayor continued to drone on, JP studied the area around them, seeking out the dark-haired beauty he so desperately wanted to corner. She was currently heading to the lake in front of the clubhouse. Alone.

When he returned his attention to the conversation at hand, the corners of Cat's mouth twitched. Her eyes shifted to the lake and just as quickly back to him. She knew exactly what he had on his mind and had likely stopped him for the sole purpose of making him wait. The conniving little—

Then he realized he was witnessing something he hadn't in years. Cat being playful.

He'd begun to worry he wouldn't see that side of her again after her husband had been killed in Afghanistan. Seeing it now made it almost worth having to put up with Doty's ramblings.

Almost.

He peered at his sister over his Oakleys, silently informing her she would have to pay, then fought the urge to cut the mayor off midsentence. It didn't seem to matter that JP had never once expressed interest in being a congressman, senator, or even a local magistrate. He was a Davenport, and that made it simple. Davenports possessed the ambition to aim for the top. Only he didn't. Not in politics.

He lifted a hand to scratch at the back of his neck and used the movement as an excuse to glance, once again, toward the lake. Dark eyes were focused in his direction.

She looked down the instant he locked on to her.

He smiled. It was time to head to the lake.

Taking pity on him, Cat finally turned the mayor's attention to someone else, allowing JP the chance to escape, and he headed straight for nirvana.

As he approached Vega, now with her back to him, she was in

the middle of stretching out her neck. She twisted her head from side to side, her eyelashes resting against her velvety cheeks, while her thick hair swished back and forth with her movements. Loose curls teased but never lingered against the smooth skin of her neck.

He studied her, understanding that she pulled at him in a way he didn't get, but he had no problem going with it for the moment. The fact was, he didn't know if he could do anything *but* go with it. He took one final, silent step forward, all the while fighting a very basic, primal urge. The one that made him want to dip forward and taste her right then and there.

CHAPTER TWO

"*C*an I help you out with that?"

Vega froze, the deep rumble coming from directly behind her. He was back.

Her mind quickly replayed their earlier conversation, reminding her he had his own agenda, and she couldn't help wondering if he was there to hear her proposition, or suggest one of his own.

Resisting the compulsion to smooth her hair and wipe away the day's grime, she pulled a deep breath in through her nose and forced herself to focus on the job, not a potential romp between the sheets. Plus, he was a politician. Fake. Always out for himself.

And she would not relive past mistakes.

When she had herself under control, she faced him.

And just like the first time, she was literally weakened by the power emanating from the man.

Life lessons be damned, she was a sucker for powerful men.

He stood close enough this time that the hairs on her arms reached out for him, and against her will, she swayed in his direction. Catching herself before harm was done, she took a quick step back and shot him a questioning look. What had he asked? "Help with what?"

He motioned to her neck. "Looked like you had a tight neck. Thought you might need some help."

Her eyes rounded. *Oh Lord, no.* She did not need him touching her on the neck or anywhere else. No matter how much she might want him to.

She managed a small smile. "No. Thanks."

He gave a single nod. "You let me know if you change your mind." He wiggled his fingers in the air between them, his eyebrows bopping up and down at the same time. "I've been told I can do wonders with my fingers."

Surprised laughter burst from her at the over-the-top flirting, the sexual tension easing but not disappearing. She shook her head in disbelief. "You're quite the flirt, aren't you?"

"I do my best." His lips curved into a smile. Not the half-smile or even the slight twitch of one side of his mouth she'd seen earlier that morning. This one lifted his cheeks, showcasing his dimples and strong jaw, and showing off his perfect teeth. Oh geez, she even thought his teeth were awesome.

She had to get over this fascination.

As her laughter died down, they ended up standing there grinning at each other like goons until she made herself look away. She glanced around, wondering if there was a way to get out of this conversation, to regroup before pitching her idea, and as she concentrated on looking at anything but him, she was mortified to discover that more than a handful of people were turned toward them, openly staring.

If she wasn't careful, she'd find herself gossip fodder purely for having a private conversation with the man. And that simply wouldn't do. She'd spent as much time gracing the covers of tabloids as she ever intended to.

She moistened her dry lips. It would be best to get Darrin and do their wrap-up interview, then head back to the hotel for the night. She'd find another time to discuss her ideas with JP. She eyed the white news van Darrin had been holed up in since returning from the hotel, but there was no sign of him.

With a nod tossed in the direction of the van, she asked, "We'd like a quick interview if you have a few minutes? I'll run get Darrin."

"Wait." Before she could slip past, JP stopped her. He didn't grab her, just pressed long fingers to her bare forearm. Fireworks popped to life and shot up to her hairline. "Tell me what you wanted to talk to me about first," he said.

Ah, crud. She couldn't put it off.

"Okay." She cleared her throat and dredged her practiced speech up from her memory. No time like the present. "Mr. Davenport, with the upcoming announcement and your move into politics, I'd like to propose an in-depth, day-in-the-life interview."

No screamed instantly from his body language, but she plunged ahead, pretending she actually stood a chance.

"A piece where I would spend several days following you, showing your home life, your interaction with your family, where you live, what you do in your downtime."

He removed his sunglasses, and cold eyes glared back at her. "What kind of underwear I wear and what I eat for breakfast?"

Shock paused her at his words, but then a slight grin crept over her face. "That hadn't been my plan, but with your popularity among the females, I would expose that too, if you were willing."

"I'm not." His jaw tensed.

She swallowed past a lump in her throat and went back to her speech, focusing on a small freckle at the side of his neck instead of taking on the full power of him. "I'm not looking for anything earth-shattering, simply to give the country more reasons to love you before ever stepping foot into office. I also want to assure you that a seasoned professional would be doing the on-camera interview instead of me. My part would involve getting the footage and building the piece. Everything up to the face-to-face."

The same thing she hoped to do with the new job.

JP rocked back on his heels, his lips pursing as if in deep thought. "Why would building an entire piece on me be of interest to anyone?"

He had to be kidding! She began ticking the points off on her fingers. "You're a Davenport. For that alone, the world wants to get to know you better. They want to believe you'll one day have the fairy tale your parents shared. Two, to know what makes you tick. They want to live vicariously through you, to see who you really are, and to sit on the edge of their seats as the day comes when you fall in love and settle down to make baby Davenports of your own. And three, they need to see the historic values of the Davenport clan embedded deep in you, and to know those standards will be carried forward. They need to believe."

She smiled into his eyes, trying for a bravery she didn't exactly feel, and wrapped up her speech. "I want the world to see the man you really are, not just the pieces you allow to be seen. I want to give them a reason, other than your looks and charm, to hang their hats on you in the years to come."

His face had blanked as she'd talked, leaving her with absolutely no idea what he was thinking. Finally, he leaned in close, his warm breath touching her ear a millisecond before his words. "And what makes you think I'm all that, Vega? What make you think I believe in love?"

Her name sounded good coming from his lips. She blinked. "You may live up the playboy life, but..." She paused, not sure what to say that would come out believable.

"But?"

She silently prayed she came across as sincere. "But...people are usually more than their outer shell. With your background and upbringing, I suspect you are, too."

"And that means I would naturally believe in love?"

"Doesn't everybody...deep down?"

He shifted, giving her room once again to breathe, but the way he studied her made her fingers twitch. She had no idea what he saw when he looked at her.

"Maybe I go home every night and do nothing but down a pint of whiskey."

Her gaze raced over his torso, refusing to believe he did anything less than take care of his body day in and day out. "I somehow doubt that," she mumbled.

"Then maybe I intend to sleep with a different woman every day for the rest of my life." His eyes glowed as he let them take the same path over her body that she'd just taken over his. When finished, he curved the edges of his mouth. "Would that endear me to you, Vega? Can I put you on my list?"

She held her ground, fully aware he was taunting her, but she refused to back down. She needed this story. She needed the change. Maybe she could no longer go after her original dreams, but she could chase new ones. "We're discussing an interview, Mr. Davenport, not our separate sleeping arrangements."

He studied her again, clearly more interested in dissecting her than in taking her idea seriously. "In case you've never figured it out, I don't want the world in my business."

"I've suspected as much, Mr. Davenport, but—"

"My name is JP."

"Of course." She nodded. "My apologies."

He stared at her as if waiting for something else. "Say it." The deep voice dropped even lower.

"Say...it?" She shook her head, not sure she knew what he was asking.

He gave a slow nod, his gaze locking with hers. "My name," he spoke softly. "I want to make sure you've got it."

In an instant, the air stilled and closed in on them, holding them prisoner together in a tiny space built for one. Her heart thumped against her ribs. "JP."

The blue in his eyes deepened, saturating with color, and it took every ounce of strength she had not to fall captive to them.

She cleared her throat and restarted, determination she hadn't been sure she still owned pushing her forward. "The last thing I need you to know—and what should convince you to agree—is that I'm not like most journalists. I would never do anything purely for ratings, and I absolutely refuse to twist facts simply to sensationalize a story. In essence, I'm the exact person you'd want to do a feature piece on you."

The fact was, if she were the hard-nosed reporter she'd once imagined herself growing into, then yes. Any ugliness she could find, she'd want to dig out and share. But those dreams had ended years ago when she'd been yanked from her climb to stardom before ever being able to convince anyone she was more than a pretty face. Or more than the next glamorous woman to appear scantily clad on the cover of a magazine.

Thank goodness she'd spent those early years in so much makeup she could now get away with living her life unknown, and relatively as she wanted.

JP stared down at her, and she crossed her arms over her chest to mimic his stance. Failure was not an option. Setting her jaw, she edged her chin up and prepared to go down fighting.

"How about if…" She paused. She had nothing left to even toss out.

One side of his mouth twitched as he watched her struggle to come up with a tactic that would work. He looked as if she were merely his entertainment of the moment.

"How about the fact it would be in your best interest? After all, the governor *is* planning to name you as the state's next senator. Good publicity would only help override anyone's objections."

"Who says I'm accepting?"

That stopped her. Was he serious? No way would he not accept the seat and follow in his father's footsteps. Right? Not only his late father, but he had cousins, uncles, and even an aunt or two who were or had been involved in the politics of this country over the last hundred years. Heck, he even had an uncle who'd been president.

She blinked up at him. "You are joking, right?"

The dark slash of his eyebrow lifting was his only response.

Wow. She didn't know what to believe. "Then maybe you'll allow me to create a story about your reign as Atlanta's Businessman of the Year, and why you *won't* be accepting the senatorial seat?"

"Nothing is decided yet, so I wouldn't know what kind of story I wanted." He paused. "If I wanted a story."

A sigh slipped out to stick in the muggy afternoon. "Okay, fine. I'm begging. This is clearly important to me, so tell me what I can possibly do to allow me into your life for a few days. Whatever it is, whatever you want, I'll do it."

"Now that, Ms. Zaragoza, is one heck of a proposition." Heat and mischief swirled in his eyes. "I can honestly say that I would love to have you in my life for a few days."

His deep voice washed over her, instantly lighting trails of fire throughout her body. She wasn't naive enough to miss his meaning. But she also wasn't naive enough to not know what a bad idea sleeping with him would be.

"I'm quite serious, *Mr. Davenport.*" She waggled a finger back and forth at him, praying she could hold up the bravado a few minutes longer. "But I won't be prostituted out. Anything else, though, name your price."

"Okay, then, here's what I want to know." Somehow, he pulled out an even more impressive look of superiority. "What is it exactly, using me like this, would do for *you*?"

"*Use* is a harsh word."

"Then how would you define it? Because you have to admit," he went on with an apologetic shrug, "I'm a Davenport. There isn't a lot of gain in it for me."

Annoyance turned her away from him, pushing her a few steps toward the lake. Her nerves were stretched thin. Facing him, she knew she had to lay it all on the line.

"Here it is," she began. "I need a new job. My station is downsizing, and though my position is safe for the moment, it's boring. Our Atlanta affiliate has a position open that would offer more chances for travel, more excitement, and it would take away the concern over losing my job in Savannah. If I can get enough footage of you for an hour-long special, the job should be mine."

Something seemed to have piqued his interest. "And why is it *your* job, in particular, that's in danger? Are you not any good?"

She straightened. "I'm very good. In fact, the station's chief photographer would be more than happy to back that up by discussing some of the many times I've saved their butts over the years."

"Then why *your* job?"

Normally, she appreciated a straight shooter. Today she wished the man would back off and let her keep a few secrets. "It's simple. On the smaller budget the station will have, they'll need every photographer in the field also willing to be on camera."

This lifted both his brows. "And you don't wish to be on camera."

It wasn't a question, so she gave no reply.

"Can I ask why?"

Pain from the past almost overwhelmed her. She was not made for the camera. Not anymore. She had to keep reminding herself of that. With what remaining strength she could muster, she uttered, "I don't want to be in front of the camera. That's why I need this job. They'll accept me as I am."

He didn't respond as he once again studied her as if able to see something no one else could. She silently prayed all he saw was a plain, makeup-free camerawoman standing before him—and not the former up-and-coming model who'd been splashed across magazines worldwide. It was amazing how much different she'd looked in full makeup, but that never kept her from squirming anytime someone looked too close.

"Vega!" The shout came from the other side of the clubhouse, and they both glanced in that direction, releasing her from the tension engulfing them. Darrin had finally emerged. She let out the breath she'd been holding.

"Interview time." She paused until JP once again looked her direction. "You will allow us a few minutes of your time, won't you? To go along with the golf tournament?"

"Of course."

"And the other..." She begged with her eyes. "Please consider it."

A shadow passed briefly over his face before he said, "How about dinner instead?"

"Dinner?" The change of subject threw her at first, but then she wondered if maybe she hadn't completely lost out on her chance. "To talk about me shadowing you?"

It probably wasn't obvious to anyone watching, but JP leaned his body farther into her space. "Surely you can tell how attracted I am to you, Vega. And unless I'm completely mistaken, the feeling is mutual."

Her body instantaneously blazed, her center burning the hottest. She licked her lips. "I'm not interested in getting involved with you."

"Neither am I."

"Then—" Ah. He was talking about a night only, maybe two. The touch of his thumb on the inside of her wrist weakened her knees, but she managed to keep from sinking to the ground. He chuckled, his thumb moving back and forth over her erratic pulse.

"Have dinner with me tomorrow night if I promise to reconsider?" The low voice set her body on tremble.

"You would seriously reconsider?" It might turn out to be a wasted effort, but how could she walk away without at least trying?

"Absolutely." He pulled back and peered at her. "But no guarantees."

Oh, how she wanted to go out with him, and it had nothing to do with an interview. "I'm not sleeping with you for a story," she whispered in a hurried breath. Darrin was nearly to them.

JP said nothing, merely watched her. His eyes, though...they were deep and penetrating, and she saw something she wasn't sure she'd ever thought possible from a man like him. He seemed to want her to agree to dinner as much as she wanted him to allow the interview.

She glanced away to catch Darrin stop and give the mayor a good-ol'-boy pat on the back before she brought herself back to reality. Being seen having dinner with JP Davenport was out of the question.

With regret for more reasons than she wanted to acknowledge, she murmured the words that would effectively end both her career dreams and her inappropriate fantasies. "I'm sorry, but I won't be seen out on a date with you."

"Ouch." JP took a step back and rubbed a hand across the center of his chest, humor filling his eyes. "Am I that unattractive?"

"Hardly." The muttered word brightened the glow in his features. She crossed her arms over her chest and smirked at the ego trip her admission had given him. "I won't allow unsubstantiated rumors to be spread about me, and being seen with you would, without doubt, result in rumors."

He nodded his head in concession, then produced a low hum that came from his throat. "We could make them fact?"

Vega narrowed her eyes, and he threw back his head and

laughed out loud. Once the laughter ceased, his posture relaxed, and for the first time since they'd begun their conversation, Vega felt as if it was the real JP standing in front of her instead of the playboy the world knew.

"Then how about at my place?"

"Your place?" she squeaked. She shook her head. "I don't think so."

He grew serious in thought. "My sister's house, then? She has a lovely, *private* home, and I'm sure she wouldn't mind having us over for dinner."

Cat's house? Vega pictured the woman they'd interviewed early that morning. She'd been every bit as nice and down-to-earth as JP was a flirt. Guilt poked at her for even considering intruding on the woman without being properly invited, but she was having a very hard time turning down this opportunity.

"You don't think she'd mind?"

"Not a chance." His tone wasn't entirely convincing, but she ignored the fact.

With a chaperone, there'd be no risk of tossing her inhibitions out the window and doing what every woman who came within the man's circle of space wanted to do.

JP studied her, his features suddenly as frozen as a stone sculpture, and she found herself wondering if he actually wanted her to say yes or no. But for one more chance to talk the country's golden boy into his first personal interview? She had to try. She nodded.

"Thank you for the opportunity." She felt as if she was walking straight into the devil's den. "I would love to accept dinner with you and your sister."

CHAPTER THREE

*J*P lifted his mobile phone and stared at the small screen as if he could conjure up a call from the woman who'd been on his mind for the last twenty-four hours.

"Mr. Davenport?" The intercom on his desk broke into his thoughts.

He pushed a button. "Yes, Beverly?"

Beverly Brubaker—his staunchest supporter and long-time family assistant—refused to call him by his given name. Though she'd seen him at his worst as a kid, from the moment she'd stepped foot in his office seven years earlier, she'd addressed him as nothing but "Mister."

"I spoke with the Montessori school. They wanted confirmation you're okay with the change of schedule for next week." Beverly was also the only person outside immediate family who knew his secret. At least his oldest secret. "I assured them there was no problem, then moved your one o'clock back to ten in case it ran long."

"Thanks, Bev. You're the greatest." JP straightened from the intercom and flattened his back to the Italian leather of his chair. The Montessori school was a huge reason he had no interest in politics. Along with the fact that he preferred the thrill of high-dollar real estate developments, he hated to stop his work with the school. Accepting the senatorial seat would not only take time away from that but would also offer his entire life up for inspection. As it stood today, though the media was aware he visited the school on occasion, they had no idea his reasons for stepping foot in the halls of the century-old building. He intended to keep it that way.

With an audible grunt, he pushed from the chair and crossed to the floor-to-ceiling windows.

Peering out over the bustle of Atlanta, he considered the other secret that reporters would salivate over. The one he wouldn't act upon until he had all the facts. Only then would he make a move, bringing Beverly into this new part of his life as well. It would be required in order to protect his family. He shook his head. The woman deserved more money than he paid her.

He took in the sight before him, skyscrapers filling his view. Office buildings, condos, hotels, all with their glass windows gleaming in the midday sun, clustered proudly around the city. His chest expanded at the image. Not only did he own the forty-story building his office and penthouse were housed in, but several others dotted throughout the skyline as well.

The glass-and-steel scene was even more magnificent after dark. He groaned, remembering the previous night's darkness, and braced one hand against the warm glass. The vista in front of him had barely registered in the wee hours of the morning. Instead, it had been Vega. Her lithe body and curvy hips, eyes tilted up just the tiniest fraction at the corners, and dark hair, down and flowing around her bare shoulders. She'd filled both his fantasies and his dreams.

This morning she'd also haunted his shower, and now here she was, smack-dab in the middle of his business day, too. He had to get her out of his head. Lifting the hand still clutching his phone, he searched his contacts for the number she'd shared. As he tapped to bring up a blank text message, he chastised himself for his actions—though he didn't stop them. He was behaving like an uncontrolled teen drooling over the first girl to give him the time of day.

7:00, right? You got directions from Cat?

He hit Send and stared at the device as he waited. Texting a woman simply because he couldn't wait to see her—to get his hands on her—was not normal operating procedure. He preferred to have more control over his urges. He scowled in disgust, the frown disappearing the instant three little dots appeared on his screen.

His phone vibrated to signal her return message.

Yes, thank you. I'll be on time. Thanks again for the opportunity to discuss.

All business? That's the way she thought she could play this?

Irritation flared, making the custom-tailored jacket suddenly seem tight. She was coming over knowing full well he would have her in his bed before the night was over. All business wouldn't cut it. He thumbed out a quick reply.

Wear a skirt.

The thought of Vega's long legs, bare in a short skirt, stoked heat through his body. He slipped a finger in the edge of his Armani shirt and ran it around the collar. He still had no intention of allowing her into his personal life with a damn video camera, but he'd been unable to walk away without making sure he saw her again. The fact that he'd promised to reconsider when he had no real intention of doing so sat heavy in his gut, but he consoled himself with the knowledge that she was as aware as he the reason for the invite.

How he'd get his hands on her at Cat's dining room table, especially with Cat's two children present, he had no idea. But he was excellent at thinking on his feet.

His phone and intercom both buzzed at the same time. Glancing down at the phone, he moved to the desk. "Yes?"

"Mr. Davenport, Lexi Dougard is here, insisting on seeing you." Beverly's clipped tone was unmistakable. She didn't care for the woman.

Neither did he.

He, at least, knew why.

Lexi Dougard was a roadblock that needed to be taken care of. Only, she was either a very good con artist, or she held the card capable of ruining both his political career and his family's name. Not to mention what it would do to his mother.

He glanced down at the waiting text message and temporarily pushed thoughts of Lexi and his mother to the side. Right now, he had an exciting, beautiful woman on the other end of a text.

```
Will it help me win the interview?
```

He loosened his tie.

```
Couldn't hurt.
```

"Mr. Davenport?"

JP jerked back to the intercom. He hadn't answered Beverly. "Give me a couple minutes then show her in."

He pulled his jacket off and settled into his chair, the hand holding his phone poised in front of him as he waited. His breath released the instant the device buzzed.

```
I'll wear one if you'll answer a question
of mine.

Ask.

Why did you text me? You know I got direc-
tions. You were standing right there.
```

His gut seized. Vega was calling him out. Refusing to let him pretend he wasn't desperate to see her. Brazen.
He liked it.

```
Because I haven't stopped thinking about
you for a second. Make it a short skirt.
```

The door to the office opened, and he centered the device flat on the desk as the stylishly dressed, barely twenty-five-year-old woman entered his office. Beverly backed out of the room without a word, and Lexi began to prattle on as if being a part of his life were a longtime occurrence. She ended her monologue by explaining how she had no intention of tipping the valet at the front door because he'd been so rude to her.

"Honestly, JP. You really should look into hiring more personable servants."

JP's shoulders tightened. He never referred to any of his employees as servants, whether here at the office or in his personal life. He motioned to a chair in front of his desk, but she headed for the sitting area instead, her cloying perfume swirling in her wake. He merely rose and followed, gritting his teeth over the thought that this woman had held money for all of seven years now—his *father's* money—yet she acted like one of the snooty women he'd spent most of his life around.

His way of dealing with those women was to either sleep with them or outright avoid them—sometimes even good sex couldn't overlook certain personality traits. This time, however, he had no desire for the first, but also couldn't do the second.

She made herself at home, sinking into the dark-brown leather of the couch as if she intended to stay a while. He didn't sit.

"What can I do for you, Lexi?" His cell phone buzzed across the room, but his texting games would have to wait.

"The test results."

"I haven't received them yet. I made it clear I'd contact you when they arrived."

"No, silly." She dug into what he recognized as a multi-hundred-dollar bag at her side and came out with a large envelope, the flap on one end folded back. "I have them."

He didn't outwardly react. "I gave explicit instructions for the lab to send the results to me."

She shrugged, her fake-tanned shoulder wiggling under her sleeveless top. "And I told them that I wanted a copy, too. I picked them up about thirty minutes ago." She waved the envelope in the air between them, a predatory gleam on her face. She had what she wanted, and they both knew it.

Truth be told, he'd known it the instant he'd seen the picture of her son two weeks ago. Blue eyes, dark hair, the boy looked just like him.

The kid really was his brother.

He returned to his desk and pressed the intercom, wanting his own copy of the results in case she really was that good a con artist. "Beverly, has anything been couriered over from the lab I mentioned last week?"

"Not that I've seen," she replied. "Should I call them?"

"Please." He paused, knowing the time had come to bring

Beverly in on everything. "I'm waiting on test results. Get them faxed over, then bring them right in."

"Yes, sir."

The room grew quiet until Lexi broke the silence, her voice trying, but not quite as confident as it had been a few minutes earlier. "You'll give me money now, right? I don't have to go to your mother?"

Damn woman. His back teeth ground together. She'd shown up two days after rumors had broken that the governor planned to announce him to fill his cousin's senatorial seat and had demanded money from the second she'd stepped foot into his office. If he didn't pay, she'd explain to his mother how his father had slept with a seventeen-year-old while on the campaign trail. He couldn't let his mother lose the respect she'd always held for her husband, no matter what kind of mess the man had left for JP to clean up.

But he wasn't simply playing Lexi's game, either.

"Let me get this straight, first." He turned back to her, remaining behind his desk. "When you told my father about the pregnancy, you didn't want your child thrust into the spotlight of our family?"

"Right."

"And this is still your wish? You don't want it known he's a Davenport?"

"Yes." She nodded. "He doesn't need that kind of attention. He deserves to grow up normally."

"Right." He nodded, not quite believing her story, but understanding the sentiment. "You just want enough money to raise him as if he *were* a Davenport. To *put him through the best schools*, you said."

Cold eyes stared back at him, but she didn't reply. He wondered if she knew where he was headed with this line of questioning.

"Yet my father already paid you over a million dollars, not the quarter million you previously claimed."

At her look of protest, he held up his hand. "Save it." His voice was flat and hard. "I know it as fact because I had you investigated. Around the time you would have gotten pregnant, two large deposits hit your account. One for a quarter million. A couple weeks later for another million. What I can't figure out is why that wasn't enough to put your son through school. The kid is only seven. We're talking elementary school, not an Ivy League private college."

She stuck her probably touched-up nose in the air. "It's expensive raising Jackson's son."

JP eyed her, hating even more than usual that he carried his father's name. "I'd say it's expensive raising you."

"How dare you," she blustered, coming up off the couch.

"How dare I?" His hands clenched at his sides as he fought the anger coursing through him, but he was unwilling to lose control for this leech. "I dare because you've shown up here, now wanting *my* money. And I'll tell you, Ms. Dougard, I won't spend my life being blackmailed for something my father did. He may have had no problem paying you off, but unfortunately for you, he died before you could come back for more."

Beverly entered before Lexi could form a response. The look on her face said it all. The kid was a Davenport.

He took the paper and gave her a tight smile. "Thanks, Bev. When Ms. Dougard and I are finished, I'll need some time with you, please."

With the thought of working out a way to pay for the boy's education through a company-sponsored scholarship, he'd need his assistant's help to make it happen. Setting it up through the business would be less traceable back to him in the event a nosy journalist was to get insight into his finances.

"Certainly, Mr. Davenport," Beverly muttered.

Realizing the disappointed look in her eyes said that she assumed the kid was his, he gave a quick shake of his head and murmured, "Dad's. Not mine."

A sigh and a nod came from Beverly. "I'll be at my desk if you need anything more, sir."

The room once again fell silent as the door clicked softly behind her. He stood straight, head bent, and confirmed the results. His father—who'd been part of a supposed fairy-tale marriage—had cheated on his wife with a seventeen-year-old volunteer and hadn't been careful enough to keep from getting the girl pregnant. White-hot rage started at the soles of his feet and moved upward, gaining speed as it traveled his body until he wanted to dig up the man's remains and shake him as if he hadn't been dead and buried for the last six years. He needed to pay for the pain his wife would feel if JP didn't successfully keep this from her.

His mother may have her own faults, but she'd loved her husband with everything she'd had. So much so that she'd as much as turned her back on her own sons when they'd needed her the most, all for a man who wasn't worth it in the end. She'd stood by him, supporting everything he'd done until the day he'd died. To find out now it had all been a lie would crush her.

No matter how frustrated JP often was with her himself, he could not let that happen.

Yet mixed in with the anger coursing through him was guilt. He lived his life as honestly and cleanly as he could, and he didn't care to ever carry around guilt. This kid was his brother. Shouldn't he do better than to write him off as easily as his father had?

He locked his gaze on Lexi, at the now-apprehensive look in her own eyes. She no longer stood as straight and determined as before, suddenly looking as uncertain as he felt. Were they doing the right thing for the kid?

As he continued to study her, he watched her eyes flit back and forth, seemingly battling with something on her mind, before finally hardening her features. "So? What are you willing to do? I'll need enough to get him through private school and then college. I want only the best for my son."

"No." JP shook his head, but there was no fire in the movement. "The investigation showed you've blown through most of the money he gave you, so I'd classify you as not financially mature enough to handle a similar lump sum. I'll make arrangements to cover the best health insurance and school every year, but that's all. You've already purchased a house, and you have no mortgage or bills other than utilities. As long as you get yourself a job, there's enough remaining in your account that you'll be fine. Let Beverly know what school to send the check to, and the money will be wired directly."

"You can't do that."

He shot the woman a look that said he was done with her, then picked up the mobile phone from his desk. He had a beautiful woman with the most amazing brown eyes waiting on him. "I assure you I can, Ms. Dougard. I'll take care of your son through college, but I won't ever give you a dime. You've swindled enough out of my family. And if you insist on going to my mother…" He paused, silently praying she didn't choose that option. "I guarantee you nothing about the child will be kept secret any longer. He'll be thrust into the limelight, no different than the rest of us. Like a Davenport really lives his life."

Looking down, he dismissed the woman and punched the button to display the text message.

```
The only short skirt I brought requires my
five-inch stilettos. Think you can you
handle that?
```

All the blood left his brain.

A vision of Vega flashed through his mind in that instant. But it wasn't so much her long, slim body he focused on. Instead, it was that brief moment when she'd been explaining how she wasn't made for the camera. Up until then, though she'd clearly been fighting her attraction to him, her entire being had exuded confidence and determination. But in that instant, her eyes had flickered along with her voice, and everything about her had become vulnerable.

He didn't know the story but would bet all the money he was about to pay for his father's kid that there was something there. A history that still haunted her.

He scratched the back of his neck as his mind churned through the possibilities. Maybe she'd had a shot in front of the camera before and blew it? Or maybe something had happened in her teen years? Teen scars were often painful to overcome.

He smirked at the irony. Scars when you were six were equally hard to overcome.

He studied the last message, as if by doing so he could see the answers.

Whatever it was, he couldn't imagine it would have the potential to affect his public reputation if they were seen together. Chances were slim, but with the announcement just around the corner, he had to think of such things. He wondered if there was even a minute chance he should call a halt to the full-fledged pursuit he was about to open on her?

And then he almost laughed at the thought. She was the first woman who hadn't dropped at his feet just because he'd looked her way. No way was he not chasing after that.

The sound of someone clearing their throat got his attention, and he looked up to find Lexi standing in front of his desk.

He sighed. "What is it, Ms. Dougard? Shouldn't you be gone already?"

She nervously wound the fingers of one hand through the strap of her bag. "I…uh…"

"What?" he snapped, all patience gone.

"I need extra money, Mr. Davenport."

"Well, you won't get it."

"You don't understand. It's for my son."

"Of course it is." He crossed the room to the door, this time to personally escort her out.

"It is," she pleaded. "He needs tutors."

JP opened the door and glanced into the reception area. "Ms. Brubaker, please see that Ms. Dougard finds her way out of the building."

"Certainly." Beverly jumped to her feet and came to Lexi, putting a firm hand around her elbow, but Lexi twisted from her grasp and backed away from both of them with a panic-stricken look.

"Please," she begged. "Please help me. I don't know where else to go, and I don't know how to do this myself. He needs help. Tutors. They say he even needs hours of specialized exercises every day just to be close to normal."

JP froze, his hand still outstretched on the doorknob.

Lexi continued, frenzied now. She shook her head from side to side, backing away until the windows stopped her. She stood there, the impressive skyline at her back, tears streaming down her cheeks. "I can't do this by myself. And I can't be there like he needs if I have to get a job to support us both. Please. I don't know what else to do."

With precise movements, JP pushed the door closed, its click flashing a twenty-four-year-old memory. They'd just moved into their house in DC, and his mother had been explaining that his grandmother was moving in and would now spend the afternoons with him instead of her. *Plus,* she'd said, *your grandmother will work with you on special exercises to help make school more fun.* Then his mother had closed the door on the way out. On her way to go be with his father.

He and Beverly exchanged looks as if both knew exactly what the problem was. Beverly hadn't been there that first day, but she'd soon been brought on to the family payroll as his mother's assistant. Given that his mother had gotten regular reports on his progress, Beverly had quickly become aware how severe his dyslexia had been.

They both turned to Lexi now, still plastered against the window, hugging herself. JP was the one to speak. "What's he been diagnosed with?"

Tears—he was pretty sure honest ones—continued to leak from the corners of her eyes. "They said dyslexia. Severe dyslexia." She shook her head. "I don't know if I can do this."

He nodded then but fought the urge to cross the room and wrap the woman in his arms. Though she was still his worst nightmare, she was also human and appeared scared to death. "I understand you're scared, but you can do this." He paused before continuing. "You *can* do this, Lexi. And I'll help."

He wanted to say he would personally help the child since he knew exactly what he would be going through for years to come, but doing so would absolutely cast the boy and the situation into the public eye.

And end the political career his mother so wanted him to have.

"I know a school that's great with learning disabilities," he said. "We'll get him in there, and I'll find the best tutors."

Lexi sniffled and nodded, suddenly looking more like the teenager his father would have been swept away with instead of the overconfident woman who'd first walked into the room. "Thank you. And I'll get a job, I promise. I'm not really as heartless as you think. I just messed up. I'd never had money before, and I just spent too much. I'll get a job and pay my own way. I just need help with Daniel. Please. I want him to get the best help he can."

So did he, though he'd never met the kid in his life. "We'll work it out. You worry about Daniel right now. But I do need one promise from you."

She nodded, chewing on her lower lip. "What's that?"

"When you do get that job, get one so you can be home with your son after school. He's going to need you there."

CHAPTER FOUR

"This is it, miss." The rideshare driver shifted the car into neutral and turned to smile at Vega, one arm thrown across the back of the seat. His smile was innocent but a little too wide as he took in Vega's legs. Why she'd allowed herself to be goaded into wearing this skirt and heels was beyond her. It wasn't like anything she'd worn in years. This outfit hugged her body in the way material was made to do, the rich silk reminding her she was soft and feminine.

She'd bought it last year when visiting her mother in Mexico. The wild blues and greens were as enticing as the water surrounding a hot Pacific island.

She tapped the app on her phone to complete the tip and stepped from the car.

"I'll be in the area," Patrick, the driver, tossed out. "If you need a ride back, maybe I'll catch the request."

"Sure," she mumbled. "Thanks." She *would* need a ride back, but hopefully only after she'd secured the interview. That's why she had on this outfit, she kept telling herself. It was also the excuse she'd given when she'd caught herself boldly text-flirting with JP earlier in the day.

Wear a skirt.

The three simple words had jolted her. In an exciting way. The man wasn't afraid to ask for what he wanted; that was for sure.

And she'd decided her chances of securing the interview would be enhanced if she went along and wore a skirt. She'd show him he wasn't the only one who could play games.

Though he wouldn't get what he was really after, her heart pounded at the thought of sleeping with him. Huh...*sleep*. She shook her head, unable to imagine getting naked with the man and ever calming down enough to fall asleep. She didn't make a habit of avoiding men, but as a rule, she tended to date the more ordinary ones. Those who blended into the crowd. To have someone the caliber of JP desiring her was quite a turn-on. One, she reminded herself, she had to ignore. She smoothed her hands down the front of her skirt and shook her head as if the action would clear the JP-induced fog that had taken up residence since the day before.

Drawing in a deep breath, she let it out slowly and peered up at the massive structure in front of her. Heavy wood-and-glass doors graced the entry sitting atop the wide, semicircular steps. Two-story columns bordered the doors, antique brass lights centered in each. And floor-length windows enhanced the dark-red brick façade of the mansion. It quietly announced dignity and elegance.

Finally coaxing her legs to move, she put one foot in front of the other, her years-old python-skin Alexander McQueens crunching softly across the stone driveway. They'd had to stop at the gate to get buzzed in, so she was confident someone waited near the front door to usher her inside. She ascended the steps, the slim skirt climbing her thighs, and prayed she didn't embarrass Cat with her less than professional attire.

Before she reached for the doorbell, the heavy door swung open.

"Vega." Cat greeted her warmly and pulled her into a quick hug, catching Vega off guard. "I'm so glad you came."

"Really?" Vega didn't have time to get her arms around Cat before she was released. Cat had been friendly enough the day before as they'd interviewed her at the golf tournament, then again earlier today when she and Darrin had covered the charity women's luncheon Cat and her mother had hosted, but Vega hadn't been able to decipher if the warmth had been real or merely part of her role as director. She'd had no clue what to expect showing up tonight. The genuine smile had Vega relaxing and looking forward to the evening. "I was worried this was too much to ask. It's quite an imposition."

"No, no." Cat ushered her in. "I'm thrilled to do it. And oh my goodness, you look awesome. JP is such a hardnose. It's about time someone got to him."

"Thank you," Vega said, pleased with the compliment but unsure about the JP comment. "But I wouldn't say I've *gotten* to him." She stepped farther inside the house and took in the opulent, yet comfortable atmosphere. A gleaming marble floor lined the foyer, with pedestals running along each wall. But instead of priceless art, each held a different child's art project. She glanced back at Cat and smiled. "JP simply promised to discuss the possibility of an interview project."

Cat snorted in an unladylike but totally casual manner. "And *that's* why you have legs a mile long tonight. Purely a business dinner."

Vega couldn't hide her embarrassment. She wasn't fooling anyone. "Of course," she muttered. She should probably apologize for the unbusinesslike clothing, but the fact was, Cat didn't seem to mind.

"Come on." Cat motioned behind her before turning to lead the way. But before she took a single step, she glanced back. Then she slowly tilted her head to look all the way up at Vega. "Good grief, you're as tall as my brother tonight. This might be a new experience for him."

Vega gave a self-conscious grin, her shoulders hunching slightly. "These are the only heels I had with me that could… uh…*compete* with this skirt."

"And that skirt definitely needs an extraordinary pair of heels." Cat lowered her eyes to the shoes, then let out a low, impressive whistle. "And I'd say you found them. You've got excellent taste. I might have to beg your help for a shopping trip while you're in town. I've been less than enthused about my style for the last while, and lately I've been feeling that something special might be just what I need to pull me back to the land of the living."

She was referring to the well-known fact she hadn't had an easy go of it since her husband's unexpected death three years earlier in what had been labeled a "friendly fire incident." Joseph Carlton had been a highly decorated sergeant major in the Army, and though he hadn't been born a Davenport, it had been widely speculated he would follow in his in-laws' footsteps once he retired from the military.

"Of course," Vega murmured. "Maybe we can make that happen."

Certain the suggestion of shopping was merely a conversational topic, Vega gave the expected pleasantries, but was shocked at the pang that rattled around inside her over the thought it would never happen. Even if Cat truly meant the words and sought her out, being seen in public with Cat would be almost as risky as being with JP. And of course, it wouldn't only be Vega who got hurt. She couldn't do that to this woman.

"Now," Cat began. "It's time to take you to the man you came to see." She raised her eyebrows suggestively, and Vega couldn't stop the heat rising to her cheeks.

"Really, it's a business din—"

"Sweetie," Cat said, somehow managing to look down her nose at her even though she was a good five inches shorter than Vega—without heels. "I saw the way you were checking out my brother yesterday. Not that I blame you or are bothered by it. You seem nice. I hope you rock his world. But don't be pretending you aren't at least thinking a bit of the same thing I'm suggesting." She winked. "Now straighten your shoulders, and let's go make an impression."

Vega smiled a real smile for the first time that night, accepting the friendliness being handed out, and Cat shook her head and mumbled, "The man has no idea what he's in for."

She led them through a set of open double doors into an informal family room where Vega made out muted murmuring coming from around the corner of a wide, thick couch. One of the voices was a low, deep rumble, the others clearly coming from children.

Nerves settled in Vega's feet, keeping either of them from taking another step.

Cat nudged her forward. "Come on. I want to introduce you to my kids before the three of us head out."

"What?" Vega whispered, her breath growing shallow. "You're leaving? I assumed you were eating with us. I thought…"

Her words died as she came into view of JP and caught sight of him playing with Cat's two small children. The girl was beautiful. If Vega remembered correctly, she was six.

"She looks just like you." Realizing that didn't express the full compliment, Vega glanced at Cat, taking in her blonde hair and the Davenport-blue eyes that both kids also owned. "She's beautiful."

"Thank you," Cat murmured.

But it was the boy to whom Vega's attention was pulled. He was younger, maybe four. However, the media had never mentioned he had a disability. It hadn't been obvious the few times he'd been on camera, but the jerky movements of his right arm implied a neurological disorder of some sort. Slight, but undeniable. The way JP played with him was the most tender thing Vega had ever seen.

The big, bold, take-charge man sat cross-legged on the floor, his suit jacket tossed on a nearby chair, with the boy sitting on his lap. They both gripped the same helicopter and "flew" it in the air, JP explaining the intricacies of the vehicle in a softly modulated voice. All the while, the girl seated behind him combed his dark hair, securing twisted clumps with tiny pink clips and rattling nonstop about a television show Vega knew was a current favorite among little girls.

She had the urge to back out of the room and leave the house. This was not the man she expected JP to be. He was a politician, for crying out loud. Not yet, maybe, but there was no doubt in her mind he would accept the position and soon start a long-lived, successful—if you called any political path that—career. Politicians did not sit on the floor and play with their niece and nephew so candidly unless there was a photographer in sight.

And then it hit her. She was a photographer.

Had he expected her to show up with a video camera, or was he simply planting seeds of ideas for the interview?

"JP," Cat spoke softly. His wide gaze swiveled to hers, a grin in place from ear to ear at the same time Cat said, "Your guest is here."

The grin disappeared, and his eyes widened as he sought out Vega's gaze. He made contact, seemingly embarrassed at first for being caught letting his niece treat him like one of her dolls, but then shrugged good-naturedly. He pulled both kids close and planted a kiss on their chubby cheeks. "Uncle JP has to go now."

Both kids complained, but it wasn't real. It seemed to be part of a game they played. When they collapsed into his lap, he snaked a hand over each of them and tickled their bellies, sending them into fits of giggles before tenderly rubbing their blond heads. They finally settled on either side of him while JP removed the clips and threaded his hands through his thick, dark hair, bringing it into submission with ease. He rose to his full height, and Vega's heart rate increased. His presence filled the room.

After scooping up the discarded jacket, he shrugged into it, all while eyeing Vega from across the room. His gaze took in every inch of her bare legs, then traveled up over her tight skirt and matching bright-blue shirt, pausing at the deep V, where the tiniest hint of cleavage peeked out. Her toes curled in her python-skin shoes when his gaze swept back down and landed on her feet. They were both aware of what the heels did for her legs.

He moved toward her, and she couldn't help returning the appraisal, admiring the way the tailored, pin-striped suit framed his body. She was here for dinner, she reminded herself, not to have him for dinner. Or be the main course herself. His gaze implied he had a hard time remembering as well. He stepped to her side, and the same woodsy scent she'd noticed before pulled at her, attempting to lure her closer.

"Impressive," he murmured for her ears only.

"Wow," Cat's youngest said, his innocent voice the epitome of youth. "You're bigger den Uncle P."

Vega laughed softly and took in her height against JP's. She did have a couple inches on him. "Yes, but only for tonight. See." She briefly slipped out of one heel and placed her foot flat on the smooth wood floor, bringing her back down to a more respectable height. "It's just the shoes."

The little girl was in awe, her eyes brightening as she gazed at the brooch on the vamp of each shoe, but the boy suddenly seemed less impressed.

Without warning, the girl made a beeline for the crystals winking from Vega's feet, her hands outstretched as if desperate to reach the jewels as quickly as possible. "Pretty."

"Becca!" Cat's reprimand came an instant too late. Although

most of Becca froze with her mother's command, one finger gently traced the outer curve of the hardware on one shoe. Her face slowly turned toward her mother, but she didn't relinquish her touch on the bauble.

"I don't mind, Cat." Vega shook her head slightly, her voice soft, almost laughing. "Really. I always appreciate meeting a young lady with exceptional taste in shoes."

"Exceptional taste or not," Cat muttered, "those are darn expensive, and Becca's fingers spend more time these days in dirt than soap and water."

Vega laughed with ease. "Then you should feel better knowing this pair is several years old."

They were the last she'd purchased on her modeling income. Wearing nothing but sensible clothing and shoes for the last few years, Vega should have gotten rid of these along with the remainder of her collection a long time ago. But as a shoe enthusiast from the instant a modeling job had stuck her in designer heels, she'd been unable to separate herself from the footwear even though she'd refused to wear them anywhere but the comfort of her own home.

A masculine chuckle in her ear pulled her attention back to JP, and his blue eyes almost made her forget the subject at hand. He nodded toward her feet, and she looked down to see Becca now sitting on the floor, the girl's own sandals discarded nearby.

"Can I try?"

"Becca!"

Cat and her daughter both spoke at the same time, Cat clearly mortified that Becca didn't yet have the grace not to ask a total stranger if she could try on her shoes.

"Do you know how to walk in heels, Becca?" Vega would have squatted to the child's level if not for fear her skirt would rip up the back. Instead, she rested her hands on her thighs and bent her knees a fraction as she peered down at the girl.

Becca nodded, her blonde curls dancing around her face. "I wear Mommy's all the time."

Vega glanced at Cat and saw she'd given up on being humiliated by her daughter's behavior. She shrugged. "Since she learned to walk."

"That long, huh?" Vega continued to Becca. "Then I guess you do know how to walk in heels."

Becca nodded and scrambled back to her feet. "I'm a good walker. I promise not to hurt them. Tyler can't walk in them, though. He falls down." She crinkled her nose and looked at her brother, still sitting on the floor and flying the helicopter, as if his status as a male made him worthless as a sibling.

Vega slipped a foot from one shoe, and JP's hand connected with her elbow, his fingers strong and hot through the sheer fabric of her sleeve. After she reminded herself to breathe, she slid off the other shoe and noticed her eyes were now level with the angled ridge in the middle of JP's throat. His fingers remained wrapped around her elbow.

"Look at me, Mommy!" The girlish squeal squeezed Vega's heart. She'd once been that innocent and free, that certain that happiness was a given.

Becca marched back and forth, her tiny feet crammed into the toes of the shoes so that she barely wobbled. The heels clomped behind her with each step, and Vega felt an ache in her chest. She was approaching thirty and had yet to find anyone she trusted enough to consider settling down with, much less settling down to have a child with.

Tyler inched closer as if realizing he was no longer in the middle of the action.

"You can't do it, silly." Becca flapped her hand at her brother as she clomped toward Vega. "Boys don't know how to walk in heels." Hot heels apparently brought out the big-sister attitude in the girl.

"Tell Vega thank you." Cat scooped up her son and waited for her daughter to comply. Once she had, Cat smiled warmly at Vega. "I appreciate the attention. As you can see, she does love girly shoes."

JP held tight as Vega once again slipped into her heels, then finally, almost reluctantly, his fingers trailed down the back of her arm before disappearing. The fire from that soft touch roared through her body and filled her ears to the point she barely made out Cat's words as she said her goodbyes and headed to the front of the house.

JP disappeared with them, the temporary silence giving Vega a chance to pull in a deep breath. She inhaled until her lungs burned, then let it out. Rubbing her hand up and down the arm where he'd touched her, she looked around the massive room with the high ceilings and authoritative elegance, and nerves hit her, pooling in her belly. She was in the home of one of the Davenports. With Jackson Parker Davenport Jr. himself.

Dinner.

Get the interview.

Nothing else.

"I love the skirt." JP stood in the middle of the open French doors, his admiration clear in his heated look. "I think I even like you being taller than me."

Vega played it off, giving him a slight curtsy and dipping her eyelids. "As you wished."

He growled, low and dangerous. "You are a tease, Vega Zaragoza. But I do like it." He motioned down the hall. "Our dinner awaits. Shall we?"

She crossed the room, suddenly unsure how to walk in the spikes as he devoured her every move. When she passed in front of him, he touched a hand to the small of her back, and fire licked from his heated fingers into her body, toasting all sorts of hidden places.

"What was it you wished to talk about again?" he asked, his voice as coarse as gravel.

"You know full well what I'm here to talk about."

"Honey, at the moment, all I know is how bad I want those legs wrapped around me." His fingers drifted lower, but he remained a gentleman.

She stopped in the threshold of the dining room and took in the scene. The ambience was far too intimate. Two place settings angled together on one corner of the twelve-person table. Gleaming china trimmed in gold, flickering candlelight, and elegant crystal all beckoned.

Seduction.

And she had seen this particular play before.

She wiggled her fingers together in a nervous gesture, unable to control the action, and reminded herself that this time was different. This time she was older, not as naive, and no one was hiding anything. They both knew exactly why the other was here.

She wanted the interview.

He wanted her naked.

Gulping, she moved forward and wondered which one would get their wish.

CHAPTER FIVE

"*I*t was a rotten thing to lure me here then send your sister out for the evening." As JP held out her chair, Vega's voice was soft and low, almost intimate, and not at all as she'd intended.

"Wish I could take the credit."

She looked over her shoulder to see if he was lying and found light-blue eyes burning steadily back at her. The look indicated he was telling the truth. It was Cat's doing.

But he hadn't tried to convince her otherwise.

"The hair is amazing." His fingers feathered across her bare neck as she lowered to her seat. "I'd love to see it down sometime."

She fidgeted at his touch, quickly recovering by reaching for her water glass. He kept touching her, each caress traveling way beyond the barrier of her skin, and it was quickly driving her mad. She shouldn't be here. She had no business playing this game.

"Thanks," she murmured, lifting her hand and patting the intricate twist that was far less severe than her normal ponytail. "I prefer it up."

The fact was, she *had* to wear it up. Her hair—along with her legs—had been her calling card in her modeling days, and though it had been years since she'd been on the cover of any magazine, she still felt vulnerable at the thought of being seen with her hair loose. She'd only recently taken it back to its natural color.

JP disappeared through a swinging door without additional comment and promptly returned with two plates and a decanter of salad dressing. A bottle of wine had been tucked under one arm, and a corkscrew dangled from his fingers.

With a flourish, he presented the salad. "Mustard vinaigrette okay?"

"Absolutely," she practically purred as she took in the first course of the meal. The presentation was so professionally done, he'd either bought outside food, or more likely brought in a chef to prepare it for them. She tossed a quick glance at the kitchen door, wondering if there was someone currently stashed away in there.

JP drizzled the dressing over their salads and poured them each wine before settling into his chair. He held his glass up for a toast.

"To the beginning." *Clink.*

She paused, her glass still pressed to his. "Of what?"

"Whatever this is." The twinkle in his eyes tied her stomach into a pretzel.

After a sip that exploded on her tongue and, alone, almost had her promising to do whatever he wanted, she murmured, "*This* is a discussion about you allowing me to shadow you."

"This," JP began, reaching for his fork and spearing a mix of crisp colors, "is whatever we make it."

And at that moment, she honestly had no idea what she wanted to make it. The chemistry between them was like nothing she'd ever been a part of. Why couldn't she throw caution to the wind? It wasn't as if she'd ever have such an opportunity again. And they could keep a single night discreet.

She dug into her salad, but her nerves insisted food was not the best idea. After two bites, she reached for her wine.

She *couldn't* sleep with him.

Right?

She cast her eyes to the side to find JP's fire-blue gaze lingering on her mouth. Her stomach wrapped around her knees. If she did sleep with him, where would she go from there? Because, no doubt, someone who exuded that much testosterone would put anyone else to shame.

With effort, she decided to remind them both why she was there. She reached for the bag she'd carried in with her and slipped a folded piece of paper from an inner pocket. "I spent time this morning outlining my vision and how I see the interview being laid out."

She slid the sheet onto the glossy table, but he ignored it, jabbing his fork through the outer skin of a ripe tomato instead.

"I thought getting your feedback would be a good place to start," she tried again.

Silence.

After chewing as if making sure to attain the digestively recommended twenty-one chews per bite, JP balanced his fork on the edge of his plate and topped off her glass of wine. "Let's get to know each other first. Put business off until after dinner."

When she opened her mouth to protest, he cut her off.

"If I'm going to give real consideration to this idea..." His lips flattened briefly as if the thought were utterly distasteful. "I need to know more about you first." He turned the full power of his gaze to her. "I need to be able to trust you."

Trust?

Sure.

She doubted that was his true intention, but she didn't see any other way to go at the moment. She nodded. Fine. If he wanted to talk, they'd talk. But it wasn't just going to be about her.

She started the questions, turning the conversation on him. No sense not taking the opportunity to shed some light on kernels of information. After all, understanding the man better would help her produce the best program possible.

He backed off the flirting, and they began to talk, then he soon brought out the next course. The New York steak crusted in a pepper rub and red wine sauce placed a stranglehold on her remaining nerves, making them momentarily lose out to the incredible taste of the succulent meat.

"This is fantastic," she murmured, more to herself than to JP, but she didn't miss the predatory gleam in his eye. The pride of a man who knew he was winning over his prey.

She definitely had to find out the name of the chef and visit his restaurant on occasion. Surely a few infrequent visits to the occasional five-star wouldn't break the bank. She closed her eyes as she chewed, savoring every hint of flavor while also recalling how easy it was to become used to such delights. If she wasn't careful, she'd redevelop her expensive tastes.

It wasn't as if she couldn't dip into the savings left from her previous income, but she'd always held back, worrying she'd someday need the money for items far more important than good food and better shoes.

Dinner passed, and she found herself shocked at the ease with which they carried on a conversation. He'd spoken about everything from his first memory to some of his more recent business deals and why he'd made them. She'd shared moments of when she'd been a kid, as well as snippets about her mother and father, all without mentioning either that her father had been killed in the line of duty or that she'd had to go into modeling to support her mother.

Their conversation had been far more than the chitchat and innuendos she'd originally expected, and though she wouldn't use anything he'd said without his permission, her respect for him had grown leaps and bounds. It couldn't be easy growing up a Davenport, especially when choosing your own path instead of following immediately in the family tradition.

"You said you were only six when your family moved to DC? That must have been exciting." She waited as JP refilled her wine-glass. He emptied the bottle into his, but barely enough for a few sips poured out. She held hers up in silent question. Did he want some of hers?

JP's lips tilted, his eyes hooded. "You drink it. It seems to be doing wonders for your nerves. And to answer your question, yes, we moved there for school years, then went back to Atlanta during the summers. But no, I wouldn't exactly call it exciting."

"No?" He was right. The wine had done wonders for her nerves, though relaxation hadn't been exactly complete. She glanced at the remaining food on her plate, then at his empty one. "Do you want the rest of my steak? I don't think I can eat any more."

"You didn't like it?" His voice was low, pulling her toward him as if tugged by an invisible wire, and the atmosphere seemed to change. The moment became softer. Warmer.

She found herself helpless to retreat.

His Adam's apple bobbed. During dinner, he'd removed his jacket and tie and opened the top button of his shirt, and she now found herself eyeing the spot just above that open V. She had the strongest urge to put her tongue right there.

"It was delicious," she said, her words so low they could barely be heard. She tilted her head, watching his throat rise and fall with every swallow. "In fact, I can imagine only a couple things I'd like better."

―――――――

VEGA'S WORDS had an instant reaction below his belt. Had she meant them as the come-on they'd sounded? Any other woman and he'd have no doubt. But this one had confused him since the moment he'd met her.

One minute he thought she was playing the normal man-woman games, wanting the exact thing he did. The next, she slid an annoying sheet of paper across the table with enough notes on it that even he had to acknowledge she was here to get the interview—even if she might also be open to sleeping with him.

He watched her gaze clear, then dart to his in horror as she realized how wanton her words had sounded.

Yep, that's what he thought. She might be thinking she wanted in his bed every bit as much as he wanted her there, but she wasn't ready to go down without a fight.

"I...uh...I'm sorry," she finally mumbled. "I meant..."

He couldn't take his eyes off her, humored by the way she tried to find some explanation for the slip.

With jerky movements, she shoved the paper closer to him. "If you'll just take a look at my notes, you'll see how I've done exactly as promised." Her tongue peeked out to touch her lips before continuing. "And...um...will ensure those who aren't in love with you already *will* be by the end of the hour."

She took a deep breath that didn't seem to settle her down at all, then jumped right back into her spiel, her words coming out so fast they practically tripped over each other. "I'd like to capture you in your everyday activities. At the office, playing golf or whatever you do in your downtime, possibly a business meeting, charity work..."

He didn't want to talk about an interview that wasn't going to happen.

"Don't worry, Vega," he spoke softly, and her relieved gaze rose to meet his as if understanding he meant not to worry about how she'd come across a moment earlier. He wouldn't hold it against her.

But as quickly as his words had soothed her, her obvious relief shot ire into his gut. What was so wrong with the thought of them coming together and having a good time, anyway? It wasn't as if there was anything wrong with him. He narrowed his eyes on her, deciding he preferred her as off-kilter as he felt. "I know you didn't mean to sound like you wanted to go straight to the nearest bed. We can have dessert first."

Fire heated her dark eyes, and though he knew he was being an arrogant jerk, he couldn't stop himself. "But we probably shouldn't use one of Cat's bedrooms. That would be uncouth."

A gasp filled the air and Vega's mouth dropped open, and he instantly chastised himself. He was better than that.

"I apologize," he muttered, looking away to stare at the artwork on the other side of the table. "That was uncalled for."

His attraction to this woman was screwing with his head, making him act like a spoiled rich *kid* instead of the successful, upstanding adult he'd worked so hard to become. "Please..." He motioned in her general direction, uncertain what to say other than, "Continue."

After ten seconds of silence, her words once again started up, rattling about the damn interview as if he hadn't just insulted her. He kept his gaze trained on the painting, careful not to clench his jaw, but from where he was sitting, an in-depth interview now would be the worst possible thing for his fucking "budding" political career.

There was the knowledge of Lexi and her kid to worry about. Plus, though he'd been around politics his whole life, he knew precious little about the day-to-day business of it—and cared even less. Not to mention that he just liked having a small piece of his private life his own.

Damn, he was so tired of this. Tired of knowing he had to give up his life to live that of a "true" Davenport. Tired of worrying about the fact that if he didn't play his cards right, the family name, which had been built on morals and "doing the right thing," was about to go down in flames. And just damn tired of being a Davenport.

He simply wanted to be himself for once.

Do what he wanted, see who he wanted, and freaking have someone interested in him just because they liked him and not because of who he was or what he could do for them.

But that wasn't the life he'd been born into.

As Vega continued talking, doing her best to avoid looking at him, he returned his gaze and studied her. He compared her look tonight to yesterday. Something didn't add up. Today her clothes weren't baggy in the least. In that way, she was showing off her beauty, but the thing he found the oddest was that she still wore no makeup.

Not that she needed it. Her long lashes and smooth skin were things of beauty as they were. But most women would play up all their features.

And then there was her hair. He couldn't figure that one out either. When he'd mentioned it earlier, she had pointed out that she preferred it up, but he wasn't so certain that was the truth. It felt more like she wore it up as some sort of shield. But from what? And what would he have to do to get her to take it down for him?

He shifted his gaze to her lips and got lost in the subtle movements as she spoke. Most women, if they had that mouth, would do everything possible to call even more attention to it, thereby having every man within a thirty-mile radius drooling at her side. Exactly as he was doing now.

With a groan, he shifted in his seat and readjusted himself. Her mouth drove him out of his mind. It was probably a good thing she *didn't* paint it red and fuel his fantasies even more. If that were possible.

His fingers curled around the stem of his wineglass until he wised up and pushed the glass away. No need snapping it in two and looking even more an idiot than he'd already painted himself tonight.

It had started the moment she'd walked into the house. Initially embarrassed with her seeing him let his niece make his hair *pretty*, as Becca would say, embarrassment had taken a back seat when he'd seen the glow in her eyes. She'd been impressed, and he'd wanted to stand up and thump his chest.

Instead, he'd stood and gaped.

He mentally hung his head like a dog who'd been reprimanded. It was time to do the right thing and quit fantasizing over this intriguing woman whom he apparently couldn't have. No matter how much he wanted her, he couldn't let her sleep with him thinking that would win her the interview.

Working hard to focus, her words reentered the conscious part of his brain.

"...and then there's your family. I know you all are close, so I'd like to get something with just you and your mother as well as all of you. Casual and laid-back."

His mother was rarely casual and laid-back. Every conversation centered on politics, which she brought up with an intensity he hadn't seen in her since his father's first days running for president. Too bad the man had let cancer take him instead of hanging around to clean up his own mess.

"I also thought I could capture you with Cat and the kids. Maybe as you were when I came in tonight?"

"Leave Becca and Tyler out of it," he bit out, unintentionally sharp, but the mention of his niece and nephew had him suddenly questioning if he should have been so free with the family stories he'd shared tonight. She was a journalist, after all. Though she was normally behind the camera, she clearly went after stories, or they wouldn't be there tonight.

Dammit. He'd run his mouth off all night as if he hadn't even known that fact.

Her silence tugged at his conscience. He hadn't meant to come across as a brute, but backtracking now wasn't something he was willing to do either. Instead, he stared at her, daring her to do anything but acknowledge his directive.

After a pause, she glanced down at her hands, now folded demurely in her lap, then back up at him. She nodded. "Okay. I just thought…"

Her words trailed off as she looked toward the living room and gnawed her bottom lip.

"Thought what?" He gentled his words, but the tone was still clear. *Don't mess with my family.*

"Well," she began, but stopped to clear her throat. She faced him once again, her eyes no longer holding the determination she'd worn since starting her little speech. The tip of her tongue poking slightly through her parted teeth got his body's attention.

Lifting one eyebrow, he remained silent, waiting for her to explain.

"It's just…when I came in, the picture you made with Becca and Tyler was exactly the type of thing people love to see. I thought maybe you'd…" She shrugged and dipped her eyes. As if finding her resolve in the depths of her uneaten steak, she straightened in her chair and boldly locked her gaze on his. "I thought maybe you'd staged that scene to subtly suggest a potential one for the interview."

He studied her face, turned on anew at the resolve currently etched in her features. She'd just insulted him, yet she stood by her words. Flat-out wrong words, but he liked that she had the guts to say them to his face. He allowed a real smile to form, wishing for the first time in years he could have the freedom to get to know a woman. "You think that's the kind of person I am? Entertaining two small children for the sole purpose of publicity?"

A brief lift of her shoulders. "Most people would do similarly if presented the opportunity."

"Most people?" He leaned back, putting a gap between him and the table, and wondered what had happened in her past to give her so little respect for people in general. He wanted to peel back the layers to find those answers himself. "Including you?"

"No." She spoke quickly, vehemently. She shook her head and swallowed a large gulp of her wine. He'd had the idea to open another bottle of the imported Cabernet Sauvignon when he'd seen how much she enjoyed it, but he hadn't wanted her getting more than a little tipsy. "I'm a what-you-see-is-what-you-get kind of girl. If I want something from you, I'll come right out and ask for it."

Stubborn pride gleamed from the depths of her gorgeous eyes, showing him more about her than he'd managed to figure out until this moment. He leaned across the table, closing the gap to a narrow breadth, and was rewarded with a small hitch in her breathing. "That's something you're proud of, isn't it, Vega?"

"Absolutely," she answered, almost hesitantly. "For instance, as you pointed out yesterday," her words came out breathy as if his nearness made her nervous. Or excited. "I may be currently looking to *use* you, as you say, but only in the sense to be beneficial to both of us. I'm not trying to hide what I'm doing—when you asked, I told you—but I'm also honestly looking to help you in return. That concept goes beyond most people's imaginations."

"And you think that includes me?"

"Well..." Her lashes flickered. "Given who you and your family are...yes."

If he were a less confident man, her bluntness would put a dent in his ego. And what a paradox she was. The bluntness went totally against the hesitant, almost shy woman her downward glances sometimes indicated.

"Do you have such little respect for my family?" he asked, not questioning her impression in thinking he might have been raised the way she'd implied, but rather, trying to understand how she'd come to that conclusion

"That's not it at all. I have great respect. But I also suspect you know how to work people for your benefit. You wouldn't be so successful today if not."

She made an excellent point.

"I think you have a bad habit of making assumptions, Vega." He reached over and trailed the tip of a finger along her jaw, enjoying the feel of fresh, clean skin with no makeup between him and her. "You might want to consider working on that little flaw of yours. It could lead you astray."

Her chin lifted, and her eyes blanked. "Or it could be exactly the right path."

Interesting. It was almost as if something else was trying to make its way into their conversation, but he couldn't quite put his finger on what that might be. "Confident in that assertion?"

"It hasn't failed me yet."

"No?" He settled back in his seat, unsure why he was pushing this line of questioning, yet unable to back away. "Never?"

Something zipped through her gaze, but she maintained her bravado. "Never."

That brief flash struck him as hollowness, the kind caused from pain, and he went with his gut. "Not even with whatever happened in your past?"

She jerked back, clearly shocked by his abrupt change in topic, and her momentary loss of control confirmed it for him. Something definitely haunted her. Something painful, and if he had to guess, something that involved a man.

Feeling suddenly guilty for poking at her past, and not sure he wanted to know the details anyway, he changed the subject before she found the courage to answer.

He lowered his voice, hoping she would shift closer to hear. "Then how about this one? I believe I made it perfectly clear yesterday what I'm after. I don't recall hiding behind the fact that I find you very attractive." He picked up her glass and drained it. "Did you somehow miss that?"

The smooth skin of her throat rolled with a gulp, but she attacked the change of subject with fervor. "You also said you'd reconsider my idea. Are you telling me that was a ruse? That you never intended to hear me out?"

He studied her mouth as she talked. "I heard you out. That's what you've been so diligently doing instead of simply enjoying the excellent meal before you." He slipped his hand over hers, startled at the spark that spiked up his arm, but managed not to show his surprise. "But I'm sorry to say—" He stopped, held one finger up.

"What?" She flipped her hand over, their palms touching, and he couldn't keep from caressing his thumb into the dip of her hand.

He shrugged. "You almost caught me, there. Total honesty, right?"

She nodded. "Always."

"Then, I'm *not* sorry to say, you won't be following me around with a camera anytime soon, sweetheart. My unequivocal answer is no."

Her lids lowered, and air slid from between parted lips. He called upon all the control he'd learned over the years not to close the distance between them and press his mouth to hers right then and there.

"Let me ask you, then." She pierced him with a narrowed gaze. "Did you really give it serious consideration?" The lady did not give up easily. "You see, I think we're about to prove my point after all. You brought me over here, promising reconsideration."

He stilled. She did have him there, but his nature refused to let him back down. "The better question is, did *you* really expect me to?"

The truth flashed through her eyes, along with embarrassment. She glanced away, seeming to realize for the first time that her hand was under his, and yanked it away to smooth over the very lovely skirt she'd worn just for him.

"I had hoped you would, of course," she spoke softly.

His smile arched farther up his face. "But you didn't really think I would, did you?"

She wanted to lie. He would bet both his Atlanta and New York penthouses on it. She wanted to lie more than anything she'd ever done. But would Ms. What-you-see-is-what-you-get do it? And when she did, should he call her out on the fact that she was no different than anyone else?

Pink suddenly colored her high cheekbones. She crossed her arms over her chest and met him head-on. "No. Honestly, I did *not* think you would seriously consider it. I had hoped, had wished, even, but when it came right down to it, you're a Davenport, a *politician*," she practically sneered the last word. "So, no, I didn't really believe I would be given a fair chance."

The slur against his family name should have made him furious. Any other time and with any other person it would have. But instead, as she sat trembling with rage, he was able to see past the insult to catch something else she probably didn't mean to share. Hurt.

Pain and agony screamed back at him from every inch of her. From her too-wide gaze, her rigid jaw, to the overly taut tension running through her from head to toe. Whoever had hurt her in the past had done a real number on her.

He didn't want to know.

Opening his mouth, he tried to find the right words to end the evening and call off the games he'd apparently been the only one playing, but instead found that he couldn't do it. He couldn't casually shove her out the door when she was hurting so badly. He had to help.

Reaching one hand out, he had no real idea what he intended to do, but he stopped at her upraised hand, her flat palm facing him.

"Whatever you're thinking, just stop. I know your type. Just because I didn't think you had enough integrity to truly give me a fair chance doesn't mean I came over here to have sex with you, either. So get that absurd notion out of your head. *I...*" She jabbed a finger to her chest as her words continued to steamroll out of her. "*I* came over hoping to somehow change your mind no matter what I thought of you."

She tossed down her napkin and rose from her seat. "Now I believe you mentioned something about chocolate? Stupid as it is, after tasting the other food, I'm not about to leave this house before I at least get whatever amazing concoction is hidden behind that door."

Suddenly as cool as she'd just been riled, she tilted her nose with a dignity that kept him quiet and in his seat, and stated, "Don't get up. I'll get it."

CHAPTER SIX

*A*fter escaping to the kitchen, Vega braced her hands on the counter and sucked in deep gulps of air. Her entire body shook with the anger coursing through her as she replayed the last few minutes through her mind.

Of course JP hadn't planned to hear her out. She'd known that as surely as she'd known she had zero business thinking she could play his game. Text-flirt, short skirt...who the heck had she been kidding? She'd never been good at games and clearly still wasn't. That was, after all, why she was behind the camera instead of in front of it.

With an audible groan, she flipped around and slumped against the counter, realizing she was far too tall to even appropriately slump. She yanked off both shoes and with a guttural growl, had an arm raised to throw one across the room before she remembered what she had in her hands.

Her absolute favorite pair of Alexander McQueens.

How stupid would it be to not only chuck them across the room, but to do so because of another human being.

Fire bathed her anew at the mere thought. Disgust battled to overpower the anger. She knew better than to trust. She absolutely knew better.

Yet Mr. Charm-and-Smarm in there had somehow gotten under her skin at the golf course, and though he'd never actually encouraged her to trust him, she'd very much wanted to. She'd wanted him to be different. But what she didn't understand was why.

Gritting her teeth, she shook her shoes at the closed door separating her from the despicable man, and realized there was yet another emotion whirling around inside of her. Disappointment.

Lowering her hands, she gently tossed the shoes to the rug stationed in front of the sink. Then she faced facts.

That achy spot widening behind her ribs was disappointment in the man who had invited her here for the sole purpose of sleeping with her. She had really thought he might be more than the playboy the rest of the world knew him to be. More than the sleazy, slimy politician she knew all of them were.

She had wanted him to actually...what? See the real her? Care for her?

Stupid!

She yanked open the refrigerator to find two of the most awesome-looking dessert cups she'd ever seen. And yes, they were chocolate. At least something good would come of this evening. With barely a thought to the fact that if she was going to eat the dessert the man provided, she should at least take his out to him, she shoved the plastic covering from the top of one, rummaged around in a couple drawers until she found a spoon, then dug in.

Oh, and did she find heaven.

Man. She closed her eyes and savored the taste of the creamy mousse. Digging a little deeper, she found a rich, chocolate cake. The quality of the ingredients was definitely as superior as the rest of the meal.

Four quick bites later, she calmed down enough to open her eyes and face the real issue she'd been doing her best to ignore.

She dipped the spoon in, swiped the deliciousness off with her tongue, and bobbed the curved end toward the door as if warding JP off. In the span of a few short sentences, he had unearthed the past hurt she'd lived through when she'd first found out Ted was happily married and had been lying to her from the start.

More chocolate.

Three bites later, the spoon clinked against the empty crystal. With a huff, she shoved aside a bowl on the counter and replaced it with the now empty dessert flute while once again replaying those minutes through her mind. JP had looked at her for an instant as if he'd understood.

But what had he understood?

Her pain, most likely. She nodded. That was all he'd seen. She'd let her guard down, and he'd seen the hurt cross her face as she'd remembered.

Turning away, she snatched open the refrigerator and decided to totally blow her calories for the week. If a person didn't live once in a while, what was the damn point?

With no guilt whatsoever, she dug into JP's dessert.

As she licked each spot of lusciousness off the heavy spoon, she finally noticed the general dishevelment of the kitchen. A chef would have cleaned up before leaving.

At least a good chef. She slid another bite between her lips and silently noted that whoever had prepared the meal was definitely good.

Scanning the entire area, she took in a dirty broiler pan on top of the stainless-steel range, a top-quality skillet and another pot pushed to the side, and an apron tossed haphazardly in the corner behind a butcher block of knives. She stepped closer to the stove and lifted a lid to peek inside. The remains of the potatoes they'd eaten. Peering back at the door, she studied it as if she could see through the solid wood. Had Cat cooked all this for them before leaving?

Because surely it hadn't been JP.

Not that she didn't think men cooked, but men like JP? The last thing he would ever need to do was cook his own meals. He could afford anything he wanted, and probably never bat an eye at the cost. Plus, he'd brought her here for sex, not to impress her with a fancy dinner.

At the thought of sex, she remembered how much his simply looking at her turned her on. She dropped her head back and stared at the ceiling. Despicable or not, the man was hot, and her body didn't seem to care about his character. She needed to get out of there now, before she calmed down completely, lest she find herself once again vulnerable to his charms. Because like him or not, it had been a long darn time, and her body was well aware it could have one heck of a night if she would just turn her mind off.

Her phone and purse were at the table. She couldn't simply waltz back in and order a rideshare without having to talk to the man. But if a car were already here, she could breeze through, grab her stuff, and go.

Slipping another bite between her lips, she searched the room until she spied a landline phone tucked onto the corner of a desk. Padding across the floor, she enjoyed the cool slate against her bare skin, then snatched up the receiver. She tried 411, hoping it still worked for providing information, and located a cab company. With a car now on the way and the guard at the gate made aware to expect them, she turned back to the room and surveyed the area. She had to spend the time waiting somehow. Because she wasn't about to go back into that dining room until she absolutely had to.

Just like she clearly wasn't getting out of Savannah anytime soon.

She'd go home, her figurative tail tucked between her legs, and explain to her boss how she'd stretched the truth just a tad. She'd assured him the interview was as good as in the bag. Bob had always been her biggest supporter, so no doubt he'd forgive her and hopefully do whatever he could to save her job. She simply wished it hadn't all ended like this. She'd really wanted the chance.

Facing the mound of dishes before her, she gave a quick nod. Chores focused her, and she needed to pull herself back together. Plus, there was no need leaving such a mess for Cat.

Setting the partially eaten dessert beside the sink, she turned on the water and went to work.

JP EYED the kitchen door for the tenth time in the last few minutes. What was she doing in there?

His hands rested across his lap, fingers twined, thumbs tapping together, as one possibility after another played through his mind.

One: he'd ticked her off so much she'd bolted through the outer kitchen door and left. Eyeing the bag resting against his sister's dining room chair, he didn't think she'd leave without that, no matter how mad she was.

Two: she wanted him to follow her into the kitchen?

No.

He shook his head. It had become painfully obvious she wasn't playing games. She didn't want him anywhere near her at the moment.

Then three: whatever memory he'd caused to resurface had hurt her even worse than he'd thought.

Wide, panicked brown eyes flashed through his mind. That was it. Something had hurt her badly. He pushed back from the table and stood, reminding himself it was none of his business. As quickly as that thought entered, another followed.

It didn't matter. She was hurting.

He crossed the room and pushed lightly against the door until he could see exactly what she was doing.

It was neither his one, two, or three.

With her backside facing him, he scanned the woman. Arms up to her elbows in a sink full of bubbles, her do-me-now shoes were tossed to the side, and her pink-tipped toes curled slightly inward. A soft song drifted from the high-end under-the-counter radio, and her long, lean, perfect body swayed, just the slightest, to the country song currently playing.

A warm gush of emotion JP didn't recognize filled him. He stepped quietly into the room and held on to the door until it closed behind him. He then leaned against the wall and watched.

The chorus of the song started, and Vega began to hum so softly he at first wasn't sure it was her. As the next verse began and the hum grew to singing, he cringed, recanting his thought. No one could honestly call that singing.

Taking a break he was very thankful for, she snaked one arm out of the bubbles and scooped up a bite of dessert, filling her mouth so no treacherous noise could escape.

And that was when he noticed the other dessert cup sitting on the counter as well. Empty.

The woman had snuck off to the kitchen and was eating his dessert as well as her own?

He silently crossed the room to stand directly behind her. "You're eating my dessert."

A squeak came from Vega as water splashed and she whirled to face him. A clump of bubbles now clung to one cheek. She wiped at it, looking as sweet and innocent as one of the Disney characters Becca loved so much, and JP found himself flooded with conflicting thoughts. Kiss. Hug. Devour.

Protect.

"What are you doing in here?" She breathed the words into the space between them.

He wanted to close the distance and bury himself so deep he couldn't find his way out for a week. Instead, he touched her cheek with the back of his fingers and willed his desire down to a flicker. "I came to apologize."

Her eyes fascinated him. They went warm with his words, then immediately reversed to cold. "Apologize? I doubt you even know what the word means."

She didn't trust him. Good. She probably shouldn't.

And he couldn't help but touch her again. He traced a fingertip over the line of her jaw, to the point of her chin. "I'm sorry I was playing games, Vega," he whispered. "That's what I'm used to with women. It's what they expect."

"I didn't come to play games." Her voice trembled. "I mean...I suspected you were toying with me, but I wasn't just...I didn't just..." She huffed then, her warm breath bathing his jaw. "I really came for the interview, JP."

"I know." He nodded. "And like I said, I'm sorry I didn't take you seriously. I should have made my stance on the interview clear before and not pushed for anything more."

Her body relaxed as if all the air inside had been released. She leaned against the sink. "Thank you."

He studied her, more than a little interested in what made her tick. He hadn't expected her to admit she'd known he was playing games but came anyway, and now she'd said as much twice. Such forthrightness was rarely found in his world. The thought reminded him of their earlier conversation and made him wonder what kind of situation she'd gotten involved with that had hurt her so deeply. "I'm also sorry for whatever happened in your past that I reminded you of tonight."

And the dark eyes once again closed down. Vega shoved her arms deep in the bubbles and began to scrub. "You have nothing to apologize for there. The past is just that. Over. Finished. No discussion needed."

"No?" He tilted his head and studied the stiff *back off* sign she was posting in every direction. "If I'm not mistaken, it isn't over for you."

Silence.

"You can talk to me about it if you want." He shrugged and picked up a clean pan, suds still clinging to it. He held it under running water. "I've had my own hurts." Not that he would be sharing them. "Maybe I can help."

She didn't reply, just watched him through shut-down orbs.

But if the posture read correctly, and along with the pain he'd already witnessed, she definitely wasn't over whatever it was. She hurt, and she hurt right now because of something he'd said. The fact she wouldn't let him help riled him. Not that she and he were anything other than acquaintances, but for some reason he wanted her to let him in.

"Okay, then," he began. "Let's talk about the more important topic of the moment." He grabbed a dish towel and dried the pan, then couldn't resist leaning into her as he reached around her to snag the spoon from the dessert. As their bodies brushed, his tensed in accord with hers. Uncomfortable awareness arched between them each and every time they touched.

With a bite of chocolate now on the spoon, he straightened and blanked his own eyes to match hers. He held the utensil between them, moving it slowly back and forth, smiling as her gaze flickered between it and his face. "Why are you in here eating my dessert, Vega?"

Before he could guess her intentions, her mouth covered the chocolate, her eyelids closing along with her lips. She moaned as he stood rooted in shock. He wanted that sound to come from her throat at his touch.

He had to get a grip. The evening was over, otherwise his apology meant nothing.

Vega licked her lips and smiled a tight, frightening smile. The curve of her mouth said she had herself completely back under control, and therefore felt she once again held the upper hand. "I'm eating your dessert because you're a cad and don't deserve it."

His body went instantly from a flicker to a full-blown blaze, and no matter what his dwindling brain told him, he couldn't stop from trying one last time.

"I'm a cad, hmmm?" He started with the top of her head, now a few inches lower without her shoes, and trailed his gaze over the hair pulled smoothly back into some sort of sexy, messy style. Then he moved over her face, his gaze grazing the smooth forehead, cheeks, the edge of her nose, but barely alighting on her eyes or full mouth, no matter how they called to him.

Tilting his head, he eyed her long, slender neck. He dipped forward, as if to press his mouth to the spot pounding beneath her ear, but stopped inches before touching her. He was rewarded with her own body swaying forward on a soft gasp of air.

"Mmm," he murmured. Leaning back, he continued his perusal down her body. He'd perfected the technique years ago. Seduction by touching every part of a woman's body with nothing but his gaze and the thought of what he could do to her. Only this time he was having a heck of a hard time not simply reaching for what he wanted. This time he honestly wasn't sure if he was the one in control or not.

He tightened his hands into fists when his gaze crossed over the hem of her skirt, wondering what her thighs would feel like against his palms, and couldn't contain the movement in his slacks. Although he wasn't looking, he felt her gaze clinging to his crotch, and he surged higher.

A soft whimper hit his ears, but he trudged onward, dragging over every square inch of her long, long legs until he ended at the toes curled under her feet.

Slowly, he scanned back up to find her lids heavy and her lips parted. Whatever this was between them, he had to explore it.

Shifting, he leaned back against the counter. "Come here."

She tensed, her intent to deny him obvious. Then something changed.

Uncertainty flashed across her face. Her shoulders widened, and she studied every part of him. But it wasn't the physical scrutiny he'd given her so much as it seemed she was studying his insides. Trying to figure out if he was worthy of her, maybe? No doubt he wasn't.

The question was: Did it matter? Did she want him enough to push aside their differences and indulge?

After what seemed like hours, her eyes darkened and melted. She reached for the spoon hanging from between his fingers and dipped it back into the cup. Coming up with the last bite, she brought it to her mouth, her tongue darting out to swipe along the edge, barely lifting anything off.

He quit breathing, his gaze following the speck of chocolate as it disappeared between her lips, and realized something he'd never thought he'd acknowledge, even to himself. He was desperate for this woman. This woman whom he'd barely met and who so blatantly wasn't looking for fun and games.

She set down the flute and held out her arm, offering him the last bite. After a gulp, he opened his mouth and let her feed him the decadent dessert he'd learned to make from the best chef money could buy.

He fought everything inside him that wanted to moan, both at the taste and the thought of the woman feeding it to him. When he remained silent, she angled her head in concentration as if trying to figure out what she could do to get him to lose control. Finally, she took a hesitant half-step toward him, one arm whispering against the side of his hip with her movement.

And he snapped.

Wrapping a hand around her waist, he dragged her flush against him, yet not nearly as close as he needed her. Every soft curve fit perfectly against his harder planes. He wanted their clothes gone. Now.

Without asking, he gripped her chin and brought her mouth up to his. He slanted over her, intending to ravish, but he couldn't do it. She wasn't like the others. With ragged control, he hovered there, lifting his gaze, silently begging for permission.

Her eyes didn't answer. They merely stared, daring him to make a choice.

Then a horn outside the house made it for them.

The sound stiffened Vega's desire-melted body, and she shoved out of his arms. "My cab is here."

"Stay." His voice was hoarse. "Let me take you back to your hotel."

She shook her head, not looking at him. "I can't."

"Vega," he murmured. He reached one hand out for her, but she skirted away. Shoes in hand, she pushed the door open to go back through the house.

"Thanks for dinner." Her voice, muffled from the other side of the swinging door, startled him into action, and he followed. He had to see her again.

"Vega." His sharp command stopped her as she reached the front door.

She turned to him, her features cool and blank.

He eyed her as he crossed the room to stand before her. If he hadn't just seen her seconds earlier, every inch of her plastered to him, he wouldn't believe she'd ever been aroused. He sighed. "You're going to pretend that was nothing in there, aren't you?"

"I'm sorry," she mumbled, suddenly looking less unaffected. "We shouldn't...I mean I..."

"It's okay." JP closed his hand gently over hers, bringing it to his mouth and pressing a light kiss to her knuckles. "I'm confused, too. But we'll figure it out. Let me send the car away."

She shot him a mixture of sadness and regret. "He's already here."

"So tell him to go away."

"No." She shook her head. "It's best if I go. This can't go anywhere, JP."

Frustration flared in him. His intuition told him she was right; it was best if she returned by herself, and they both forgot they'd even met. That way he didn't risk once again trying to talk her into something she wasn't ready for, and also didn't risk getting shot down twice in one night. But what if tonight was all she gave him?

Unable to accept the idea, he silently pleaded for her to be unable to walk away so easily. This thing he felt, whatever it was, she felt, too. He had no doubt about that.

He stepped forward, backing her into the door, his body barely brushing hers. A soft breath touched his neck. He used a knuckle to nudge her face up, letting her see his certainty.

"I will see you again," he murmured and planted a soft kiss on her forehead.

The horn outside honked again, and emotions danced over her features. Sadness, regret, acceptance. "You won't see me again, JP. Other than behind the camera at the gala tomorrow night. And since it's the last event for the fundraiser, I go home early Sunday morning."

"No."

"No?" One perfect brow edged upward as she gave a husky chuckle that sounded way too final. "I'm afraid you don't have a choice. You may be the great, almighty JP Davenport, but you don't always get your way." She shrugged against him, and he pressed harder into her. "Since I didn't get the interview, my job here will be done at the conclusion of the gala."

Blinding fear he didn't understand gripped him. She couldn't leave. He wasn't done with her. He roved his gaze over her perfectly unmarked skin, as clean as the day she was born, and wondered what it was about her that made him desperate to know more. "It's Friday night. Surely you don't have to return to Savannah until Monday. Stay for the weekend. Let me take you out. For real this time."

She shook her head. "I already told you. I won't go out with—"

"Dammit, Vega. One dinner."

She remained silent, the back of her head resting again the front door, her polite, controlled expression pissing him off as much as her refusal to go out with him.

"Why not?" he growled.

"It's simple." She pushed at his chest, and he let her create space between them. "There would be no reasonable explanation for me to be seen with you. Therefore, anything we do would be caught and displayed in some trashy paper."

"So? It happens all the time."

She chuckled, nodding. "I know. Probably every single time you step outside your door."

He didn't understand what the big deal was. Yes, the paparazzi were an inconvenience, but it wasn't like showing up in the tabloids with him would ruin her life. He hated to be a jerk but considered pointing out it would more likely open more doors for her than shut them.

Before he could share his thoughts, she held up a hand. "Stop. I can see what you're thinking. But what you don't get is that the people who show up in those magazines—the *normal* people— often get dragged through the mud for no reason of their own, no matter who they get photographed with. And if there isn't a story to be found, one gets made up. So no, I have no interest in that."

"The articles can get shut down."

"Maybe. And maybe it would already be too late. But unlike you, I don't have the unlimited means to snap my fingers and have a lawyer put a stop to it. Plus, I value my privacy enough not to put myself in the situation to begin with. I won't risk having myself plastered all over the tabloids, talked about as if anyone has any right to discuss my private life and drag me through the mud, simply for a good time." She shook her head. "With anyone."

He glared at her, fully aware he was damn close to groveling, and strong men didn't grovel. And then it came to him. "At the end of dinner tomorrow night, there's an auction. Every year I end up being the final sale, silly as it may seem. A day with Jackson Parker Davenport, Jr., treated to every indulgence a woman could want." He finger-quoted the last sentence as that's how it was advertised, then dropped his arms to his sides, completely out of ideas. "Buy me."

Dark eyes faded to black. "I've seen the results of prior years. Even if I wanted to buy a date with you, I can't spend money like that."

"I'll pay," he gritted out. "Whatever it costs." Damn. His father would roll over in his grave if he heard the way his son was begging a woman to go out with him.

"JP." Vega took his hands in hers and peered up at him, as sincere as he'd seen her. "I can't. Buying you would cause the exact opposite of what I want. You'll just have to trust me on this."

The cabbie laid on his horn, and they both stepped away from the door. JP opened it a couple inches so the driver knew she was on her way, then his chest deflated. He wasn't ready for her to leave.

With a finality he didn't accept, Vega pressed a light kiss to the corner of his mouth.

"I like you, JP," she whispered. "I think you're a better guy than you give yourself credit for, but it ends here." After slipping into her shoes, she smoothed her hands over her hair and gave him a tight smile. "Thanks for a lovely dinner."

CHAPTER SEVEN

"*H*ere we go again," JP uttered as he held the door to his childhood home open for his sister to enter before him.

Reaching up, she patted his cheek as she passed. "Poor baby. Another night of the most rich and eligible—and some not eligible—women of Atlanta, all vying for your undivided attention. How will you ever survive?"

He pushed the heavy door closed behind them and scowled, only half-serious. "You know the auction is not my idea of fun. I don't know why I let you two talk me into this every year."

Cat turned to him, her long green gown flowing with the movement, and pointed a finger at him the way only older sisters knew how to do. "You know exactly why. It's the item that brings in the most money every year. And don't even think of backing out after you let yourself be dragged into politics either."

Her mention of what he'd soon be doing took all the fun out of teasing her about the auction. He wasn't lying; it wasn't his idea of fun. In fact, it was darn near embarrassing. Yet she was right. How could he not like all those women hooting and hollering over the idea of spending the evening with him? Not to mention, running the bid up to such numbers some years he was awed by the action. So he went along with it for the good of the charity—and for his ego. He could think of worse things to be doing.

But the thought of going up for bid *after* he became senator? That sent a fizzle of terror down his spine. He'd soon have to watch his behavior much more carefully than he already did. Being caught in the tabloids as the most eligible Davenport was one thing, but being there as a Georgia senator? He shook his head with disgust. Attention from the paparazzi was only going to get worse.

"I don't know why you're going along with it, you know," Cat said. He wasn't sure if she was referring to the auction or the political position, but since the former was her doing, he could only imagine she was referring to the latter. He ignored her.

They asked the housekeeper to inform their mother that they were there to escort her to the gala and were ushered into the formal sitting room. Since the final event of the weekend was highly covered by the media, it was an important time to ensure they arrived giving the correct appearance. One family, standing strong. JP knew his mother wished every year that his brother would come home to attend as well, but Bennett was career military, and no one could fault him for that.

In his mother's mind, no one could fault her for being so driven and pushing JP so hard to be in politics either. He didn't always agree, but he also didn't let it be known. He had a position in this family, and his father had instilled in him a long time ago what it was. He was to be strong, never show weakness, and above all else, carry forward the Davenport name.

He might be forced into bearing the political Davenport name, but no one was going to coerce him into another kind of heritage if he wasn't ready. That's one of the reasons he dated so many women. He wanted it clear to his mother that she may drive one part of his life, but she couldn't have the other. He'd do only what he wanted in his personal life.

Vega Zaragoza's face as he'd been about to kiss her the night before popped quickly to his mind, and he almost groaned aloud at the thought of what he wanted to do with her. But that was purely lust. He was almost certain of it. Though something about her definitely pulled to him in a way he wasn't used to. He only wished he could figure out how to convince her to explore it with him. Surely being seen in public with him wasn't so bad that she could walk away from the heat that literally spiked between them. Yet, it appeared that's exactly what she planned to do.

"We both know politics isn't anything you honestly aspire to," Cat tried again when her first comment didn't get a rise out of him. She settled herself gently onto the seat of a Queen Anne-style chair, one of a set passed several generations down through their family, and sent him a knowing look.

"Be quiet." He leaned back out of the doorway, making sure neither their mother nor Cynthia, her twenty-something house-keeper, was within hearing range. Once he confirmed all was clear, he shot his sister a dark look. "Don't say that in here."

She laughed. "Why should you care? You don't owe her this."

"Cat, stop." He had no idea why she was badgering him on the matter tonight. She knew as well as he did that he had a duty to uphold. "It's not worth even thinking about."

Cat was referring to the many times as a kid his mother's ambitions had led her to being somewhere else when he'd thought she should be there with him. He'd gotten used to it, though, and mother and son had gotten beyond the strain it had put on their relationship. At least, he had. Mostly. He wasn't sure his mom was even aware how many times he'd wanted her there to begin with. As a child with dyslexia, having a mother who was proud of you even though you weren't perfect would have been nice.

"I'm just saying, she's upset you enough times over the years, JP.

You know I love her to death, but you shouldn't let her opinions matter in this. It's too big." Cat had lowered her voice, but discussing this in his mother's house still made him nervous.

"Let it go, Cat. I'm doing what I've always known I would someday become."

"You're not Dad, you know. I think she forgets that too," Cat urged. "You may look like him, and you may have had this *role* instilled in you over your whole life, but you don't have to do it. *It's your life.*"

No, it wasn't. It had never been. Not when he'd wanted to be like all the other kids in school, and not when he'd wanted to attend hockey and baseball games instead of political dinners. Though he had managed to drop out of law school and chase some of his own dreams. At least for a while.

"Drop it, Cat. It's what I want."

A sound on the grand staircase caught the attention of both of them, and Cat rose to stand at his side as they watched their mother make her entrance. She wore a gown of floor-length navy, an air of superiority surrounding her that no one would dare argue with, and a sparkle in her eyes that had JP worried. She really was a good woman, but sometimes she was just a little hard to take.

"Mother," Cat gushed, rushing forward. "You look stunning tonight."

Emma kissed Cat on the cheek then arrowed her gaze in JP's direction where he remained by the sitting room door. "No compliment for your old mom tonight?"

In answer, he offered her his elbow and frowned down at her after she slipped her arm through his. "You look like you're up to no good, Mother. I'm not sure why I'd want to compliment that. Usually your antics do nothing but cause me trouble."

She shushed away his worries, which only made him frown harder. "I'm merely thrilled to have the excuse to dress up, is all."

"Oh, please." He called out a goodbye to Cynthia, who he knew enjoyed the attention from him, and waited for a returned comment and a slight giggle before he turned back to his mother and Cat. "What are you talking about? You dress up all the time. I have it on good authority you were both dressed to the nines for the women's luncheon yesterday."

He escorted them both to his waiting SUV and ushered his mother inside the front seat. Once they were all seated, she continued where they'd left off.

"You really are like your father, Jackson. He also never knew the difference between an elegant luncheon and a formal dinner. Especially one where everyone attending will know that my son is about to become the next senator of the United States."

Ah, so that's what had her so worked up tonight. Fantastic. Another opportunity for her to live vicariously through him.

Cat snorted from the back seat. "He doesn't need any ego building, Mother. He already has half the women of this town tweeting about who's going to win him in the auction, and then whether she'll go home with him *tonight*, or if he'll choose someone else for that particular honor."

His mother peered over the back of her seat before shooting her son a look. "You really need to start thinking about settling down, Jackson. This continual frolicking will have to stop soon anyway. It's unbecoming for a Georgia senator."

"Yet you sign me up for the auction every year," he said drolly.

"Well, yes, it's a tradition. At least until you're married. But that doesn't mean you have to continue to date a different woman every night. No one wants a roving senator, no matter what his last name."

Instead of being pulled into the argument, he thumbed a button on his steering wheel and turned the radio on.

His mother lowered the volume and shifted in her seat to face Cat. "Who do you have your money on?"

"Come on," JP mumbled, not taking his eyes off the road. "It's bad enough you both talk me into this, but do you have to act like it's my fault you get the women all worked up?"

Another snort from the back seat. "It's not us who've got them going. Your reputation speaks for itself. Whatever it is you do on your dates, I've never heard a single woman sing anything but your praises." Cat scooted over to the middle of the seat and leaned forward, putting her face between the seats in a way he remembered seeing her do as a child. "Except to complain that you can't be talked into more than the occasional night. Really, JP. You're getting older. How do you maintain the stamina?"

"Seriously?" he gritted out. "Can we talk about something else for once? Every single year it's the same thing. I pick you two up because you insist you can't arrive at the gala alone, yet I get berated the whole way there. Geez," he grumbled. "Pick a new topic for once."

His mother craned her neck to get a good look at his face, and he caught a pinched look etched around her mouth. "Is everything okay, Jackson?"

He nodded. Everything was just fine. Why wouldn't it be? He didn't have the life he wanted. He couldn't get the woman he wanted. And his mother continued to have visions of his world turning out just like hers and his father's had—with the supposed perfect marriage. Only, he knew better. He knew about Daniel.

Cat piped up from the back. "He's upset because the woman he wants to bid on him tonight can't. She'll be there working instead."

He threw a hard stare into the rearview mirror, accomplishing nothing but making Cat giggle.

"I'm right, aren't I?"

He liked that she definitely seemed to be coming out of her mourning period for her husband, but why she had to continually taunt him was a mystery.

His answer was another shift of his thumb, pumping music

into the cab of the vehicle, this time louder. His mother sat back and looked back and forth between the two of them.

"Is she right?" She had to raise her voice to be heard over the music, and he didn't even feel bad about it. "Do you have your eye on someone, Jackson?"

"For crying out loud." He jabbed at the wheel, and the music silenced, then he took a hard right and shot up the interstate on-ramp. "Cat's just pecking for information on my date last night."

"I'm not pecking," Cat said smugly. "I know exactly how it went. You had dinner at my house, and when I returned, she was gone, and you were there doing the dishes. Alone. I doubt you ran over to her hotel after tucking Becca and Tyler into bed, either."

"Interesting," Emma murmured. "Who is this woman, and why don't I know about her?"

"I don't make a habit of introducing my dates to you, Mother."

"Yet I'm typically fully aware of who you do and do not go out with. I don't recall hearing a thing about this one."

"It was just last night." He couldn't get to the gala fast enough.

"Uh-huh. And the evidence is usually posted somewhere on the internet before you climb out of her bed the next morning. Which has to stop, by the way. You have a new kind of reputation to build now. We need to focus on that." She eyed her daughter. "They had dinner at your house?"

Cat smiled, the look of a sibling having something over on the other. "She refused to be seen in public with him."

A horn honked as the car jerked into another lane.

"Be careful, Jackson." His mother patted his forearm, and he couldn't help but tense beneath her hand. "Don't get us killed just because last night didn't end the way you wanted." She turned back to Cat. "Who is she? And what do you mean she'll be there working tonight?"

"That camera lady from Savannah. The one who was at both the golf tournament and the luncheon yesterday. You remember?

Long dark hair in a ponytail? Gorgeous mouth and legs that could make any man beg?"

"Can you give it a rest?" he snarled.

"But let me tell you," Cat said, ignoring him.

If it wasn't for the fact he was pathetic enough that he wanted to hear whatever she had to say about Vega, he would make it clear that she needed to stop.

"The woman has style," Cat continued. "Gorgeous pair of Alexander McQueens. And her clothes were straight out of a fashion magazine."

"Alexander McQueens?" his mother asked. "How does she afford them? I wouldn't think videographers made that much."

Cat shrugged. "She said they were several years old, so who knows. Maybe she had her a sugar daddy at some point."

The idea was not a pleasant one, though he also couldn't bring himself to believe it could be true either. Vega seemed much too self-sufficient to let some man pay her way.

"You don't think that's what she's doing with Jackson?" his mother began, and red flags waved madly inside his head.

"No, Mother," JP said. "Stay out of it. She's not after me or my money. Trust me on this."

"Cat?" his mother asked.

He caught Cat's shrug in the mirror. "She could have us both fooled, but that wasn't the impression I got at all. I actually really liked her. Much more real than his normal dates."

"It wasn't actually a date," he grumbled, hoping to put an end to the entire conversation. "She wanted to talk about doing a behind-the-scenes interview, digging her nose into my personal life and sharing it with the world at large. And anyway, I already Googled her. The only thing out there mentions some of the awards she's won for her work in Savannah."

"An interview?" his mother asked.

"I told her no. Absolutely not."

"Let's think about this first," she mused.

"No, Mother. I don't want an interview. I'm not doing an interview."

"But with it only days from you taking office, this could be the right time, Jackson. The world wants to know more about you. It's all part of the process, son."

His jaw hardened. He might be playing her game, but he didn't have to act out every scene. "It's not going to happen."

"Well, I think it's a good idea," she stated, as if that was all it would take to get him to agree.

With a quick flick, music once again filled the space. He was finished with this conversation whether anyone else was or not.

He'd be a senator, and he'd continue to pretend he was as perfect as his mother and father had always wanted everyone to believe. But he wouldn't open the only part of himself he held private for the world to pick over. He had the right to keep at least that much to himself.

CHAPTER EIGHT

*L*ike him or not, she needed to stay away from JP Davenport.

Vega panned the camera around the ballroom at Atlanta's Fox Theatre as the attendees took a break from dinner and waited for the auction to start. She tried very hard to avoid focusing on the man whose words had kept her lying awake most of the night, but found her zoom returning time and again to study him.

He wanted her to buy him.

And she wanted to.

Right. She closed her eyes and mentally flung her head from side to side as a cartoon character might do to clear the cobwebs. What she needed more than anything else was attention from the media, so why not just waltz right up and make an exorbitant bid for the main attraction? She snorted.

"What's with you?" Darrin asked.

"What's what with me?" She glanced down at him. She stood on a riser, the camera attached to a tripod to get the best view of the crowd. Her position put her a good eight inches above him. He stepped one foot beside hers and brought himself up next to her.

"You're all weird tonight." He motioned to her hair. She'd secured the majority with combs, while flat-ironing what was left to within an inch of its life. The part that wasn't twisted up on the sides reached the middle of her back, and Darrin had been staring at it all night. "Your hair is different, not in that ponytail thing you always wear. And your clothes aren't as baggy. You keep mumbling to yourself, and now you're snorting. What's going on?"

She eyed him. "Do you have a problem with the way I look?"

"What I think about your looks isn't important." He scanned her body, and she heated with embarrassment under his perusal. "But, yeah, you look great. Your face is a little plain still, but even then, you're hot. So what's the deal?"

Hot? Her stomach rolled. Just what she needed, Darrin thinking she was hot. She turned her back to him and peered through the camera. Magically, it found JP, and he was scowling at her. He'd done that several times throughout the evening.

"I felt like doing something different with my hair," she finally answered, her back still to Darrin.

"And the clothes?"

It was just black slacks and a white top. She shrugged. It didn't matter that she'd spent the morning out shopping for them. "We always dress nicer for formal events."

"And you always remain baggy. Seriously, if I'd known your ass was so fine, I'd have asked you out years ago."

Vega swiveled around. "And I would have said no, same as I would today."

"Right." He grew quiet, and Vega returned to watch JP. He was now talking to some gorgeous woman. He smiled and gave the woman a one-armed hug. She stood there fluttering her hands around, touching him way more than she should, while Vega's blood pressure neared boiling.

"Check out that babe with Davenport," Darrin stated.

She ignored him, but she couldn't take her eyes off JP. A few minutes later he left the woman's side and exited the room.

Good. Maybe he'd stay out for a while. She turned to Darrin. "I need to speak to Cat and Mrs. Davenport for a few minutes."

He nodded. "I'll go with you."

They made their way across the floor with Vega keeping one eye out for JP's return. She wanted to express her thanks for their interviews and hospitality, as well as wish them well, but had felt keeping her distance from JP was equally prudent. Since she wouldn't be doing as he suggested and bidding on him, no additional conversations with the man had seemed necessary for the evening.

She hated that she hadn't won him over on the interview, but after the strength of what filled her every time she was near him, both physically and emotionally, she needed to get away from him anyway.

"Vega." Cat rose from her seat.

The women hugged a hello, but JP's mother had stepped away before Vega made it across the floor. Instead, Governor Chandler stood by the table.

"It's nice to see you again, Governor." Vega nodded at the man as she and Darrin stood within their small circle.

"I wanted to tell you, Vega," Cat began. "We appreciate the extra effort you've gone to this weekend. We get decent coverage from the local stations, but having a bit more devoted attention always brings in even more money. So thank you."

Vega blushed under her praise while at the same time ignoring Darrin's evil stare. He'd gone with her the day before to the luncheon, but, again, hadn't stuck around longer than was necessary for a short interview. Vega had stayed, questioning many of the participants afterward and generally beefing up the story to highlight the foundation more than she'd originally done.

"You're welcome," she said. "Since we're in town specifically to cover the events for the foundation, we've simply had more time than our local affiliate, is all."

"Well, we all appreciate it," the governor spoke up this time. He was a good-looking man, both powerful and charming. "The Davenports are one of the oldest families of the state, and they do terrific things through their foundation. More coverage can only help."

At sixty-two, Governor Chandler had been in politics for thirty years. Though he'd lost his wife—a favored "Southern belle" from an old Atlanta family—over ten years earlier, his popularity hadn't dampened one bit. In fact, he'd gone on to secure his position in the last election with an overwhelming lead and didn't look to be stopping anytime soon.

"I wonder," Darrin chimed in, using his on-air voice. "As governor, do you think your support for the Davenports help keep them on the map?"

"Son." Governor Chandler shook his head. "If that's what you believe, you might want to read back through history. My support behind this good family likely does nothing but help *me* out." He chuckled. "The Davenports don't need me speaking for them. They're a dynasty all on their own."

"Of course." Darrin's face blanched of color, but he wisely chose to say nothing else.

"Ah," the governor's voice changed to one of more familiarity. "Here's the lady of the evening now."

Vega smiled as Emma Davenport stepped into the group. It was clear she was a force. She wore the air of a gentle Southern woman, but the hold of her shoulders and steel in her gaze proved she was so much more. Few tried to get anything over on her, and even fewer succeeded. "Tsk, tsk, Douglas. Don't be telling such fibs. This is Cat's night. She's the one who's done all the work."

"Oh, right," Cat said, giving her mother a quick hug. She was the complete opposite. Sturdy and strong, yes—she'd had to be as a widow and single mother to two young children—but the sharp edges of the older Davenport were missing. Cat was warm and open whereas her mother was all business. She was the typical Southern mom. "I may have worked hard, but Mom is the backbone. Without her none of this could happen."

There was clear love but also admiration for the matriarch of the family.

"Cat, dear, you must want something out of me to be handing out such accolades so freely. I'll be sure to keep my eye on you this evening."

"I don't know," Governor Chandler said. "I think she's right on target, Emma. You hold everything together far better than I would guess Jackson Sr. ever imagined."

Mrs. Davenport's eyes dimmed for the briefest second as she no doubt relived some fond memory of her husband. The couple had lived out a romantic fantasy in the eyes of the country for over thirty years, until his untimely death six years earlier, only four months after being diagnosed with pancreatic cancer.

"Douglas," she said, patting his arm. "You, too, are such the flatterer, but I assure you, I am not the right target this evening. My son is the one you should be buttering up to. He's the one who'll soon make you proud. Jackson will be a great leader. Exactly like his father."

The conversation turned to JP and his political future, but Vega didn't miss the gleam of yearning in Governor Chandler's eyes as he snuck in a long look in Emma's direction. So the governor had a thing for JP's mom? Interesting.

She wondered if that meant Emma returned the sentiment.

Taking in the sturdy, no-nonsense lady, Vega would guess either she had no idea of his desires, or she was determined to squash them.

"Now tell me, dear," Mrs. Davenport began, turning to Vega.

"What is it you've done to my son in such a short time as to beguile him with you?"

Vega's eyes grew wide as the entire group turned to her. JP was most definitely not beguiled by her, but that didn't stop everyone from staring.

The governor studied her, likely trying to figure out if she was good enough to fit in with the Davenports. Mrs. Davenport's expression remained pleasant but closed down to the point that Vega couldn't figure out what she was thinking. And Cat smiled the smile of a new friend.

Darrin's eyes narrowed into slits of jealousy.

Ignoring all but Emma, Vega turned to her. "Thank you for the compliment, Mrs. Davenport, but I certainly wouldn't say I've beguiled anyone."

"Please." Mrs. Davenport waved her hand in the air in front of her, the diamonds of the wedding ring she still wore flashing with the movements. "Call me Emma. There's no need to be so formal. And do make sure you step out from behind that camera long enough to enjoy the auction tonight. We have so many fabulous items up for bid. Maybe you can find a nice souvenir to take home to Savannah that interests you."

Vega didn't meet the questioning look she could sense Darrin throwing her way. He wanted to know how she'd become such "good friends" with the Davenports, but it was none of his business that she'd had dinner at Cat's house the night before. "Thank you, Emma. We'll make sure and do that. I've heard such positive feedback from this event over the years, I'm just thrilled to be part of it tonight. And don't worry, if I bid on anything, I'll still make sure you get excellent coverage for the foundation."

"No doubt you will," Evan Martens spoke as he joined the group. She'd met Evan briefly after the golf tournament two days before. He was quite the player and had tried out more than one line on her. She had passed on all of them.

He stopped slightly behind her now, and she glanced over her shoulder at him. He was good-looking with his short dark hair and obviously fit body, but all his polish and shine didn't hold a flicker to JP's hotness.

Before she could begin to dwell on Mr. Hot himself, or all that had happened between them at dinner the night before, she shut the memories down.

"Good evening, Evan," Emma said, the look on her face not entirely welcoming.

He gave a quick nod. "Mrs. Davenport, Governor. It's good to see everyone tonight."

Evan stepped farther into the circle as the conversation picked back up, closing the distance between him and Vega. He touched a hand to the small of her back, and she cut her eyes to him, wondering what he was up to, but didn't want to be so rude as to call attention to his too-personal manner.

The group chatted while Vega attempted to put a small bit of distance between her and Evan. She then took the opportunity to merely observe, joining the conversation only if asked a direct question. Unlike Darrin, who jumped in at every available opportunity.

She would prefer to excuse herself completely, feeling both out of her realm and perfectly at ease at the same time, but couldn't bring herself to step away. Doing so meant she would need to make the phone call she'd been avoiding all day. Her boss had left a message earlier, wanting to ensure the interview was a go.

JP entered the room at that moment and caught her eye, causing her breath to stick in her throat. She hadn't talked to him since she'd practically run from his arms and preferred to keep it that way.

With any luck, he'd head in another direction. She watched him take in the crowd around her, then land on Evan standing to her side. The lack of distance between them seemed to be what JP's gaze fastened on.

In the next instant, his powerful legs propelled him in their direction.

"If you all will excuse me," Vega murmured. It was time to make that phone call.

She moved to a quiet corner of the room and turned her back to the crowd. Bob would be disappointed she hadn't managed to secure the interview, but updating him now was a better use of her time than sticking around to talk to JP.

Pulling out her cell, she pulled up the number with jittery fingers. She'd hung everything on this chance, and now she had to admit she couldn't pull it off. She would be stuck following Darrin around forever.

"WSAN, Felicia speaking."

"Hey, Licia, it's Vega. Is Bob around tonight?"

Her boss soon came on the line, his voice booming and comforting, all at the same time. "Vega. How's it going? What have you gotten on Davenport so far?"

Gotten on him? She squinted as if doing so would help her see through the phone and into the man's head. "Sir? As in something juicy? That wasn't what I'd planned to do."

"Sure, sure," he said. "You planned a day-in-the-life feature piece, I know. And the Atlanta station will love that, too. But he's a politician, Vega." Bob's voice lowered, taking on a more fatherly tone. She'd worked for the station for six years, and from day one Bob had taken her under his wing almost as the father she'd lost as a teenager. "Don't forget that. He can't be as clean as he appears. Even if it's simply that he skimps on Christmas bonuses or refuses to put up a tree at the office. Anything you get, no matter how minor, will be golden."

"Yeah." She gulped. "About that." Vega caught sight of Darrin out of her peripheral vision. He was eyeing her as if she were editing footage to show only his bad side.

"What about it? You need more time? Sure. We expected that. You just let us know how much time you need, and you've got it."

"But..." Something about his voice sounded like they didn't even need her back at the station. "I thought I had assignments waiting for me for Monday. Shouldn't I hurry back?"

She wondered what she was doing by dragging out the facts. She needed to just lay it on the line that she'd failed. She couldn't get the interview. But in the silence, she also picked up on a strange tension crackling over the distance.

"Bob?" She hated the unsure tone of her voice.

"The orders came down, Vega," Bob said, his voice now grave. "We definitely have cuts. Unless I can get you in front of the camera, I can't use you as a video journalist any longer, kid. I'm sorry."

"Bob, come on," she pleaded. She was about to not only fail to secure the job she wanted in Atlanta, but also lose the one in Savannah? She couldn't let that happen. "I'm your best photographer."

"Honey, you plan to get the Atlanta job and move there anyway. It's what you want, remember? This is why I went to bat for you with them."

She felt the spirit drain out of her. The past couple of days around the Davenports and covering events in the city had given her more life than she'd had in years, and now she wasn't only losing the chance for that, she was losing the pitiful existence she'd made for herself in Savannah as well.

For once she'd like to just say "screw you" to everybody and go for what she really wanted instead of worrying about the crap some jerk had once done to her.

"You do have the interview, right?" Bob suddenly sounded worried for her. "Tell me you got it."

She couldn't admit it. Not just yet. The time would come when she had to, but not right after he'd fired her. She'd finish this assignment feeling as if she had some shred of dignity. Instead of admitting what a complete failure she was, she smiled, trying to force happiness through the phone. "Of course, everything is lined up. I just assumed I'd have to come back home and finish the interview later next week, is all. I thought I was needed back there first."

"I'm sorry, hon. My hands are tied. We can keep you on a couple weeks, but getting this interview wrapped is important for you. Unless you want to change your mind about being on camera…"

She shook her head even though he couldn't see the movement. They'd had that conversation many times already, and he knew her stance on being in front of the camera.

He let out a sigh. "Okay, then. They're still holding the other position for you, so focus on that. We can make do here without you."

Before she could come up with anything else to say, someone on the other end called out, and Bob had to go. She hung up and lowered her hand.

Her life was in shambles, and at the moment she wanted nothing more than to climb under her covers and turn the world back thirteen years. Back before her father had been killed in a drug bust, and back before she'd been sold the line of crap that modeling would be the best thing to ever happen to her.

Wanting to escape from it all, she crossed her fingers that no one was paying any attention to her and slipped through the side door.

She found herself in a hallway. Able to make out people laughing and talking at the far end of the corridor, she hurried in the opposite direction until she found another turn, this path deserted and leading to large windows overlooking the Atlanta skyline.

Reaching the windows, she stepped to the side and squeezed between a five-foot potted plant and glass that appeared to glitter from the city lights twinkling on the other side of it. She needed to get her head wrapped back around the job she was here to do, and not the fact it would be the last job she ever did for the station. Possibly for any station.

Maybe it was time to take a step back and come up with a *real* plan. Something exciting.

At the thought of exciting, she pictured JP.

Breathing in and out through her nose, she closed her eyes and rested her forehead on the cool glass, picturing him as he'd been the night before. At first arrogant and certain he could literally charm the pants off her, then coming into the kitchen to apologize and ending up helping her with the dishes. She rolled her forehead back and forth against the glass. She couldn't figure out who he was.

Then the night had ended with him practically begging her to go out with him. Who would've ever thought that possible? She couldn't get over his actions, especially in the kitchen and playing with his niece and nephew. Those were not the actions of the man the world thought he was.

Unless he had such a big ego it was still all a game to get her to sleep with him. Do whatever it took to win her over.

Maybe he couldn't handle the word *no*?

"Hiding?" The deep voice came from directly beside her. She neither jumped in surprise nor opened her eyes to greet him. She'd somehow known he'd follow.

"I don't need to hide, JP." *Liar.* "I'm simply enjoying the view of the city."

He chuckled, and the hairs on her arms lifted. "With your eyes closed?"

She smiled a small smile but didn't open her eyes. "Can't you see with your eyes closed?"

"Depends on what I'm looking at." The voice inched closer. "I can close my eyes and see how beautiful you were last night with your head thrown back and your neck bared. Right at the moment you thought I was going to taste you."

She fought to keep her breathing steady at the reminder.

"And I can close my eyes and imagine how perfect you feel with your body pressed to mine."

She could do that with her eyes open.

"I can also close my eyes and know how right it's going to be when we make love."

"JP," she whispered. She didn't lift her head but turned in his direction and looked at him. He had his head resting against the glass as she did, facing her. His eyes glittered in the reflection of the city. He wore the gleam of a man out to get what he wanted. "We've discussed this," she said. "We won't be going out. Plus, I'm not into being a notch on someone's bedpost."

"Then you'd better stay away from Martens." His tight voice gave him away, and she peered closer at him.

The man was jealous. Though nothing had changed that would allow her to be with him, a sizzle of hope bounced around inside of her, lighting all the places she would best forget she had.

Jealous!

But was it at the thought of Evan sleeping with her—not that he was going to—or was it simply that being with Evan would mean Evan "won" instead of him? The flare of excitement fizzled. She shrugged and stood up straight, facing him. "Not that it's any of your business, but if I wanted to sleep with Evan Martens, there's not a thing in the world you could do to stop it."

That got him. His eyes narrowed, and he leaned in so close she breathed his aura with each lungful of air.

"If anyone here is taking you to bed, it's me." His voice was hard. Matter-of-fact.

She licked her lips and swore she could taste him. "Thank you, but I'll make my own decisions."

"The last thing Martens cares about is you, Vega."

She laughed out loud. "And you care about me?"

A voice came from the other room, announcing five minutes until the auction started. Neither turned toward the sound.

"Maybe I do."

His uncertainty stopped her from replying with another snippy comment, the confusion in his gaze matching her own.

"You don't care about me, JP. You don't even know me."

"But I want to."

She studied him, her heart thudding in her chest. "Why?" she whispered. "Why does it matter when you can have any woman you want?"

He broke eye contact then, turning to scowl out the window. She held her breath as she waited for his answer. She didn't want it to matter, but she couldn't stop the desire. Not only sexually, but something that ran deeper. Something that seemed to call out to her and say that they were two souls fighting the same battles.

Yet that made no sense.

He was a Davenport, for crying out loud. He had everything he wanted at his disposal, could snap his fingers and get the world to jump. He'd soon be the country's next hero.

She, on the other hand, had very little of what she wanted. She'd made so many mistakes that she'd not only run her mother back to her home country, but she'd been forced to let her own dreams drift away as well.

She and JP couldn't be more unalike.

Without making eye contact, JP picked up her hand and lifted it to his mouth, pressing kisses to each knuckle. "I have no idea," his voice was low, "but I'm not ready to let whatever this is end tonight."

He turned to her, tucking her hand between both of his and resting them against his chest. "You said last night that you believe I'm better than I give myself credit for. What did you mean by that?"

That wasn't what she'd been expecting. She went back in her mind to those parting words, recalling the hint of something she'd seen in his eyes every time she'd been around him.

She took a half step forward, bumping the toes of their shoes together, and lifted her face to his as she thought through her answer. "You're highly successful. A selfless, charitable man. And the person the whole country has expected to do well since the day you were born." She wrapped her free hand around the outside of their intertwined ones. "And you've always met everyone's expectations. Only...I think you're living behind a protective layer."

His features didn't change. "How so?"

"You play up the persona of playboy to keep anyone from getting too close to the real you. But why?"

"I don't."

"Really?" She squeezed his hands, caressing a thumb over them. They were big and strong, and she found it incredibly odd that she was the one holding him when what she'd wanted for years was someone to hold her. "You're saying you really are the shallow, date-them-once-or-twice man you'd have everyone believe? That you don't want more than that? That you don't deserve more?"

His jaw twitched. "If you don't think I'm that person, then why not go out with me?"

She blew out a breath of air. "I have far more reasons not to go out with you than not wanting to be dumped after getting me into bed, but we're talking about you right now."

"Fine." He nodded once. "Go on."

With a bluntness that surprised even her, she said, "I think you're afraid to try for anything deeper because you fear you won't live up to your parents' love affair. That by not finding the same thing, you'll somehow be a disappointment. I guess the question is, who are you worried about disappointing? You mother? The country? Or are you simply afraid you'll dig deep enough you have to admit to yourself that you're as hollow as you pretend to be?"

CHAPTER NINE

"*W*ow." The shock of her words knocked JP out of the trancelike state he'd been in.

He dropped her hands and put a foot of space between them. Of all the things he'd thought she might say, bringing up his parents' love life hadn't been one of them. And wouldn't she get a thrill if she knew that what the world thought of as the perfect relationship had in fact been trite and cheap in the end?

"That's some story you've imagined in your head." He'd been really close to again begging her to buy him.

Vega turned her hands, palms up. "So prove me wrong. Explain why it seems you've never had anything more meaningful than a one-night stand, or at the best, an extended weekend."

"I'm not that bad."

"No? When was your last relationship that lasted longer than a weekend?"

He set his jaw, wondering how he'd gotten himself into this conversation when all he really wanted was to take her to bed. "I've had plenty of relationships that lasted longer than a weekend." He named a couple of well-known women he'd dated.

Vega shook her head. "From what I heard, those were merely bootie calls."

The women in question would have liked making them more than that, JP thought. *That should count for something.*

He eyed the woman standing in front of him, wondering why he'd thought following her out into the hall like a lovesick puppy would get him anywhere. "We'll have to agree to disagree on this subject."

She shrugged. "Whatever."

"Dammit, Vega. I didn't come out here to argue with you."

She raised an eyebrow. "Then what, exactly, did you hope to accomplish?"

Her words probably weren't meant as the challenge his ego took them, but he could no more ignore it than he could the chemistry that tied them together. Without giving her time to guess his intent, he reached forward and captured her face. This time he didn't stop to question whether she would allow the kiss.

He just took it.

JP's LIPS pressed into Vega's with hard intensity, jolting her to her toes and clogging the breath in her throat. His hands were splayed against the sides of her face, and for seconds, neither of them moved, nothing but his lips and hands touching her.

Then as if on a coiled spring, he pulled back, gaping down in bewilderment, his expression saying he was experiencing the same things she was feeling at the moment. Fire, fear, and a frightening desperation for more.

The breath she'd been holding burst from her lungs, and she quickly sucked in another, her chest rising and falling between the two of them as they remained frozen, staring at each other. JP's gaze flickered to her mouth and back to her eyes. Then again. Not knowing whether to come back for more or run as fast as he could in the opposite direction.

She made the decision for him. She edged up her chin, her lips trembling. "More," she whispered.

His eyes flamed. Then, as gentle as the first time had been hard, he angled his head and lowered his lips.

He pressed a soft, closemouthed kiss to hers, lingering only for a second. Pulled back and made eye contact. Then he swooped in for another touch, this time a swipe along her bottom lip was all he took, nipping the flesh softly before retreating.

She rose onto her tiptoes, wanting more, but he merely touched another tender kiss to her lips. He pulled back, his blue eyes now so dark she couldn't make out which emotions played through them and which didn't.

As she stood, still within the hands holding her, she wet her lips and slipped her hands to the front of his chest. The rough texture of the tuxedo jacket sent a shiver down her spine as she imagined its coarseness caressing her naked skin. Then she slid her palms under the lapels and flattened them on his chest, warming at the feel of his heart thundering beneath her fingers.

He was clearly as turned on as she. Then why wouldn't he take more?

She met his gaze and understood. Their touch was more than he'd expected, too.

She gave a little nod. "Kiss me, JP," she whispered. "Like you mean it."

With a groan, he finally lowered his head and latched on as if never intending to let go. His tongue pressed hot between her lips and, at long last, slipped inside.

"Vega," he moaned, breaking for breath. He shifted them both, angling his head to taste her from the opposite direction. Her hands inched higher, reaching his neck. When they connected, she wrapped her arms around him and pressed her body to his. Then clung as if no longer able to maintain the strength to stand on her own two feet.

The sensations swamping her made her head spin.

With another grunt, JP walked her backwards. When she bumped the wall, he used his body to press her into it. His hands roamed lower, down her back and over her rear. He gripped her, spanning the width of her hips, then yanked her forward to join with the hard ridge straining from him. She wanted to touch without the barrier of clothes. She wanted it all.

Too soon, his grip loosened, and his fingers went on another journey, all the while his lips and tongue plundered, seeking out every inch of her mouth as if certain her secrets were hidden deep in the warmth.

His hands flattened under her shoulder blades, holding her breasts tight to his chest long enough to inspire her with the idea of lifting her legs and wrapping them around him. Before she could raise either limb, he was off on his next exploration. His hands flittered over her sides and around to her front, never landing, merely skimming, his staggering breaths bathing her as his thumbs crawled up her front and swiped at the undersides of her breasts. At the touch, he tensed.

Their lips parted. Barely.

Instead of going higher, his hands dipped, gripping the material over her stomach and holding on. His clenched fingers screamed fear of going further, yet terror of not continuing.

"Vega," he pressed a hard kiss to her lips.

Their chests rose and fell in sync, the tips of her breasts touching him for a split second before moving away, then doing it all over again. "Yes?"

"Baby." One hand lifted to cup her jaw, his voice scratchy. His fingers shook as they explored the crest of her chin then across her bottom lip. "This…" He paused and pressed another kiss to her mouth, his thumb tugging downward to give him complete access to sample her. "We need more of this. Need to see what it is."

She couldn't disagree. She'd never experienced anything like this kiss. It—JP—completely engulfed her, made her forget why she fought it. Not even with the man she'd once thought she'd loved had it ever been this wild and untamed. This urgent.

The thought of Ted brought her back to the present, and she lowered her head, a soft groan ripping from her in anguish. She pushed away from JP, attempting to find enough space to think, but he maintained the hold on her shirt, keeping her close.

"Don't," he pleaded, the word drawn out between them. "Don't pull away."

She shook her head. "We can't. We shouldn't be out here. Shouldn't be doing this."

His body stilled, the fingers at her waist clenching then letting go, and she hesitantly peered back up at him. Blue eyes flickered and changed until she could once again make out something more than desire. Finality.

His face began shutting down, masking the heat that had been so clear only seconds before. He was accepting it was over. The thought fired panic through her entire body.

She should agree. Not want to scream for him to come back.

She could do neither. The thought of not exploring this thing between them almost had her pleading, begging for him not to look at her like that. She wanted the hot and hungry man who'd been clinging to her only moments before as if his life depended on it.

"JP?" She didn't know what she was asking.

The pads of his fingers smoothed over the curves of her face, one finger lingering to draw a line from the middle of her forehead, over her cheek, and ending at her mouth. He gave her a tight smile. "I won't do this alone. Change your mind and I'll pay whatever you bid. And I'll figure out a way to keep the press out. I guarantee."

Then he was gone, leaving her to make her own sense of what had just happened. The man had been vulnerable in her arms. Literally shaking at the power of holding and kissing her.

And she'd pushed him away.

She slumped against the wall. She'd had to do it, for both their sakes.

SIXTY MINUTES LATER, the final auction item was announced, and the room erupted with a buzz. A high-pitched, all-female buzz. Vega panned the crowd to capture the excitement for the man of the hour, then settled back on him as the bidding began. The gorgeous woman he'd been talking with after dinner lifted her hand in the air to start the bid.

Vega's heart pounded as she watched a ridiculous number of women vie for an evening with JP. Old, young, it didn't matter. It appeared everyone wanted a date with the next Davenport up-and-comer. And said date spent the time preening on stage. Making sure they saw exactly what they'd be getting.

Finally, the hands began to whittle down. Women dropped out of the race, shaking their heads to indicate they couldn't go any higher, until only two remained. They both rose to their feet. The first bidder and another woman Vega had barely noticed before now.

She was in her early thirties, well-built—and not afraid to advertise the fact—and wore the look of a woman confident in both her looks and her ability to win this current item. The worst part, she was even more beautiful than bidder number one. The woman's pitch-black hair flowed in waves down her back, perfectly setting off her deep-purple gown and amazing curves. Vega shifted behind the camera, suddenly feeling drab and dowdy.

"You know who that is, don't you?" Darrin whispered from her left.

"Who?"

"The bombshell looking like she intends to go home with Davenport."

He had to be talking about Purple Curves. "I've no idea." Though a memory niggled at the back of her mind. It felt like she *should* know who it was, but she'd only caught a glimpse of her face. Enough to let her know the woman was gorgeous.

Vega zoomed in on JP as he caught sight of the final two bidders. Number One waved her hand in the air to bid, and after smiling at her, JP turned to Vega's camera and gave a polite don't-make-me-do-this smile.

"It's Greta Kirby."

Vega pulled away from the eyepiece and gaped at Darrin. "The one who posed in Playboy, then married that old guy who just died? The *rich* old guy?"

He gave a wink. "That's the one. Looks like she's on the prowl for sugar daddy number two." He nodded toward the camera. "Better keep watching, this could get ugly."

Vega studied the woman. It was her. She'd been blonde when Vega had known her before, as well as during her brief marriage, but Vega recognized her from her modeling days. Greta had been a few years older, but the two of them had worked together once during a shoot.

Greta bid, and Vega watched JP's eyes take in his other possibility. They roamed way too long over the woman's surgically-altered body before the sexiest smile Vega had ever seen was tossed the other woman's way. Vega's stomach hit the ground. If he wanted that woman, then he could have her.

A soft whistle rent the air beside Vega's ear. "Looks like a match made in heaven."

JP turned to the camera again and looked straight at Vega. This time, one eyebrow arched as if to say, *Now* that *I could do.*

Fury filled her head like the sound of a jet taking off. She would not stand there and watch this any longer. She turned, intending to leave, but Darrin blocked her path.

"What are you doing?" His whisper was harsh.

"I need to go."

He motioned to the camera. "Get back up there. This is the best part of the night."

She shook her head. Not even the threat of losing her job could get her to stay. Hell, it wouldn't matter after tonight anyway. "You do it."

Before he could object, Vega made a dash for the ladies' room, hearing the bids continue to go up behind her. And then one of them stopped.

Her heart stopped as well.

"Any more bids?" the announcer asked.

She peeked out of the corner of her eye to see who had won him. Purple Curves—*Greta Kirby*. Bile rose in her throat. Vega looked at JP and found him watching her.

"Going once."

She swallowed. She couldn't buy him; everyone was watching. She tried to move, but her feet were rooted to the spot. JP's lips pressed into a straight line, disappointment obvious.

"Going twice."

What good would it do? One night with him?

It wasn't like she could even use it to talk him into the interview. He'd said no.

His eyelids dipped slowly, but right before they broke contact, she caught something that kicked her in the gut. JP turned to the woman who was about to win him and gave her a brilliant smile.

Vega had seen hurt in his clear blue gaze.

She raised her arm in the air to get the auctioneer's attention.

CHAPTER TEN

"Seventy-eight thousand to the lady in black and white. Woo-wee, ladies and gentlemen. Don't go anywhere just yet. We have a new bidder in town."

Every single eye...and camera...turned to Vega as the auctioneer crowed. What in the world was she doing?

Panic began low in her belly, and sweat broke out on her upper lip. She had just done the one thing that was her top priority *not* to do. She'd called attention to herself. In a big freaking way!

As she stood there, unable to move or even blink, she sought out JP and found his gaze glued to hers. A new look colored his features now, but the fear shredding her from the inside kept her from being able to decipher what it might mean.

Oh my God. Oh my God. Oh my God.

Staring into JP's eyes kept her from running screaming from the room, but nothing, it seemed, was going to save her from the bright lights she'd just stepped right in the middle of. But she *had* stepped in them, so she wasn't about to get out of this until she won that damn date. And kept that money-grabber's hands off him.

Greta upped her bid, and Vega once more signaled to top it. She wasn't even looking at the auctioneer at this point, only at JP. And he at her.

As the bidding slowly climbed, thousand after thousand, the fear began to change to something else. Something Vega hadn't felt in a long time. Pure, unadulterated excitement. She might have been standing there doing the stupidest thing she'd ever considered, but oh, the outcome was going to bring a rush of joy unlike anything she'd ever felt.

She wanted JP. He wanted her. And as soon as the other woman sat down and shut up, they could figure out what came next.

Vega gave a nod to bid one hundred thousand dollars, and a whoosh went through the crowd. If she wasn't mistaken, the highest bid up until this year had been eighty-five thousand.

And she'd just bid one hundred.

Panic once again flamed inside her as the silence stretched. Everyone in the room turned to Greta to see what she would do. Even the auctioneer seemed to be out of words.

Slowly, like a man-eater closing in on her prey, the other woman raised her hand, eyed the piece of meat she intended to purchase, and clearly enunciated the words, "Two hundred fifty thousand dollars."

Oh. My. God.

Reality hit Vega like a rush of ice water poured down the front of her overheated chest. She was in the middle of the Fox Theatre, in the center of what seemed like every camera in Atlanta, and she could either up a quarter-million-dollar bid, and thus have to explain not only why she wanted to win JP so badly, but how she came up with the money. Or she could step away and figure out some story to sell so she didn't look like she'd been doing exactly what she had been doing.

Fighting over a politician in public.

With a gracious smile, she turned to the woman and dipped her head in concession. Purple Curves had won.

Now *she* needed to find a way out of there before having to answer too many questions.

* * *

VEGA DROPPED her head to the portable desk in the back of the news van and moaned. She could not believe how this night had ended. Bad enough she'd thrown herself into the middle of the auction, but she hadn't even won. Afterward, she'd had to stand there as reporter after reporter had sought her out to ask who she was and how she felt about losing. And every last bit of it had been her own fault.

Darrin rapped on the desk beside her head. "Let's get back to it."

"Ugh." Vega lifted her head. "We can't possibly put me out there like that. We have to edit this."

He shrugged. "What's the big deal? You clearly have the hots for the guy, and you got carried away. He's a Davenport. It's the news. Bob will have our throats if we give him anything less than this. Plus, it's terrific."

Darrin reversed through the footage that had just made Vega pound her head. Though he wasn't a photographer, the man had done a fantastic job. The camera had been positioned on JP, so he'd caught the flare of joy turned to predatory heat.

He'd then sought out the bidder who'd put such a look on JP's face. None other than Vega herself. He had zoomed in on her. Hair touching the middle of her back, eyes glowing, a woman on a mission. Though she'd worn no makeup, the passion on her face as she'd bid, chin raised, lips full, had reminded her of the more famous shots in her modeling days. The ones her agent had promised would move her to the top and keep her there.

119

Back and forth Darrin had captured them, Vega, JP, and Greta, until finally it had been clear the other woman wouldn't take no for an answer.

Once she'd bid, Darrin had instantly focused back on Vega and had caught the defeated look on her face perfectly. She'd given her conciliatory nod, and the camera had returned to JP, who wore the same look that had been on her own face only seconds before. Defeat.

The footage was perfect. Exactly what she would have done. And there was no way to *not* use it in the broadcast.

"It isn't that I have the 'hots' for him, as you keep saying. I was doing this for the station."

"Get real." Darrin's normally deep, smooth *television* voice changed to something tight and unrecognizable. "You were doing this for you. Look at your face in that shot. You seriously want this guy."

"No." She was flat-out lying, and she knew Darrin was as aware of it as she. "Well," she conceded. "Sure. I mean, he's hot. What's not to want? But like I said earlier, it was for an in-depth interview I'm working on."

She refused to admit defeat with the interview, allowing Darrin to blab the information to Bob before she got a chance.

A muscle jerked in his jaw. "So you're finally taking Bob's suggestion to shoot for an anchor position."

Ah...that was his problem. He thought she was going for his job. "Of course not. I'm not kidding when I say the last thing I want is to be in front of the camera."

"Then I don't get it. Why an interview? And how would you have come up with that kind of money if you'd won?" His voice took on an edge she'd never witnessed. "Did Bob get the station to spring for it? I don't see him doing that unless you agreed to be on camera. We both know you're his pet project, and he wants you out front."

"Absolutely not." Geez, he needed to let up on the anchor thing. She hadn't realized he was so insecure. "I've been playing the stock market for years now, and I have to say, I've gotten pretty darn good." At least that wasn't a lie. Not completely. Though most of her remaining nest egg was directly from her modeling days. But had she won, she still would have made JP pay her back. She wasn't blowing all her savings for one night with him.

Two nights, maybe.

She silently kicked her inner voice in the shin and told it to forget about JP. No matter how hot their chemistry, it wasn't going to happen.

"And what?" Darrin asked. "You were going to blow it all right here? For an interview that you claim you don't even want to make?"

She sighed. "I want to create the interview, Darrin. That's all. I want to get the footage, find out about his homelife, his downtime, all the things no one has been able to get, then pull together a one-hour special that someone else—you, even—could anchor. But to answer that devious mind of yours, what would be in it for me would be a photographer position with the Atlanta office. I want out of Savannah."

"That's bullshit. You want my job."

"Oh, get over yourself." Vega stood and paced the small space. She wanted to be away from the jerk. Darrin had been nothing but a pain in her butt since the day she'd met him. "Your job wouldn't interest me if it was the only way to put food in my mouth."

Again...not entirely true. But not because she wanted to eat. She'd done without food many times.

No, her secret desire to be in front of the camera was purely because she thought she could make a difference. She wanted to do pieces on the underprivileged. To bring those people and places to the focus of others' eyes.

Thanks to her past, she'd never get that opportunity, but maybe with a larger station she could eventually get the chance to create the specials, even if she wasn't actually the on-air face.

"I don't care what you say. I think you're hiding something."

Darrin stomped away, the back door of the van slamming behind him, and Vega pushed thoughts of him out of her mind. She needed to finish the edits and transmit them to the station so she could drown her sorrows in the bottle of vodka she'd talked out of the bartender in the hotel.

A man-eating, money-grubby slut had won the man she'd suddenly figured out she wanted. It seemed an alcohol-induced coma was highly deserved at the moment.

She reran the footage, laying in the last of the sound bites while also looking for ways to downplay her actions. All without short-changing the station. They may be getting rid of her, but she owed Bob. She wouldn't do anything to damage the station's reputation.

He had offered her her first job out of school, an unknown in the world of television photography, and he'd been a staunch supporter over the years, going to bat with corporate when they'd wanted to force her in front of the camera years ago. Most field photographers had to be on camera these days. She'd proven herself by getting some of the best stories and doing the best legwork of anyone at the station.

Now, because of her actions tonight, the station was already getting only half the good stuff. She couldn't shortchange them anymore. The after-auction interview with JP and Greta had been done, but everyone had been just as interested in Vega. She'd ended up on stage alongside them, had pasted on a fake smile, told her story about hoping to use the date to learn more about him for an interview, and how she'd been willing to part with her hard-earned money to take the chance. And WSAN and their Atlanta affiliate had both gotten very little screen time due to Darrin being unable to both run the camera and interview her at the same time. He'd had to resort to capturing footage while other reporters threw out questions, occasionally tossing in one himself from behind the lens.

And to think, last night she'd been worried about being seen having a single dinner with the man.

JP had tried having a conversation with her before she got away, but his date wouldn't allow it. She'd just paid good money for his attention. Ever the public figure, he had been aware she was his priority of the moment.

Vega had quietly slipped off the stage and out of the building without so much as a backwards look. Her time in Atlanta was over. And her time with JP should have never begun.

THUMP. *Thump. Thump.*

Early the next morning, Vega rolled over in bed and grabbed her head. Dang, it felt like something was knocking directly on her skull. She'd had far too much to drink.

She did a mental head-slap when the night's stupidity crept back to mind, then tucked one arm under her pillow and wiggled around to the side of the bed where the sheets were cooler. More sleep would delay having to relive it.

Thump. Thump. Thump.

She cracked open an eye and peered through the darkness. That noise had not come from inside her head. She eyed the wall separating her room from Darrin's. Had he gone out and talked a woman back to his room last night? She smirked. Probably.

Sighing, she pulled a pillow over her head and wondered if that's what it would have sounded like if she'd won the date with JP. Because there was no doubt he would have seduced the panties right off of her.

And she would have wanted him to.

She squished her eyes shut as tightly as possible, willing sleep to overtake her. Maybe she should find that bottle of vodka and finish it off. Surely she could drink enough to blank out the past twelve hours or so. Maybe even enough to forget the jealousy that had roared through her at the thought of that gold digger getting her paws on JP.

With a growl, she pounded the pillow covering her head, disgust making the shots of vodka threaten to reappear. She had no one to blame but herself. After all, she was the one who'd stepped into the minefield. And, as if to ensure the television exposure was as bad as it could possibly be, she'd done it beside JP Davenport.

Freaking perfect.

Thump. Thump. Thump.

"Vega! I know you're in there. I checked at the front desk. Now open this door."

She sprang upright, instantly alert. The thumping was at her door. The voice, of course, JP's. She swung her legs to the side of the bed, her head fuzzy, but not the full hangover she'd assumed, and checked the bedside clock.

"Vega!"

The raised voice was suddenly too much. Abandoning every other thought, she marched to the door, flung it open, and scowled. "What in the world are you doing here? It's five o'clock in the morning."

JP faced her, clean-shaven and fresh. He wore a dark suit and the wickedest grin she'd ever seen. "Morning, darlin'. Time for our date."

Vega grumbled under her breath and turned her back to him. "I didn't win a date. Go away."

That she walked away from the door without closing it made it clear she didn't expect him to do as she'd said. She would never admit it, but she didn't think she wanted him to go away. She'd made a fool of herself for this man, and apparently, she wanted more.

Sighing in disgust at her own thoughts, she clicked on a lamp, crumpled into the nearest chair, and peeked at him through her lashes. Dang, he looked good this early in the morning. How did he do that? "What are you doing here, JP?"

He entered and softly closed the door behind him, then stood with hands on hips, staring at her. "I figured you deserved credit for bidding last night, so I'm here to take you out anyway."

She opened her mouth to tell him she didn't want a pity date, but he spoke first.

"I have my plane waiting, enough fuel to escape, and all day to play."

She gaped. He had his plane ready to take them away? "Even if I wanted to go out with you, I really couldn't now. We were all over the news last night. We'd be recognized in an instant, and I still don't wa—"

"But you didn't win," he interrupted. "So no one will be expecting to see the two of us together."

The reminder of who did win and the fact that it meant he'd soon be taking *her* out did nothing to improve her mood.

"Plus," he began, opening the closet door and rummaging around in her clothes. He passed over each article as if not finding what he was looking for. "You do want to go out with me."

"No, I don't," she grumbled. She did. More than anything in the world. But no way would she admit that to the man who had women fawning over him with every step he took.

He glanced over his shoulder. "You suck as a liar, you know. What's the matter? Are you jealous of Greta?"

"No!" Vega shot him a scathing look. What a jerk. Like there couldn't be something other than jealousy to make her not want to go out with him.

"Then what? Oh, wait." He faced her. "Are we back to whatever makes you not want to be seen with me—even though you publicized your infatuation last night?" His wink and wicked smile softened his teasing.

"Stop it," she moaned. She lowered her head in dejected shame. "I can't believe I let everything get me so carried away. Can we just forget about it already?"

"Oh, no way." His voice grew heated. "You looked hot standing there bidding on me. I can't let that go. Now tell me, what's really the issue? And what's the reason behind why you don't want to be seen with me?"

She fiddled with the loose hem of her cotton sleep shirt, just then realizing how she'd answered the door. She gingerly touched a strand of hair and wondered how bad her bed head was. "Let's put it this way." She met his gaze. "I'm not exactly the type of woman *you* want to be seen with. Trust me."

His lips flattened as he stared at her. "You still won't tell me what you're so afraid of?"

Not *if* she was afraid, but *what* she was afraid of. She shook her head. Her past was of no concern to him.

JP studied her again, then with a decisive nod seemed to make up his mind. He stepped into the bathroom, leaving the door open, and the sound of running water soon filled the space. "I brought disguises," he called, raising his voice to be heard over the water. "We're going to Anguilla, so no one will even expect to find me there, much less the both of us. You have nothing worthy of the Caribbean in the closet, so we'll get you some clothes when we get there."

He exited the room, a wet washcloth hanging from his hand, and headed her direction.

She pulled her knees to her chest and wrapped her shirt over her bare legs, pulling away from the cloth marching her way. Did she look so bad he felt the urge to wash her? She patted her hair once again, hoping he wouldn't bring out a brush next.

"What's that for?" She nodded to the cloth.

JP kneeled in front of her and grasped her chin. He began gently rubbing the damp terrycloth over her cheek. "You have chocolate on your face, sweetheart."

Her shoulders slumped. "Of course I do."

Too tired to push him away, she sat there and let him administer to her. "Along with my alcohol-fest at two o'clock this morning, a chocolate bar and I came to an understanding."

One side of his mouth tilted at a sexy angle. "I take it you won?"

She liked his hands on her face. "Barely."

When finished, he sat back on his heels and inspected his work. His features softened. "I like your hair all mussed up like that."

Wickedness simmered in his eyes, but he didn't make a move. She dropped her head to the back of the chair, alert enough now to question what was going on. What was he trying to do? Woo her out of her clothes? She didn't need to be wooed. She'd gone to that dance before, and it had ripped her apart. If this was just about the attraction, it could be handled without all the extras.

"Why are you doing this, JP? If all you're after is sex, we can go at it right here in this room. There's no need for the plane. No need for the seduction." She shrugged, self-conscious, her voice now a whisper. "You've proven more than once that I'm powerless to the chemistry between us."

He didn't answer at first, instead rising to return the cloth to the other room. When he once again towered in front of her, he tucked his hands in his pant pockets and peered at her, giving away nothing in his expression. "You had every intention of buying a date with me. That's what I'm giving you."

"And I'm giving you an out."

"An out? Because you'd rather I disappear?" JP's low voice was hypnotic, a master at seduction. But she also detected the same vulnerability she'd seen at the auction the instant before he'd looked away from her. "Is that really what you want?" he asked.

She locked her gaze on his. "If I said yes?"

The fight behind his eyes was clear. He wanted to take charge, demand she follow his plans. "If you really want me to go, I'll walk out the door and never bother you again."

Yes. Yes. Say it, Vega. Yes.

If she didn't say yes, she would not only soon be naked with him, she might like it so much she wanted more. She swallowed. "One day?"

His jaw twitched. "One day."

She silently cursed her life. One had to be enough. More wasn't an option.

"I'll be ready in thirty minutes."

CHAPTER ELEVEN

The turquoise waters and bright sun of the Caribbean greeted JP as he descended the steps of the plane. The four-hour flight—most of it spent watching Vega sleep on the couch—had been uneventful, though not even close to his original agenda.

When he'd set out for her hotel that morning, his plans had been to coax her on board, then once lifted to the skies, into the bedroom—and not to sleep. He'd figured, why not start off by confronting facts. They both wanted each other, so they might as well take the edge off.

But the instant he'd heard the uncertainty in her voice, the whisper that sounded like shame for the fact she was powerless to their attraction, he'd known this trip wasn't about him. And it wasn't about them.

It was about her.

He had no idea what had happened in her past, but he'd suddenly found himself near desperate to learn. He wanted to know everything, but he wanted her willing to share it. He wanted her trust.

Turning, he smiled at the sight of her inching down the steps behind him, taking in the scenery as he'd done mere seconds earlier. She wore a floppy hat and oversize dark sunglasses, every strand of the glorious hair he'd ogled that morning tucked up underneath, and her standard-issue baggy cargos paired with a pink, short-sleeved pullover, also too big.

He'd hoped the islands might be a first for her. He'd looked forward to seeing her excitement at what lay ahead, but from the tight expression and lack of amazement, he was guessing this wasn't her first trip after all. And quite possibly, not only had she been here before, but there just might be bad memories associated with it. *Well, damn.*

"First thing on the agenda is to buy you new clothes." He'd act cheerful whether he was or not.

She whipped her tinted lenses in his direction. "I don't need clothes. These are perfectly suitable."

His words had been meant to take her mind off whatever was troubling her, but he also wanted to see her in properly fitting clothes again. How could he not after witnessing perfection?

Last night's outfit hadn't been anything special when compared to the other women in attendance, but the form-fitting tuxedo shirt and low-riding black trousers hugging every curve had set him on fire from first glance. The clothes, along with watching Evan attach himself to her side, had been what had sent him chasing after her. But their kiss had been even more surprising than his actions.

He couldn't remember ever being so tempted from a simple touch of the lips. Then he'd gotten his hands on her. If he hadn't grabbed hold of her shirt and stopped his exploration, he'd have had them both naked within minutes. In that very public hallway.

She'd felt everything he had, too. There was zero doubt about that.

If he'd pushed, she'd have gone along willingly with whatever he'd suggested, and damn the consequences.

He reached for her when she stepped to the tarmac, closing his fingers around hers, and tightening when she attempted to pull away. He wanted her in his hands. Since this might be all he got, he wasn't giving it up easily. He nodded at her legs. "It's too hot here for anything but shorts. Plus, I suspect there isn't a single swimsuit in that purse you brought."

Her forehead pinched as if she were narrowing her eyes on him behind the sunglasses. "You promised to do nothing to make me stand out." She lowered her voice as the pilot and copilot exited the plane. "I don't want to buy clothes that'll draw attention to me."

"If you don't want to stand out," he began, and tapped her bottom lip with his finger. He wanted to kiss that mouth. "Then you'll be in shorts. A bikini top would be preferable as well."

"Preferable to you, maybe." Her mumble reached him as the pilots neared.

He pressed his mouth to her ear, nipped her lobe, and whispered, "I'd prefer you naked."

"Sir," began the captain, a man who'd piloted a Davenport plane for over twenty years. "You'll call when you have your return time?"

"Absolutely, Michael. You two have a good time. I have rooms reserved at the resort."

The men moved off to care for the plane, and Vega whirled on him. "Rooms? Were you planning for us to stay overnight?"

He opened his mouth, trying to figure out a way to suggest spending the night might be a good idea, but she interrupted him, her voice tight. "This is just a date. One day, remember?"

"We're here to have a good time, that's all." JP rubbed his thumb across the back of her hand to calm her. "We can stay or we can go, whatever you want, but I can't ask them to make two flights in one day and not have a place to rest in between."

"Oh." Her fingers wiggled in his hand. "Okay. But I'll want to go back tonight."

He nodded. "I'm aware of that."

He led them to the car Beverly had reserved, tugging at the ball cap on his head. He'd been uncomfortable with the thought of disguises, but with Vega's refusal to share her secrets, he'd decided to do this to make her more comfortable. Besides, it would be fun being incognito for a day. It had been years since he'd gone anywhere and not been recognized.

After several moments, each of them lost in their own thoughts, a tremulous sigh echoed from Vega. "They won't tell anyone we're here, will they? The pilots?"

He squeezed her hand. "They're loyal. Nothing to worry about."

Tension radiated from her, worrying JP, but he had no idea how to fix it. After climbing into the sedan and leaving the airport, he pulled to the side of the road and faced her. "Did I mess up? Should we not have come here? I wanted to give you a great day, but I can tell something's wrong."

Vega looked out the side window, the tension easing, but sadness replacing it.

"Vega," he spoke softly. He removed his sunglasses. "Look at me, please."

Several seconds passed before she turned to him. When he continued waiting, she finally reached up and pulled her own glasses from her face.

"Thank you." He picked up her hand and turned it palm up before placing a kiss in the middle of the soft skin. He ran a finger back and forth over the spot. "I want this day to be great for you. Tell me what's wrong and I'll fix it."

His words seemed to jolt her from wherever she'd been. She blinked and smiled. Slowly, but at least it reached her eyes. "I'm sorry." She pressed her hand to his cheek, her palm cool against him. "Thank you for this. It's lovely."

"I'm not looking for gratitude, here, honey."

The devil played in her eyes now. "No? I wonder what you are looking for then?"

She leaned across the space and pressed her mouth to his, then tilted her head and parted her lips. He knew he should pull back but couldn't. Instead, he cupped her around the neck and drank from her, fighting the urge to take more.

With a heavy breath, he separated from her lips and pressed his cheek to hers. "That's not it either," he whispered.

"No?"

He leaned away and fiddled with their now skewed hats until they were both once again pulled low on their heads while watching desire being reflected back at him. But there was something else there, too. She suddenly looked far younger than her years. And the sadness was killing him.

"Don't get me wrong," he said. "I want to make love to you in the worst way possible, but that's not why we're here."

"Yes, it is." She shifted her gaze to the hand he still held.

"No." He touched a finger under her chin and nudged her back to him. He needed her to see the truth in his words. "We're here because I want to spend the day with you. Because I want you to spend the day with me. I knew you wouldn't give me that in Atlanta."

She nodded as if believing him, but her eyes remained lost.

"How about if I promise not to touch you again? Will that prove it?"

Her brown irises deepened to a rich chocolate, half flirt, half resignation. "What would be the point, then?"

JP didn't know what to say. Since he'd met her, though she might not have been too thrilled with the chemistry that burned between them, she'd at least acknowledged it was a two-way street. Now she acted as if he intended to use her while giving her no choice in the matter.

And then it hit him. He closed his eyes with frustration, afraid Vega would see it as something else. When he had the anger under control, he cracked open his lids. "Whatever happened in your past, sex played a role, didn't it?"

Her eyes turned black. She remained silent.

"What happened? Did he use sex against you somehow? Force y —" Pain ripped through his chest. "Because I'll—"

"No." The word barely sounded. "I slept with him voluntarily."

Relief came close to smothering him. The thought of another man's hands on her was bad enough, but hands that'd had no permission to be there was unthinkable. If that had been the case, he would have to personally hunt the man down and take care of the situation.

He removed the hat from her head and pulled her to his chest, wrapping his arms around her. "Then let me in," he muttered. "Let me help. Did something happen here? Is that it? I'm sorry. Say the word, and I'll take you back home."

VEGA ENJOYED BEING PRESSED to JP's chest so much she almost forgot the man was waiting for her to speak. She felt cared for and protected in his arms. Something she couldn't remember feeling since her dad had died. And she didn't want to wonder if there was an ulterior motive, but she couldn't help it. He'd made it clear more than once that all he wanted was to take her to bed. Heck, until she'd stepped out of the plane, that's all she'd thought she wanted. A day of hot sex and wild passion, then back to her normal life. Her normal, boring, about-to-lose-her-job life.

But when she'd caught sight of the water, felt the salty air touch her skin, she'd been transported to the past and had suddenly been angry at the fact JP was just like *him.* Not married—she was smart enough to make sure of such things these days. But he only wanted her for a good time. When would she be more than that to someone?

The last time she'd thought she was, she'd been gullible and apparently desperate for love. That's all she'd ever come up with for falling for the lies. Gullible and desperate.

Until this week, she'd been certain she'd overcome both those flaws. Looking at the man, though, who'd stood at the bottom of the stairs waiting for her, she'd realized she liked him. Not just the insane attraction, but actually liked him. From what she could tell, he wasn't a bad guy. His sister loved him. His mother couldn't be more proud.

But as he'd held out his hand to her, what she'd seen instead of the good guy was a man willing to humor her just to get what he wanted. He was used to women falling at his feet, and when she hadn't immediately followed suit, he'd rolled out all the tricks to get her there. Not that he'd ever done anything to make her think he wanted more than a good time. He'd never promised her more. Yet she'd found herself suddenly hurt over the fact that today was all he was offering. When would it be her time to have more?

With determination, she pushed her maudlin thoughts away and reminded herself that whether she wanted more or not wasn't what was important. Today was what she had. And today she wanted to make love to this man.

She wasn't about to waste time worrying over what couldn't be. Like him, she'd take what she possibly could and not look back.

"There's no need to go home," she murmured, finally bringing herself to answer his question, and trying her best to put a happy lilt in her voice. She pushed off his chest, his arms still looped around her. "I'm sorry I flaked out on you there. I'm okay."

She tried to turn away, but JP wouldn't let her. "What's going on, Vega? You can't just ignore this and pretend everything's okay. I'm right, aren't I? Something happened here?"

"Not here." She slipped her fingers through his when he

released her to reach for her face. "It was a different island, but I haven't been in the Caribbean since."

"And how long has that been?"

She believed he was asking out of concern; she really did. But the last time she'd trusted someone with everything, he'd not only broken her heart, he'd dragged her image through the mud, paid off her friends, and ended her dreams. She wasn't ready to give over that power again. She might never be.

Leaning forward, she pressed a quick kiss to JP's mouth. "It was a long time ago. How about those clothes? Let's go shopping."

JP didn't immediately start the car. "I only want to help, you know."

"I know." Her smile was bright. "It's just that it's not worth talking about."

Something passed through his eyes for an instant that Vega would swear was hurt, but that didn't make sense. Her not answering his question wouldn't affect him one way or the other.

She smiled again and leaned on the console between them, breathing in his scent. "Let's go shopping," she whispered. "I need a bikini."

A SHORT WHILE LATER, Vega's eyes widened behind her dark lenses as JP opened the double doors of the terrace. She crossed the white tile and took in the brilliance of the early morning sun sparkling over Maundays Bay. It was simply stunning.

He'd rented a suite at an exclusive resort and had convinced her that it made more sense to shop in the resort boutiques, then change their clothes in the room before heading out for the day. In fact, given the activities available on the grounds there, she wasn't sure at this point if there was a need to go anywhere else. They had everything she could possibly want.

She dropped her purse on the chaise and pulled off the hat and glasses to toss down with it. Then she stepped to the edge of the patio. The crystal-clear water was almost too perfect to be believed. It was as if the sand beneath was painted the most beautiful shade of aqua.

"Do you like it?" JP stepped to her side, his voice so smooth she almost felt as if she could melt into it.

"It's..." She crossed her arms over her chest and rubbed a hand back and forth over her upper arm, nervous to voice how much she liked it. When she'd left the Caribbean for the last time eight years before, she'd honestly never thought she'd return. There was nothing quite like looking out over the tranquility of a white sand beach and slow, lapping waves. The sailboat in the distance framed by the mountains of St. Maarten added the finishing touch. "I must say, I was prepared for the beauty I knew I'd find here, but this is sheer heaven."

He handed her a champagne flute, and she raised her eyebrows in question.

"Mimosa," he answered.

Perfect. She couldn't believe she'd been worried about whether JP was or was not like Ted. She had a charming companion, a location to die for, and nothing but a day of luxury stretched before her. She would make the most of it and would not expect more from it than it was. "Thank you for bringing me here."

Eyes very similar to the waters fifty feet from them glistened back at her. "I'm glad you said yes."

So was she.

"So." He sipped his own drink then motioned to the beach before them. "How about we get changed into our swimsuits? The first activity I have planned begins in less than twenty minutes, so we should get going."

He'd held off on sharing what he had laid out for them to do today, and she found she liked that. It added to the adventure. She tilted her head back and finished her drink, then smiled up at him. "I'll be ready in five."

```
Little brother, you watching the news this
morning? You're leading the way on all
stations.
```

JP READ the text from his sister as he waited for Vega to join him. It had been over five minutes, but he didn't care. As long as she remained relaxed and happy, he could wait all day. He'd been a nervous wreck since she'd gone a little weird on him in the car earlier, but he hadn't seen another sign of that side of her since. They'd shopped, laughed, and he'd caught more than one intentional flirt. He couldn't be happier with the way the day was turning out.

His thumbs moved over the keys of his phone.

```
Out of town at the moment. Why have I made
the news this time?
```

```
The auction. The stations are smitten by
the young camera lady who didn't quite win
the prize. They're as taken with her as
you seemed to be.
```

Well, who could blame them?

He shared most things with his sister, but he wasn't about to tell her the young camerawoman had won in her own way. Or more aptly, he had won. He also had no intention of telling Vega she was apparently the big story of the day. He suspected that would not go over well.

Cat sent another message before he could reply.

Where are you? And who are you with?

He shook his head. Not on her life.

None of your business. Let me know if the
media gets out of control.

Cat replied that she would, then tacked on another comment to address his "none of your business." Something a proper lady shouldn't say. He laughed, then looked up as Vega stepped out of the bedroom from changing her clothes, and almost dropped his phone. The woman was a goddess in a white bikini.

"Wow," he murmured. At least, he thought the word passed his lips. At this point, he couldn't be sure. Tanned skin and perfect curves had definitely been hidden under her baggy cargos. He wasn't sure he could stick to his plans and not ravish her at the first possible moment.

He swallowed. The bikini wasn't as revealing as what most women he spent time with would wear, but even with its slight modesty, it couldn't hide what she typically concealed. "You look amazing."

A timid smile crossed her lips before she glanced down at herself. "Thank you."

"No, seriously." He shoved the phone in his pocket and crossed to her, then turned her around to face the mirror on the other side of the room. "Look at yourself."

He stood behind her, his body bigger and stronger than hers, and watched her take in the two of them. They looked good together. They both had dark hair, his slightly darker than hers, and both had a nice, tanned color to their skin, but that was where the similarities ended. She was soft where he was hard, and she was thin and shapely in all the places he wanted to explore. He was broad behind her and, though only a few inches taller, seemed to take up twice the space she did.

His hand came up to skim along the edge of her hip where a purple wrap hid part of her from his view. The fringe from the swath of material tied at the other hip dipped down over a long toned thigh, and he gritted his back teeth to keep from begging her to take it off.

Dark eyes took him in as he scanned over every inch of her. She was simply magnificent.

He lifted a hand to the hair pinned at the back of her head. "May I?" he asked. He wanted to get his fingers in that dark mass in the worst possible way. He could make out captured curls just dying to spring free.

Her slim throat moved with a swallow before she once again glanced away. "I'd rather not."

His chest deflated. He nodded. "Okay. How about a massage then?"

Her gaze shot up to meet his in the mirror. "A massage?"

She thought he meant one he'd give to her; he could read it on her face. And even better, he could see that she wasn't settled on giving him a definite no. He intended to show her a perfect day, though, and although touching her at ten o'clock in the morning might make for a very *good* day, it wouldn't do anything toward ensuring she saw and experienced all Anguilla had to offer.

"The beach." He nodded toward the open door as he spoke, fighting to get the words to come out without sounding like a teenager going out on his first date. "I've arranged a private massage on the beach for both of us to start off the morning. Sound okay?"

Dark eyes melted, and he knew he'd struck gold. Now if only the rest of the day would go so well.

They grabbed their hats and sunglasses and made their way through the flowered landscape to the tables awaiting them at the edge of the water. When she climbed aboard and lay on her stomach, then reached behind her to untie the strip of white holding her breasts out of sight, he was certain his knees would forget how to work.

Without another word, he lay on his own table in the same position, pulling his t-shirt over his head before settling down, and buried his face in the headrest. Having Vega less than ten feet from him with no top on was going to be the death of him.

Desperate to think about something other than the bare, side curves of her breasts, he grabbed for the first thing that came to mind. "Tell me about your childhood. What was your mother like?"

What was your mother like?

Since when did he ask a woman anything about her mother? Such questions would only lead to similar ones directed back at him. The last thing he wanted was to be caught whining about how he'd often wished his mother was around for him more instead of out playing politics with his father. What a pansy.

The masseuse began on his shoulders, and he pulled in deep breaths as he focused on relaxing, while Vega remained silent to his right. Unable to keep from looking at her any longer, he turned in her direction and was instantly sucked in to the beauty that lay across from him. She lay facing him, her hat and glasses tossed to the ground, her eyelashes resting upon her cheeks, and her dark hair the perfect complement to her skin. She might try to downplay her looks on the job, but the woman was beautiful. She topped anyone he'd ever gone out with.

"My mother is a good woman," she finally said, keeping her eyes closed as the masseuse worked over her bare back. Hands swooped down to the curve of a very nice rear, and JP had a hell of a time pulling his eyes from the dip in the small of her back.

The hands on him pressed hard into a knot in the top of his shoulder, and he once again forced himself to breathe, easing the tension from his body. Staring at Vega's near-nakedness was doing nothing to help him relax.

"She would have never been caught not working hard when I was growing up," Vega continued. "And from what I understand, she keeps the same habit today. She's honorable and proud, and I only hope to someday have her see the same in me."

He couldn't imagine her mother not being blown away with the daughter she'd raised. "You don't visit often?"

Longing drifted through her eyes as her lashes lifted, and he held an almost desperate wish that he was close enough he could reach out and touch her.

"A couple times a year," she finally said. "But that's not enough. She lives in a small village in Mexico, and I can't get away to visit as often as I'd like."

"Did you grow up there?"

She shook her head. "No. We lived in Texas."

She turned her head to face the other direction, and he got the message: the conversation was over. But he wasn't ready for it to end so quickly. Her soft voice mesmerized him.

"Tell me about your father," he asked.

The sound of the waves was his only answer.

After several long seconds, he caught the eye of the woman at Vega's side and couldn't miss the what's-your-next-move-now look she gave him. Clearly, he'd struck out with that line of questioning. Maybe if he gave something in return…

"My dad was in politics my whole life but got serious about it when I was six. He had very strict rules about being a…" He paused, almost saying *being a Davenport*, but remembered just in time that they weren't alone, no matter how much it felt as if they were. Vega once again looked at him and he finished, "…about being a son of his."

Her gaze flicked to the woman now working on his calves, and he could read what she was thinking. They needed to be careful or their identities would be figured out. He wouldn't mind so much if that happened; he was used to it. But he had promised Vega anonymity. A nice tip would hopefully convince the ladies to keep any secrets they uncovered to themselves.

"What was that like?" she asked softly. "Growing up with him."

He shrugged one shoulder, unsure why he'd even brought it up but strangely wanting her to understand. Only, it sure would be easier to have the conversation if there weren't two strangers currently in their presence. He nodded to the masseuse working on Vega, and she got his meaning.

Both women excused themselves, murmuring that they'd give them a few minutes alone.

"Thank you," he said. "Ten minutes, please."

They nodded and hurried away, then he rolled to his back and stared at the unflinchingly blue sky.

"It was like being groomed to be the next in a long line of perfect men. I wasn't allowed to show the tiniest bit of weakness, even as early as six."

She laughed. "I can't imagine you not coming out of the womb with perfection stamped across your forehead. Seriously, weren't you always this way?"

The words made him smile. He hoped she always thought him perfect. It was certainly easier than letting her see his flaws. "Afraid not. But I do work hard at it."

She rolled over to match his position, and he turned to watch her movements. She'd grabbed the extra towel to drape over her chest as she flipped, and he let out a soft groan when he caught sight of it.

Light laughter floated up from her, and he grinned. He was fairly certain her breasts would be the kind of beauty that should be carved in stone.

"It sounds lonely," she said, picking up on the truth of the matter far easier than he'd expected.

"Yeah." He raised his arms and propped his head on his hands, suddenly thinking of his half brother and what the boy would feel like growing up with the same disorder he had. "But I had Cat. We were always close."

"What about your older brother? Was he not groomed in the same way as you?"

He squinted against the brightness of the sun as he thought about the question. No, actually. Bennett had not been treated to the same "training" as he had. Maybe his parents had known from an early age that Bennett had been made for the Army instead of Washington.

The ladies came back to finish the massages, and conversation drifted off as he and Vega relaxed under their skilled hands.

At the end of the hour, he thanked them and tipped them soundly, then he was left with nothing but him and Vega and a long, glorious day stretched out ahead of them.

He shoved his hands in the pockets of his swim trunks and kept his distance from Vega. All that golden skin was beginning to test his willpower.

"So what next?" he asked. "I'll leave this one up to you. We have our pick. Horseback riding, fishing, sailing, swimming." He winked. "Building sandcastles?"

She turned from him to look out over the water, and a rightness settled deep inside him. He may have twisted her arm a bit to get her here, but he couldn't regret his actions. There wasn't another place on earth he'd rather be.

With a wide grin, she whirled back around. "Is there some place we could go parasailing?"

His brows shot up. "You're an adventurous one?"

Her grin only grew. "It's rare I get the opportunity, but yes. I do like my share of excitement."

Then excitement would be the order for the day. He offered his elbow and gave a slight bow of his head. "Then come with me, my dear, and I shall make your dreams come true."

A pure giggle erupted from her, and he couldn't have felt more like a man.

CHAPTER TWELVE

*V*ega and JP had been shopping for the last couple of hours, after they'd parasailed, jet-skied, then toweled each other off after a quick dip in the ocean, and Vega was finding it harder and harder not to search for excuses to reach over and touch him. As it was now, she was picking through a bin of hats just so she could run her hands over his hair.

Coming up with a winner, she removed the cap he wore and replaced it with the stonewashed bucket hat. "It's more exciting than this baseball cap," she said.

He eyed himself in a mirror with distaste. "I don't believe it's my look."

Vega raised her cell up in front of her to take his picture. They were goofing off more than shopping as they tried out unusual handmade items or local favorites, but she was having a great time. "Bring the strap around front."

"You've got to be kidding me." JP chuckled but did as she asked. The longer they'd played on the island, the more relaxed they'd both become.

When he had the strap sufficiently tightened under his chin, she snapped the picture, giggling at the face he made. Her own personal souvenir. "Take off your glasses for one."

He did as she asked, and she captured another picture, this time with his eyes smiling at her in a way that made her all warm inside. She grinned at the shot and held it out for him to see before moving on to the next table. Although at first she'd been uncomfortable being out in public, she'd had more fun today than she could have ever imagined. And there was still dinner and the remainder of the evening to go. Going home today hadn't been mentioned again.

"What's good for the goose, you know."

"Hmmm?" Vega slipped a lovely turquoise and lapis bracelet over her wrist and turned to see what he was talking about. He held up the tackiest pair of sunglasses she'd ever seen, his uncovered eyes twinkling at her, and waved the pink, blue, and green frames at the jewelry she'd just tried on. "It matches."

She grinned. "And with the pink, they match my new bikini, too."

At the mention of her bikini, JP's eyes heated, and his gaze lowered to the pink, sequin-edged cleavage currently on display for all to see, but specifically for JP. She'd picked it out at an earlier store, deciding she wanted something a bit more revealing than the first swimsuit had been. She'd forgotten how much she liked looking pretty and how she liked seeing appreciation from the male population. Of course, although JP seemed to enjoy the view, he'd come across as surprisingly jealous, pulling her close or gripping her hand every time a local man had whistled his appreciation.

JP smiled at her when she slipped the gaudy glasses on her face and brought out his own phone. Her heart flip-flopped at the thought he might want a reminder of their day, as well. She propped a hand on one hip and struck a pose, realizing too late she pursed her lips and set her head in a long-forgotten way.

"Wow. Aside from the tacky frames, and the fact your hair is still hidden in a brutal ponytail, this is an awesome shot." He held the phone out for her to see.

He was right. She still had it. Knowing the picture could always find its way into the wrong hands, she said, "I guess. We can do another without the glasses if you want to delete that one and try again."

"Not a chance." He yanked the phone out of her reach as if expecting her to grab it and run.

It wasn't worth making a scene over. Plus, she liked knowing he had a decent picture of her in case he wanted to think of her after she returned home.

While she moved to a jewelry display at the front counter, he studied the picture again, tilting his head in concentration.

"You have a very natural grace about you, Vega."

That's what had gotten her noticed at sixteen. "Thanks."

She tried on a couple things before putting them back. The jewelry from the islands was stunning, always reminding her of the ring her father had given her when she'd been a small child. A lovely aquamarine stone that in the right light was more like a pale sapphire, not unlike the waters edging the island. Her grandfather had given it to her grandmother as a wedding present. She'd gotten pregnant the night of the wedding and had claimed from that day forward it had mystical powers able to grant the wearer their greatest wish.

Never without it, Vega had worn it on a chain until she was old enough for it to fit her finger, only taking it off for photo shoots. She'd been almost as broken over discovering she'd lost the ring as she'd been over losing Ted, but with the media hounding her, making her lay low, she'd accepted the loss as fate and given up on ever finding it.

She certainly didn't expect to find it here, either, but the romantic design of the jewelry reminded her of it so much she couldn't help digging through the styles.

"Can I ask you something?" JP said.

"Sure." She motioned to a gorgeous bracelet under the glass counter that had a matching ring, and the clerk pulled it out for her. She held her wrist up, and the salesman clipped it on her.

JP pointed his phone at her and took another picture. "Have you ever thought about being on the other side of the camera?"

Shock had her gaping at him before she caught herself and snapped her mouth shut. She shrugged, playing for nonchalant. He couldn't actually have guessed that about her. "My boss would like me to, but I'm not cut out for it."

"He wants you to be a reporter?"

She gave a noncommittal answer as she flipped her wrist over and over, watching the blue of the stones glisten amongst the glittering diamonds.

"How about something like the interview you wanted to do with me? Not just getting the video but reporting on it? Feature pieces."

The ring was gorgeous, too, but she didn't put it on. "I'm good at what I do. Why change?"

JP reached in front of her and caught her hand, stopping her motions. "Why do you want a new job?"

"What?" She lifted a shoulder. "I told you. Savannah is boring me. I want something bigger."

"And it's not because you're not happy with what you're doing, but just because you're bored with Savannah?"

"And because my job is on the line. Why would you even think it was anything else?" She untwisted her hand from his and handed the ring back to the clerk. Its color was as close to her long-ago ring as she'd ever seen, but she wasn't comfortable paying that kind of money for it, and certainly not in front of JP. Doing that would lead to even more questions she didn't care to answer. Plus, it looked more like something to be received from a lover, not purchased for herself.

"Would you quit ignoring me for a minute and talk to me?" JP said.

Sighing, she pulled off the bracelet and, with an anguished frown, handed it back to the clerk. "Thank you for letting me try it on. It's very lovely."

"You nah like?"

"Oh." She smiled at the clerk. "I *love*. Very much. But it's not to be, I'm afraid."

JP hadn't quit staring at her even though she'd continued ignoring him, but he did when the clerk suddenly pointed at him. "Fuh you man get fuh you?"

Vega giggled and patted JP's wrist at the startled look he sent between her, the jewelry, and the man. "Don't worry, *darling*," she purred. "I wouldn't dream of such."

She moved back to a much lower-priced rack of jewelry, pulling off a lovely sterling silver bracelet with a multitude of dangling charms representing the island, and JP once again followed.

"I think you do want to be in front of the camera. You're a natural."

She grunted. "How would you know anything about it?"

"I watched you last night. You're not only stunning and graceful, but the few minutes all those cameras were turned on you..." He shook his head and turned her to him. "You were in your element, Vega. Even though I knew you were uncomfortable, I couldn't take my eyes off how perfectly you responded and held your own. You're stunning in front of the camera."

Calm, blue eyes pried into hers as she stood there trying to figure out how to answer him. What could she say? It was her biggest dream? That she wanted it so badly she'd considered purchasing the ring she'd just admired with the hopes it held the same power as her grandmother's and she would one day finally get her wish?

Yet another reason not to buy it.

"Tell me," JP urged, reaching out one strong finger to stroke up the inside of her arm. "Why do you refuse to try it?" He studied her before added, "Does it have anything to do with your past?"

Lying had never been something she enjoyed, especially since the biggest, fattest lies had been told about her, but if ever a time called for it, this was it. She blanked her faced as she'd gotten so used to doing over the years, only then realizing she hadn't been doing that with JP since he'd shown up at her door that morning.

Before she could come up with something he might buy, and open her mouth to recite it, JP stopped her cold.

"You're a what-you-see-is-what-you-get kind of girl, remember?" He spoke in a low voice, his eyes, she realized, matching the expensive stones she'd admired just a few minutes earlier. "You tell it like it is, and you don't care for people who refuse to do so. That means you can't lie to me about this, Vega."

But it didn't mean she had to tell him the truth, either. She held up her arm and shook the bracelet at him. "What do you say? How about this one instead? Want to buy it for me?"

He growled with impatience. "You can be so damned stubborn. You're not going to answer me, are you?"

She admired the bracelet on her arm again before grinning up at him with her best smile, the one that used to make men swoon. "You can't tell me you don't make a habit out of buying your women baubles?"

She turned back to the display to make sure nothing else caught her fancy, and JP stepped up behind her, his scent making her head swoon. He briefly skimmed the length of his body against hers as if considering wrapping around her like one of the diving suits they'd admired in a previous store.

"Fine," he muttered, his breath heating the back of her neck. "Ignore me. For now."

He fastened both hands to the bare skin at her waist, his thumbs pressing on either side of her spine, and touched his lips to her neck. Goose bumps lit down her arms.

He lifted his mouth to her ear. "Are you my woman, Vega?"

She shivered. Did he want her to be his woman? She glanced at him over her shoulder. "Today I'm anything you want me to be."

JP's eyes darkened, and she could tell he fought the urge to kiss her. He'd been the perfect gentleman all day, but she was tired of it.

"You going to buy me this bracelet?" Her voice was soft and husky, not concerned at all about the jewelry.

His body filled the remaining gap between theirs until his knees and thighs touched the backs of hers, the hair of his legs rough against her smooth skin. His chest pressed to her shoulder blades, and one hand slid around to span her waist. Warmth engulfed her like a cozy summer day by the lake.

"Mmm..." He nuzzled her neck. "I could, but I typically save my jewelry buying for when I let a woman know it's time to move on."

"When you break up with them?" She tsked. "Tacky." She removed her sunglasses, and with a seductive pout, peered up at him. "Surely you won't make me wait. I promise to give you a proper thank-you."

A low growl rolled in his throat. "Vega..." He bumped his erection between the cheeks of her rear. "You're killing me."

"Why, Mr. Davenport." She batted her eyes. "Whatever is that in your pants? I don't believe your constituents would approve of such behavior in public."

This time he bumped harder. "I don't have constituents."

Without explanation, she removed the bracelet and his hat and replaced their original disguises. She then dragged him from the store. As she made her way, winding through the overstuffed bins, she caught sight of herself on the TV anchored high in the corner of the store. It was a clip from the auction the night before. She ducked her head, praying no one would notice who they were, and moved faster.

"Uh...Vega. I don't think I should walk around out there right now," JP warned but followed anyway.

She led him into an alley between two strips of stores and stopped in the sunken doorway of one of the shops. As she backed into the panel, she pulled him with her. She'd dragged him from the store because she was tired of merely flirting and teasing. Because she wanted a kiss. But after seeing the video, she was almost desperate for it now. She needed to block out the stupidity of letting herself get caught on camera like that. She couldn't afford to be in the spotlight. If she was, her past would come back to haunt her, there was no doubt. There were simply too many people always willing to dig deeper than what was presented to the public.

"Kiss me," she begged.

That was all he needed. JP cupped her face in his hands and tasted her like a man handed the first meal he'd seen in weeks. When their hats and glasses bumped, he ripped them off, tossing them to the ground at their feet. He slanted his mouth over hers, searching out her secrets until her mouth felt swollen and bruised. That still wasn't enough.

She slid her palms under his t-shirt and scrubbed up his chest, his groan vibrating against her hands. She wanted him naked.

He must have had a similar thought. Within seconds, he had the string behind her neck untied and her breasts bared. Both hands gently cupped her, and his thumbs teased back and forth across her nipples. "You're beautiful."

She arched her back as his head lowered, certain she'd die if she didn't feel his lips on her that very instant. His tongue flicked out to touch, then retreated, and she let loose an animalistic growl.

He flicked again.

This time he latched on, and her back bowed, tight as a guitar string. She bit her lip and twisted her head to the side to keep her moan from becoming a scream. His tongue was the rain in the middle of a very dry desert, and she was pretty damn certain he could do that forever, and she'd be a happy lady.

He slid a muscular thigh between hers, and a burst of pleasure quivered through every nerve ending. Bearing down, she began to ride his leg. She wanted him. Now.

"JP," she breathed.

"Yeah?" He cupped her bottom with one hand and pulled her closer, squeezing the curve of her rear. She literally vibrated in his arms, so close to an orgasm her eyes crossed. This man had the power to send her over the cliff with a single touch, and she was more than happy to blindly leap.

From what she could tell, there wasn't a reason to waste another second of their day with their clothes on. Holding on to him for fear he'd let her go, she urged, "Let's go back to the room."

JP jerked his head up, her breasts pouting at his departure. His eyes gleamed with desire and triumph. The predatory male who'd conquered his prey.

A sharp whistle cut through the quiet alley. "Nice tits, lady... show me more."

The crass comment jolted them into action. JP yanked Vega's top up to cover her at the same time they both whirled to see who was watching them.

A teenager stood twenty feet away, hooting with laughter as he shook a camera in the air. "Great shot!"

CHAPTER THIRTEEN

*a*nger zapped immediately through JP. How idiotic could he be?

"Give me that camera," he growled, rushing toward the kid.

"Oh, no. All fuh me now." With a final shout, he was gone. His nimble feet were faster than JP could begin to be in his current position.

Embarrassment sickened him as he returned to Vega. She stood silent in the doorway, her top in place and her hat and glasses once again hiding her from view.

"Vega..." he began, having no idea what he could possibly say to make it better. He settled on, "I'm so sorry."

She shook her head, smiling bravely, and held out his hat to him. "No need to fret. What's done is done. He was probably only seeking a thrill anyway."

JP wanted to agree, but he'd gotten a good look at the kid's camera. It was no toy.

He shoved the sunglasses on his face. They'd been completely exposed, and he had no doubt if the kid figured out who he was, the shot would end up in a tabloid or on a celebrity website by the end of the day.

Vega's closed-down expression let him know she'd come to the same conclusion.

He glanced back in the direction the kid had run, frustrated anew that he had so majorly fouled up. He'd promised her a day of fun where no one would know who they were, but he'd delivered worse than he'd ever imagined. Not only getting caught together, but with her body literally exposed to the world.

No wonder she'd been hesitant about going out with him. Though it was the last thing he wanted, he said, "Maybe we should call it a day. I'll get Michael to ready the plane."

He had the hotel number pulled up on his phone when she spoke. "I thought we were going out to dinner."

His thumb hovered over the Send button. He looked at her.

"Isn't that what you promised?" she asked softly.

"It is." He lowered the phone, his heartbeat suddenly thundering. "I'd planned to take you to a very exquisite location here on the island. I guarantee it'll compete with anything else you've ever tasted." He paused as if giving her time to change her mind, then asked, "Are you sure?"

He had no idea what was going on behind those beautiful eyes of hers, but he'd gladly give her anything she wanted. Anything to keep the day from coming to an end.

She dipped her head and made a vague motion toward the bikini top and jean shorts she wore. "I'll need something decent to wear first."

Their day was not yet over.

Happiness so pure it felt as if he were being cleansed from the inside out raced through him. He nodded, reached for her hand, and wrapped his fingers tightly around hers when she met him halfway. "Then allow me to buy you everything you need."

VEGA SIPPED her wine and glanced around at the view from their table in the restaurant. Earlier, JP had made quick arrangements with an upscale boutique for a private appointment to find her just the right cocktail dress. She'd tried on a number of dresses, modeling each for JP, until they'd landed on one they both loved. They'd then headed to the suite for a quick shower and change of clothes, and now sat in a secluded corner of the most exclusive restaurant on the island, picking over the end of a delicious meal and overlooking the setting sun.

The ocean breeze and the long blues and purples from the sunset created romance on a level Vega wasn't accustomed to. Soft music drifted through the air, and JP sitting across from her, power emanating from every hard angle of him, only added to the ambience.

It was a dream date. A once-in-a-lifetime event.

And one she'd discovered in the alley she hadn't been quite ready to give up so easily.

Yes, she'd been furious when the boy had taken their photo. With that camera, he was working for someone or, at the very least, had every intention of selling the picture once he found a buyer. He probably annoyed all tourists in the same way, hoping to catch a celebrity. Her only hope was that it would take the kid a while to figure out whom he'd captured.

She wet her lips as she took in the rectangular-framed glasses she'd talked JP into wearing to try to hide his identity. It didn't go far as a disguise, but she found she liked the studious look on him.

"You're wishing you'd never suggested we wear glasses tonight, aren't you?" JP's deep voice soothed her anxiety. He readjusted the frames over his eyes. "Unlike you with your sexy-librarian look, I probably look like the biggest dork you've ever seen."

"Maybe I like dorks." She shot him a look, unable to contain the flirting. He'd asked her to leave her hair down, but when she'd stepped out of the room with it in a French twist and rectangular-framed glasses settled over her nose, she'd caught his quick indrawn breath and had smiled.

"You don't ever wear glasses now? I recall a few older pictures of you wearing them."

"Haven't since I entered college. Laser surgery my first semester." He picked up her hand and turned it over to trace the length of each finger with his. She'd always thought her fingers too long, but he caressed them as if he found them the most amazing parts of her. "Any pictures of me with glasses would be at least twelve years old." One corner of his mouth lifted. "You've been Googling me, Vega."

She ducked her head, her heart rate increasing with the embarrassment she'd just stepped into. Yes, she'd spent more than a few minutes since they'd met looking him up on the internet. She'd told herself it was for the story, but even she hadn't believed it. He was simply beautiful to look at, and she'd been unable to stop herself.

He chuckled softly and laced their fingers together. "I hope that means you're as smitten as I am."

A blush heated her cheeks. She glanced around as if someone would overhear, but strategically placed plants and lack of noise from other diners reminded her there was no one else within earshot. He'd paid good money for the seclusion they were currently enjoying. She met his gaze. "I've never denied the attraction I feel for you."

"No?" He squeezed her hand. "Turning a man down over and over makes him wonder."

She shook her head at him. "I don't believe for a second your confidence was ever in question."

"You'd be surprised." He stood and pulled her hand with his, lifting her arm out to him. "Let's dance while we wait on our dessert."

"Dance?" She looked around once again, this time embarrassed at the thought of snuggling up next to him in a public restaurant. "This is a restaurant, JP. Not a dance floor."

He tugged until she rose. "This is our corner of the world, and we can do with it what we choose." His arm closed around her waist and pressed her torso to his. "I choose to dance with you before I do something embarrassing like beg you to touch me."

"Oh." The heat from his body kept her from saying more, because yes, she wanted to touch him in the worst possible way. She snuggled in, wiggling around until she found the perfect spot, and grinned when he growled in her ear.

Nothing about the day had been as she'd expected. He'd been fun and flirty, but not demanding. He'd romanced. He'd wined. And he'd dined. But he hadn't once acted as if he was doing any of it for his own benefit or the outcome he was no doubt hoping for.

She'd honestly felt like the day had been about making her happy.

"You're a bit different here," she murmured, gazing up at him.

"Yeah?" He twirled her, then brought her back, clamping his arm hard around her. "How so?"

Man, he felt good. She let herself get lost in the motions of their bodies before answering. "Still just as charming, but...not quite as hard."

He raised an eyebrow, and she giggled.

Wrapping her arms around his neck, she connected her curves to his muscles and whispered, "That's not what I mean."

She rotated her hips against him, checking out his hardness in a little more detail, and couldn't keep from licking her lips when his gaze fastened on her mouth. Before things got out of hand, she eased off and returned her hand to his grip.

He didn't seem to be able to speak, so she continued. "What I mean is, you're more *real*. More down-to-earth, like you're less concerned about maintaining any sort of image."

"Less of a cold, heartless bastard?"

She laughed and let him spin her again. "Something like that."

The music swelled, and she began to softly sing along with it. JP grinned broadly, spun her in two quick turns, then dipped her low to the floor. Her world felt exactly that. Turned upside down.

"You're tone-deaf, you know." He smiled down at her, his sheer handsomeness earning him forgiveness for the insult. "But the lipstick makes up for it."

She rolled her lips in on each other, tasting what remained of the gloss she'd picked up at the boutique. Unlike the clothes, it hadn't been his suggestion, but from the number of times she'd caught him staring at her mouth, she'd been glad for the purchase. "It seemed like the night for it."

He brought her back upright and settled her to him. "Don't get me wrong, I love it, but I've had the worst time not coming across the table to see how much I could remove without my hands."

She laughed. He was good at flirting, that was for sure.

His hand kept firm pressure on her low back as he swept her around the floor, but even if he removed it, she wouldn't put space between them. She was exactly where she wanted to be.

"When will our dessert arrive, do you think?" she murmured against the side of his throat, letting her lips move seductively across his skin as she spoke.

The fist gripping her palm tightened. "We can skip it if you're in a hurry to leave."

"I was thinking maybe we could get it to go."

He stopped dancing and pulled back to study her, eyeing her in the waning light as if trying to figure out if she was saying exactly what she was saying. She wanted to strip off their clothes and move to the next course, no more waiting.

"Okay," he nodded. "Let me get the server and pay."

While waiting for him to return, she caught a glimpse of something sparkling at the edge of the ocean. Their table was sitting within thirty feet of the waves, and they'd enjoyed the sound of the water crashing against the beach throughout dinner.

She stepped to the perimeter of the open-air room and stared out into the night, trying to make out where the light had come from while praying it wasn't a photographer. Then she saw it. A young boy, maybe eight or nine, had wandered out to the water and fallen. He wore something around his neck, and as the water swept in, splashing over him, the necklace twisted and sparkled in the moonlight.

Air caught in her throat as he climbed from where the water had dragged him and began trudging up the beach. She scoured both directions for parents but came up with none. What was this boy doing out there all by himself?

With no further thought, she kicked off her heels and stepped gingerly through the hedgerow. She hurried to make sure the boy didn't get swept out with the next incoming wave. Reaching him at the same time the water did, she clung to his arm to keep him from being dragged away.

"Are you okay?" She gentled her voice to make sure she didn't sound panicked as she once again scoured the area for whoever should be watching him.

"I got water in my nose." The child tried to pull away to wipe at his face, but she refused to let go.

She began moving them both away from the water. The beach wasn't deserted, but no one seemed concerned with a missing child. Most stood in the distance, couples seeing nothing but each other. "Where are your parents?" she asked.

Without further provocation, the boy burst into tears and flung himself against her.

The force with which he hit her caught her off guard, knocking them both to their rears as yet again, the waves reached them, this time pulling *her* toward the ocean's depths as well.

"I lost them," the child wailed once the water had washed away and they both sat, soggy in the wet sand.

She sputtered the saltwater from her own face and pulled the water-speckled glasses off.

Before she could do anything more than rise to her feet, a strong arm wrapped around her while at the same time hoisting the boy up off the ground. She looked up into JP's hard features as she hurried to keep up with his long strides. She couldn't keep the grin from covering her face. "You're rescuing me?"

"What are you doing out here?" His tone was sharp enough to make her jump.

She couldn't keep from giggling. Though it might have looked scary, the boy had been the only one in danger. She was a very strong swimmer. Plus, they'd barely been in the edge of the water. But the thought of JP being scared on her behalf thrilled her. "I was helping this young man find his parents."

JP got them all to the grass, and he put the scared child down. She shrugged out of his arms and squatted down to the youth. Once they had him taken care of, she would properly swoon over the heroic measures of her date, but first things first.

The boy calmed, and she pieced together that he'd wandered away from his parents to chase a small school of shiny fish that had been swishing back and forth in the surf.

"I didn't mean to get away from them," he muttered as if knowing the trouble he would be in once they found his parents. His sobs had subsided now that the danger was past, and he turned a stubborn look up to the both of them as if daring either not to back him up when the time came.

"I'm sure you didn't, sweetie," Vega said, stroking the boy's wet hair as she caught sight of frantically moving shadows heading their way.

Two adults rushed up from the beach, making a direct path to the boy.

"Oh my goodness," the mother breathed a sigh of relief. "You scared us to death, Rickey. Don't ever walk away from us again!"

"Sorry, Mom," Rickey mumbled, his head down as he waited for his punishment.

Vega couldn't help but smile at the mix of relief and fear crossing both adults' faces. She stepped away from Rickey, and JP reached for her, planting her at his side.

He'd also pulled off the fake glasses, and since he wasn't dripping wet as she, he was easily recognizable if anyone were at all familiar with American politics or even popular celebrities.

Given that the family standing before them had a heavy New England accent, Vega wasn't surprised when the mother's mouth gaped with recognition. "Oh my goodness, you're Jackson Davenport Jr."

She looked from JP to Vega and then to her husband, her eyes round circles.

"My Rickey was just rescued by Jackson Davenport Jr.?" she continued. "I'm so honored, Mr. Davenport."

"Please, call me JP, ma'am." Always the Southern gentleman, JP nodded at the three of them. "And I can't take any of the credit. It was this lovely lady here who was the rescuer, not me."

Her husband reached a hand forward and shook Vega's then JP's hand. "I do thank you both, whoever the hero. Rickey likes to explore, and we should have known better than to take our eyes off of him, even for a second. We'll be forever in your debt."

"No problem," both Vega and JP murmured at the same time.

A crowd had formed at the edge of the restaurant, and a couple flashes went off as JP's name moved throughout the group.

The arm around her tensed, but he didn't release her. She didn't know whether she more wanted to hide because he'd been recognized, or because her sodden hair was now clutching raggedly at her nape while her dress clung inappropriately, showing far more than she'd intended anyone but JP see that night.

"We're so grateful, Mr....JP," the mother gushed. Fear for her son had subsided, and she was now enthralled with the man they'd found themselves enmeshed with. "And for you, too, Miss..."

"Thank you," Vega said but didn't offer her name. "Really, it was no problem. I just hope Rickey is more careful next time."

The boy turned a narrowed gaze up at her as if it were her fault his parents were now chiding him against the terrors he could have been plagued with. She gave the boy a quick wink, hoping that would ease his suffering.

Someone in the crowd mentioned getting a picture and story for the local paper, and JP dropped his arm to clasp her hand. He looked down at Rickey, his intention to bolt obvious. "You okay now, sport?"

The boy nodded, his eyes glowing at JP in a similar fashion to his mother's. "Yes, sir. I'm sorry for the trouble."

JP chucked him on the shoulder. "No problem. When I was little, I liked to explore, too."

"Wow. Really?"

The whole family now gazed at JP as if he'd unearthed a secret no one else had ever been privy to, and she had to fight the urge to make gagging faces at the starstruck looks.

As the crowd moved closer, JP politely finished the conversation and got them out of there, pulling her around the side of the restaurant before ducking through a cluster of palm leaves and taking a shortcut through the foliage.

"I forgot my shoes," she moaned when her feet landed on the uneven gravel of the parking lot.

"Forget them." JP didn't slow. He reached back and lifted her in his arms. "I'll buy you as many pairs as you'd like."

He hurried them to his rental and had her tucked safely into the passenger seat before she could figure out whether she liked being hoisted and carried away as if a damsel in distress. As he rounded the car, she decided she liked it, no matter how ridiculous she might have looked.

The interior light blinked on as JP slid into his seat, then darkness once again fell with the closing of the door. He sat there, his breathing increased but not strained, and she swooned even more. What she should be doing was figuring out how to go back into hiding now that she'd been caught more than once with him, but she couldn't take her eyes off the powerful man sitting across from her.

He'd come to her rescue twice tonight. First hauling her up out of the ocean, then getting them both away from the swelling crowd. And when the perfect opportunity had presented itself to take credit for saving a child? He'd done everything he could to make sure it didn't happen.

Whether she was there or not, most politicians would have certainly stayed long enough to ensure the story hit the papers.

Wouldn't they?

JP glanced around the parking lot then settled his gaze on her. "No one followed us, but I'd better get us out of here before they do."

She nodded. "We clearly suck at hiding in public."

A chuckle drifted through the space as the car came to life. He reached over and laid his hand on her knee, squeezing it lightly, and comfort swelled inside her.

Now that the excitement had passed, she snuggled deep into her seat and thought about the day as a whole. She would be plastered all over the tabloids within hours, if not already. That meant if they weren't already, someone would soon start looking into who she was and where she came from.

A smart woman would cut bait and disappear without looking back.

"Where to?" he asked as he steered the car out of the lot. "I'm sure you'd like to clean up. You can use the lavatory on the plane, if you want. I'll have Michael bring our things from the suite."

She'd forgotten how bad she must look. She peered down at herself to see that patches of her thin dress were still clinging to her, and she grimaced. The downward movement also dangled loose straggles of her hair in front of her face. She plopped her head back on the seat. "I look awful."

JP glanced at her, his expression hidden in the dark. "Not possible."

They pulled up to a light. A nearby sign reading *Airport* pointed to the left. The resort was to the right.

"So?" He swallowed. "The plane?"

He was really going to head back to the airport and take them home tonight? It would be the middle of the night before they arrived in Atlanta, but he acted as if there was nothing wrong with the idea.

And then she remembered the next day was a workday. "I suppose you need to get back so you can get to work tomorrow. I probably should, too."

He turned on his left turn signal. She thought she detected a slight slumping of his shoulders, but he didn't comment on the fact that the date was now apparently over. "I own the company," he said. "I can do as I please."

"But don't you have appointments lined up?"

The light turned green, but he didn't press the gas. Instead, he turned to her, and the hand still on her knee tightened. "What do *you* want, Vega?" His voice was low. "That's all that matters."

He really would head back without once pressing her for sex. And he had to know she'd be heading to her home, not his, as soon as they returned.

Or was this somehow part of the game?

She was so confused. She brought a hand to her forehead and rubbed. He hadn't once acted as she'd expected since she'd met him. Her chest suddenly tightened at the thought that if he turned left, they would begin the ending of their time together.

A horn honked behind them, and JP glanced in his rearview mirror but still didn't move the car. He returned his gaze to her, and she made up her mind.

"I want to turn right."

One eyebrow lifted, highlighted in the streetlight. "Something else you want to do?"

She nodded, hoping she was making the right decision. They might have nowhere to go after this night, but she wasn't ready for it to end so soon. "I want to make good use of that room you paid for."

The air between them disappeared.

"Are you sure?" His voice was tighter than normal.

"Positive." She smiled, impatient now. "In fact, if you *don't* take me to the resort within the next few minutes, I'm going to seriously start doubting your manhood."

He threw a glance toward the traffic and jolted the car forward. Tires squealed as they shot off to the right. His hand on her knee changed, heat from his fingers now imprinting into her skin, and she couldn't help but laugh out loud when he leaned over and planted a quick, hard kiss on her mouth.

"Never doubt me, sweetheart." His voice returned to its normal rumble. "I'll spend the rest of the night proving it if you need me to."

CHAPTER FOURTEEN

They entered the suite, but Vega barely had time to once again be awed by the opulence as JP pulled her through the main room. They skirted the couch and end table and bypassed the wet bar. They got to the room he'd changed clothes in earlier in the day, and when he swung open the door, she practically swooned.

"That is quite a bed." The mammoth king-sized bed sat in the middle of the room, waiting for them. One lamp was on but dimmed. A light breeze from the ocean lifted the sheer panels over the doors leading to the private patio, and the top edge of the bed's thick taupe comforter had been turned back. Mosquito netting draped romantically from the ceiling to either side of the headboard.

The only things missing were rose petals and champagne.

"That, my dear," JP began as he twirled Vega around to face him, "is about to be put to good use."

She held her breath, suddenly nervous as she waited for him to make his first move. She didn't understand the nerves. The entire day had led to this moment, yet for some reason, she felt shy and new at this.

His arms reached around her, and she inhaled him. His woodsy scent combined with the salty air was a powerful aphrodisiac. His fingers began plucking the pins from her hair and dropping them to the floor behind her, one at a time.

"I've wanted to take your hair down from the moment I saw you."

"It's already half down as it is." Her nerves came through in her voice, mortifying her. "And it has saltwater mixed with it. Nothing sexy about it now."

He leaned back and peered down at her. In her bare feet, she felt tiny next to him. "You okay?" he asked.

She shrugged, wanting to move him past the moment. "A little nervous, I guess."

It had been a long time since she'd made love to anyone, and in her wet dress and bedraggled hair, she suddenly felt very unattractive. That wasn't the picture she wanted him remembering from this night.

His hands had all the pins out, but he stopped, both hands sunk deep in the tendrils, studying her as if seeing her for the first time.

"Nervousness is not something I'd associate with you. Quiet sometimes, letting people like that ass you work with walk over you. Sometimes shocked at your own feelings…at the attraction between us. At the fact you raised your hand and bid on me," his voice lowered. "But never nervous. Just shocked that you did it." He stepped back, releasing her, and goose bumps lifted on her skin. "What can I do to help?"

God, she was getting more mortified by the moment. He was supposed to care only about himself, not worry about her. That's the way Ted had always been.

At the thought, she pulled in a quick gasp and looked up at him. "What?" he asked.

She shook her head. She wasn't about to tell him she'd just compared him to the ex who'd turned her against men like him. At least he'd come out the winner between the two, though.

And that alone made even more anxiety consume her. He *was* different than Ted, even from the beginning of her past affair. Ted had wined and dined, but he'd never asked her what she wanted nor pretended to actually care about her feelings. He'd said the words, but his actions hadn't backed them up.

She'd been so blinded by the thought of love and not being alone anymore that she'd completely ignored those facts.

"Vega?" JP lifted one of her hands and pressed a kiss to her palm before curling her fingers over his. "You've got to help me here, babe. I can see something's wrong. Tell me what I can do. Please."

The plea was too much. She didn't want to believe he was a truly good guy. It wasn't supposed to be like that. She pulled away and rubbed her hands up and down her arms. "I'm just feeling ragged from the dip in the ocean. Maybe I could take a shower and clean up first?"

"Of course." He pressed a kiss to her forehead and pushed her in the direction of the bathroom. "Whatever you need."

"Thank you," she murmured as she headed through the door, but when she turned to close it, he surprised her again.

He stepped up to her and caressed her jaw. "If you've changed your mind, that's okay, too. We've had a perfect day already. If it needs to end now, I'll take the other room, and you can have this one. Just say the word."

Her lips trembled. "Let me clean up, then we'll see where we stand, okay?"

He nodded. "Absolutely. I'll order something chocolate from room service to make up for losing our other dessert."

"That's perfect." She leaned forward and pressed a light kiss to his mouth. "Thank you."

JP CLOSED the door behind room service and carried the covered platter to the master bedroom. He set it on the desk and removed his jacket and tie. The hum of the hair dryer suddenly shut off, sending the room into silence, and he eyed the closed bathroom door, wondering what would happen next.

He'd been telling the truth. If the night needed to end now, then that's what would happen.

But he hoped like hell it wouldn't.

The entire day had been one incredible journey after another, and yes, he wanted the last stop to be with him buried deep inside her, but if not, he could live with it. He'd already had a better date than he'd experienced in the last ten years. Maybe longer. There was just something about her that put him at ease, allowing him to lose the need to constantly be "on," thus allowing for an entire day of being happy and relaxed. Those days were rare.

The bathroom door opened, and steam whooshed out, making him remorseful at being gentleman enough to stay out of the shower with her. Her hair, now dried, bounced lightly around her shoulders, making her appear to be a dark-haired angel heading toward him.

"Hi." She smiled, then looked at the floor, seemingly as nervous as she'd been when he'd last seen her. He crossed the thick rug and lifted her face to his.

"Hey." He leaned in and planted a soft kiss against her warm lips, unable to keep from doing so. Her lips had looked unbelievable glistening with lipstick earlier in the evening, but with the heat of the shower plumping them up, he had a hard time stopping with a simple peck. "You feeling better?"

She nodded. "Thanks."

"I got chocolate." He grinned when her eyes lit up. He motioned to the end of the bed. "Sit. I'll bring it to you."

Instead of the edge, Vega plopped herself on the turned-down sheets, rearranging the pillows behind her until she was comfortably seated against the headboard. She curled her bare legs under her and patted the mattress beside her. "Sit with me."

"Whatever the lady wants." He grabbed the dessert and slid it onto the bed, then kicked off his shoes and joined her. When he lifted the lid, he revealed a six-layer chocolate cake so large Vega's eyes bugged wide. He laughed out loud at the innocence of it all. "I feel like teenagers sneaking out of our parents' houses in the middle of the night, only instead of making out in the back seat of my father's car, we're doing something even more forbidden."

With the first bite already on its way to her mouth, she chose to finish its path before answering him. "Mmm, chocolate should never be forbidden."

"I agree." He forked a bite but remained manly enough to hold back a matching moan at the richness of the dessert. "I find it amazing you can eat the way you do yet remain as hot as you are."

She eyed him from the corners of her eyes, a sparkle glinting in the brown orbs. "You trying to toss a compliment in there, Davenport, or asking how I stay in shape with my appetite?"

He chuckled. "I guess both."

Another bite crossed her lips and he found it impossible not to watch her mouth in action.

After swallowing, she lowered the fork and narrowed her gaze on him as if determining if she could share the secret of where she kept her stash of chocolates. Finally, she plunged the tines back into the cake. "I do martial arts and kickboxing on a regular basis. In fact, I could probably have taken you to the ground and stolen this cake from you myself if you hadn't willingly handed it over."

He burst out laughing. Not at the idea she thought she could take him, but at the spirit coming back into her eyes. "I've never met anyone like you, Vega."

She shrugged. "I love the things I love, but..." Her teeth nibbled at her bottom lip as she fiddled with another bite. "Life has a way of taking the air out of you sometimes. It's happened to me a time or two, so I have to be careful."

Seriousness quickly settled into the room, and though he wanted to ask about the times life had kicked her down, he preferred to keep the moment lighter. This was supposed to be one fun day out of their lives, after all.

He stole the bite off her fork.

After a stunned pause, she yelped and punched him in the ribs. He cringed, pretending pain, while she snatched the plate and pulled it directly in front of her instead of between them. The serious moment was broken. He scooted closer, inhaling the fresh scent of soap and woman as they both fought to beat the other to the next bite.

"So how about your teenage years?" He won with the cake but fed it to her instead of eating it for himself. As her mouth closed around his fork, he suddenly had a hard time not thinking about the fact they were on top of a very large bed, and she was most likely naked underneath her thick robe. "Did you drive the boys crazy refusing to sneak out with them, or did you give in to the pressure?"

She lifted her shoulders in an apologetic way. "I was a good girl."

He acted shocked. "You never snuck out of your house as a kid?"

"You're telling me you did?" She licked a crumb off the corner of her mouth and grinned at him, and his gut seized. She was absolutely beautiful. "I thought you were perfect?"

"I've never claimed to be perfect." His voice grew scratchy. He scooted down to lean on one elbow, then scooped up another bite and fed it to her. This time he couldn't stop the movement behind the zipper of his slacks. His ears filled with the roar of his own blood as it headed south. "That's merely the way the world wants to see me."

"Ah." Her eyes closed for a few seconds as she rested her head against the pillows and chewed. "So you're telling me you had hordes of women, even as a teenager, and you routinely snuck out to meet them?" She peered at him from her position on the covered down. "I'll bet even then they were only too happy to let you get in their panties."

He lowered his gaze to where her panties would be and fought the urge to ask if she was wearing any. "I wouldn't call it hordes."

She snickered. "Definitely hordes."

He held another bite up in the air but kept it hovering over the cake instead of feeding it to her. "You jealous?"

She watched him from under heavy lids now, and he could barely remember what they were talking about other than panties. "Jealousy would imply that I cared."

Was it so wrong he wanted her to be jealous? "That would be bad?"

She nodded. "That would be terrible."

He wasn't so sure about that. He lifted the fork up in front of her as if in question.

"Aren't you going to eat more?" Her words were breathy.

He shook his head. "I got it for you."

"I can't eat all of that."

"Then you eat until you're done."

He waved the fork in the air, and she lifted up off the headboard, her throat stretching forward as she reached for it with her mouth. She watched him as she closed around the tines. He licked his lips and managed to hold in his groan.

After she swallowed, she spoke softly. "I'm done."

Without words, he moved the plate to the bedside table. When he turned back, she'd slipped down to lie in the same position as JP, her bare legs now stretched out over the comforter and her robe riding high on her thighs. They both lay there watching each other, a narrow foot of space separating them.

"So tell me what you were doing as a teenager instead of slipping out to make some poor sap's night?"

A haunted look crossed her face. "My dad died when I was fifteen."

"Oh, honey." He reached out, unsure how best to comfort her, and ended up tucking a strand of hair behind her ear. He pressed a kiss to her cheek, lingering against the downy skin. "I'm so sorry," he whispered. "What happened?"

When he began to pull back, she reached up and stopped him. She held his face close to hers and turned her lips upward. "Killed in the line of duty. I don't want to talk about it."

He kissed her then, certain he'd never done anything good enough in his life to enjoy the pleasure of her mouth. Her soft lips parted beneath his, and he denied himself the pleasure no longer. With an agonized groan, he slipped his tongue inside and sunk into her, closing the gap between their bodies at the same time.

They aligned perfectly. He couldn't help but press into her, his cock begging for the freedom to chase the pleasures before him. Locking a leg around hers, he made sure she felt what she did to him.

"JP," she whispered. "I'm sorry I was...weird earlier. It's been a crazy day."

He dotted kisses along her forehead and over her cheeks. His hand dipped to the hollow of her back and held her to him, tension from not taking her about to snap him in two. "You can take all the time in the world you need. As long as you know I'm here when you're ready." He tilted back and met her eyes. "Are you okay, now? I meant it when I said I could sleep in the other room. It's not what I want." He chuckled at the thought. "But I'm not an ogre. We'll do this only if it's what you want."

She nodded and reached for the tie of her robe. Then, as if in slow motion, she rolled to her back and spread the edges of the cotton.

"Make love to me, JP."

JP stared at the woman before him. She was going to be the death of him. Her beauty had been what had initially attracted him, but her vulnerability was literally making him so hard he wasn't sure he could wait long enough to see to her own enjoyment.

He had to have every last bit of her. As damn soon as possible.

Dragging his gaze from the perfect, honeyed globes in front of him, he flitted his fingers over her flat stomach before scraping his gaze up off her and admitting something he never thought he'd say out loud. "I'm afraid it'll go too fast."

She nodded. "Yes."

"Vega." A groan ripped through the air. He clamped his hands around her waist and rolled them, pulling her atop him to straddle his hips. Her breasts jiggled as he reached up to cup them both in his hands. He bounced their weight, then squeezed, battling with himself to go slow. He could barely make out anything but the hard peaks as he flicked his thumbs over her nipples. "You're amazing." He didn't like being this out of control. "Give me a minute. I need to calm down. I want to make sure it's good for you."

Her hands moved to his shirt and undid the buttons with amazing speed, then she yanked the tails from his pants and slid her palms over his chest, all shyness gone. "It's been good since the first second you spoke to me." She leaned forward, touching her lips to the underside of his jaw and her breasts to his chest. "Now take me," she whispered.

And it was over.

He groaned, out of control, and worked feverishly to remove all his clothes as she shed the robe and waited on the bed for him, splendidly naked. He grabbed a condom from his wallet and tossed it on the nightstand, then kneeled on the bed, situating himself between her legs. He wouldn't take her yet, but he couldn't put off touching her any longer.

With firm hands, he gripped both knees and yanked her down the bed. She opened before him, and he locked her legs around his hips. He then leaned over her, pressing against her so that her heat touched him, and his head swam. If he wasn't careful, he would pass out from lack of blood circulating anywhere near his brain.

"You're incredible." Forcing himself to slow, he sucked in steady breaths, one after another, and lifted off her, sending his fingers on an exploration of the long, perfect extensions of her body. His palm roamed over the back of a thigh and down to her calf, the firmness of the narrow muscle tightening his body even more. He gritted his teeth and slid upward. Everything about her was both soft and hard, innocent yet sexy as hell, and burning hot.

He traced the dip behind her knee, then over the top of her thigh, taking his time to make sure he enjoyed the strength of it, before using his thumb to follow the bend of her leg and hip.

"Later," he murmured, dipping his head to stroke his tongue over one nipple, "I get to explore all these places with my mouth."

His hand slid over her hip to the curve of her rear, and she moaned. A soft, low animal noise that had him gripping the sheet with his other hand so hard he pulled the corner free from the bed.

Her breath hitched when his fingers slid down the cleft of her bottom. He buried his face between her breasts and spoke without moving his jaw. "I want to make sure you never forget me, Vega."

One finger continued sliding, reaching for the moisture waiting for him just around the curve.

"Can't imagine how that could be possible," she panted, her voice soft and drugged.

When he reached her core, he anchored the base of his palm against her and used his middle finger to toy over her. She trembled beneath him.

"God, I want to taste you." He closed his lips over her mouth and at the same time pressed one finger inside her.

Her body bowed, her muscles clenching around him, tensed and squeezing until he thought she might climax at that very moment.

With a grunt, she pulled her lips from his. "JP?"

He peered down at her, seeing her through the heat in his own eyes. "Yeah?"

"Fuck me already."

His body heated to boiling.

She shoved the condom toward him. "Put it on."

He ripped open the packet.

Vega's head rested on the pillows, her dark hair spread out on the white sheets underneath her, and her hands began to move downward as he worked. She slid along her sides, gliding over her own skin as if unable to wait for him. Dipping lower, she trailed her fingers to the tops of her thighs, her long hands practically framing the spot where she wanted him.

His fingers froze as he watched her, unsure how to perform the simple act he'd done hundreds of times before. He'd intended to make love to her as many times tonight as she'd allow, get her out of his system, then see her back to her own life. He didn't know what pain she hid from, and other than wanting her to share so it might help her to overcome it, he'd told himself he didn't care. But at that exact moment, he realized what a lie all of it had been.

There was no way he would be able to let her out of his life so soon. He wasn't sure at the moment how he ever could at all.

His fingers fumbled, but he finally got the protection in place, then he trailed his hands over her legs and up to her own fingers, his movements slow. He was almost sick at the thought that she would most definitely walk away from him the next day.

"JP?" Solemn brown eyes searched his. "Is something wrong?"

He shook his head, unable to utter a word. Anchoring his hands on either side of her, he held himself up so he could watch as he took her. Her legs widened, tucking him perfectly into their V, and with one smooth motion he disappeared.

"Ahhh…" Vega's eyes rolled to the back of her head, and liquid fire shot between his shoulder blades and down his spine, jerking him into a tight arch above her. Her mouth opened; her bottom lip became a beacon. Her breasts rocked as he once again lunged forward.

Slowly, he moved in and out, fighting the urge to pound, and watched as her trimmed pelvis lifted to meet each thrust. Her body turned a heated pink beneath his, and her breaths shortened, pants matching his own, and all the while he pumped, practically desperate to dip and catch a turgid nipple between his teeth.

His arms shook with his resistance. If he captured her now, he was done.

She slipped her hands behind him and dug into his buttocks as her chest curved upward, her body taut, and he almost laughed out loud. Who was he kidding? It was already over. For both of them.

"Vega." His voice was tight, close to losing control. She didn't acknowledge him. "Vega," he repeated urgently.

Her eyelids fluttered until a sliver of black gleamed up at him.

"Look at me, baby. Look at me." He ground himself against her. "Let me see what I do to you."

Glazed eyes remained trained on him, and an overwhelming desire consumed him. He would do anything to satisfy this woman. Pushing them both higher, he pumped, meeting her thrust for thrust, while never taking his gaze from hers.

And then it was there, ready to shoot them both to the pinnacle, and he collapsed. He fell on her, holding his hands on either side of her head to keep her from looking away, and surged.

"Vega," he cried, the guttural sound seeming to come from somewhere else. He pumped twice more, then let out an anguished cry as he emptied himself. His shoulders and neck tense as he kept his eyes trained to hers.

She jerked in his arms, uncontrollable spasms shaking her, tightening her thighs to the point that he wondered if she would hurt herself. Her eyes begged him to release her, but he didn't. He couldn't.

Her mouth opened with silent screams as they both stared, trembling in each other's arms until there was nothing left.

When the moment calmed, he latched on to her lips, unwilling to show her any more of what was in him. He kissed her until no breath remained anywhere in his body, then dropped his face into the curve of her neck and panted. He'd known it would be like this. This powerful. This instant need for more.

And he knew whatever her demons were, he had to help her overcome them.

So she could be his.

Rolling off her, he pulled her to his side and tucked her against him. That meant he'd also have to let her into his life.

She seemed as content as him to say nothing, so he held her until their breathing returned to normal, then grabbed a tissue and quickly rid himself of the condom. When steady puffs of air whispered across his shoulder and her breaths grew deep, he ran a palm over her hip. "Babe?"

"Hmmm?" Her lips pressed into his neck, and his chest tightened. God, he could do this forever.

"Will you spend tomorrow here with me too? Make it two days instead of one?"

She edged a leg between his and murmured, "In bed or on the island?"

He smiled at the ceiling. "Either."

Her mouth curve against his throat. "Yes."

Happiness flooded him to the tips of his toes, urging him to spring out of bed and get busy at that very moment. He had only twenty or so more hours to convince her they should date for real. It wouldn't be easy, but he wouldn't accept anything but a *yes*.

She lived in Savannah, but they could work around that, at least for a while. He could drive down for weekends, or she could drive up. Or—something nudged him from deep inside—he could let her do the interview. That would keep her in town a while longer.

It wasn't like he would be able to keep his private life that for too much longer, anyway. Once he publicly agreed to accept the position, reporters would come out of the woodwork to dig out every piece of dirt on him they could find. Luckily, they wouldn't find much. He may have snuck out of the house as a teenager, but the media hadn't been all wrong. He'd pretty much been a perfect person all his life. With the exception that he dated too many women—which everyone knew already—and he hadn't been able to read for a good chunk of his childhood.

And that he was now keeping his father's love child a secret.

He rolled to his side and faced her. Better to try the Savannah option first. "You need to call the station and tell them you're taking tomorrow off. Will they mind?"

"No." Her body was so relaxed she'd be asleep within minutes.

He'd already called Beverly earlier to cancel his morning appointments. He would email her in the morning to do the same with the afternoon ones, as well as ask her to call the school to get Daniel enrolled this week. He wasn't one to use his name to call in a lot of favors, but for this he would.

Reaching across Vega, he grabbed his phone off the bedside table. "Tell me the number."

She shook her head and dug in deeper against his side. "It's too late."

"It's only eleven thirty." He nudged her shoulder to wake her up. "Come on. Someone has to be there you can talk to. What's the number?"

One dark eye peeked up at him. "They won't care."

He paused. "That you aren't coming in tomorrow?"

"That I'm not coming in ever." She closed her eyes and rolled to her other side, her rear now nestled to the front of his crotch. "I got fired," she mumbled.

"What?"

One slim shoulder moved up and down in front of him. "Practically." Her muffled voice barely made its way to him.

Anger on her behalf burned through him. "What does that mean?" He dropped the phone back into its cradle and rolled her over onto her back so he could see her, but she didn't make eye contact. "When did this happen?"

"Last night, before the auction." Her eyes remained closed, and her voice broke his heart. She sounded younger, more lost than he'd ever heard her. No fire in her at all.

"But you worked last night."

"I'm not officially fired yet. Bob told me the call had come down, and since he can't talk me into being in front of the camera, he's going to have to let me go."

"But you've won awards," JP said. "I've seen them."

Her eyes finally opened, and she stared up at him with dark, solemn orbs. "You Googled me, too."

Heat threatened to tint his cheeks at the unintended admission. He could tell her it had been purely about making sure she wasn't a threat to his family or name, but the fact was, the more he'd searched, the more he'd been interested in her rather than in whether she had some deep, dark secret he needed to know about. With only a bit of reluctance, he nodded to confirm her suspicions.

A slight smile touched her lips, and he had to fight the urge to lean back in and kiss her. They needed to finish this discussion, not skim over it because he wanted her again. In fact, they needed to do more than have the discussion.

"We should go back so you can go to work tomorrow. You have

to change their minds. I'll call Michael to ready the plane." He reached for the phone, but her small hand stopped him.

"Don't," she said. "It won't help."

He looked down at her, desperate to remove the lost sound from her voice. "It will help. You said it wasn't official yet. You can—"

"It will be in two weeks," she interrupted him. "They aren't even expecting me back."

Selfishness flared as he realized that meant she could stay in Atlanta while he figured out what this was between them, but that fact didn't ease the knot in his gut. He couldn't help feeling like he needed to fix this.

He reached for the covers that had gotten shoved to the foot of the bed and pulled them up. "Then we'll find you another job."

He could even rent her a place in the city if she preferred to take time off until she decided what she wanted to do next. Something told him it wouldn't be that simple.

"Maybe you'll still get that job in Atlanta you wanted. Surely they'll still consider you for the position."

Instead of answering, she rolled to her side to reach toward the lamp. He watched her smooth, narrow back stretch away from him until the light clicked off, and they were cast into shadows. A strip of light from the bathroom trickled into the room, but it didn't make it to the bed.

When she settled back under the covers, she didn't lie as close to him as she had before. He closed the distance and wrapped an arm and a leg around her, relaxing into her when she didn't protest. He curled his hand lightly around her breast. "The Atlanta job will come through."

A thin sigh slid through the night before her quiet voice hit his ears. "Since I didn't get the interview with you, I won't get the job either."

A slab of concrete settled right in the middle of his chest. He had cost her her job.

Damn.

Before he could figure out what he could possibly say to that, she drifted off to sleep, her deep breaths comforting him in a way he couldn't recall feeling since he'd been a very young boy.

He closed his eyes and held her tight. He would worry about fixing it tomorrow. Right now, he just wanted to hold her.

CHAPTER FIFTEEN

*V*ega woke to the smell of bacon and the sound of JP's voice. At first she thought he was talking to room service, then realized from the lack of any other voice during his pauses that he must be on the phone. She glanced at the clock. It was barely six. It was far too early for her, personally, to consider working, but she was curious as to whether he'd so quickly gone back into business mode now that the night was over. It was Monday morning, after all.

She slipped from the bed and edged closer, hoping to make out his words.

"She won't be pleased to hear it." Pause. "Yeah, it was pretty amazing. She jumped into the ocean without thought to anything but the kid."

He was talking about her?

"Of course she wouldn't have let him drown, but there were others around. She could have easily brought it to someone else's attention."

She heard clicking as if he were on a computer keyboard. Then he laughed.

"Cute." Pause. "Huh?" Pause. Laugh. "Yes, fine. You were right. I wanted her to win."

Who was he talking to? She grabbed the robe she'd so boldly tossed off the night before and inched to the doorway. JP stood in the living room, nothing on but his slacks, looking out the open patio doors. There was a room service cart near the dining room table, and the sound of waves crashed in the background.

He remained quiet for so long she began to think he'd lost connection. She took a step out of the room but froze when he started talking again.

"I gave it thought, but I still don't think it's a good idea. I'd rather put it off as long as possible." Long pause. "You've got to be kidding me. President isn't even something I can consider for another five years."

Vega's eyes widened.

President?

She shook her head. Of course. *President.* That was the plan, after all. Everyone had expected that for years. But it still took her by surprise to hear him talk about it. That had been one of the things about him that'd shocked her so since meeting him. He barely talked politics.

For a man about to step into the limelight, and who would someday be gearing up for a presidential run, it certainly never seemed to be foremost on his mind.

"Yes, I know. I'm a Davenport. Of course I want to be president someday."

Vega stared at the long, sinewy muscles of his back, now bunched, and noted the dry tone of his voice. He *didn't* want to be president? She flashed back to their first conversation when he'd said him accepting the senatorial seat wasn't yet decided. She'd assumed he was kidding, but was that the reason for the delay in making the announcement? Did JP not want to be a politician?

Suddenly realizing she was eavesdropping, she turned around to leave but got caught in the act.

"I've got to go, Cat. Vega's up." Pause. "Fine. Yeah. I'll think about it some more."

She faced the man she'd just spent the better portion of the night exploring and smiled as he got off the phone, awkwardness filling her at the thought of everything they'd done to each other. "Good morning," she managed.

He crossed to her and planted a kiss on her mouth that came close to having her shucking the robe and dragging him back to bed. "Morning."

"You must have gotten Cat out of bed early." She didn't want to pry, but they had been talking about her.

One eyebrow rose. "She's the one who called me."

"Oh." She rounded the food cart and peeked under a lid, finding what she wanted. Pulling out a piece of bacon, she held it in the air as she talked. "I just assumed you'd been up a while."

JP bit off the end of the crisp pork she held in her hand, then grinned at her shocked gape. The man had a bad habit of snatching food out of her hand. But then, she kind of liked him being comfortable enough with her to do that.

"I have been up," he began. "I routinely rise at five, so when I woke, I got some work done, then decided we would both probably need more than chocolate cake." His eyes glinted at the implication of why they might need reenergizing. "Cat called before I could serve you in bed."

The naughty look on his face made her wish she'd stayed in bed. "Something wrong with Cat?"

He motioned to the computer screen on the corner workstation. "We made the internet."

Anxiety straightened her spine. She'd known being out with him would cause this to happen. She took in the picture on the monitor and let out a breath that it was only one of her looking

191

like a drowned rat while he stood by her side, holding her hand. The caption indicated they didn't know who she was, but that would be righted soon enough. Someone had wanted this up overnight, but as soon as they put two and two together and reviewed the video from the auction, she'd be found out.

She glanced up at him. "The alley? Anything show up from that?"

"Not yet."

Yet. They both knew it was only a matter of time.

Nodding, she crunched on another piece of bacon and scrolled down the screen. There was another shot of them darting off toward the trees, but not one of him carrying her across the parking lot.

She smiled at the memory. "Sorry I lost the shoes you bought me yesterday. They were really nice shoes."

He stepped up behind her and circled her waist. "And you looked really good in them."

"I did, didn't I?" She giggled. She'd tried to talk him into a less expensive pair, but he'd insisted they were the ones that went perfectly with the dress. And she did like awesome shoes. She tilted her head back and squinted up at him. "I imagine the dress is ruined, too."

"Not even on my radar." He pressed a hot, openmouthed kiss to her mouth, and she turned in his arms, but he ended the moment before it could develop into something more. "Let's talk about your job situation. I've been online most of the morning—"

"No," she interrupted vehemently. The last thing she wanted to do right then was think about the fact she had nothing to go back home to. "We're here to have fun, right?"

He gave a slight nod. "Yeah, but we need to talk about this. It was my fault, so I should—"

"You should do nothing. It wasn't your fault, JP. They were planning cuts whether I got the interview or not."

"But if I'd agreed..."

His words trailed off because they both knew what would happen if he'd agreed to do the interview. She'd have created a potentially award-worthy piece and gotten a new job. But none of those things would happen now, and she didn't want to talk about that either.

"Maybe you should reconsider being on camera," he started.

Pain clustered in her midsection. If only things were different. She shook her head. "It's not an option." She slid her hands up over his chest to link around his neck. "Can we get back to that kiss, please? You kind of left me riled up."

His lids lowered as she could see him fighting with himself on whether to let her change the subject or not. With a muffled growl, he finally gave in. "Fine, but this conversation isn't over."

He pressed his mouth to hers so that they picked up right where they'd left off, and with the flick of a wrist had her sash untied, then had her stripped bare a mere two seconds later.

She looked down at her naked parts. "You're awfully good at that."

"I've had some practice." The smile coming back at her was worthy of the devil himself.

Jealousy reared its head, but she fought the urge to show it. As she'd stated the previous evening, being jealous meant she cared. She might not be able to turn off her feelings, but he certainly didn't have to know about them.

The last thing she wanted was for him to think she would be one of his fawning women, doing anything and everything to get a few more measly minutes of his time.

It was simple. She was enjoying the date she'd humiliated herself to get. When they got home, she'd go back to her life, and he'd go to his. Liking him or not would never come into play, and the fact that she'd known she was in way over her head when she'd darted off to hide in the shower the night before certainly didn't matter either.

"Lots and lots of practice," he teased, his voice low and sexy. He trailed a finger around the base of one breast until she whimpered and pushed into his hand. He closed over her, shooting a path of heat down her body. "You're still not jealous?"

She shook her head. She was definitely turned on though. "Doesn't matter to me. I've slept with plenty of men, too."

His eyes turned stormy at the admission, but she wasn't about to tell him she could count the number of her lovers all on one hand. Without warning, he picked her up, and she squealed in surprise. She clutched her legs around his waist as he began striding, carrying her through the rooms until he reached the master bath where he deposited her on the cold countertop.

She yelped again, rearing up off the granite, but he didn't let her escape.

He pressed his hands to her hips and pushed her down, holding her there and leaning his agitated face into hers. "How about if I tell you the thought of you with other men *does* make me jealous?"

She eyed his square jaw. It had a little twitch toward the back on the right side. Was he trying to tell her *he* cared? She licked her lips and turned her nose up in the air, refusing to accept such. "It's ego. I'm sure you say that to all your girls."

"Vega." He shot her a frustrated look. "Honey. You can be a pain in the butt when you want to, did you know that?"

Reaching inside the shower, he kept one hand on her, holding her down on the counter, and used his other to turn the knob. He then picked her up and unceremoniously dumped her under the freezing water. He closed the door and held it shut as she squeaked and squealed and jumped around, trying to keep the stinging water from turning her to ice.

"Let me out!" She banged her fist on the shower door.

"Tell me the thought of me with other women drives you crazy."

"Never."

He lost his pants and stood on the other side of the glass door, and she totally forgot the cold water or the fact that she could adjust the temperature herself if she was so inclined. Though he was acting jealous, it was clear there was a much stronger emotion churning through him at the moment.

She swallowed and licked her lips. She hadn't had nearly enough looks at that thing the night before.

"Want to join me in here?" she asked.

His fingers wrapped around the top edge of the shower door and gripped tight. "I hear the water's cold."

"Not so much." She couldn't take her gaze off his burgeoning dick. "It's getting warmer by the second."

She slid her hands up over her breasts, catching her nipples between thumbs and forefingers and pinching. She moaned as she tugged, then tilted her head down to watch as she let go, and her breasts sprung back into position. She repeated the action once more just because it felt good.

"Come in here and play," she taunted.

He shook his head. "I can play out here," he scratched out.

One hand released the shower door and lowered to grip himself, then began moving slowly back and forth, tantalizing her with its rhythm. Calling to her. He didn't pick up speed, just stroked, over and over, as she continued to watch.

A drop of fluid appeared on the tip, and she groaned. She sucked the end of a finger into her mouth and brought her gaze up to his, locking on to his dark pupils as she slowly pulled the finger deeper behind her lips, letting him know what she wanted to do to him.

His jaw tensed. "I'll join you if you'll admit the thought of me with other women makes you jealous."

KIM LAW

Her head moved slowly back and forth, and she released her finger. "Why does it matter?"

She reached to the side without taking her eyes off him and adjusted the knobs, turned the showerhead so it wasn't hitting her so directly, then picked up the bar of soap. No way was he winning this round.

"I just want the truth," he said. "I thought you were a what-you-see-is-what-you-get kind of girl."

"What makes you think you're not getting the real me?" Her hands rolled the soap between her breasts until they were foaming with bubbles, then she dropped the bar and slid both palms once again over her breasts. She closed her eyes as she soaped them, rubbing and squeezing them together until her nipples stood as erect as him.

Next, she rested her head on the tile wall behind her and roamed her fingers up over her neck, letting out a tiny breathy moan as she traveled.

Without missing a beat, back down she went, touching and teasing herself until she found the spot he'd finally gotten around to touching with his lips in the early morning hours. She was more than ready for more of that. She slipped her fingers between the trimmed hair and cracked open her heavy lids to watch JP watch her pleasure herself.

His hand had quit moving.

"Vega," he warned. "You're asking for trouble in there."

"I'm not asking." She moaned as her fingertip brushed over her engorged flesh. She spread her legs farther apart for better access. "You wouldn't join me, so I'm simply taking matters into my own hands."

He groaned, and she smiled at the steam that collected on the door where he breathed.

"You still not planning to join me?" One hand roamed back to her chest to fondle her breasts while the fingers of the other

196

worked harder down below. "Oh," she panted out, far more turned on than she'd intended. She'd simply wanted to drive him as crazy as he'd been driving her.

His grip over the edge of the still-closed shower door shook it in its tracks as his gaze jumped back and forth between her hands. "You're so damn hot."

"Uh-huh." She rested against the wall and worked herself faster, losing strength in her knees. Her other hand repeatedly pinched her nipples until she couldn't keep from rolling her head back and forth. "Come in here with me, JP. Please."

The words were barely out of her mouth before the door was wrenched opened and he had her in his arms. He gripped her butt and jerked her to him, pressing his jutting cock hard to her stomach. When she pulled her hand away, he clasped her fingers in his and led her back.

"Don't stop. I'll help."

Together, the two of them slipped back between her folds, teasing and flicking as her body tensed with the motions. She was on the verge of an explosive orgasm, and her knees were losing the battle to hold her up. She pressed back into the wall and planted her heels, trying to keep herself from slipping. "I'm going to fall."

"I won't let you." His arm closed around her waist like a vise. "Wrap your arm around my neck and hold on."

She did as instructed but that left her breasts bare. JP's eyes gleamed down at the soapy mounds a second before his mouth dipped, and he went after them. His teeth closed around a nipple and bit down, and she raced toward a climax she wouldn't have been able to stop if she'd wanted to.

"JP?" she panted. Her entire body shook with tension, so tight she wasn't sure she would survive what was coming next.

"I've got you, baby. Let it go." He sucked her deep into his mouth while lifting a knee to grind their fingers harder into her. He nudged upward in fast thrusts then switched to circling motions as the orgasm ripped out of her and tore through the room, pulling screams from the back of her throat.

He held her up, helping her ride the wave until there was nothing left to wring out of her, then rested her limp body against his. She straddled his leg, and he brought his hands up to cup her face. His kiss seemed to pour every ounce of emotion he had into her, while she fought the pressure of tears against the backs of her eyes. She was going to miss him so much.

When the kiss ended, she could only cling to him and hope like hell they got to do this enough times today that she could pull the memories out for years to come. Because she had no doubt, it was going to take years to recover from him.

CHAPTER SIXTEEN

Several minutes later, Vega's breathing slowed, and JP lowered his leg to allow her to slide down his body. He gritted his teeth as her soft curves mapped over of him. What she'd been doing in the shower had been the sexiest thing he'd ever seen. And he'd been pretty certain parts of the previous night couldn't be topped.

He shuffled her under the water and rinsed her off, then toweled them both dry, reigniting himself as he used the cloth to touch every part of her.

"I can't get enough of you," he mumbled between kisses.

"You won't hear me complain."

Her lips were swollen and her eyes glazed, but she reached for him, ready for more. She wrapped her long fingers around the erection that had yet to disappear, and he couldn't contain the automatic thrusting motion.

"Let's go back to bed and take care of that for you," she whispered.

Not needing a second invitation, he stooped and hauled her up, fireman style. Her laughter stroked his ego as his long strides ate up the space to the bed. After dumping her in the middle of the mattress, he stared down at what had turned out to be his sexual dreams come true, thanked whatever God had lined up their meeting, then climbed in after her.

VEGA COLLAPSED TO THE BED, her body once again damp with sweat, her head hanging off the edge of the mattress. "I'm going to need more sleep."

"We both are," JP agreed. He wrapped an arm around her and pulled her up until she lay curled into his side. "You've worn me out."

"I doubt it." She burrowed her nose in his neck, her words slurred with sleep. "You have the stamina of a bull."

Oh, the woman was good for his ego. Not wanting to leave her, but uncomfortably aware they'd each only managed to eat a couple pieces of bacon before he'd carted her off to the shower, he tucked the covers gently around her and rose from the bed. "I'm going to dispose of this." He nodded to the sagging protection on his crotch. "Then bring in the food to see if anything is still edible."

His stomach growled as he padded across the floor, hers replying in a matching orchestra.

The giggles following him from the room made his mood soar. He'd just had the best day and night of his life, and though she may not be ready to admit she cared, Vega was clearly enjoying herself as much as he was. He tried not to mentally gloat, but her happiness had to be in direct correlation to spending time with him. No doubt after the night they'd just shared, he could talk her into hanging around Atlanta to see where this thing between them could go.

Whistling, he returned to the bedroom with the trays of food and stopped at the sight of her sneaking a bite of chocolate cake off the plate that remained by his side of the bed. "Really? Even for breakfast?"

Her grin lit the room. "If I want cake for breakfast, I can have cake for breakfast. Plus, even stale from sitting out overnight, it's better than cold eggs will be."

"You're right, there." He scooted into bed and settled the plates between them. "But I also got French toast and fresh fruit. Surely they'll be edible."

"Mmm…" She edged closer. "You do know how to treat a lady."

He wrapped a hand around the back of her head and brought her mouth to his. Her lips automatically parted, and he slipped inside, stroking as if they hadn't just completely devoured one another. He nipped at her lip and pulled back.

"Is that all it takes to win you over?" His voice was hoarse with the power of her. "Feed you well?"

"It's certainly a start." She removed the plate covers, and her eyes lit up.

"Seriously," he began, laughing as he talked. "How do you not weigh three hundred pounds?"

She shrugged. "I told you. Exercise."

"And you've always had such discipline?"

The tip end of a strawberry disappeared between her lips as she lowered her gaze. She chewed slowly, then doused the toast in syrup before finally answering. "I went through several years where I wasn't allowed to eat things like chocolate or syrup. Or at least, only in very…*very* small portions."

"Wasn't allowed?" What did she mean? "As in…what? You and your mom didn't have money for food, or your portions were controlled because you were, what? In jail? Worse?"

"Worse," she mumbled around a bite of food. When she looked up at him, she must have registered the shock on his face because she laughed out loud. "No. Not *really* worse than jail. I…" She stopped, then gave him another one of her *it doesn't matter* shrugs before continuing. "I did some modeling when I was younger. They were real sticklers about how much I weighed."

He dug into the food, beginning to worry she'd eat his portion as well as hers. "So I was right. You are made for the camera." He inhaled the cinnamon-flavored bread as he chewed, studying the woman before him and trying to figure out what else she wasn't saying. "Why didn't you tell me?"

"It was a long time ago. Not something I talk about."

Right. Only, it still felt more raw than that, or she wouldn't be spending so much time avoiding his gaze. "So what happened?" he asked. "And why not take the modeling to reporting the news? Or a television host? Or whatever you want? With your looks, it wouldn't be hard to snag any job in front of the camera that you desired."

"I just don't want to, okay?" She was closing down.

"Don't," he pleaded. He stopped her fidgeting by catching her hands and holding them until she looked up. "Don't close down on me. Just answer me one question."

Her eyes made no promises.

"Do you sometimes think about being in front of the camera instead of behind it? I know you want more out of your career. Is that the something you're really wanting?" He was pretty sure that whatever pain was in her life must have come during her years of modeling, but he wouldn't push for that, just yet. Baby steps for now.

After several long moments, she tugged her hands from his. She played with a strawberry, balancing it on the tip and twirling it around on a plate. "I used to think that's what I wanted, but I don't anymore. I got a taste, and I didn't like it."

"But modeling is different than being on TV." He cocked his head, wondering. "Or is modeling what you really would rather be doing?"

"No." The angry word punctuated the air. "It's the last thing I want. I didn't even want it when I was doing it."

"Then why did you?"

She flicked the berry with her finger, and it rolled across the dish. "I was sixteen. We needed money. I was told it would end all my troubles."

What she left unsaid was that it had more than likely created her troubles. He wanted to demand answers, to find out who had hurt her and where he could find the bastard so he could make it right, but that wasn't his place. He needed her to share on her own, first.

Then he'd find the jerk and stomp him into the ground.

But one thing was certain, even if she wouldn't say it. She *hadn't* given up on her dreams of being in front of the camera. She was just too natural at it for it not to be a part of her life.

He thought of his earlier call and how Cat had encouraged him to let Vega do the interview. She trusted her. He did, too.

But that didn't mean he could give her an interview.

Though Cat thought it was a good idea, he wasn't ready to commit to something like that, but he wished he could. If for no other reason than he'd love to give that to Vega.

"Can we quit talking about me now?"

He smiled at the petulant way she asked the question and reached over to snatch a bite of mango from her plate.

"You have got to stop stealing my food."

He popped the fruit in his mouth and grinned at her, feeling lighthearted and happy, and realized he hadn't only been good for her. She was good for him.

"It's a good thing today is our last day together. I wouldn't want to have to eventually drop-kick you for taking my food."

Her tone was fun, but her words brought the light moment to a crash. He took one of his berries and fed it to her, a feeling of dread sitting low in his gut before he ever asked the question. "How about if today wasn't the last day?"

She shook her head. "We can't hide out down here forever. Plus, people know we're on the island. Going out would be out of the question now."

"I'm not talking about staying here." He rubbed a thumb over her bottom lip and leaned into her space. "Let's date when we get home." He kissed her. "See where this goes."

Wide eyes stared back at him, the rejection kicking him in the gut without her uttering a word. Not wanting to hear it vocalized, he pressed a finger to her lips.

"We'll talk about it later."

She continued to stare as if he'd lost his mind. Quite possibly he had. What other reason was there for ending up begging her to like him every time he saw her?

"Just think about it, okay? With the job situation, you don't have to immediately return to Savannah. But even if you did, we could easily see each other on weekends."

Her head began to shake, and he stopped her with a look.

"Don't turn me down without giving it some thought. Plus, I listened to what you said about me the other night, and I didn't like the picture you painted. I don't want to be that person anymore." He leaned in close and made sure she saw the honesty in his eyes. He didn't want to be the playboy, doing nothing more than looking for the next hot piece of ass. He wanted more. He wanted Vega. "You and I are good. Together we could be amazing."

He didn't know where all that had come from, but he didn't regret putting it out there. They were good together. And she stirred feelings in him he hadn't known he could have.

However, the bullheadedness in her eyes said it didn't matter he'd just laid his heart on the line. When the day came to an end, she was going to stomp all over it.

Anger threatened to replace his good mood. Not solely at her resistance, but at their situations. If he wasn't who he was, if he wasn't plagued by paparazzi with every step he took, she wouldn't be so hesitant to be with him. Maybe then, she'd even be the one begging to be with him instead of the other way around.

Unable to tolerate the thought of them ending so soon, he decided to turn the tables. There was one way to ensure she'd be by his side for a few more days. And he was going to make damned certain not to leave her a choice in the matter.

Mentally crossing his fingers, he prayed that his sister was right, and he opened his mouth. "I'll do the interview."

Shock registered across her face. "What?"

"You still want me to, right?"

"Of course I do."

He nodded. "Then I'll do it. We can do the face-to-face following the press conference Saturday night, and it can be aired whenever after that your station thinks best. But I get complete discretion to require changes to the final copy if I don't approve."

She sat in the middle of the bed, her uncombed hair damp and tangled around her face, naked the way God put her on the earth, and her mouth hanging open far enough he could see her back teeth. And he found her the most beautiful person in the world. He only hoped he hadn't made the biggest mistake of his life by putting his trust in the wrong hands.

"So do you want to?" he prodded.

"Why did you change your mind?"

Not even with this could she be anything but difficult.

He shook his head, ready to shake her. "Cat thinks it'll be a good idea."

She eyed him as if that wasn't a good enough answer. Now he had to beg her to do the interview she'd come after him to get? He could not figure this woman out.

When she continued silently watching him, he picked up her

hand and pressed his lips to her fingers. "And I do too, Vega. It'll be good for both of us."

She blinked as if coming out of a trance, and a small smile began to form on her gorgeous mouth. He loved the pure pleasure she evoked when she smiled.

"Can I ask you to consider doing one thing, though?" he asked.

She nodded. "Anything."

"I want you to do the face-to-face."

"I told you—"

"I know what you told me. I've heard every word you've said to me since I met you. But I'm telling you, I think you want this." He squeezed her hand. "I think you *need* this. So just consider it, okay?"

Her tongue darted out to lick her lips as she studied him. Finally, she replied, "You'll do it even if I say no?"

He studied her a moment before finally agreeing. "I'll do it even if you say no."

The smile once again blossomed across her face, and hope filled him that the upcoming week would bring something special to his life he hadn't even known until now he'd been missing. He had five days until the announcement—likely only five days left with Vega—and he intended to make the most of them.

CHAPTER SEVENTEEN

"*T*wenty minutes until descent." JP's tone was low as he entered the living room where Vega was on her cell with Bob. They'd spent another day on the island but were nearing Atlanta now, late Monday night.

She dragged her gaze from her lap where she'd been scribbling notes—plans for the footage she needed to obtain—to find him hovering at her side. He was crisp and polished with a clean black suit once again in place. She inhaled. And he smelled wonderful. She nodded that she'd heard him.

"I need to get off the phone, Bob. We're about to land."

He'd called because he'd seen the beach pictures that had now made it to all the news channels. It hadn't been hard to watch the clips of the auction and see that it was the same person with him in Anguilla. "You're sure you're okay?" Bob asked.

He didn't know the story behind her life but knew enough about her that he understood that being caught soaking wet, and with one of the country's highest-profile people, was not anywhere near being on her bucket list.

"I'm fine, honestly. I just seem to keep making a spectacle of myself. Hopefully today's pictures will be the last incident." Not that she believed that at all. There were still topless photos out there waiting to surface, but it wasn't like she could tell him that. It would be mortifying enough when it came out.

"And you don't need anything for the interview?" Bob was sending someone to trade out the news van for her car in the morning, but she'd keep the equipment she needed out of it.

"Just the hotel room, please. If you don't mind. Can you extend it through Saturday?" She had not been looking forward to explaining how she'd failed to secure the interview after all, so she had been thrilled to be able to discuss her plans on the call instead.

He chuckled. "No problem, kiddo. I'm sending that bill to the Atlanta station anyway. For all they know, they're stealing you from me. I might as well make them pay something for it." He paused, then his tone turned more serious. "As you get segments ready, send them to me for a second set of eyes. I'll do everything I can to make sure you get the job you want."

Her heart grew heavy at the thought she would soon be working for someone other than him. "Sounds like a good plan, Bob."

He'd been there with her since she'd begun this career, and far too often she'd had to rely on him as more of a surrogate father than merely a boss. She spent holidays with him and his family when she couldn't get away to see her own mom and had dinner with them at least once a month. She'd miss that.

"I'll get off here now and let you get back to that young man you've snared," he teased, but she could sense his worry beneath it. "You be careful, okay?"

She nodded, a tear forming in the corner of her eye. He knew as well as she that JP had only been a fling. She might have to cry on his shoulder a bit after she wrapped up the interview and stepped away from JP for the last time. "Will do."

They ended the call, and she got herself under control as JP lowered himself to the couch beside her. He stretched his long legs out while she studied the man she'd become so close to over the last couple days, amazed at how much more she wanted to know about him. And not purely for the story.

Before she let herself get carried away, she slammed shut her personal thoughts and glanced back at the notebook in her lap. She tapped the eraser of her pencil against the paper in a rhythmic fashion.

"Good call with Bob?"

She looked up and nodded. She'd told him a few stories over the last couple days revolving around her job, several including Bob, and he'd picked up on the fact that the man was more father than boss. "He's just worried about me."

"I can understand that. You've probably surprised him a time or two the last few days."

She chuckled under her breath. "I've surprised *me* the last few days."

JP's large hand reached over and squeezed hers. "I've loved all of it." He paused, as if sensing something was on her mind. "You doing okay?"

Again, she nodded. She was, but she couldn't help but worry about what else was to come. "Can I ask you something?"

Stretching one arm along the couch behind her, he shot her a hot look as he leaned in and whispered, "Want to know if we can make love in the air one more time before we land?" He wiggled his brows. "It'll have to be a quickie, darlin'."

His warm breath bathed her neck and made her smile. In the last twenty-four hours, he'd more than proven himself as they'd not only made good use of the bedroom aboard his plane, but they'd also christened the dining room table in their hotel room, the kitchen counters, and multiple locations on the private yacht they'd rented for the day. When not exploring each other, they'd spent time snorkeling and riding Jet Skis.

For the first time in years, she'd felt like part of a couple. And she'd liked it. She had to put a stop to it, though, before it got out of hand. She knew from experience how bad it could get.

She sighed and leaned into his embrace. "Any idea if that alley shot made the tabloids yet?"

Her only hope at this point was to pull together an interview so extraordinary that even if every detail of her past was once again exposed, no one would think twice about what she'd done beforehand.

Slim chance.

JP squeezed her to him before leaning back in his seat. "I checked internet sites about an hour ago. I didn't see anything other than those shots from last night. If it shows up, though, it'll be okay. We'll handle it."

Her eyebrow twitched, and his mouth twisted in a grim line.

"I know," he sighed out the words before smiling. "It's your breasts, and I shouldn't be so flippant."

She loved his smile. "That's not what I'm worried about." And honestly, her breasts being exposed was the least of her worries. She cradled his jaw, caressing the five o'clock shadow. "I don't want it to hurt *you*."

He smirked. "What? You don't think the governor will be impressed with his political appointment being caught face-first in a pair of naked breasts?"

She wanted to smile at the forced joke, but the matter was serious. She instead lowered her hand from his face. "I'd think you'd be worried, too."

"Of course I am. Nobody wants to be splashed around the world in an unsavory manner such as that."

Yet it seemed to her that he wasn't as worried for political-career reasons as he should be. It could change the governor's mind completely, no matter how clean he and his family were.

Then there were all the other reasons he didn't even know about that would hurt him. Everything about her past.

He must have picked up on the shift in her thinking because he reached out to wrap a loose piece of her hair around a finger. "Tell me what else we're looking at, and I'll fix it before it causes a problem."

She shook her head. "You can't fix it. It was a long time ago."

"Sweetheart." JP picked up her hand and pressed a quick kiss to it, then kept it held between his hands. His eyes pleaded with her. "Let me in. Let me help."

He couldn't help. That's what she'd been unable to get him to understand. Her mind drifted off on all the ways she'd messed up and how it still unfairly affected every part of her life today. If the affair came out, so would the lies.

"Vega?"

She blinked, refocusing on his face.

"Talk to me."

He seemed so concerned and had been so sweet with her the last two days, but she couldn't risk letting him in any further. She had to keep some things to herself, and that included her past and her heart. She couldn't afford to be crushed again.

And good guy or not, she would be the ruin of JP. He wouldn't want her in the end.

She pulled out a fake smile. "Thank you for your concern, really. But it's not anything I can't handle. I do have a question for you, though."

The look on his face said he didn't approve of her refusal to let him into her life or her quick change of subject. "We agreed no interview questions until tomorrow."

"Yes, but this is something I just want to know." It was something she'd thought about several times as she'd made notes on him and his family.

Reluctantly, he nodded agreement for her to ask her question.

She glanced down at her notepad, then back up to him. "You have an older brother."

"Yes, Bennett."

"And your family is heavy into tradition."

He eyed her as if trying to figure out where her line of questioning was leading. "You know they are."

"Right." She nodded. "So I'm wondering why *you* got named after your father instead of your older brother."

If she hadn't been staring so intently, she wouldn't have caught the change in the blue of his eyes. But the warm glow turned just the tiniest bit chilly. "Honestly? I have no idea."

"You parents never told you? Did you ask?"

"I asked." He sat up straighter, pulling slightly back from her. "My father informed me I had been given the honor because I would be the one to follow in his footsteps."

"Ah." She blinked as another thought came to mind. "That's kind of rude toward your brother, isn't it? Did your father tell him the same thing about you?"

"I would imagine."

Wow. No wonder the eldest had disappeared into the Army and rarely came home. She studied the man sitting before her, now far more distant than the mere inches separating them, as another thought popped to mind. It was a big one, but she had to ask it. "Then can I ask you one more question?"

He didn't nod agreement, but he didn't say no either.

"I've gotten the feeling from a couple things you've said, that maybe you don't really want to go into politics?"

The planes of his face hardened. "Of course I do. I'm a Davenport, aren't I?"

"See? You just did it again."

He barked a laugh. "I did nothing, darlin'. I simply agreed that I want the life that's been laid out for me."

She tossed her notebook on the small table at their side and shifted around to face him. She gripped his hands in hers. "You said the words, but there was no passion inside you. What's going on, JP? Is this what you want or not?"

His jaw twitched. "Don't forget this whole conversation is off the record. And that I approve the final version of the interview. Air anything I don't agree to and my lawyers will bury both you and the station."

She sighed. "I signed the papers your lawyer faxed this morning, remember? I know the rules. But I'm not asking this for the interview. I'm asking for my own reasons." She softened her tone and reminded herself that she'd have to shut down those reasons just as soon as the plane landed. She couldn't keep caring about him as she was. It would hurt too much at the end. "I'd simply like to understand. Is this what you really want?"

He stared at her so long she became certain he wouldn't answer. Watching his eyes change as his mind coursed through his own thoughts intrigued her, reminding her of the previous evening when he'd made love to her for the first time.

He'd insisted she let him see into her soul, to see what his touch did to her, but she wondered if he'd realized what she'd witnessed in him as well. It hadn't just been sex. Not for her or him. She was certain of that. She didn't know what else it was, exactly, but he'd let her see it was definitely more than just about bedding her. Yet another reason it had to end when the plane landed. She wouldn't be able to stand watching his feelings change when he learned who she was.

They'd go back to being professionals. She'd create a piece benefiting both him and her, then she'd continue with her life—while secretly cheering him on from a distance.

Finally, he laced his fingers through hers. "We should get to our seats and buckle in."

Once settled, he surprised her by answering her previous question. "Honestly, I have no idea if this is what I want. It's simply…

my life. It's what's expected of me. I'll be the next Georgia senator. From there..." He shrugged. "Who knows what's next."

She clicked her seat belt around her. "But what do you want?"

JP's strong profile stared straight ahead, and she couldn't take her eyes off him. His throat worked, his Adam's apple bobbed, then he finally spoke. "I like running my company. The takeovers, seeing new buildings go up, making a hell of a lot of money. I love everything about it. I've also taken care to get the right people in place to keep it moving when I'm not there day in and day out."

The whir of the jet engines filled the silence until Vega asked, "But?"

"But..." He sighed. He turned his clear gaze to her. "But there's more, outside of business, that I want to accomplish. Something more personal."

"And you can't do this if you're a senator?"

"I'm not sure."

The plane began its descent, and she caught the flash of the lights of Atlanta before they circled over and headed to the small airstrip outside the city. "Will you tell me about it? Maybe another person's opinion would help."

He grew quiet. "Maybe I'll show you later in the week."

The thought sent a flutter through her body. "Something for the program?"

"Probably not." He twisted his head in her direction and frowned. "We'll talk about it later."

Moments later, the plane coasted to a stop, and they gathered their purchases from the island. When she stepped outside, Vega was startled to catch sight of a dark figure just outside the small hangar, his hands to his face and a flash going off.

"Damn," JP muttered, seeing the photographer the same instant as she. He ducked his head and stepped in front of her, hurrying them both to the waiting town car.

Sliding quickly in behind her, he slammed the door, the tinted windows making them safe from further photographs. "I'm sorry, babe. It never occurred to me anyone would get past my security like that."

She hadn't thought so either. "It's okay."

Unless they wanted to ram into the building and run the man down, it would have to be okay.

She said the only thing she could think of. "Maybe it won't show up."

Silence reigned over the interior for several seconds before JP stated flatly, "You don't believe that any more than I do."

She shook her head. "Nope."

"We'll deal with it." He smiled and reached across the seat to hold her hand. "Together."

She didn't feel like telling him at the moment that she dealt with things alone.

"I know you've got your hotel room for the rest of the week, but I thought you could stay with me."

Vega froze, shocked. It had never crossed her mind that staying with him would be an option, though she knew she should have. Their chemistry hadn't yet fizzled, and JP liked to get what he wanted. "I'm not sure that's the best idea."

"At least tonight, Vega." JP's hand tightened around hers. "We're not finished. You know it as well as I do."

"It's after dark, and I have a lot of preparations before showing up at your office in the morning," she said, working up the nerve to put her plan into action. "Plus, I need to switch out vehicles with a colleague in the morning. It would be best if I go on to my hotel."

JP's jaw clenched. "Is this because we were just seen? I can guarantee it won't go beyond the airport. I have a private entrance to my place so no one would possibly know who, if anyone, arrived in this car with me. There's no reason not to come back with me tonight."

There were plenty of reasons. She had to retreat now, or she wouldn't be able to. Even if his feelings grew for her to the point that they tried something as crazy as a relationship, they'd always have the issue of her background between them. She looked away, threatening tears choking her voice. "I can't, JP."

Even not facing him, she felt his anger. It vibrated through the car. He leaned forward and lowered the glass panel, instructing the driver to take them to her hotel. "I'll give you tonight, but you know as well I as do that we have something here. Maybe it can't go further than this week; maybe it can. But we need time to find out."

"It can't," she whispered.

His eyes flared. "I won't accept that."

"Can I ask you something?" She was pretty sure she already knew the answer but hearing it would help keep her focused on ending it. "Did you only agree to the interview so you could sleep with me a few more days?"

JP's eyes grew dark in the shadows of the car. A flash under a passing streetlight showed the hard angles of his face, and she couldn't stop a shiver from echoing through her.

"You know it's more than just sleeping together, Vega."

"But did you? Is that the reason you agreed?"

A low growl filled the back seat of the car as he raked a hand through his hair. "I don't like people invading my personal life. I've never hidden that fact."

"So if I refuse to see you again?"

"You won't refuse."

She didn't respond.

They rode in silence for several minutes, neither willing to acknowledge what was happening between them.

Vega watched storefronts flash by one after the other and finally spoke as if talking to herself. "I love the city after dark."

"Then you would love it from my place." JP's anger was only

marginally controlled in his tight voice. "I'll show it to you tomorrow night."

"And if I say no?" She had to make him understand it was ending tonight. Right now. She couldn't walk into his office tomorrow, spend hours watching him through an eyepiece, without having this decided. "If I refuse anything further, will you cancel the interview?"

"Dammit." He slammed the side of his fist against the door. "No, of course I wouldn't go back on my word. I promised to do it for you. I think you need this to see that you want more out of life than just being behind the camera. You need to be in front of it." He turned to her and cupped her cheek, his gentleness surprising her. "You need to confront your fears, Vega. I want to help you do that."

"I'm perfectly happy where I am. Who I am."

His stormy eyes drilled into hers. "Is that right?"

She nodded.

"And that means you're perfectly happy with a couple days and nothing more?"

"We knew that's all we had going into this."

"Unacceptable." The word was hard and cold.

The limo stopped under the awning of the hotel, but she didn't immediately move from his hand. She knew she needed to, but she'd lied. She was not ready for this to end. When she saw his intention to kiss her, she couldn't resist meeting him halfway.

"JP," she murmured, lifting her mouth to his.

His mouth crashed onto hers, his heat engulfing her and his tongue threatening to destroy her resolve to step out of the car and walk away. He closed the distance between their bodies. She arched forward, returning his passion kiss for kiss, not caring that she wasn't pulling in enough oxygen to remain cognizant. If this was it for them, she had to have one last kiss before walking away.

He palmed her rear and pulled her onto his lap, his fingers

branding her as they flew over every inch of her body. Before she knew it, her shirt was open, and his mouth was on her body. Her head strained backwards as she fought to get closer.

She sent her fingers on a journey of their own, sliding across his heated flesh, gripping the muscled back she'd so thoroughly explored only hours earlier, while he unfastened the front opening of her bra. She sprang into his hands, warmth and rightness gushing through her veins.

"JP..." Gripping his shoulders, she surged into his mouth.

"You can't walk away from me. Not when we have this." His hand lowered to her shorts and fumbled with the buckle long enough to allow a vestige of rational thought to enter her mind.

What were they doing? Her breaths panted out of her as she looked around, wide-eyed, at their surroundings. The driver had to know what was going on back here.

She pushed against his hand, pausing his movements. "Stop."

The word was barely more than a whisper and absolutely filled with uncertainty, but his movements ceased instantly. His ragged breathing matched hers, and she almost cried out in pain at the thought of climbing off his lap and out of his car.

With shaking hands, she reached to refasten her bra, but he pushed her hands out of the way. He closed the undergarment and smoothed her shirt over her without saying a word. All the while, a muscle ticked in his jaw.

When finished, he dropped his hands to the seat and glared. "We are not done. I'll see you to your room tonight, but don't plan on it happening again."

She lifted off his lap and scooted to the edge of the seat, no longer able to look at him. "Please, stay in the car. I can see myself to my room."

"Vega." His hard voice pulled her gaze back to his. "Say it. It's not over."

She shook her head and whispered, "I can't." A tear slipped from the corner of one eye.

After exiting the car, her bag slung over her arm, she couldn't keep from leaning down to look in one last time. Though he was still the man she'd played with in the sun the last two days, he now wore the air of the stoic businessman with the reputation for getting everything he went after.

"Thanks for everything." Her voice was soft. Sad. "I'll be at your office tomorrow morning at eight."

"And tomorrow night you'll be in my home."

Vega bit the inside of her lip to control her emotions. "No. Tomorrow night I'll come back here, exactly as I will every day this week."

The stared at each other, both unwilling to give in.

Her smile shook as she lifted the corners of her mouth. "You're a good man, JP."

She stepped from the limo without another word and rushed into the building before she burst out in tears. The last thing she wanted was to end things, but what they'd had wasn't real. It couldn't be. They were purely chemistry and excitement.

And if she told herself that enough, she might eventually believe it.

CHAPTER EIGHTEEN

*J*P stormed into his office the next morning, still fuming at Vega's refusal to admit they weren't over. He also had to acknowledge that part of his anger stemmed from the fact that no matter how he'd tried, she'd refused to budge on talking about what had happened in her past. He needed her to open up to him. They couldn't move ahead if there wasn't trust between them.

A niggling voice in the recesses of his mind questioned why he hadn't yet told her of his own past. The dyslexia that had always been there, tainting everything he did. He consoled his guilt with his knowledge that he would show her the school this week, as well as tell her of his plans to fund programs across the country. No one should grow up ashamed of themselves.

But at the moment, his fury boiled from the fact he'd let her disturb his morning routine. Though he'd barely gotten any sleep, he'd risen at the normal early hour, and his frustrations had caused him to slam things a bit too much. The coffee cup breaking when he'd set it in the sink should have been his warning. He hadn't heeded the message, however. When he'd stepped into his shower, he'd rung the glass door on its frame. It had promptly shattered, thousands of glass crumbles falling into a heap and water spilling over the room.

He was only fifteen minutes late, but he was never late.

Beverly looked up when he neared, a smirk on her face as if she already knew about his bad morning. "Something eating at you, boss?"

Her use of the less formal *boss* pulled him up short. "Why would you ask?"

She shrugged. "Just find it odd you've spent your life keeping the media out, and yet there was one here with video equipment when I arrived this morning, swearing you'd given her permission to follow you around the whole week."

"She's already here?" His gaze shot to his closed office door.

"Has been for thirty minutes. And quite a fetching young lady, I must add." Beverly snickered. "Something tells me she's the reason for your sour mood this morning."

He growled. "She can be annoying."

"Most sharp ones can."

He pulled his gaze back from his office door and studied Beverly. "You typically have good instincts with people."

"The best."

"And I take it you like her?"

She gave a short nod. "I think she's great. Possibly enough to bring you down to a human level."

He wouldn't have put it that way, but he thought Vega was good for him, too. He just had to show her that as well. "Can you call my cleaning people and a repairman, please? The master bath needs cleaning, and the shower door has to be replaced. Today."

"I'll get on it."

"When's my first appointment?" He moved toward his door.

"Nine o'clock."

"Don't disturb me until then."

When he entered, the first thing he noticed was that Vega was wearing more new clothes. These fit as well as the ones they'd purchased on the islands. She turned when the door clicked softly behind him.

"JP," she started, her voice holding a breathlessness he liked. She cleared her throat and began again. "Thank you again for this opportunity. I hope it's okay that your assistant let me in so I could get set up. I wanted to get some shots of you starting your day."

"Of course." He couldn't take his eyes off her. She was gorgeous. Though her hair was once again clamped to the back of her head, she wore a glow from spending the last two days in the sun.

She inclined her head toward the camera positioned on the tripod. "All right if I start?"

"Certainly."

"Okay, then." She seemed nervous. She hit a button, and a small red light came to life and glowed from the camera. "Go on about your business exactly as you normally would, please. Just pretend I'm not here."

Like that was possible. He crossed the room and sat at his desk as if this were any other day, and he wasn't simply waiting for the right time to prove they weren't over. "I see you fit in time for shopping."

A hint of pink touched her clear skin as she glanced at the trim-fitting dress. The top was a wraparound style with a single button at her waist, while the bottom hugged her curves and ended modestly above the knees. The orange was bright, but not overly so, and complemented her complexion perfectly.

"The hotel boutique was still open last night," she explained. "This seemed more appropriate than cargos since I'll be with you for appointments and site meetings."

He flipped through the messages Beverly had left from the

previous day. "You know there are things I won't allow you to record, right? Some of my dealings are confidential."

"Of course." She fidgeted in place. "I appreciate this opportunity and will do whatever you say."

He looked up at her, doing his best to bank the desire to stride across the room and take her up against a wall. "Anything at all?"

She didn't pause at the loaded question. "Anything concerning the interview."

This wouldn't be easy. Clearly, she still had her mind wrapped around the thought that what they'd discovered over the last two days was over. He'd simply have to show her she was wrong.

Moving his mouse, he woke the computer and logged into his email. Beverly had flagged the items he needed to attend to and had also sent an email marked *personal*. He opened it to find a link to a tabloid site. Those links rarely produced anything he enjoyed seeing.

Glancing over at the camera, he found Vega chewing on her bottom lip as she watched the flipped-down viewfinder. Though she could no doubt see him on-screen, she wasn't looking directly at him, and that annoyed him. He wanted her as aware of him as he was of her.

With a quick click of the mouse, the link brought up the shot they'd been waiting for. He and Vega making out in the alley, her bikini top down around her waist.

Luckily, her head was at an angle making it difficult to determine who she was, but there was no doubt it was him enjoying a naked breast. This was not a good way to start off a political career.

On the other hand...damn, she had nice breasts. Ones he'd personally like to see again as soon as possible.

"You might want to take a look at this." He motioned to his monitor.

Vega's gaze zoomed to his. "I don't want to get on camera. If I do, I'll just have to edit it out."

"Then turn it off."

Tension crackled as he watched her trying to decide whether to do as he said or not. She was no idiot. He was pretty sure she could figure out that whatever it was very likely had to do with her. She didn't turn off the camera, but she did finally slide out from behind the tripod and head his direction.

He waited until she stepped behind his desk, then rolled back to give her space.

She leaned in, fire flitting through her eyes before they smoldered and turned a dull brown. "I told you this would happen. Being together was such a bad idea."

"Nothing about you and me is a bad idea." He pointed to the picture where, thankfully, her exposed side was mostly covered with his hand. "Even that wasn't a bad *idea*, just wish we'd thought it out a bit more so we didn't get caught. I'll no doubt be hearing from my mother soon."

Before he could finish his sentence, his desk phone rang. He shot a glare at the closed door, wishing Beverly had followed his orders and not bothered him. He couldn't seem to get anyone to do what he wanted anymore.

But since she'd sent a call straight through, that meant it was either his mother or an emergency.

He glanced at the call number and picked up the receiver. "Hello, Mother."

"Have you seen the internet this morning, Jackson?"

Ignoring her for the moment, he studied Vega, who looked at the photo one second longer then quietly moved away. Her shoulders drooped as if the world had sat down on them.

"All of the internet, or something in particular?"

"Don't be a smart-ass." His no-nonsense mother was in full force this morning. "Have you seen it or not?"

"Looking at it as we speak."

"Do you know what this looks like?"

He chuckled. "It looks like I had a really good weekend."

She went dead silent, and he waited. He may be doing what she wanted with his life, but that didn't mean he was playing her games.

A long sigh finally filled the void. "That's all you've got? You had a good time?"

"I did have a good time. Excellent, in fact." He snuck a quick glance at Vega, who was now looking out the window over the heart of the city. She was using one finger to trace a pattern against the glass. It looked as if she were outlining the other buildings.

"There isn't a name tied to this one yet, but clearly you went away with Vega. I assume it's her?"

Since Vega had been identified in the beach shot, as well as the clip he'd caught on the news that morning of the two of them exiting his plane, it would look even worse if this were with a different woman. Might as well come clean. "Yes, Mother. It was Vega."

Vega's shoulders stiffened.

"And you're letting her do the interview now." It wasn't a question. Probably she'd gotten the information out of Beverly.

"We actually just started filming, so if you don't mind..."

"Wait." His mother's voice was tight. "I'm glad you're doing the interview, Jackson. Really. I think it could be excellent coverage for you." She paused before continuing. "You get final approval?"

"Of course."

"Then I think it's an excellent idea..."

"But?"

"Well..." It wasn't like his mother to beat about the bush.

"What is it, Mother? I'm busy, and I have a meeting in less than an hour I need to prepare for."

"You're sleeping with your interviewer, Jackson. That will look bad as well."

He didn't comment. He knew she was right, but there was nothing he could do to change the fact. "Anything else?"

"I just think that…well, Vega seems nice enough, but maybe she isn't the right one to be hanging around with…that way."

"That way?" He could not believe just because he was letting his mother talk him into office, she now thought she could dictate who he did and did not see. He may never have lived up to her expectations since he hadn't been able to read in his youth, but she did not get a say in his choice of women. "You mean you don't think I should sleep with her, or you don't think I should bring her home for dinner?"

At the question, Vega spun around. Eyes wide, she shot him a hard look.

He winked at her.

"There's no need to get snippy, Jackson. You know I'm only looking out for you, same as always. I only want what's best for you."

"Yeah?" What *she* thought was best, she meant. "Well, staying out of my love life would be best for me, Mom. Anything else you wanted?"

He heard the soft release of air as she opened her mouth to respond, then clearly thought twice about whatever she'd been intending to say.

"Fine," she said. "It's your life, and I can't tell you how to live it. I have no problem with young men having good times, but you've got to think about where you're having these good times these days. This picture of you and her out in public like that…it doesn't look good, Jackson. Imagine what people will think. Imagine what Governor Chandler will think."

"Beverly has already called our lawyer to get it taken down." He would make sure of that fact, but given how well Beverly did her job, he was confident it had already been handled. But he had no idea how to make this better in the governor's eyes. "Anything else?"

"Just be careful. This is what you've wanted for so long. Don't damage it before you even get started."

He stared at the receiver, amazed as always that she actually thought this was his dream. But he couldn't disappoint her by telling her the truth. He scrubbed a hand through his hair. "I'll call the governor. Any chance this will affect his decision?" He shook his head because he knew better than to think it wouldn't matter. "Do you think it's *already* affected his decision?"

"I'll talk to him," she said. "I'll run a little cleanup, but he believes in us. He has for years. Surely this won't be enough to pull his support. But you have to be more careful in the future, Jackson. He can't let too many situations like this go."

JP nodded, resignation filling him at the big mistake sitting in front of him he needed to correct. "I'll go over, get an appointment with him. I'll make sure he understands it won't happen again."

His mother got off the phone, and he turned to Vega, who still stood gaping at him.

"You were talking about me?"

He waggled his eyes, trying to force himself into a better mood. "Who else have I been caught in public fondling the breasts of lately?" Actually, ever. He was normally very careful about such things.

"But you told your *mother* it was me. Couldn't you at least have kept that part a secret?"

He shrugged and stood. "It's not like it won't be confirmed soon enough anyway, probably already is."

"I don't get why you aren't mortified." She flapped her arms in the direction of his computer. "You have my naked breast in your hand!"

"Not at the moment." He stood, but when she stiffened, he changed his course and moved to her camera instead of her.

Leaning down, he glanced through the eyepiece and repositioned the lens until Vega filled the center of the shot. "Though I wouldn't mind putting it there again."

"Stop it." She glanced back at his desk, gnawing on her bottom lip once again. "What do we do to clean this up? Will your lawyer really get it taken down?"

He zoomed in on her face. She was even hotter when riled up. "Probably within the hour. But you know it'll pop up somewhere else." He couldn't take his eyes off her mouth. "And even with the X-rated version taken down, someone will still have a cleaned-up shot out there."

She paced to the desk and back to the window, and he followed her with the camera.

"You look awesome, you know. Did I mention that?"

Vega glanced over at his words and pursed her lips. "Quit messing around, JP. I had that perfectly lined up where I wanted it."

"I like recording you."

"Well, the point of the recording is to capture footage for the interview."

"And I told you, you should be a part of the interview." He peeked out over the top. "You should watch this later. You glow on camera."

For a second, she stared directly into the lens, her brown eyes deep and intense as thoughts ran back and forth through her mind. He would have paid big money to know what she was thinking. She then dismissed her thoughts as easily as she did him and turned back to the window. "I told you how this was going to play out. It's all about you. Not me."

"And I asked you to consider doing the live portion yourself."

"I already considered it."

"I don't believe you."

She sighed, a long, frustrated sound. "It doesn't matter if you believe me or not. I considered it. Case closed."

He flipped the switch and turned the camera off, then moved to the window to stand behind her. Reaching one arm around her and resting it on the glass, he put his body within inches of hers. "Okay," he whispered. "Case closed." He nudged his nose against the back of her neck. "For now."

"What are you doing?" She stiffened. Her tone said outrage, but he also caught the slight tilt of her neck.

"I'm going to point out some of the sights to you." He lifted a finger to one of the more popular attractions of the city, his forearm brushing against her. She caught her breath but followed the direction of his finger.

"That's the Bank of America Plaza. And those two structures there," he continued, using his other arm to circle the other side of her, inhaling her tropical scent. "Those buildings are mine. Fifty floors, condominiums on top, offices and retail on the lower levels."

"I know what you're trying to do, and it won't work."

He ignored her, not stopping his train of thought. "The buildings are public knowledge, though. Probably not something you want to explore too much in your program."

She nodded, unspeaking. A curl slipped loose and swayed with her movement.

He wrapped the tendril around one finger. "You didn't torture your hair as much today."

"I felt like a bit of a change." One hand lifted to the back of her head. The loose updo was attractive, but nothing like seeing all of it haloing her as she rode him, her head thrown back in passion.

He trailed a finger down her neck. "I like it."

"JP." Her voice shook, as did her body. "Seriously, I'm here to work. Stop messing around."

His finger dipped under her collar and teased along the base of her neck. They were so not over. "I'm not messing around. I love touching you."

She took a step to her right, putting space between them, and shot him a short glance. "I meant what I said. We had a great time the last couple of days, but it's over. Let's not pretend it could be more."

She sucked at pretending she wasn't affected by him, but her insistence on doing it suddenly riled. "Then you won't mind that I'm going out with Greta tomorrow night?"

Her shoulders tensed, but her voice remained unaltered. She crossed her arms over her chest and studied the buildings outside his window even harder. "Of course not. She did buy you, after all." Her eyes cut to him. "That's what you're talking about, right? The date she purchased?"

He studied her. He would be completely furious if she were going out with another man. For any reason. "So you're still not jealous? You don't care if I'm going out with her?"

"Of course not," she murmured, not quite as confident as she'd sounded a second ago, and turned back to the view.

He once again moved into her space. "Then you'll have no problem recording it."

She stilled. "Why would I record your date?"

"Seems that's a behind-the-scenes sort of thing you might want."

"Oh." She gulped. "That is a good idea." Only the expression on her face didn't seem to be saying the same thing at all.

Heat from the late-morning sun warmed the windows, drawing him forward as easily as she did. He wanted to strip her bare and lay her out in the sunshine, then feast on her until they both passed out from exhaustion. "It's a date, then."

She nodded. "It's a date for you and Greta. I'll just be a bystander."

"And you won't be jealous."

She shook her head.

"Liar," he whispered. He leaned in and nuzzled her ear. "You'll be watching us through your camera. Like a voyeur. You sure it won't bother you at all?"

The corners of her mouth tightened, and he couldn't help but smile. She was definitely jealous.

"Can we just get back to work now?"

"Sure." Only he didn't move away. He lowered his lips and nipped at the side of her neck. "As soon as you admit you're jealous."

"Seriously, JP." Her eyes closed. "We have a lot to do today."

"Okay." He grasped her chin, tilting her head in a way that gave him clear access to the delectable slope of her neck. "But before we work, I need to show you something."

As he skimmed over her skin, tasting her light flavor, she moaned. "What do you need to show me?"

"This." He closed his arms around her, and she melted back against him. "We're good for each other, Vega." His mouth swept over her ear, nipping at the lobe. "There's no need to deny it."

"We shouldn't." Her moans mixed with his as he slid his flattened hand down the front of her, in search of the hem of her skirt. His palm crossed her mound, and her head lolled against his shoulder. When he reached the bottom edge, his fingers crawled underneath, then headed upward for her panties. Though he couldn't see them, he'd learned what she liked. They would be lacy, mostly transparent, and tiny. When he landed on the miniscule scrap of material, he knew he was right.

"You're so wet." He feasted along her jawline as she angled her head for him. "So hot. You know you want me as bad as I want you."

"Uh-huh."

His other hand opened the top of her dress and the front clasp of her bra in one fluid motion. He pulled one rounded breast out, lifting it in his hand and exposing her for the world to see—if anyone were to look through the upper-floor window.

"I want to make love to you right here. With the sun streaming in on you." He flicked her nipple, and she ground back into him, her hips rocking against his erection. "You're so beautiful in my hands."

"Your assistant," she breathed. "She might catch us."

He bit down on the tender skin at the base of her neck and drove his fingers under the damp material of her panties at the same time. "She wouldn't dream of opening that door." He flicked his thumb across her core.

"JP." She gasped. Her hands lifted, reaching behind her to grab either side of his head. She curled into him like a satisfied cat. "You should stop. You're not proving anything with this behavior."

He slipped a finger inside her. "I'm proving that you're mine."

"Only…" Her head rolled against his shoulder once again as if unable to bear its own weight, and she shuddered in his arms. "Only that our attraction is strong."

"Strong is a ridiculous word for this." He tugged at her underwear, fighting the urge to rip it from her body and take her up against the window. "I'm proving that you drive me as insane as I drive you, Vega. I'm desperate for you."

To show her what he meant, he dragged her skirt up to her waist and gripped both hips. He pressed into her, his erection aching for release, and knew she felt it when he throbbed between her cheeks.

"Let me love you, darling. Let me have you."

Her body trembled. "One last time?"

His fingers flexed involuntarily. "I want it all, Vega."

"Yes." She was breathless. "Yes, all." She leaned forward and pressed her palms to the glass, her rounded backside toward him. "Now."

With a growl, he yanked down the hot yellow panties that

barely covered half her butt, then freed himself. His body sprang forward, perfectly aware where it was headed, and he gripped the sides of her hips. He entered her in one hard push. Both of them stilled, letting the sensations roll over them, before a rush of air burst simultaneously from their lungs.

Reaching around her, he found her breasts and made sure they swung free with her movements. "God, I love these."

He watched her reflection in the window as he thrust, burying himself to the hilt. Her mouth gaped. Her nipples beaded.

"Incredible," he groaned. He slid in and out of her wetness, digging his fingers into her hips as he moved closer to his climax.

She pushed back into him, her fingers splayed wide on the glass, giving her the perfect anchor to grind against him. His knees weakened.

"Fuck, you're hot. I can't wait much longer." He dipped one hand to her crotch and the other to her breasts, his palm crossing over the bare skin of her stomach. He plucked at a nipple, and her rear lifted farther into the air.

"Faster," Vega panted, and he lost his mind. Thrusting for all he was worth, her body gripped him so tightly he was certain there was no way he could wait for her.

He brushed his fingertips over her clit, and she moaned a long, low animal cry. He pressed harder, pinching and swirling his fingers until she began to tremble in his arms.

"Now, JP. Now."

With an animal sound ripping from his throat, he crushed against her, holding her as she shook in his arms, and pumped himself dry. He buried his face in her neck, wondering how he'd let this become so much more than physical, but the fact was, he couldn't imagine a life without her in it.

Within moments, their breathing slowed, and he couldn't keep from smiling wide. He might have just found the woman for him. She was gorgeous, opinionated, and the hottest damn thing he'd ever seen. And he flat-out couldn't get enough of her. He pressed one last kiss to her neck and lifted his face to catch her watching him in the reflection of the glass. "That was—"

"The dirtiest thing anyone has ever done to me." Vega's sharp whisper shocked him. She pulled away, leaving him standing there as if lost.

CHAPTER NINETEEN

"*What?*" What had happened? JP stepped back as Vega scurried away. She'd been as heavily into that as he was. He gingerly tucked himself back into his pants while she fastened her bra. "What's the matter?"

"What's the matter?" she shrieked, her hands flapping in the air as she spoke. Cold eyes faced him. "I'll tell you *what's the matter*. It's bad enough you put me in a position where Beverly or anyone else could have walked in on us, but you just used me, that's what."

"Of course I didn't use you. We were both involved in what just happened."

"Is that so?" She yanked the yellow lace up with jerky motions. "I'm here to work, JP, not to have a quickie against your office window."

"You weren't complaining two seconds ago." He raised his voice.

"But I didn't mean for that to happen."

He lowered his voice and pulled a deep breath in through his nostrils in an attempt to control his rising anger. "It just shows we can't control this thing between us."

"No." She shook her head, and what little hair had still been up fell. "You were just showing that you can bend me to your will. You walked in here, all alpha dog, and you took what you wanted."

"I did not force you." His anger once again matched hers. He'd never forced himself on any woman. "You wanted it, just like I did."

She took long strides to the connecting bathroom but didn't close the door. He could see her messing with her hair as she continued to berate him. "Of course I did. I never said we didn't have chemistry." She stepped from the bathroom, her outer appearance semi-normal, but the emotion radiating from her screamed that she was anything but calmed down. "You entered this room with the intention of having sex with me this morning, didn't you? There wasn't one single uncontrolled action on your part."

"Of course not." But he had, and he knew it. He hadn't intended to take her if she'd said no, just like last night. He would have stopped. But she had to understand what they had wasn't ordinary.

"Don't you dare lie to me." Stomping up to him, she thrust a shaking finger in his face, and that's when he saw she wasn't just angry. Her eyes swam with unshed tears. She was hurt. "I do not tolerate lies and people using me, JP. That happened once. I won't stand for it again."

"I didn't…" He captured her hand, but she yanked it out of his. And then he realized something he'd not been prepared to accept last night. He still wasn't prepared. But he also couldn't hide from it. They might be over. He might have actually pushed hard enough he'd lost her.

His heart thudded against his ribs, squeezing with fear. What was it about her that made him do the stupidest things? He mentally kicked himself. "I'm sorry."

"Right. That's convenient." She whirled around and headed to her equipment. "How about we just get back to…" She froze; not a single muscle on her body moved. When she spoke, her voice was cold and controlled. "Did you reset the view to capture us on camera?"

Honestly, the thought had entered his mind. "Of course not."

Dead brown eyes were once again in his face. No words, just Vega staring him down as if he were more disgusting than a chunk of rotten Brie left out in an Atlanta summer. "Then why were you messing with it?"

"Babe." He reached out a hand, but she jerked away before his fingertips could even graze her. Okay, he was tired of the drama. It wasn't like he'd done anything without her consent. He may have come in conceited and demanding, yes. But he hadn't done one single thing she hadn't fully participated in. "I was watching you, that's all. I wanted you to be able to look at it later and see how perfect you are on-screen. I don't think you realize that. And of course I didn't record us without your knowledge."

He paused before saying the next words, knowing it would prove he'd gone to the window with an agenda. "I turned the camera off."

Wide eyes watched him for ten long seconds before they blinked and something resembling normalcy came back into play. Without another word she crossed the room and stepped behind the camera. "We'll record a few more minutes of you going through your normal morning routine, then I'll disappear until your first appointment."

He stood in the middle of the room wondering what the hell had just happened. Not a thing about the last few minutes made any sense to him. They both wanted each other. They both enjoyed each other.

But they could no longer be together.

So said she.

Fuck it, he didn't need this trouble. He moved behind his desk and tried to pretend she didn't exist. Only there was something very important he couldn't push from his mind.

"You might want to do something with your hair," she snipped. "It looks like some fool has been running her fingers through it."

JP stared at the woman he'd just realized he was in love with and wondered what he could do to fix this mess. He hadn't thought of his plans to seduce her this morning as using her, but that's exactly what he'd done. He'd arrived with a purpose. To show her it wasn't over. Probably no better than whatever the jerk had done to her.

He moved to the bathroom and took a moment to clean himself up, then returned to his desk. "I know I messed up just now, and I'll say it again. I'm sorry. Honestly. There's no need for you to run off until my meeting."

Vega didn't say anything, but he could see her watching him from behind her camera.

"I don't know what he did to you," he started, unsure how to apologize in a way to make it right. "But remember I'm not him. I'm just a man, and I make mistakes like most of us do. That's all I did this morning."

She nodded. "And that was too much."

The intercom on his desk buzzed before he could reply, and he had to stop himself from shoving the offending item to the floor. Why did Beverly continue to disturb him?

"Yes?" he barked into the speaker.

"Mr. Davenport, Ms. Dougard is here and has asked to see you. She says it'll only take a few moments of your time. This morning is the only time we can work her in."

Reality slammed back into him. The mother of his father's secret child was waiting to see him, and he had a nosy journalist with a video camera watching his every move.

"Is she alone?"

"Yes, sir."

At least she hadn't done something stupid like bring the kid up here. With a parting glance to Vega, he replied to Beverly. "Ms. Zaragoza was just about to step out until the nine o'clock meeting. I'll see Lexi after she leaves."

He stood and nodded at the door, ignoring the scathing look Vega shot his way. No doubt he'd just pissed her off even more by dismissing her, but it couldn't be helped. He had no idea why Lexi would be here, but he couldn't afford to ignore her.

They stepped to the door, and he wrapped his hand around the knob but didn't open it. "You are coming back, right?"

She glared at him. "You think that just because you used our chemistry against me I'll run out of here and forget my job? No way. You promised me an interview. After that stunt you just pulled, I dare you to try to get out of it now."

"I'm not saying I want out of it," he ground out, the seemingly permanent state of his clenched teeth making his head throb.

"You sure about that? Clearly you only want me around for sex."

"I don—"

"And you definitely won't be getting any more of that."

He closed his eyes and rubbed his thumb against his pounding temple. How in the world had everything gotten so out of hand? "Fine. I get it. I screwed up."

"Exactly. You screwed up. And I don't give second chances."

"Just…" He paused as he tried to find the right words to let her know she was so much more to him than she thought. He'd never had a woman get so in his face when he crossed the line. Call him out and make him own his mistakes. One who so easily got him to live in the moment and forget the life he was supposed to be living. And whose smile made the whole world feel right. "Maybe we could—"

"Huh-uh," she said. "*We* can't do anything anymore. I'm here for a job. That's all I'm doing." She shoved his hand off the doorknob and opened it herself but looked back at him one last time and whispered, "Make sure you don't forget that again."

She stormed from the room, taking a quick glance at Lexi as she passed.

After the door to his outer office swished closed behind her, Beverly turned to him, her disapproval clear. "Not quite the outcome you'd hoped for, sir?" Her tone left no doubt that she was wise to exactly what he'd been doing behind closed doors.

Damn. Why did everyone suddenly think they could stick their noses in his business? And he certainly didn't need Beverly rubbing it in his face that he'd been an ass and had royally screwed up. "Nothing for you to worry about, Ms. Brubaker."

Her eyebrows arched with the formal use of her name, but he didn't stick around long enough to allow her to make him feel like an even bigger jerk. He took in the woman waiting to talk to him, her eyes as wide as saucers, and hoped like hell she didn't put two and two together as well. He didn't need to give her another excuse to try to blackmail him.

"Lexi. Come on in."

She hurried to scoot past him and had a seat in one of the chairs in front of his desk. He narrowed his eyes on her. Something was different.

And then he got it. She seemed more "normal" than last time. Her perfume wasn't as overpowering, her clothes—though still nice—were not over-the-top, and she wore an air more of what-can-you-do-for-me   instead   of   let-me-show-you-how-I-can-screw-you.

She was definitely different than the last time he'd seen her.

He closed the door and rounded his desk. Once he sat, he steepled his hands and tried to keep his voice from showing his full frustration. "What can I do for you, Lexi?"

Lexi licked her lips, then dug some papers out of her bag. "I got the information from the school. Daniel has been admitted already. He starts Thursday."

JP's favor had paid off. Daniel would be going to the Montessori school. It was the best place for him. "Great. I was informed all would be set up this week." At her continued look of uncertainty, he asked, "Is there a problem? I assure you this is a terrific school for him."

"I guess I'm just nervous." She picked at her manicure. "I was wondering if you could go to the school with us."

"Excuse me?"

A blush stained her cheeks. "I just mean...I know he's not anything to you, but you know these people and..."

Fantastic. Now the blasted woman wanted him to take care of her with more than just money. "Lexi," he spoke gently. He shook his head to make his point. "I can't go to the school with you, or someone will wonder if we have some kind of relationship."

"If anyone asks, I'll just tell them you're a friend."

"And they would take one look at your son and me together with you, and not only assume he was a Davenport, but assume he's mine. I can't do that. I don't believe that's what you want either."

At his words, her eyes grew large. "I hadn't thought of it that way."

She chewed the corner of her mouth and suddenly looked no older than a teenager. "I'm just nervous, and I know Daniel will be, too. He doesn't always do well with change."

JP leaned his forearms on his desk. "I'll tell you what. I plan to be at the school Thursday afternoon anyway, reading to the kids. I do that sometimes."

"I know." She nodded. "I remember seeing a picture of you, and the headline said you participated in things like that."

"Yes. Occasionally." He was doing his best not to think about the kid, scared and feeling alone, heading into a brand-new school. It wasn't his kid, and he shouldn't have to worry about him. But he couldn't keep from it. "So I'll tell you what I'll do. I'll make sure that Daniel is brought into the room while I'm there, then I'll introduce myself to him and help him to feel at ease. Will that help?"

Her wide amber eyes blinked. "Yes. I would appreciate that a lot. Thank you."

She gathered up her papers and suddenly jumped from her seat as if realizing she'd overstayed her welcome. "I'm sorry to bother you without calling, but I got all this in the mail and didn't know what to do."

"It's fine." He stood with her. "And you and Daniel will both be fine."

"Yes." She nodded. "Maybe." She headed to the door but stopped and faced him once again. "I got a job already."

"Did you?" Good for her.

"The school offered me part time, working in the office." She smiled up at him, and he suddenly worried he'd gone too far in helping her out. "I really appreciate everything...JP." Her lashes fluttered. "Is it okay if I call you JP?"

Yes, he'd definitely done too much. He opened the door for her to leave and made sure she couldn't easily touch him on her way out. "I'll see Daniel Thursday afternoon, Lexi. You try not to worry, okay?"

She nodded, her smile no longer quite as bright. "I promise."

Suddenly, she threw herself at him, and his arms automatically closed around her, steadying them both.

"Thank you so much," she gushed.

He wedged some space between them. "You're welcome."

When she pulled away, he saw that Vega had returned to the outer office. She stood beside Beverly's desk as if the two women had been having some serious girl talk—probably scheming his demise—eyeing him steadily.

Both women flicked a gaze over Lexi, then returned to settle on him, and with great clarity, he suddenly understood the phrase "if looks could kill." Personally, he was glad they couldn't.

JP LOOKED up at the sound of a door opening, expecting to find Governor Chandler motioning him back. Instead, he found Evan Martens, hands deep in the pockets of his charcoal suit pants, whistling as he walked toward the exit.

What was he doing here? And how had he gotten an appointment earlier than JP?

When JP had called the day before, the governor had been out of town, but the receptionist has assured him she was putting him down for the very first appointment of the day. Yet at barely eight in the morning, Evan Martens had already been here and done that.

Glancing over at the receptionist, JP caught the sour look on her face and fought the urge to ask what the man had been doing here. It would be wasted breath. He knew exactly what Evan had been doing here. Same thing he'd be doing if their positions were reversed. Evan had seen an opening and had jumped. No better time than on the heels of a boob shot to convince the governor that he had the wrong man pegged for the job.

Didn't make JP's ire any less, but he couldn't fault Evan for his actions.

"JP." Governor Chandler now stood at his door, a grim look marring his face. "Come on back, son."

The endearment was a positive. He guessed it took more than one major screwup to kill off years of close family ties. No doubt his mother had also come through yesterday and called him as well. She had a way of defusing the situation better than most he'd seen.

"Thank you for seeing me this morning, Governor Chandler."

He nodded at the seat in front of his weathered desk, and JP sat down. "Seems you've been a busy boy these last few days. Making my life somewhat difficult, I must say."

JP nodded, feeling like a kid being called to the principal's office. "I apologize for that, sir. I thought we were…" What could he say? He'd thought they were alone so it was okay to take a woman's top off in public? At a loss, he merely shrugged and knew he wore a look of embarrassment. "Honestly, I got carried away. It won't happen again. I know it looks bad, but with that being the only thing out there like that…"

He paused, out of ideas of how to go forward. That picture may be the only black mark against him in the media, but it was a big one.

Chandler pulled a fat cigar from a box on his desk. He didn't light it, simply rolled it between two fingers.

The silence was deafening. "If I may, sir. I saw Evan Martens come out of here a few minutes ago, and I've no doubt what he was doing. He wouldn't be—"

"I'm not putting him in office, son, so don't even bother." Chandler put the cigar to his nose and smelled it. "I've got more sense than that."

A soft laugh came out with JP's exhalation of breath. "Good to hear. I thought so, but…"

He let his words fall off again. What could he say—that he was afraid he'd left the man no other option?

With a deep sound of regret, Chandler put the cigar back in the box and laced his fingers together on his desk. He peered over the surface at JP. "What do you know about Ms. Zaragoza, son?"

"Vega?" JP readjusted to sit up straighter in his seat. "Well, I know she's excellent in her field; she's won many awards. She prefers to stay out of the limelight—this past weekend notwithstanding—and she somehow talked me into doing an interview mere days after I proclaimed to my mother that it was one I'd never agree to do."

Chandler's brows rose at the last statement. "Pretty sure I know where your head's been these last few days. Can't say as I blame you for changing you mind."

Humiliation engulfed him. Yes, wanting Vega had played a role in his decision. A bigger role than he'd like to admit. And the man had just called him on it. JP didn't go to the trouble of acknowledging the statement, instead determined to sell Vega in a better light. But he realized there were too many holes in her background to do it. He could tell him how sweet and vulnerable she was, while at the same time so opinionated and hardheaded she could make your head spin. He could point out that merely being in her presence gave him a sense of himself he hadn't felt since a very young age. He could tell the governor all sorts of personal things about her, but something told him that wouldn't convince the man she wasn't a threat to either of them.

And that's when he realized that he really had been living with his head in the clouds. He trusted Vega; there was zero doubt in his mind. She'd never do anything to intentionally hurt him or his family. She was a beautiful woman with an even more glorious soul. Yet she was also hiding something. Something that she, at least, felt was big.

Potentially it was big only in her mind, but as a soon-to-be leader of the country, maybe he should have worried more about her background before he'd gotten involved with her. Before he'd let himself get in the position of being taken down by anything she could be hiding.

He scraped his hand across his mouth and cleared his throat. He didn't want to go behind her back and look into her background; that wouldn't show the kind of trust he needed to win her over. But he could see that if he did so, it would make the other man in the room feel a lot better about the situation.

Some things simply had to be done a certain way.

"I've no doubts about her, sir," he began slowly, knowing he was speaking only on faith, because he refused to risk what he and Vega could have together for Governor Chandler or anyone else. And yes, his mother would be the first to tell him to get a background check done immediately. "I understand that this photo looks bad. And I recognize why you might question what kind of woman Vega is given the depth of the decision I hope you're still prepared to make. But I'm sitting in front of you today, telling you that she's one beautiful person, both inside and out. I know that's not a lot to stand on, but it'll have to be enough."

The governor sat back in his seat and contemplated the situation, studying JP as thoroughly as JP had ever done to either his allies or his competition.

Finally, he pulled that cigar once again from the box and brought it back to his nose. He inhaled deeply. "You're a good man, JP, from a good family. And I honestly believe you'll be good for this country. But you can't go around getting caught in such positions. *I* can't stand behind someone who does so." He pointed a heavy finger in JP's direction, and a finality crossed his features. "You'll guarantee never to be caught like that again?"

JP let out a huge rush of air. "Without a doubt, sir. Trust me, I don't like it any more than you do. The media this week has been ruthless."

"It hasn't been a boat ride for me either," he mumbled. "The number of calls to this office more than tripled this week. Poor Janie out there is ready to skin me."

"I do apologize for that. As you know, I try my best to remain under the radar as much as possible. I obviously failed at that this week."

The simple understatement broke the tension in the room, and Chandler guffawed with laughter. When he calmed, he pulled a lighter from his pocket and lit the cigar. After taking several long puffs, he mumbled something about not giving a crap about smoking regulations.

"I would agree," Chandler said. "You failed heartily on that front. But I'll also tell you one thing more, if you'd like to hear it."

JP nodded, having respect for what the man had to say. "Absolutely. What's that?"

The governor inhaled then blew out a perfect O of smoke. "Your dad would be real proud of the way you stood up for yourself today, son. Real proud. And I am, too. Right or wrong, we'll go with your gut and move forward together."

JP wanted to let the words about his father not matter, but the fact was, he'd so rarely made his dad proud, he couldn't help but be pleased by the comment. "Thank you, sir. I appreciate all of it."

Chandler nodded then snuffed the cigar out in a heavy cup he pulled from his bottom desk drawer. "Better air this place out before Janie reports me." He flipped on an air purifier sitting on the corner of his desk. "I'll take care of things on my side, son. You take care to keep your nose clean."

JP stood, the meeting at an end, and reached his hand out to shake. "I can promise you that."

"THANK YOU SO MUCH." Vega smiled into the phone at the compliment Bob had just doled out. She'd spent last night pulling together the first day's footage, and so far, he loved everything she'd sent. "I added the audio clip of me because...well, I was just messing around last night and wanted to see it pulled together a bit more. Plus...I couldn't sleep."

She couldn't sleep because she'd been missing JP.

Regardless of how angry he'd made her the morning before, after spending the remainder of the day with him, then returning to a lonely hotel room at the end of a long, tension-filled day, she'd done nothing but toss and turn, wanting the man there by her side.

Of course, she'd still wanted to make him pay for using her as he had. But then, payment could come in the form of being naked and serving up her every desire. Who's to say she couldn't be the one to use someone for a change?

"It's terrific, Vega. As good as I knew you'd be. I want you to seriously consider doing this one yourself." Bob forged ahead as if they hadn't already had this conversation a hundred times, always ending with her saying no. "I've been talking to Atlanta, and I think when they hear this audio, you won't just get the job, but a nice, fat raise to go along with it."

"Except then they'd want me to be on camera out in the field."

"But, honey, you're honestly fantastic. So good, in fact, there's zero doubt in my mind you should forget video journalism and go straight for anchor. You'd be an instant hit."

She flopped back on her bed and sank into the rumpled down comforter. She didn't want to be an anchor. If she ever got up the nerve to actually go for what she wanted, sitting at a desk reading from a teleprompter wouldn't be it.

"I need to go, Bob." Having another repeat of this conversation would get them both nowhere. "I'll be getting clips of JP around town today, hanging out at his favorite places and such, then I'm accompanying him on a date tonight."

She thumped her fist against her forehead at the snarky tone her voice took on at the mentioned date. Bob wouldn't miss that.

"A date?" Pause. "That'll be great for the show."

"Yeah, I'm sure he'll more than turn on the charm. Women viewers will eat that up." She uttered the expected words, then held her breath, knowing he wouldn't leave it alone that easily.

"So what happened in Anguilla...that's over?" he asked after several seconds' pause. He hadn't mentioned the second photo that had come out, but she had no doubt he'd seen it. The man couldn't have missed it.

Along with the photo—a cleaned-up version, thank goodness—practically every step she'd taken the last couple of days had been broadcast on around-the-clock news stations, along with every trashy tabloid out there. They'd figured out she had secured JP's first behind-the-scenes interview and were now playing guessing games as to whether it was because she was sleeping with him or not. At least it seemed to keep them from digging too deep into her past, but she knew it was only a matter of time.

"Yes, it's over. I know you're probably disappointed in me, but..."

What could she say? Some men she just lost her head over?

"Not disappointed, honey, just concerned. It's not like you to get caught..." He cleared his throat. "...as you did. Heck, it's not like you to do anything of the sort. I just want to make sure you're okay."

Tears escaped the corner of each eye as she lay there staring up at the rotating ceiling fan. She pinched the bridge of her nose to try to keep more from falling. "Yeah, I'm good."

"And you're okay with this date tonight?"

She couldn't stop the painful laugh that escaped. "It's exactly what I knew it would be, Bob. Sunday and Monday was nothing serious. Just a good time."

He chuckled. "If you say so, but I have to admit, you raised your hand Saturday night like a woman on a mission."

She groaned. He'd already brought up the auction when they'd talked on the plane Monday evening. "Don't even bring that up again, it's history. We're calling that episode...heck, we'll call everything from then through Monday, temporary insanity. Every girl deserves that at least once in her life, right?"

Easy laughter was her answer. "Sure does, kid. And I'd say

you've paid your dues over the years. You deserved a momentary lapse. Tell me before you go, though, who's his date with?"

She smirked at the irony, knowing Bob would get it as well. "Greta Kirby."

This time, instead of a light chuckle, she got a full minute of rollicking laughter. And she couldn't say she blamed him.

By the time Bob finally had himself under control, Vega was beginning to snicker at the situation herself. Of course the first man she'd gone gaga over in years, she'd end up having to watch—to record!—on a romantic date with him and the woman who'd beat her out.

Not that she thought JP would let himself get trapped by Greta for anything more than one night, but he was a man. And Greta was a very good-looking woman. Vega wouldn't be surprised to find out they ended up exactly how she and JP had ended Sunday night. Buck naked and eating chocolate cake crumbs off each other's parts.

The pain that seared through her at the thought did nothing to improve her mood.

It was time to wrap up the conversation. "I really do need to run. I'm meeting JP for lunch at his favorite diner. I'll send more video later tonight or in the morning. I think this will shape up to be a very nice program."

"No doubt it will," Bob said. He then turned his voice serious. "I may not be able to keep you down here in Savannah, kid, but that doesn't mean I'm not still watching out for you. That includes the job situation, as well as the men in your life. You be careful with this one, okay?"

She appreciated his concern more than she'd probably ever told him. It was nice to know at least one person in the world had your back.

"Thanks, Bob."

CHAPTER TWENTY

*V*ega snapped her pen in two and silently cursed as she hurried to keep the ink from dousing her skirt. Yet another new skirt. At the rate she was buying clothes, she'd need a second new job just to pay for her wardrobe.

She glanced up to find JP watching her from the driver's seat, and she practically hissed at him. How she'd come to be sitting beside him as he headed to pick up Greta for their date, she had no idea. This wasn't at all what she'd envisioned for the week, though the logical part of her brain did point out what a fabulous opportunity it was. An in-depth interview of Atlanta's hottest playboy wouldn't be complete without seeing him in action on a hot date.

"Problem?" He reached across her to the vehicle's glove compartment and pulled out a package of tissues.

"You're my problem," she muttered, yanking the tissues from his hand before her ego let her cause a bigger mess than she already had. As it was, the ink was contained to her palms, turning them a lovely dark blue. No need spreading it anywhere else.

JP didn't reply. Instead, he began humming under his breath to the country song playing softly on the radio. The chorus of Chris Young's "Losing Sleep" began, leaving Vega to wonder if he was thinking of being wrapped up in the sheets with her or with Greta.

"I still don't know why you insisted I go with you to pick her up. I could have met you two at the restaurant. That would make it easier for me to disappear later when I've gotten all the material I need." Or all she could stand. Plus, it wasn't like she'd forgotten that Greta was out to catch a man and had all the right parts to do it. Vega didn't need to see it from the first second it started.

"I told you. When I asked if you joining us tonight with your camera was all right, Greta got overly excited. I think she's looking forward to being on camera more than the date with me."

"I doubt it." She didn't mean to say that out loud, but JP's chuckle indicated he'd heard.

"Jealousy becomes you, babe. I like it."

"I'm not jealous." If she were the jealous type, the feeling would have flared up when JP had kicked her out of his office yesterday morning to entertain the gorgeous redhead. The girl had looked barely twenty, and Vega had been a little taken aback at catching her in JP's arms before departing, but she supposed that was the norm for someone like him.

If she hadn't been so furious with their prior actions in his office, she'd have called him out about having sex with her one minute then kicking her out to hug on another woman the next. Instead, she'd spent the remainder of the morning reminding herself that who he hugged didn't matter to her. They were over.

She rooted around in her bag as if looking for something, hoping JP would return his attention to the road, but he didn't take the hint.

"I would be jealous if our roles were reversed." His voice was perfect tonight. Deep, gravely. Sexy. "And if I had to watch, I'd punch the guy in the face."

Why wouldn't he take the hint? She did not want to talk. "I'm perfectly fine."

The SUV slowed at a stoplight, and he turned on his signal. They were outside an elegantly gated community in Buckhead. Greta certainly knew how to live. But then, that's what you got when you married a billionaire fifty years your senior. The poor man had been gone only a few months, and his widow was already on the prowl. The thought rippled a cold wave down her spine.

They crept up to the guard station, and JP rolled down his window.

"Mr. Davenport," the man practically announced. "Ms. Greta is expecting you."

With a buzz, the gate opened, and they drove in...and the knot in Vega's stomach twisted and grew to the size of Texas. She did not want to see Greta Kirby, and all her assets, fawning all over JP.

So okay, maybe she was just the teeniest bit jealous, but dang, it had only been thirty-six hours ago she'd been ass-bare, thrusting back against the man herself. Now he was going to spend the evening entertaining one of the most stunning women—even if she was considered a joke—in Atlanta. And said woman was no doubt going to be putting everything she had out there.

Vega glanced out her side window as she wondered if he'd be receptive to what Greta offered, then wondered if there was any man alive who could conceivably say no. Of course he'd be receptive. He was single. *They* were over...not that they'd ever really started. And he was a young, virile man. Yep, he'd go to bed tonight after a full couple of days, sandwiched on either end by a naked woman unable to say no to him.

Fury returned at the thought of how easy she'd been yesterday morning. Had she learned nothing over the last eight years?

And she still couldn't believe he'd made love to her up against his office window! Not that she worried anyone would've had a long lens in the building across the street, *and* had it pointed JP's direction at that exact moment, but she had to be more careful.

She'd done much better today, but then, he also hadn't been turning up the wattage of his charm and blasting it her direction. He'd been different since she'd blown up at him. Flirty, but not pushy. Charming, but more in the polite way. And still powerful, yet far more subdued. More as he'd been over the weekend, yet not exactly that either. His actions had actually made it more difficult to resist. Only, he hadn't actually made another pass.

Her foot tapped on the floor mat as she replayed the previous morning and the moments leading up to her blowup. He had entered with the sole purpose of seducing her, totally ignoring her prior dictates that they were over and coming after her as if he had a point to prove. Granted, he'd proven it. She didn't have to like it, but he'd made it clear she couldn't be alone in a room with him without succumbing.

She didn't want to imagine what she would've done next if she hadn't caught the flash of a predatory smile in his reflection as they'd finished. Her warm fuzzies had immediately turned frigid, and she'd felt as used as when she'd been with Ted. Only this time it had hurt more.

Then had come the horror when she'd thought he'd recorded them. It had taken several seconds to calm down enough to think rationally, and even then, she hadn't fully believed him until she'd checked the camera to find that it had, in fact, been shut off.

The car stopped, and JP turned to face her. His eyes ran the length of her body, landing on the five-inch heels she'd worn to their first dinner. They were the closest things she had with her to power heels, and if she was going to be hanging out with two of Atlanta's most beautiful people, she wasn't going to go into it looking like a total loser.

His gaze raked back up the length of her and landed on her lips. No doubt he was noticing that she'd once again applied lip gloss.

But good grief, a woman could only be expected to stand beside someone such as Greta for so long without fighting back.

"You've got the hottest legs I've ever had the pleasure of enjoying." His mouth quirked, and his eyes steamed, then he quickly switched gears. "Make sure you have that camera pointed at the door before she answers. I think this is her big premiere."

Vega rolled her eyes and stepped out of the car. She leaned into the back seat for her equipment as JP came around to help. Straightening, she handed off her camera and began arranging the lighting to capture the "first moment" of their date.

"I don't know why she wants me here," she mumbled. "If she wants to be on camera so bad, why not just sleep with a producer somewhere? Then *bam*, she'd be given the chance."

JP ignored her ranting, which she appreciated. She didn't need him pointing out her petty jealousy yet one more time. He leaned back against the car and eyed the front door as if not really wanting to go up there himself. Or maybe that was just her imagining it.

"I would have paid the quarter million, you know," he spoke quietly.

The dark of the night laid shadows across his face, but she could make out his strong profile and the slight angle of regret in the tilt of his lips. This was the first time since they'd returned that she felt as if she was fully getting the man who'd swept her away and done his damndest to make her fall in love with him.

She softened her tone to match his. "I couldn't do that. There would've been no way to explain it, and you wouldn't have wanted to admit that you paid for your own date. Doing so would've ruined all future auctions."

One side of his mouth lifted as he crossed his arms over his chest and dropped his head back to stare at the night sky. "They might already be ruined."

"Why?" She peered closer, wishing he'd look at her so she could read what he was feeling. He sounded so sad. "Will it be inappropriate once you're in office?"

Assuming the backlash from the topless photo didn't keep him from landing in office.

"That's one reason."

Another beat passed between them as she waited for him to expound, but then, as easily as the melancholy mood had shrouded him, it lifted, and he pushed away from the vehicle. He shot her a wink. "Make sure you get this, babe. No doubt she's looking as hot tonight as she was Saturday."

With those words, he was off and striding to the front stoop of the million-dollar home, a soft whistle drifting back from him. He was once again whistling Chris Young, leaving Vega with no doubt of whose sheets he was thinking of.

"It would serve you right if she stepped out in a turtleneck and a skirt down her to ankles."

He glanced back at her and waggled his eyebrows up and down. "I'm sure she doesn't own a single piece of clothing anything near that modest." A wide grin showed his gleaming teeth. "Lucky me."

Jerk.

But he was right, no way would Greta not step out with a low-cut gown, shimmering and showing every body part her husband had paid for.

JP knocked on the door, and Vega readied the camera. She zoomed in tight to make sure she got the start of the "dream date."

After keeping him waiting the proper amount of time, the door opened, and Vega almost dropped the camera at what stepped out.

Greta wore a vintage pink suit, as prim and proper as Jackie O had ever been, with a straight, modest skirt and button-up jacket, a pillbox hat with matching bow slapped on the front...and pearls around her neck. She fluttered her eyelashes in what Vega could only assume was her attempt at innocent lure and presented JP with the back of her white gloved hand.

Vega kept the shot trained on the two of them but fought an all-out laugh at the look of strangled shock covering JP's face. He would kill her for including that in the final version, but he looked so adorable, she had to try. That picture alone would endear him to women across the nation.

With as little intrusion as possible, Vega captured the couple as they strolled to the car, Greta's hand resting demurely on the inside of JP's elbow, the most innocent smile curling her lips that Vega had ever seen. This woman had done a complete one-eighty in more ways than one. From the look of things, Greta was taking tonight as her opportunity to convince JP she would make the perfect politician's wife.

From the green hue to his face, he registered this fact. And didn't agree.

For Vega, the night couldn't have been more perfect.

After JP deposited Greta in the front seat, Vega flipped off the camera and hurried to gather the remainder of the equipment.

He stepped to her side. "I'm sure you think this is funny."

"No." She blinked up at him, as innocent and demure as Greta. "Hilarious."

He eyed her, clearly intent on saying something snarky in return, but then his eyes hooded, and his gaze stroked her mouth, and Vega very nearly swayed forward, right into his arms.

She caught herself and shot him a look that should have turned him to cinders. Instead, he smiled like a kid on Christmas morning, a glint flashing in his eyes. "I could have you naked behind my car in thirty seconds if I wanted," he whispered.

What a complete ass. Using her elbow, she jabbed him in the gut to move him out of the way. She opened the back door and shoved her camera inside. "The portable light will be enough when we get to the restaurant. I'll use that so you don't have to waste time helping me instead of devoting your full attention to your date."

She climbed in beside her camera and turned to slam the door in his face, but he beat her to it. The door jarred to a stop in front of her. At least she was done with him for a few moments. Except he opened the back door on the other side and thrust in her lighting.

As he stooped over, he gave his one-hundred-watt smile to Greta, who'd glanced back at him. She then turned to Vega with a straight face. "Make sure you don't miss a second of tonight. I want this recorded for me, if not for the interview."

The back door closed, and JP settled into the front seat. Greta placed her hand over his forearm, and once again glanced back at Vega, her eyes wide and gullible. "It will be aired in the interview, won't it? I want the country to live our first date with us." She sighed and brought her gloved hands to her chest. "It'll be so romantic."

Gag.

Vega fought the urge to show her true feelings and managed to settle back against the thick leather, trying to pretend she wasn't a third in a very uncomfortable situation. Greta refused to let her have that small dream.

"And then there's the whole aspect of you and me. I mean, who would have guessed the woman who was bidding against me for the man of my dreams would be here recording our first date together? The people will love the irony."

Vega blinked. Man of her dreams? Since when? Before or after her husband was in the ground? And *the people*? This woman probably already had her inauguration gown picked out, as well as the names of their two point three children.

And dog. Don't forget the presidential dog.

Nausea bumped and gurgled in Vega's gut at the thought. She should not be here. Surely there was something else she could be doing to boost her career without having to torture herself by watching another woman play dress-up with JP.

As if reading her mind, he readjusted his rearview mirror until their eyes met in the reflection. If she were reading the look correctly, he wished he was anywhere but there, too.

Too bad.

At least one of them had the potential for ending the night on a high note. Vega would go back to her hotel, alone. While JP and Greta would...

She glanced up at him as he circled around the driveway and headed back to the main road. What *would* they be doing by night's end? She closed her eyes and swallowed down her disgust.

Yes, jealous was a nasty, ugly thing. And yes, it had her in its tightest grip.

THE SEA BASS WAS PERFECTION, the restaurant couldn't have been more high-end, and the company...wasn't whom he wanted.

JP took in the woman perched across the table from him, one hand placed purposefully in her lap and the other picking daintily at her food, and wondered what had happened to the curves Greta had on display Saturday night. Not that he really cared about her set of curves, but that had been the only thing he'd looked forward to about this date. Rumor had it Edward Kirby had hired the best surgeon money could buy and bought himself some first-class parts. The least the woman could do was display them a little.

That would have made teasing Vega about the date much more fun.

He tossed a quick look to the corner of the room where she stood, trying to pretend she didn't exist. But the thing was, every damn man in the room had eyed her more than they had their own dates. Those heels and the softer sweep of her hair highlighted some of her best features.

Not that she had a bad feature from what he could tell. And he'd thoroughly inspected each and every one himself.

His dick twitched at the thought of Vega naked, so he pushed the picture away before Greta caught him with a hard-on and assumed it was made for her.

"What are we doing next?" Wide eyes blinked across the table at him. She was maintaining an excellent job of keeping up the role of "little lady," but he was tired of it. He wanted to stir things up.

"I thought it would be polite to invite Vega over to eat."

Greta's hand fluttered at her throat. "But how will that look? I mean, we're on our first date, Jackson."

And their last.

"I want it to be perfect, you know?" she continued.

He reached across the table and took her hand, knowing the visual would look romantic on camera, then leaned in and tried for a sultry look. He needed to give her her money's worth, after all. "We brought her with us, Greta. We can't really keep her at the camera all night and not feed her." He gave her a warm smile. "Wouldn't we look more chivalrous inviting her over?"

"Oh," she murmured, clearly liking the idea of being a charitable host. "You're right, of course. Please, yes. Go invite her to join us."

He gave her hand a slight squeeze and stood without hesitation. Vega had been too far away for far too long.

When he headed her direction, she poked her head out and narrowed her eyes at him.

"What are you doing," she whispered as he reached her side.

Before she could slip back out of reach, he circled her wrist with his fingers and leaned down to whisper in her ear. "I missed you."

She twisted her arm until he let go. "Go back to your date."

"Huh-uh. Not without you." He peeked over at Greta and waggled his fingers. She returned the gesture. "Greta and I would like you to join us."

"I am *not* joining you for dinner. You're on a date, JP. I'm just here to record it."

"Ah, come on. Don't be like that. We want you to join us." He leaned in once again to whisper in her ear, only this time he grazed her with his lips and felt the pop of electricity down his body. "There are other photographers here, you know, just waiting for the money shot. Greta and I want to make sure we look courteous to our own personal historian."

Vega stiffened underneath his mouth, and the tension sizzled around them. He quickly straightened when it occurred to him what it would look like when he escorted another woman back to his date and he was clearly sporting a raging erection. Though everyone knew it was a bought-and-paid-for date, that didn't mean he could be outright rude to the woman.

He put a couple inches between himself and Vega. "I'm not leaving this corner without you, so if you'd rather you and I not end up on the eleven o'clock news instead of me and Greta, I suggest you politely come along."

He may have sense enough to keep his hormones under control for the moment, but that didn't mean he had the mental capacity to stay away from the fire.

Vega studied him, then Greta, then the other patrons in the room. She didn't say whether she knew he was lying when he said there were other photographers around, but he wasn't about to tell her that no way would the restaurant allow them inside the dining rooms. The manager went to great lengths to maintain privacy, and JP had had to work miracles just to get Vega approved to be in the room with her camera.

After what seemed like hours, she finally relented. She sighed and flipped the switch to stop the recording. "Fine, but I'm buying the most expense entrée on the menu."

He grinned at her. "I already ordered it for you."

Yes, he'd intended all along to have Vega at his table tonight. If he couldn't have her in his bed, he'd take whatever he could get. He winked. "It should be arriving within minutes."

CHAPTER TWENTY-ONE

*a*s they made their way across the room to JP's own
personal Jackie O, Vega couldn't stop the nervousness
from gurgling deep in her belly. After watching the two of them
ooh and *aah* over each other for the last hour, she had to have lost
her mind to be joining them. And JP was so full of crap. There was
no other person in this room with a camera. This restaurant
wouldn't allow it.

But she was starving, and the smells in this place were to die
for. When she sat, a fat lobster was plopped down in front of her,
and her mouth instantly watered. She looked at JP, unwilling to let
him off the hook for even a second. "Wine?"

Before the word was out of her mouth, a glass was placed on
the corner of the table and the sommelier held out a bottle of
Grüner Veltliner for JP's inspection. An Austrian wine that, she
knew from past experience, perfectly complemented boiled
lobster dipped in garlic butter. She held in the moan at the thought
of the upcoming flood of sensations to her taste buds and was
immediately taken back to their dinner at Cat's. The wine-steak
combination had been utter perfection.

Upon returning to the hotel, she'd looked up the wine, thinking she might order a case for herself. The stuff wasn't cheap.

The sommelier poured a taste and waited for JP's approval, then filled her glass. That's when Vega noticed the bottle already on the table that he and Greta had been drinking was something else. He'd ordered this just for her. She glanced at him, and his eyes locked on hers. Yep. Just for her.

A slight cough came from the other side of the table, reminding Vega that she was interrupting Greta's date.

"I'm sorry, Greta." Vega smiled, hoping the woman hadn't noticed the moment the two of them had just shared. "I didn't mean to ignore you. Thank you so much for inviting me over. I've gotten some terrific footage of the two of you tonight."

That was all it took to settle Greta's jealousy.

"Really?" She flipped her long black hair over her shoulder and slipped into the harlot look she wore so often, before apparently remembering she was playing a different role tonight. She quickly masked her face and gave Vega a soft smile. "Thank you so much; you're so sweet. I was just telling Jackson how special this will be for us some day. Our own history being recorded as it happens."

Vega almost laughed out loud at the look on JP's face. It pinched as if he'd just swallowed a lemon.

Greta continued to blather on about what a great team she and JP could make together and how she "knew people" and would be the perfect philanthropist by his side. JP's eyes glazed over, and Vega almost felt sorry for him.

But then, she didn't.

He might be stuck in the middle of a difficult situation for a few hours, but that didn't mean he wouldn't get to enjoy the payoff at the end. At the thought, it became difficult to swallow the bite of lobster she'd just slipped between her teeth. She settled her hands in her lap and pretended the testosterone to her left didn't exist.

After forcing the bite down her throat, she focused one

hundred percent on Greta. "Tell me more about yourself. I know you were married to Edward for what…five years?"

Greta's faced glowed, and if Vega didn't know better, she'd think the woman might have actually loved her husband. "Yes. Five wonderful years." She sighed. "Eddie was the greatest."

As if realizing her words might bruise JP's ego, Greta quickly reached across the table and patted his forearm. "Though you're every bit as great, darling."

JP closed his hand on top of Greta's and stared into her eyes, giving her a dazzling smile. "I'll do my best tonight to prove it."

Vega shifted to turn her body more toward Greta. "Tell me about your life with him, if you don't mind. I can't say I followed your every movement, but I do recall seeing it mentioned that he took you somewhere pretty exotic for your honeymoon?"

Pleasure burst on the woman's face. "Yes. We went to South Africa."

Vega's eyes bugged. "South Africa?" A Playboy Playmate and an eighty-year-old, trekking across the game reserves of South Africa? She had a hard time picturing it.

Greta blinked over at JP. "You don't mind if I share some of this with Vega, do you, darling? She might want to use it for her story."

Not a single touch of humor was visible as JP politely dipped his head. "Please, go ahead. She should get as much about you as possible."

"Thanks," she breathed out, then turned to Vega and completely forgot about her date. "It was the most amazing trip. Not only the wild animals, but the people we came in contact with. Their sense of community over there was unlike anything I'd ever seen."

She went on to explain their entire trip, and Vega couldn't help but be a little jealous. It had been years since she'd thought about doing anything so adventurous. Of course, when she had considered it in the past, she'd wanted to take her video camera and help bring attention to some of the communities in need there. Communities that had the most amazing vistas and cultures, but where many of the residents were also starving and dying at the same time.

The way Greta described her honeymoon made it clear the woman wasn't nearly as empty-headed as the world believed. Why she fed that persona, Vega had no idea, but there was definitely a brain inside her head.

Vega remained focused on Greta as her storytelling moved into another adventure she and her husband had taken. This one in Alaska. When JP jumped in to share details of some of his own trips, the two of them laughed easily together, making Vega once again feel like the third wheel. That was okay though—she was the third wheel. She dug into her succulent lobster and pretended nothing about the situation bothered her.

"It sounds like you love adventure as much as I do." Greta's fake eyelashes fluttered at JP. She dipped her head modestly then looked coyly back up at him. "I'd love to take a trip with you. It would be like starting a whole new chapter in my life."

He chuckled. "I'm not sure I could keep up with you, Greta. You sound like more woman than I'm used to."

"Oh," she giggled. "You silly thing. You do like to stroke a woman's ego, don't you?" Her gaze suddenly shifted to Vega's. "Wouldn't you agree? The man likes to stroke a woman's ego?"

A commotion in the front of the restaurant got their attention, and as the three of them turned to see what was happening, the restaurant manager stepped to JP's side, a look of concern registering on his face.

"Excuse me, sir. We have a situation with the paparazzi outside." He glanced at Greta as he spoke to make it clear the situation had to do with who they were. "I apologize for the interruption, and I assure you we're getting it under control, but I did want you to be made aware of the disturbance."

JP nodded and rose. "I'll help."

"No need, sir, I just wanted to—"

"I'm the cause, Miguel. I'll help." He nodded to Greta, then landed his gaze on Vega. "Please excuse me, ladies. I'll be right back."

As he walked away, uncomfortable silence settled over the table before Greta once again turned her focus to Vega. Her polite expression was beginning to crack.

"Wouldn't you agree?" Greta's voice changed from perfect hostess, taking on a slight note of annoyance.

At a loss as to what she was talking about, Vega asked, "Agree with what?"

"That Jackson likes to stroke a woman's ego." Her blue eyes glittered behind her lashes. "Or better yet, likes to stroke a woman's naked breasts."

Panic lit a fire in Vega's low belly. She could not believe the woman intended to bring up that photo here tonight. The stink was just starting to die down. Before she could figure out how to possibly reply to the question, Greta jumped back in, rage flashing across her face.

"I cannot believe you did that," she sneered. "Did I not make it clear at the auction that I intend to have him? I'm more his style, my dear. Not you. Not you at all. You're nothing more than a cheap piece of trash." She laughed, an evil sound that made the skin down Vega's spine light up. "You really thought flashing your boobs would get him long term? Not a chance."

Anger mixed in with the panic now, but Vega didn't let it overtake her. She could not afford to make a scene. Doing so would look like nothing more than a fight over a man, and that was definitely the type of situation that would appeal to the cameras trying to make their way inside the building.

"I apologize, Greta." The words stuck in her throat, but if she had any hope of calming the woman down before this conversation got out of control, she had to be placid. "Being caught like that certainly was not my intention."

"Is that so?" Sculpted eyebrows rose, and the polite, serene expression Greta had worn all night was now completely gone. "Then you'd better be careful, *Ms. Zaragoza*. Keep it up and you might find yourself portrayed even worse than a few sleazy shots in the tabloids. There are evil people out there, you know? Keep prancing around in public with him, and before you know it, you could become the next social media sensation."

An instant chill swept Vega from head to toe. Greta was merely tossing random threats out, but she'd hit on Vega's biggest fear. With the ease of cell phones these days, it would be so easy to get caught in a compromising position if she weren't careful, and have it go viral.

Calmly placing her napkin on the table, she rose. "Excuse me."

She needed to escape the fear roaring to life inside her as her past tried to make its way forward. When she turned to head for the ladies' room, JP stood in her path. His features were set in stone as he shifted his gaze from her to Greta.

She skirted around him, shaking off his hand when he reached out as if to stop her. Behind her, Greta shared how she'd missed him in the three minutes he'd been gone, her tone changed instantly back to sweet and demure.

JP muttered something in return, but Vega couldn't care less what it was. She had to get away.

She hurried to the restroom where she hid in one of the floor-to-ceiling stalls for several minutes until she had herself once again under control. This was merely an assignment. She could do it, and she could do it without letting one of the subjects get her riled up. She had to, in fact, or she'd have no job come the end of the week.

After splashing water on her overheated cheeks, she reapplied lip gloss, nodded to herself in the mirror, then tipped the attendant and stepped from the room. Right into JP.

Without a word, he closed his hand around her arm and steered her from the hallway to a small, private section off the side of the kitchen.

"Are you okay?" he asked when they stopped, and she nodded. She suddenly was.

He'd come after her.

Worry creased the space between his brows, and she reached up to smooth the area. "I'm fine," she whispered.

The two words lessened the tension in his shoulders, letting the air out of his chest.

"You should go back to your date, though," she made herself say. *Before she gets even more jealous*, she wanted to add but didn't let herself. In actuality, she couldn't care less how jealous Greta got, but she did suspect the greater the jealousy, the harder Greta would play the game.

"I don't care about her right now," he said. "She upset you. I need to take care of you first."

His hand loosened where it still gripped her upper arm and slid down, stopping when he reached her hand. He laced his fingers backwards with hers so that the backs of their hands were facing each other and caressed his thumb along the outside of her forefinger. He then leaned in to speak in low tones.

"What all did she say? I only caught the end of it."

Vega shook her head. It didn't matter. And she couldn't explain that the biggest problem was her fear that not only would she manage to get herself dragged through the mud again, but she'd take him with her.

"There was nothing sleazy about that picture of us, Vega." He touched one finger to the underside of her chin when she didn't say anything, silently edging her face up to his. "I told her that. You know that too, don't you? What we had...what we *have* is not sleazy."

Going for a smile, she gave him all she had. He was sweet to try to comfort her. "I had my top off, JP. Even you've got to admit that's fairly sleazy—"

"It's not," he urged. "*We're* not."

She shook her head and fought back the tear that wanted to escape. If only things were different, she'd love seeing where they could go. "It doesn't matter. That's not what I'm so upset about anyway. Not exactly."

His fingers squeezed hers. "Will you tell me what it is, then? Tell me and I'll fix it. Are you afraid someone will do like she said? Put something online?"

She gave a half shrug. It was close enough. She had enough people following her these days that one little misstep and she would definitely go viral.

"If it happened, I'd pay whatever it took to get it taken down. And I'd make certain that whoever was behind it never tried anything like that again. You know that, don't you? I'd take care of it."

His urging was almost more than she could bear. She focused on the intensity of his face and couldn't help but fall a little deeper for him. Life was sometimes so unfair.

As if sensing her turbulent thoughts, he put his mouth to her ear. "Stay with me tonight. Let me make love to you."

She wanted to say yes more than any other time in her life, but she couldn't keep letting herself fall into his arms. Every time she did made it even harder to walk away. With an enormous pile of regret, she glanced away from him. She had to make herself say no, but she couldn't do it while staring into his eyes. She almost laughed at the thought. She wasn't sure she could manage it without staring in his eyes either. That's when she saw the waiter standing slightly behind JP with his cell phone up in front of his face.

"Oh my God," she whispered.

JP swiveled to see what had caught her attention, then cursed at the same time as the man realized he'd been discovered. The man shot off through the kitchen, the phone disappearing inside the front pocket of his pants as he wound his way through the food stations. He was wiry and fast, but they'd both gotten a good look at him. He would be caught; Vega had no doubt.

JP tossed her a quick look, frustration and apology clear on his face. "I'll be right back."

"Yes," she nodded. "Go."

After he disappeared, she returned to the ladies' room and splashed more water on her face, terrified over how difficult it was becoming to keep telling him no. She needed to get away from him but knew she couldn't. Not yet. But she could tonight, at least.

Knowing it might upset him when he came back and she was gone, she didn't let that change her mind. It was time to take care of herself and let him get on with his life.

Pulling out her cell phone, she ordered a rideshare. The show would have to be done without the remainder of his and Greta's date. And he'd have to get over the fact he couldn't control her actions. He had a woman waiting on him tonight, and even if he wanted to, he couldn't get out of the rest of this evening.

And she wasn't going to sit around and watch another second of it unfold.

Especially after she'd just realized she was already more than halfway gone for him.

CHAPTER TWENTY-TWO

*V*ega glanced at the clock for the third time in the last ten minutes. JP was now thirty minutes late for work. She sat in his outer office waiting for him and was beginning to wonder if he'd even come home from his date the night before. According to Beverly, since he didn't have traffic to contend with —he lived in the penthouse on the top floor of his office building —he was practically never late.

But he definitely was today.

The phone on the assistant's desk rang, and Vega turned her attention to the notebook in her lap. She tried to concentrate on what she had left to do for the interview instead of listening to the phone call, but she couldn't help overhearing the one-sided conversation with yet another reporter. Apparently, whatever had happened after she'd left the night before had been newsworthy.

She hovered a finger over the browser icon of her phone, fighting the urge to do a search for JP and Greta. She did not want to see what turned up...yet she did.

Before she could bring up Google, her phone vibrated in her hand, and she let out a burst of air, thrilled for an excuse to keep from searching for something that would only upset her. With a shaky finger, she answered the call from an Atlanta number she didn't recognize.

"Vega...this is Greta Kirby."

Irony had a very bad sense of humor.

She closed her eyes and thumped her head against the wall behind her chair. Could she please get past this week already?

Pulling in a giant breath of fortitude, she forced a pleasant tone to her voice. She had the impression that pissing Greta off would not be a good thing. "What can I do for you, Ms. Kirby?"

"I'm so sorry about our little misunderstanding last night, dear."

Ha! *Right.*

"And I hate that I didn't get a chance to right it before you had to leave," Greta continued.

Vega listened to the sugary-sweet voice on the other end of the phone and wondered what she was up to. After returning from the bathroom the night before, Vega had thrown out an excuse, taken her equipment, and waited just inside the front door of the restaurant for her car. All before JP had reappeared.

What Greta could want now or even how she'd come to have Vega's phone number was a complete mystery.

"I am so sorry about that, Greta. I got a call and had a slight emergency." She didn't feel the need to fill in the silence with any other words. From what she could tell, there was no reason to even be talking to the woman.

"Well..." Greta cooed. "I called hoping to make my behavior up to you. Thought maybe we could meet for lunch. Wouldn't that be fun?"

Fun? It would be like jabbing a dull ice pick in her eye over and over again.

Vega cast a longing glance across the room to Beverly sitting behind her desk, engrossed now in something on her computer screen, and wished she'd continued eavesdropping instead of taking her own call.

"I'm sure there's no need for that, Ms. Kirby. All is forgotten." She'd so rather be talking to JP's assistant than JP's date.

"I refuse to take no for an answer, dear. Let's do it. A girls' day out!"

Vega blinked several times as if her brain were rebooting. Why in the world would Greta want to have a girls' day out with her?

She decided to approach the situation in a different way than just a flat *not on your life.* "That sounds like loads of fun, but I'm not sure I'll be in town long enough to make it happen."

Beverly glanced up from her computer, her eyebrows going on a hike to her forehead. She must not be above eavesdropping herself.

"Oh poo," Greta whined. "I was so hoping you'd say yes. You see, I don't have many friends here in Atlanta, and since Eddie died, well, I get lonely. And I do so regret my nasty comments last night. JP and I talked about it, and I see that I was out of line. What happened before the two of us got together is simply none of my business."

Vega stared straight ahead, willing JP to show up, or Beverly to toss her an excuse, or the danged building to catch on fire. Anything to get her out of this conversation without making an enemy. Greta had money, and Vega had learned long ago that money could cause more than one kind of problem. Especially for someone with an agenda.

Vega only wished she knew what Greta's agenda was.

She opened her mouth and mumbled the only thing she could think to say. "I won't be working with JP much tomorrow. Maybe we could do something in the morning."

"Oh!" Greta squealed so loud Vega had to pull the phone away from her ear. "That would be perfect. How about I meet you at the Hilton?"

A twitch pinched the back of Vega's neck.

"How do you know where I'm staying, Greta?"

"Huh?" Greta stammered a bit then giggled. "Oh, Jackson mentioned it last night. He was worried, hoping you'd made it back after you left, so he called the hotel and confirmed you'd returned. That's how I got your phone number too," she added in a rush. "I sort of sneaked a peek at Jackson's phone after we..." Giggle. "Well...later in the evening."

After what? Was she trying to suggest that she had postcoitally snuck JP's phone away just to get Vega's phone number?

Something wasn't making sense here, but the thought of Greta having the opportunity to get JP's phone when he wasn't looking sent such a gush of nausea through Vega, she made an excuse and got off the phone before she was caught throwing up her breakfast.

It wasn't her business what the two of them had done at the end of the evening, and it would never be her business. She was here for the interview. Which, for the most part, would wrap up today. They had a trip to the school where he volunteered, then dinner that evening with his family, along with confirmation with the governor that JP would, in fact, accept the senatorial seat.

Tomorrow would be spent pulling everything together, then Saturday, the press conference announcing it to the world.

Getting the press conference would conclude her time with JP, but hopefully start her new job in Atlanta. One, she fervently hoped, that did not put her in JP's path too often in the future.

She closed her eyes and rested her head against the wall, taking in long, deep breaths to steady the irregular rhythm in her chest. It didn't matter that JP was late to the office, and it didn't matter if it was because he had been up all night trying his best to experience everything an ex–Playboy Playmate had to offer. It was his life and his choice.

But she wanted to rip out both his and Greta's eyes. Or worse.

A soft *hmmm* drew her attention to JP's admin, who was still engrossed in the monitor, and Vega couldn't help but wonder what had piqued her interest.

She'd chatted with Beverly multiple times over the last few days and had found her to be a truly lovely person. She was utterly loyal to JP but wasn't above snickering with Vega over some of the shenanigans he'd gotten himself into over the years.

Vega rose from the chair and began to pace the small waiting area. "I'm surprised JP wasn't already working when I got here this morning." It was a conversation they'd already had, but she had to do something. Waiting was driving her out of her mind.

Beverly looked up from the screen, her glasses perched on her nose and the devil dancing in her eyes. "From the looks of these photos, I'm suspecting he had a late night."

Disgust spread through Vega like a nasty fungus. She wanted to go over and check it out for herself, to see just how bad it was—hopefully going a long way to turning off her own fascination with him—but it would be rude to butt in without being asked.

"Of course, that normally doesn't stop him from getting to work on time." Beverly chuckled and shook her head as she continued staring at the screen. "Come over here. You've got to see these."

Vega hurried to the desk. No, she didn't really *want* to see pictures of him and Greta, yet she couldn't make herself not look at them. She stepped to Beverly's side and glanced at the monitor, then leaned in and gaped.

It couldn't have been a more perfect picture of an upstanding politician and the little wife standing by his side. Vega couldn't tell where they were, but they'd clearly carried a crowd with them. JP stood before everyone, many of them photographers, but he was front and center, tall and powerful, and Greta stood discreetly by his side, hands folded over each other, and a pure look of adoration as she gazed up at him.

JP with the tailored dark suit he'd worn the night before and Greta in her Jackie O finest. It was truly a gem. Vega had no doubt Greta already had the shot printed and framed.

"Check out these others," Beverly said, then began scrolling down the screen.

One after another, there were the two of them. Entering an upscale jazz club, then coming back out of the club later. In the first one, JP had one elbow slightly askew with Greta's arm slipped into the bend. In the next, they stood on the sidewalk after exiting, JP's hands in his pockets, Greta's head resting on his shoulder as if they'd just come from the most romantic evening.

There were several more in different night spots over the city, all similar, and all with Greta cuddling close to him. The man had certainly done his job as perfect host for the evening. The governor couldn't be upset with these because there wasn't a single thing vulgar or unseemly about them. They were simply two perfect people out enjoying the beginning of a lovely relationship.

"At least it'll take their minds off that shot of him and me," she mumbled, her irritation showing itself.

Vega froze, realizing that though everyone knew it had been her in the photo, this was the first time she'd talked about it to anyone other than JP. And she'd been the one to bring it up!

Might as well try to make it a little better since it was now out there. "I'm sorry about that picture," she said, her cheeks tinting with heat. "If you'd asked me last Saturday night which of us would be the one to bring the man to a low like he's never seen, I would have sworn it would be that one." She pointed to the perfect pictures on-screen.

Beverly cackled with laughter. "Don't you dare apologize. I loved it! The man needs someone like you in his life."

"Are you kidding me?" Vega gaped. "He has *plenty* of women in his life. Not that I want to be in his life anyway. It was a one-time thing."

Beverly eyed her as if she didn't believe her protest, then went back to the screen. "I want to show you something. Check these pictures out in detail. And look close."

Vega dragged over a guest chair to sit, and Beverly once again started scrolling through the pictures.

"What am I looking for?" she asked.

"Just look at the two of them. What do you not see happening in those pictures? In every single one of them?"

Vega squinted at the computer as if doing so would make something clearer, but all she kept seeing was JP and Greta, Mister and Miss Perfect, cuddling all over each other. Wait...she leaned closer. She took the mouse from Beverly and scrolled back to the top to start over.

The admin plopped back in her chair in a queen-of-the-castle manner. "You see it, don't you? They're all like that. Every woman he's photographed with."

Vega turned her head and looked Beverly straight in the eye. "Every one of them looks as if they're close, cuddling even, but there isn't one single picture where he has an actual hand touching her in anything more than the most cursory fashion."

His hands were either in his pockets or at his sides. She pointed to the screen where he'd been holding the car door open for her. Greta was once again leaning into him, a wide smile on her face, but JP had one hand on the open door and the other holding a gift bag they'd apparently picked up on one of their many stops.

"Exactly. He sometimes will have a steadying touch to their backs, but he never has his fingers clasped around anyone, and rarely does he even touch a woman in public."

"Wow." Vega settled back into her chair. "I can't believe I never noticed that."

"And where were his hands in your picture?"

She blushed madly. They both knew exactly where his hands had been. "That was different. We were kissing."

"My point exactly."

"Okay, wait." She stood and began to pace again. "What are you saying? That though he goes out with—*and sleeps with*—all kinds of women, he always makes sure not to be photographed in even the tiniest compromising position?"

Beverly dipped her eyes in acknowledgment.

"Yet he let himself get caught like that with me?" Vega pierced her with her gaze. "Why?"

A shrug. "He's different with you."

Vega blinked. Well, that was interesting. Only…She scrunched her nose up in thought, then shook her head. "No, that doesn't count. We were wearing disguises, and no one was supposed to even know we were on the island. He only let himself act that way because he didn't think anyone would be looking."

"Sweetheart," Beverly began as if explaining to a small child. "I hate to break it to you, but you aren't the first woman he's tried to disappear with for a weekend. He's been caught before when no one knew he was there, yet even then, there was never any public hand-holding."

The thought that she might be somehow different to him than other women was nice, but she had a hard time believing it. They were just chemistry and a good time. She shook her head, feeling a slight pang at the thought that even though that's all they were, it was over. "Still doesn't matter. JP and I were just a weekend thing."

"Why is that?"

What a silly question. "First of all, because he *never* gets more serious than a weekend, but mostly because he's too…" She paused, trying to figure out how to explain, then ended up flapping her hand at the screen. "Public."

Beverly returned her gaze to the pictures. "And you don't like being public, I take it?"

"Exactly."

Another click brought up one more photo. "Then you have a funny way of showing it," Beverly murmured.

Though the server at the restaurant had likely gotten fired, he had managed to get payoff for his trouble. There in the grainy, low light were JP and Vega, heads close together as he whispered in her ear, their hands clasped together at her side.

She swallowed a gulp, while Beverly laughed so hard she snorted.

Could she not get a single break? Being caught together like that—while he was out with another woman—would look as bad as if they'd been caught kissing in the back hallway instead of merely talking.

The outer door swung open, and JP entered with authority. He took one look at the two of them and fastened on Beverly. "Don't you have work to be doing?"

Beverly straightened. She wore the air of being reprimanded, but the gleam in her eyes gave her away. "Yes, Mr. Davenport."

JP narrowed his eyes on her, doing an excellent impression of someone who'd woken up on the wrong side of the bed and insisted on taking it out on everyone around him. Vega wondered if that meant his night had ended badly.

She could only hope.

"I'll be in my office." The door rattled in its frame behind him, leaving Vega wide-eyed and wondering what had just happened.

She edged back to the other side of the desk, then stood there, wondering what she was supposed to do next. He was the one who'd suggested she come to his office until they headed to the school, but with him not even acknowledging her, then closing himself off behind his door, she wasn't about to sit there waiting all day. Even if she did care to tolerate his mood.

"I think I'll—"

"Beverly," the phone speaker squawked into the room.

"Yes, Mr. Davenport?"

"Send Ms. Zaragoza in."

Ms. Zaragoza? Apparently, they were back to formal names. She supposed that's what happened after he slept with someone else. Her irritation level inched higher.

Beverly peered over her glasses. "You going in, or should I tell him you left already?"

She was thinking the same as Vega. Why should she go in there just because he commanded? Vega glanced at the closed door, sure she hadn't done anything to deserve his mood, and equally certain she didn't want to be on the other side of it. She was the one who should be furious, not the other way around.

"I would say not to take it personally," Beverly began. "But he's arrived in that mood every day this week." She shrugged. "Could have something to do with you."

"Yes, well. He could learn to put out the effort to be civilized, too." Especially after he'd just had a long night with another woman. "I'm leaving."

Vega turned to the chair she'd been sitting in and began gathering her things. The sound of a door swinging open behind her stopped her movements. She peered over her shoulder. JP now filled the space where the door had been, and his blue eyes were focused purely on her.

"Would you come in here?" His tone still commanded, but she could see he was trying.

She so didn't want to go in there. She couldn't fully escape him —they did have to film the activities scheduled for the day—but the thought of being near him at the moment wasn't a pleasant one. In fact, it was darn near torturous.

She glanced at the outer door, wondering if he'd refuse to continue or renege on the whole thing altogether, if she just left.

"Please."

Damn. That did it. She still couldn't say no to the man, no matter what, and certainly not when he said *please.*

With a great show of reluctance, she grabbed her remaining items and slunk into his office. He stood at the entrance and let her pass, then followed her in, closing the door behind him, this time more gently.

Once they were alone, she stood in the middle of the room, her arms wrapped protectively around her stuff, and waited.

"Sit down, Vega." His deep voice came from behind her a second before his hands reached around and lifted the camera and her backpack from her arms. He pressed his fingertips to her shoulder, nudging her toward a chair. "Sit."

With a drawn-out sigh, she finally did as asked. He circled his desk and sat facing her, and she found herself unable to look him in the eye. Knowing he'd been with Greta the night before hurt way more than it should have.

She tried the view out his window, but that just reminded her of what the two of them had done up against that pane a couple days ago. Finally, she settled her gaze on the shelves lining the wall to his left.

"Why did you run out like that last night?" The underlying anger in his voice was enough to swivel her head back in his direction.

"Are you kidding me?" she asked. "We'd just gotten caught being photographed *again*...while you were on a date with another woman, and you think I should have sat back down with her for round two?"

"You could have let me know you were leaving. I was worried."

Right. Greta had mentioned he'd checked on her before he'd done who knew what to the other woman. She supposed she was supposed to be thankful for that small bit of worry. She stared at the shelves again and snorted her disgust.

"What does that mean?" he asked, the tension in his voice slightly subdued. "You don't think I would worry about you?"

"I don't think it was the topmost subject on your mind, no."

"What is wrong with you this morning?" He slammed a hand on his desk, making her jump but getting her attention back on him. "I'm the one who should be pissed here. I had no idea you'd run out."

"You should be pissed?"

"I had to make up an explanation to Greta."

"You think you're the one who has a right to be angry?"

"Then I had to call in all kinds of favors to get the hotel staff to make sure you'd gotten back safely. And all the while—"

She stood and leaned over the desk, putting her face in his. "Since when have I become incapable of seeing myself back to my own hotel?"

He rose to mimic her pose. "Since I can't stand not knowing what you're doing every single minute of the day."

"That's a load of crap."

"That's the reality, lady."

They were standing nose-to-nose, screaming at each other, and hadn't heard Beverly come in. She cleared her throat during the brief silence, and they both whipped their heads around to the door.

"I'm sorry." She looked at the floor as she spoke. "The governor is on line one, Mr. Davenport. He's insisting he speak with you."

The door closed behind her before JP could utter a response.

He turned back to Vega, their heated breaths mingling, and locked his gaze with hers. She didn't know what was going on here, but she was sure she didn't like the look in his eyes. Moving away from the tension, she settled back down in a chair, wishing he'd do the same. Instead, he continued hovering over his desk.

"What is it that's really bugging you, JP?" she asked. "Of course I left last night. I was more than embarrassed when Greta brought up that picture of us, then we got caught again in the back room, and if that wasn't enough, the entire evening had already been uncomfortable. I couldn't take it anymore."

"Why not?" Childlike belligerence was the closest she could come to describing his tone.

She glanced away, not wanting to show him her pain, but then decided it might be the only way to get him to back off. Lifting her chin, she faced him. "I know I don't have the right to care, but I find it incredibly difficult to sit with you and another woman on a date."

"But you knew it wasn't a real date."

"I knew it wasn't likely to go past last night, yes. But that doesn't mean..." She hated herself for being jealous. She took a deep breath and licked her lips before continuing. "That doesn't mean you wouldn't see to it that Greta got her money's worth."

Confusion marred his brow. "What do you mean? A good date? Of course I'd show her a good time. I took her to the finest restaurant in Buckhead, then to every club I could think of. I made sure we were seen together all over the damn town, just so we could be splashed in every tabloid that exists. That's what she wanted, after all."

Vega shook her head. "That's not all she wanted. And I'm smart enough to know a man like you would have a hard time turning that down. If I were guessing, I'd say it would be darn near impossible."

Emptiness permeated every molecule of her being. She couldn't be with JP, and she'd just admitted she didn't want him to be with anyone else either. How stupid was she?

He pushed off his desk and came around to stand directly in front of her. He held out his hand. "Will you stand, please?"

She shook her head, not looking at him.

"Vega?" The word was gentle, but she still resisted.

"Don't say anything," she begged. "I knew you'd sleep with other women. That's who you are. I just..." She shook her head and rubbed the spot on her chest that ached. "I didn't know it would bother me so much."

JP squatted in front of her. She let him turn her face to his, but she refused to make eye contact.

"Baby?"

One lone tear slipped out of the corner of her eye. "Stop."

He kissed the tear away, which only released another in its place.

When she shoved against him with her fists, he merely wrapped his arms around her and held her tight. She buried her face in her arms, now crumpled between them.

"I'm sorry I was mad this morning," he said. "I just wanted you with me last night instead of her."

She nodded, drowning in humiliation.

"And I'm sorry I made you go through that. I shouldn't have insisted you come."

Her tears dried, but she kept her forehead pressed to the hardness of his chest. She didn't want to walk away from him and never look back.

"And I'm sorry I didn't realize what you were thinking."

She wasn't sure what he meant, so she glanced up.

He pressed a gentle kiss to her mouth, clinging for several seconds before letting go. "There is no way I would ever sleep with Greta, sweetheart. None. And I made that clear when I dropped her off at her house last night." He gave her a half-smile. "But, man, it's good to see the jealousy in your eyes."

She tried to hide in his chest again, but he wouldn't let her.

"It means you care, you know?" he whispered.

"Mr. Davenport," the phone crackled.

His arms tensed around her.

"It means I'm an idiot," she muttered.

"No." JP brushed loose strands of hair back from her face and closed his mouth on hers one more time.

He held there, firm pressure but closed lips, letting her know the choice was hers. She wanted to resist. So very badly. Yet her mouth opened, inviting him in.

With a groan, his tongue stroked hers, and he pulled out every trick in the book. Within seconds, he had her pliable and ready for surrender.

"Mr. Davenport." Beverly stood inside the room again, and Vega jerked out of JP's arms.

"I need to go." She stood, more confused now than she'd ever been. "I'll be...back...later."

JP watched her from his squatted position, his gaze telling her something she refused to hear, then rose to take the call.

CHAPTER TWENTY-THREE

*T*he buzz of the city faded as the SUV left Peachtree and headed northeast. Vega watched the passing sights in silence, while JP kept his hands on ten and two and didn't take his eyes from the road. It all seemed perfectly normal and polite, only she couldn't get their morning argument out of her mind. She suspected he was dwelling on the same thing himself.

Whatever had been going on in that room had left her utterly drained. His frustration over her leaving the night before, as well as her jealousy—thank goodness he *hadn't* slept with Greta, after all—had all been a mask covering something else. Something more intense. Something that had caused panic in her midsection every time he'd stared into her eyes.

Taking a quick peek across the car, she studied him. This was the first time she'd seen him during business hours in something other than a suit, and she wondered what was so special about the school they were heading to that would bring out the difference. His khakis and navy polo were nice, and certainly looked just as terrific on him as three-piece suits. But different.

Then she wondered if he really was different with her, as

Beverly had suggested. She wouldn't have seriously considered it before, but pictures didn't lie. After she'd escaped his office, she'd pulled out her phone and looked up every tabloid shot of him she'd been able to locate. He was never photographed doing so much as holding hands with any of them. Occasionally he'd lean in close to hear or speak, putting a hand to the woman's back, but still, nothing personal.

The car turned off the road into a school entrance, and JP headed toward the back of the building. She peeked behind them and saw that the photographers who had been on their trail continued straight, stopped from following by a security guard at the school entrance. JP made a left turn and slipped in under the building via the service ramp.

"Do you always park underneath the building?"

Once parked in a marked-off spot, he turned the car off. "Yep."

Their conversation had been about that deep since they'd left the office.

He reached for his door handle, but she stopped him with a hand to his arm.

"Can I ask you something about this morning first?" Her question was spoken softly. She wanted to know what that had been. The panic flaring through her had made her want to run, yet at the same time, something good had been filtering in as well.

His jaw twitched before he shifted to face her. One thigh hitched up on the seat in the space between them, and his body visibly relaxed, almost as if he'd been waiting to talk about this very subject. The warmer hue in his eyes suddenly sent her into retreat mode once again.

Maybe she needed to rethink this before bringing it up. Or not bring it up at all.

But she had to say something now that she'd started. She reached for the only other thing that came to mind. "What was the call from Governor Chandler about?"

The glow in his gaze shut down. "That's what you want to talk about?"

She nodded, swallowing the fib. "Was he upset?"

"You are a master at avoidance, aren't you, woman?" JP laughed, a short, harsh sound. "Okay, fine. We'll talk about the governor, for now. Yes." He gave a single, decisive nod. "He was upset."

Her chest deflated. "I was afraid so. Was it because of the pictures of Greta, or…"

He leaned the side of his head against the headrest and watched her, his blue eyes steady. "Or?"

She shrugged. What was she supposed to say? She was worried the governor had read too much into the picture of him and her. "Was he upset over the other one? The one of you and me talking."

"The other one."

She held her breath. "How upset?"

He picked up her hand and held it in his. "He ranted for a minute or two. Pointed out how inappropriate it was to be seen having a moment with one woman when I was already out with another one, no matter that the first one was obviously not a real date."

"Surely you told him it wasn't a moment. We were just talk—"

He leaned forward and seared her with a fast, hot kiss. When he pulled back, his voice was deeper. "It was a moment. And everyone who sees it will know that."

She licked her lips, tasting him. She really had to quit letting him kiss her like that. "We've got to go into repair mode. We've damaged your reputation enough. What can I do to help?"

Without warning, he leaned over and laid another fevered kiss on her, exploring her mouth until she could no longer pull in breath.

"Just keep giving me reasons to have moments, and I'll be fine." His voice was gravely.

"You've got to be serious, JP. Governor Chandler might pull his support if we get caught again." She motioned toward the opening of the parking garage. "They follow us everywhere."

He nodded. "Chandler and I are okay. He'll still be there tonight to make it official on camera. But yeah, he's getting frustrated. We'll be more careful."

"So we're in agreement. We have to stop…" She waved her hand back and forth between them. At his quirked brow, she sighed and let her hand drop. Who was she kidding? They couldn't just *stop* whatever this was. Not when they had to be around each other every day anyway. "We just have to be more careful in public. I won't be the cause of your downfall."

"That sounds fair." He reached up to caress a finger over one cheek. "All I have to do is figure out a way to keep my hands to myself."

"You're already failing," she whispered. The soft laugh that followed changed the mood inside the car, and suddenly all she could think about was the fact that they weren't exactly in public at the moment. And she wanted one more kiss.

Without giving herself time to think, she shifted on the seat and went to him. She closed her mouth over his and kissed him with everything she could muster. A strange power came to life inside her when he didn't take over, instead letting her lead the way.

Bringing her hands up to cradle his face, she poured her soul into the kiss. She may not be able to be with him fully the way she wanted, but she hoped this showed, in some small way, how much she cared.

When the kiss ended, she slid back down into her seat and suggested they should go inside the building. She was terrified he'd want to dissect that kiss if they didn't get out of there.

Without words, JP stepped from the car.

She followed, but when she reached for the back door, it was locked. "I need my camera."

"You can't record in here." He spoke low, his steady gaze burning a hole in her.

"Why not?" She tugged on the locked door. "Everyone knows you make occasional appearances here."

"Have you ever seen those appearances on the news? Anywhere?"

"As a matter of fact," she said, ready to prove him wrong, but then realized that no, as a matter of fact, she had not. "Then why show up if not for publicity?"

They crossed the garage to the elevator, and once inside, he jabbed a button to take them to the first floor. "It's not for publicity. Additionally, you can't use anything you see or learn here in your segment."

"Then why let me come in the first place?"

He cut his eyes to her, and she couldn't tell whether it was annoyance or disgust peering back at her. A ding announced their arrival, and JP motioned for her to exit before him.

"Mr. Davenport." An older woman rushed from behind the desk when they entered the front office. "Thank you so much for rearranging your schedule. The kids would have been terribly disappointed had our mix-up caused you to be unable to make it."

"Ms. Halloway, you know I'll do everything I can to be here each week." JP turned on the charm and had every woman in the office giggling within minutes.

He came here weekly? Interesting that no one had ever caught on to that fact. That was why he parked underground, to hide from view.

"Ms. Halloway." JP lost a bit of the charm as he turned toward Vega. "This is my friend Vega. She's doing a special report on me, so she's following me around with a video camera this week."

The principal's eyes widened.

"However, she will not be filming anywhere in the school."

Gray-blue eyes shifted from Vega to JP, then suddenly twinkled from behind small wire-rimmed glasses. "Your friend, you say?"

JP looked properly caught. "My friend. Will you please make her welcome?"

She gushed. "Absolutely."

Vega was beyond confused. What was going on here that was so secretive? She followed him to a classroom in which sat a group of kids, all probably under the age of ten, who were twittering with excitement. When she entered behind him, it was clear they wanted to bombard her with questions, but their respect for the man who made it a point to come see them weekly won out, keeping them on their best behavior. Vega settled into a child-sized seat in the back of the room, her knees up to her neck, to watch. Good thing she'd worn slacks instead of a skirt.

As she got comfortable, the same redhead Vega had caught hugging JP in his office earlier in the week stepped into the room with a dark-haired boy and took a direct path to JP. Both she and the child appeared nervous as the woman dragged the boy along behind her.

Vega glanced at JP in time to watch him catch sight of the newcomers. He took a shocked step back, his eyes going wide along with his stance. In the next instant, his entire body tensed, but he stooped down to speak to the boy. A fake smile mapped his lips across his jaw as he held out his hand to shake the youngster's. Vega studied the pair as they talked. Something was off.

When JP straightened, he snuck a quick glance Vega's direction then looked away just as abruptly. That had been guilt splashed across his face.

And that's when she saw it. She cocked her head and studied the child standing at the front of the room, fidgeting from one foot to the other. Dark hair. Bone structure indicating a very attractive man would one day be standing in his place. And aqua-blue eyes.

Blood drained from her upper region to pool in the bottom of her feet. Those eyes were identical to two other people Vega had met in the past week. Two other Davenports.

She shook her head slowly back and forth, unable to believe what she was seeing, yet it was right there in front of her. A miniature version of JP.

He had a son.

Was this why he kept this place so secretive? She glanced around to see if anyone else was aware of what she was witnessing, but there was only one other adult in the room, and she didn't seem the least concerned with the two standing at the front of the class.

Vega's chest burned. She opened her mouth like a fish and sucked in gulps of air, all while trying to focus long enough so she didn't pass out and topple from the tiny chair. But she couldn't stop herself from zooming in on each of them, back and forth, from one to the other.

JP's head tilted down as he listened to another student, but she caught the glint of his pupils as he peeked up at her through his lashes. His jaw clenched when she caught his gaze.

Oh. My. God.

She looked around for an escape route. Was she honestly sitting there looking at an illegitimate son of Jackson Parker Davenport Jr.? Damn, it was a good thing the two of them were over. She did not need to get mixed up in the media frenzy this was bound to be.

And then her eyes widened as she realized what this meant to her. And her interview.

Oh, my. She licked her lips, suddenly feeling more like the wolf about to devour Little Red Riding Hood. Only JP was no Little Red Riding Hood, and she would have sworn she was no wolf.

The redhead—she assumed the child's mother—finally shuffled to the side of the room and settled in another chair, JP following her every move. He finally glanced Vega's way and locked on to her. She told herself to look away; she didn't want to get into this in front of all these people. But his steady, unblinking gaze held her prisoner.

After what seemed a full minute, she broke contact and stared at the tan carpet squares covering the floor at her feet. His clear gaze had repeated one word over and over. Innocent. Only, something else was in there, too.

Was he saying that *wasn't* his son?

Then whose?

And why didn't the world already know about this?

She squeezed her eyelids together, wanting it not to be as it seemed. He had looked so guilty. But then, he'd also pleaded for his innocence.

Whatever it was, she would definitely find out later. They had a long drive back to his office, then an even longer dinner after that. She would simply refuse to leave until he explained the situation.

With conscious thought, she relaxed her shoulders, pretended to ignore the giant pink elephant in the room, and focused on the remainder of the kids. All sat eagerly awaiting JP to do whatever it was they were here for him to do. She was just as eager to see what this was all about as well.

After two hours and another session, this time with older children, Vega had a vague understanding of what was going on. Every single child that had entered the room had either a learning disorder or a physical one. She watched JP talk to all the kids, sharing stories and reading to them. He then moved from person to person as they worked on their own, devoting time to each and every one. Her heart swelled at the passion the man put into this, but she could not figure out why he kept his work here such a secret.

She slipped from the room and headed to the front office.

Ms. Halloway looked up as the door signaled her entrance. "What can I do for you, dear?"

"Can you tell me how long he's been doing this?"

She gave a motherly smile. "Almost six years this fall."

Vega shook her head in disbelief. "How in the world has the press not been privy to this information?"

"Because that's Mr. Davenport's request." Her eyes said if Vega dared to do the leaking, she would personally come after her. "It occasionally is noted that he's visited. The kids like to share, you know. But if asked, we only say he stops by on occasion to read to the children."

"And what is it he's actually doing?" Vega couldn't quite put her finger on it, but there was far more than reading going on in that room.

"He's helping, dear. Helping all of them."

"With whatever disability they have." She spoke softly, trying to piece it together as she went.

"Yes. The school allows the children to progress at their own personal rate. Mr. Davenport helps more with their emotional well-being than their skills. His encouragement and patience help them understand that being different is perfectly all right."

"But why? Why does he do this?"

Ms. Halloway patted Vega's hand, a look in her eye that said she had her suspicions, but it wasn't for her to share. "That's something he'll have to tell you himself."

CHAPTER TWENTY-FOUR

"Who has a word for me today?" JP stood at the front of the room, his stomach twisting as it always did at the end of his visit. Part of what he did each week to help the kids see it's okay to do things differently, to do things in their own way, and—for some of them—not to be able to do everything was to let them try to stump him.

He'd spent years learning the tricks to overcome his dyslexia, at least to the public, but he still dealt with a few issues on a daily basis. Spelling was one of his more troublesome areas, so the kids always spent the week coming up with a word to test him.

A quiet, dark-haired boy raised his hand. JP smiled at the youngster, seeing way too much of himself in the boy. The child was the son of an up-and-coming movie star. As JP called on him, the door opened, and Vega and Ms. Halloway slipped in. He fought the urge to call a halt to this part of the day. He wasn't ready for Vega to see him at his most vulnerable.

Yet he'd wanted to bring her along today, knowing he would do this.

"Spell *baccalaureate*."

He glanced at Vega, and she smiled at him, clearly impressed with his attention to the students. He could tell she didn't realize the real issue, though. He turned to the class and began his "act" of pondering the word they'd chosen. Luckily, this was one he was pretty sure he could get.

As he wrote on the whiteboard, he knew each of the kids had the spelling memorized in their own minds. They would have studied it multiple times throughout the week until they each got it. Sweat formed on his brow from knowing Vega watched, but he pushed forward, using the marker to write out the letters. At the sound of simultaneous sighs, he glanced over his shoulder and laughed with the class. "Not the right letter, huh?"

He erased the error and called upon every trick he'd ever learned but couldn't produce the correct letter. Finally, he shrugged and asked one of the less confident boys for help. "Blaine, can you help me with the next letter, please?"

Blaine bit his lip and glanced over at Vega, who sat quietly in a chair near his. She gave him an encouraging smile, but he continued eyeing her as if terrified she would find him lacking. It was rough enough being a fourteen-year-old and noticing girls for the first time, but to have a gorgeous *woman* show up in class could be torturous.

In the next instant, Vega winked at the boy and scooted her chair over to his. She leaned her head in close and whispered something that made him smile. Again, she leaned in and spoke, this time causing Blaine to laugh out loud. Finally, he pulled his shoulders back and sat up straight. With a healthy amount of confidence supporting his voice, the missing letter was announced. He then smiled at Vega, and JP's heart swelled.

In less than a minute, she'd sized up the kid and moved in to boost his confidence. She totally got his purpose for being there. And he wanted to marry her and love her forever.

The thought slammed into him, rendering him speechless. But

he couldn't stand in front of the class gaping like a lovesick puppy. Especially when the reciprocating puppy continued to insist they were nothing more than a weekend fling. That morning in his office had almost been his undoing. He'd been grumpy as hell since returning from chasing the moronic server to find Vega missing, but when he'd figured out she'd been sick with worry that he'd slept with Greta, he could have jumped over the moon. She may pretend she didn't care, but he had no doubts she did. Now he just had to prove it to her.

With renewed determination, he returned to the board and finished out the word. The kids erupted in applause, and he smiled and held his hands out at his sides. "You guys got me again."

And as soon as he figured out a way, he'd get Vega.

He caught sight of her from the corner of his eye, smiling and clapping along with the rest of the class, but she also bore a tiny line between her brows. No doubt, from the many things she'd witnessed throughout the day. He glanced at the empty seat Lexi had occupied earlier and frowned. He'd been prepared to meet Daniel today but had hoped Lexi wouldn't come into the room at the same time. It hadn't taken more than a few seconds for Vega to put two and two together and come up with five. First, she'd seen Lexi in his office, then she'd seen her here with a boy that had features very much like JP's.

He hadn't been quite ready to expose Daniel in that way yet, but it looked like that was another of the big conversations he would be having tonight.

They said their goodbyes and left the building, and he could see the questions lurking as he pulled out from under the school. He ignored them for the moment and headed south. Right now, he needed to focus on getting back to his penthouse and starting the meal, all while figuring out how to convince Vega that she loved him every bit as much as he loved her. Or, at least, she *could* love him that much.

Time was running out for them. Tonight was the last shoot before the press conference, when attention on him would become even more visible. It might also be his last chance to win Vega over. He would be laying everything on the line before the night was over.

"Thank you for taking me today." The soft words hit his ears, and he glanced her way.

She wore black pants and a flirty, white shirt. One that tempted him to beg the opportunity to explore underneath. Her dark hair was curlier than normal and pulled back, held loosely with a clip against the side of her neck, and she once again had something shiny on her lips. A new kind of confidence seemed to be brimming just beneath her surface, making her more beautiful each day.

"I wanted you to see what I do, but I won't approve any specifics being released. These kids deserve their privacy."

"Of course." Her lips rolled inward and flattened in a straight line before she gave him a tiny smile. "You were terrific with them."

He reached for her hand, praying she wouldn't refuse him as his fingers closed around hers. He'd been giving her space, backing off to let her get to know him more as a person than the public image, but he couldn't keep his fingers from twining with hers when she didn't pull away. "I'm glad you were there."

She looked out the side window, and he returned his focus to the road.

"Those are the kinds of stories I once wanted to do," she whispered. "In front of the camera."

His breath stuck in his throat at the announcement. That was the first time she'd admitted the desire to be on camera. "About me being there or about the kids?"

"The kids." She laughed at his question as he'd hoped she would, then turned in her seat and brought one knee up on the seat between them, excitement etching her features. "They were all so great. And I'm sure you're the cause. I mean, I never met them before you started working with them, but they seem so extremely confident and proud of themselves. No doubt that's because of you."

His chest filled like a hot-air balloon. He hoped so, but he also liked knowing that Vega thought so highly of him. "In part, because of me. But the school is the best I've seen at nurturing students."

He also hoped their progress would continue without his visits. Once he stepped into the Senate, not only would he not be around every week, but his visits, if continued, would be exploited. Both he and the kids would come under tight scrutiny, and that would eventually lead some nosy reporter to one shining, yet-to-be-uncovered fact about him.

It came down to a simple question. Did he reveal his own dyslexia and keep working with the kids as he had time or stop his visits altogether? Stopping would also end his plans of starting a similar program that spanned the country.

He rubbed his thumb over the back of Vega's hand as he contemplated the right course of action and felt a tremor shake her body. He loved that she had that reaction when he touched her. It gave him hope.

Pushing his own struggles to the back of his mind, he concentrated on her. "Why not consider changing careers and focus on stories like theirs?"

She tugged against his hand, but he didn't let her go. Instead, he braked at a light and faced her. "Don't pull away from me, Vega," he pleaded. "Talk to me. Tell me why you won't even consider it."

"Quit pushing, JP, please. I've made my decision, and you know it."

"Yet I can't help but think it's the wrong one. If being in front of the camera is what you want, then why won't you go for it?"

"Seriously," she said, trying to make her voice stern, but it came out more like begging. "Stop it."

The light changed to green, and he gave her hand a squeeze before once again facing the road. "You can start by doing the interview with me Saturday."

———

FURY SCRAPED HER RAW NERVES. Why wouldn't he give it a break? She jerked her hand out of his and crossed her arms over her chest. Instead of arguing about it further, she decided to turn the tables. "How about you answer a question of mine instead of badgering me?"

He closed his fingers around the steering wheel. "Shoot."

"The boy at the school."

She paused. His knuckles turned white, but everything else about his demeanor remained calm.

"Is he yours?" The breath pushing up and out of her lungs thinned as the words came out. It wasn't that she was against him having a kid, only…why had he never acknowledged him? It didn't speak well of him if he'd kept a child hidden all these years, refusing to offer the parental support every child needs.

She eyed him, watching his jaw work back and forth as his mind raced through his own thoughts. He glanced over his left shoulder a split second before his car surged forward, and he switched lanes, cutting off another driver.

The driver of the car now behind them laid on his horn. Vega peeked back, catching him throw up his hand and flip them off, as another question slammed through her mind. If JP truly wanted them to be as close as he kept saying, then why hadn't he told her he had a son?

Her chest burned as if experiencing a record-breaking case of heartburn.

"Is this for the interview, or is it a woman asking a man she cares about?" he finally asked.

"I never said I care about you." But they both knew she did. Way too much.

He crossed back to the other lane, barely squeezing between a car and a semi. The SUV jerked as he overcorrected to keep from swerving onto the shoulder.

"Are you trying to kill us now so you don't have to answer my question?" She wanted to be angry with him for keeping this from her but knew she had no right. It was his life, and she'd said over and over she didn't want to be a part of it. She sighed, the soft sound the only one in the car. "How is it you have a son, JP? And please tell me you've only been an absent parent in the physical sense."

He shot her a look, confusion marring his brow. "What do you mean?"

"Financial support. If you've refused financial support all these years, you know that'll come out, even if I sit on the information."

And that's how she knew she loved him. She may be broken-hearted over the fact he had a kid and hadn't thought enough of her to share the fact, and she may be disappointed in him if he confessed he hadn't supported the child. But even knowing that revealing this information could prove herself as a reporter, she wouldn't throw him under the bus. She couldn't hurt him that way.

But it would eventually surface. There was zero doubt in her mind about that.

JP faced forward, his jaw clenched and both hands wrapped securely around the wheel, and turned off the road to head to his office building. And just that fast, the tension seemed to seep completely out of him. "He isn't mine."

Relief washed through her. "But how can that be? I saw him. He looks just like you."

JP shook his head. "I swear, Vega." He made eye contact, and the look reached to the bottom of her soul. "He isn't mine."

Her mouth opened, but she had no idea what to say to that.

"But he is a Davenport."

Or to that.

Vega stood shoulder to shoulder with JP in the confined space as he inserted his keycard, and they shot to the penthouse of his office building, the near-silent hum of the elevator sticking in the thick tension like a spoon in hard-packed ice cream. It had been that way since he'd declared the kid a Davenport, then promptly pulled into the underground parking lot, refusing to say more until they were inside.

She stood with her head lowered, eyeing his loafers, and wondered how much longer he thought they could go without continuing the conversation. Whose kid was he? The brother who never came home? It had to be.

Unless JP was lying.

"So." She couldn't stand the silence. "You've lived here for a while, then?"

He glanced over at her, and his lips curled up in that sexy way that always flatlined, then just as quickly kick-started her heart. "You suck at small talk, babe. And yeah, I've been here since we bought the building. Five years."

She nodded, unsure what else to say to fill the void.

"And I've never brought another woman up here," he said, his words spoken quietly as he faced the front of the elevator. "Only my mom and sister."

Wow. Her heart thudded. She hadn't expected to hear that.

The elevator finally pinged, and the panels slid silently into the deep pockets on either side of the doors.

Before either of them moved, she asked softly, "Aren't you worried I'll leak the information, JP? About the boy. All it would take is one tweet, and the world would know within minutes."

Of course, she would never do that.

He eyed her silently, and she was unable to read anything from him at all. He held the door with one hand and her lighting equipment in the other and nodded for her to step out in front of him. But he didn't answer her question. She inhaled as she passed him and got a warm thrill down to her toes for her efforts.

Stepping into the foyer, she scanned the area. Everything on this floor was as immaculately decorated as what she'd seen of the rest of the building. Stone sculpture in the center of the space, expensive art decorating the walls, and a comfortable, welcoming beige with occasional splashes of deep red covering the remainder of the space.

"It's lovely," she murmured, almost to herself. Though it didn't say much about him other than that he maintained the same image up here as he did everywhere else.

Everywhere except in the Caribbean under a poor excuse for a disguise.

And in the front of a roomful of students looking for someone to give them a reason to believe in themselves.

And in his car.

He'd looked her in the eyes, as honest as she'd ever seen him, and said the kid wasn't his. And she was one hundred percent certain he'd been telling the truth.

He opened the door, and her heart stopped beating, then a smile spontaneously bloomed on her face as she discovered that the man she'd gotten to know so well this past weekend actually lived here.

"JP," she breathed, then set her camera down on the table inside of the door and moved into the room. "This is so not what I expected."

The room opened to an enormous living room edged in windows overlooking the city, but it was the feel of the space that tugged so hard on her heart. It was as classy and well decorated as anyone would expect of a Davenport, but the formality was gone. The public persona was nowhere to be found.

There were throw pillows skewed to one side of the over-stuffed leather sofa, an imprint on the cushion indicating he spent many nights stretched out in that very spot. A remote rested on the arm of the couch, and a half glass of water sat on an expensive, but not designer, end table. The overall feel was comfort. Not the stilted perfection he typically wore so tightly around him.

The best thing in the whole space was the grand piano sitting on a platform by the balcony doors, with a well-worn seat shoved up under the edge of the keys. The whole area reminded her of the piano sitting in the living space of that old Kelsey Grammar sitcom, and though JP's furnishings were much nicer, the rest of the room reminded her of the father's comfy recliner from that show. Worn in and comfortable. Livable.

He followed her to the middle of the room and touched a hand to the spot between her shoulder blades. His fingers lingered there. "I take it you like it?"

She smiled over at him, unable to keep from it, and finally felt like she had him a little bit figured out. This was the real man. Not the stiff suits and hard-as-nails attitude. Underneath all of that, he was real. And she probably would have been better off not knowing that.

Though this side of him would be fantastic for the show, she couldn't as easily hold herself apart from this version. This was who had been with her in the Caribbean. This was who she loved.

"Let me show you the rest." He held out a hand, his gaze daring her to take it, and she laughed out loud at the relaxed man before her.

She was powerless to resist him.

"Okay." She slid her palm across his. "But I'm not forgetting that we have a conversation to finish."

He held her hand tight and pulled her in to him. "I'm not either. I promise to explain everything before you leave tonight, but let me show you my home before we have to get back to reality."

The way he said that was odd, as if his home wasn't his reality. Then as he took her from room to room, showing her little pieces of himself, she began to realize it wasn't his reality. Not one he ever presented to the world, anyway.

They stopped at the threshold of his bedroom, and she stared in at the largest bed she'd ever seen. The enormous king-sized bed was framed with a thick, heavy headboard on one end, an antique chest on the other, and looked out over a view of the city that rivaled the one in the living room.

"Wow." She could totally imagine making love to JP under the rumpled navy spread, with the city lights twinkling down on them.

Or out on the connected balcony with the breeze licking the sweat from their bodies.

"Glad you approve." His deep voice said he'd like to show her more if she'd allow him. "Feel free to look around."

She turned loose of JP and entered the room, wanting to explore the man's most private quarters, all while knowing she really didn't need to know this much about him. The shelves in the corner held pictures of Cat and the kids, along with black and whites of what were most likely their grandparents. There was also a formal portrait of his mother and father from their earlier days.

She scanned the shelves and took in the books shoved in tight to fill every empty hole. There were tomes on business, management, dealing with people, and... She cocked her head to get a better look and read the titles of the others. Psychology. Most of them relating to self-confidence or self-esteem in some way. She pivoted to where he remained standing in the doorway and narrowed her gaze on him. His eyes burned steadily back at her, but he didn't utter a sound.

Fine. He didn't want to explain. No problem.

But she couldn't help wondering if these were used in learning to work with the kids at the school, or if the man who projected such a powerful image to all who met him had once had issues of his own. Because no way did he have problems now. She'd never met a more self-assured man.

Since he clearly had no plans to answer her silent questions, she moved on around the room, circling it as an animal would its prey, but knowing all the while what she wanted to explore most was the chest at the foot of his bed. It was a style she could imagine the rich once used as they boarded ships like the Titanic to make long, cross-Atlantic journeys.

She wanted to know what he valued so dear he kept tucked away within arm's reach.

Stopping beside the chest, she had her hand on the clasp before better sense prevailed, reminding her she shouldn't be so rude. She shot a quick glance over her shoulder and asked with a look. He nodded his consent.

JP WATCHED from the doorway as Vega lifted the lid to his grandmother's chest. His great-grandmother had passed it to her daughter when she'd been a teenager. She'd then given it to him the year before she'd died.

He loved it. It was the first thing he'd moved into his penthouse.

The lid creaked from lack of use, but it opened as smoothly as he knew it would, and Vega straightened to stare down into the cavity. He didn't want to close the space between them and risk touching her in his bedroom, but he needed to look at the contents, same as she.

"Go ahead," he spoke in her ear, and she jumped as if unaware he'd moved to her side. A stack of blankets his grandmother had made filled up most of the chest, but tucked into the left corner was a metal tackle box, in pristine condition, that he'd gotten from his father on a long-ago fishing trip. He nudged his chin toward the box. "Take it out if you want."

Brown eyes blinked up at him. "It looks personal."

He nodded. "It is."

Worried eyes peered down into the space. "Are you sure you want me to see?"

The silence lingered between them as he contemplated her question. Yes, he wanted her to see. Showing Vega his past was the only way he could think to prove he wanted forever with her. But he was equally afraid that what she found would lead her to find him lacking.

He took a deep breath and surged forward. "To answer your question back in the elevator, no, I'm not worried about you tweeting my personal business." His hand reached for her and stroked a finger along the inside of her arm. "Because I trust you not to leak it."

Her eyes widened, and her teeth edged out to sink into her bottom lip. He was letting her know his life was in her hands, and he could tell that she got it. If she picked up the box, she would be acknowledging she wanted that, as well. He held his breath and waited.

She crossed her arms over her chest and continued staring down.

"What is it?" she asked. "It looks similar to the tackle box my dad used for fishing."

"My father purchased it for me the time we went fishing." He pursed his lips. "It was more of a photo op than a fishing trip, though."

"Oh." Her hand rubbed back and forth over her upper arm. "So there's tackle inside?"

"No."

"Then what?" She grinned over at him. "Love letters from your youth? Panties from the first girl you slept with?"

He chuckled and shook his head. "Not quite. In fact, I haven't put anything in there since I was ten, so I guarantee there are no panties to be found."

Her smile waned as she continued staring down at the box. Suddenly, she shook her head and took a quick step back from the chest as if she'd just figured out what she was about to do. She glanced at the clock on his bedside table.

"What time is everyone getting here? I need to get shots of you throughout the apartment and get set up to do their interviews. And I need to—"

"It's okay." He held up his hand to stop her panicked ramble. Now wasn't the best time to get into his past anyway. But they would get into it tonight. "We can do this later. Plus, I need to start dinner."

She blinked at him. "Dinner? You're cooking?"

"Yes."

"I figured you'd have something brought in. Or maybe hire a chef for the evening."

"Nope." He turned from her to go, then glanced back, noticing that she seemed more like the fragile woman he'd first met than the strong woman he was coming to know very well, and wondered if he'd somehow put that cautious look back in her eye. He hoped not. He reached out and pulled her after him. "Let's go. I actually love to cook, and I'm very good at it."

They wandered back through the house, her hand in his, and he couldn't help but smile at the crazy turn his life had taken. He was about to commit to politics, something he'd dreaded his entire life, but at the same time he planned to have the woman of his dreams by his side. Something he'd almost given up the idea of finding.

He stopped beside the piano and gazed down at her, unable to keep from tugging her closer. With mere inches separating them, he lowered his voice so she'd lean even closer, and said, "I hope you're ready for this evening, babe. I'm going to do my best to show you exactly who I really am."

Her throat rippled with a gulp. She nodded, but her words didn't match her actions. "Honestly, I'm not sure I am."

Then he would do whatever he could to change her mind. He closed the space and touched his lips to her luscious mouth but pulled away long before he wanted to stop. His pulse raced, and when her eyes darkened, he knew that she wanted more as well.

They had a lot to learn about each other tonight, and he was determined to make it happen. He had to. He intended to have her by his side from the press conference forward, and he had only two days to get her there.

CHAPTER TWENTY-FIVE

*V*ega finished arranging the seating so she could conduct individual interviews with the family, then went in search of JP himself. He'd changed back into a suit, then had been in the kitchen since they'd parted, whipping up something that smelled incredible.

She lugged her camera with her, needing to capture him in his element, but rolled her eyes at the thought that the kitchen was his element. Of course, why should he be anything less than perfect at every aspect of his life?

Speaking of perfect. She didn't know why she'd gotten such a feeling, but for some reason, she was completely certain the box in his room proved that he *wasn't* perfect. It hid something he didn't show the world.

Yet he had wanted to show it to her.

Her chest had filled with a mix of love, tenderness, and outright fear. Because if she looked in that box, she would get a piece of him he'd never shared with anyone. And she was pretty sure it was the piece she wouldn't be able to turn away from. It was the piece that would open her heart. She didn't know if she was ready for that.

So she'd changed the subject and would continue doing so until she came up with something better to do. Right now, the plan was to watch the hottest man she'd ever seen stand at a stove and cook for his family. Not the picture she would have imagined a week ago, but now she understood how perfectly it fit him.

She entered the kitchen with her camera on her shoulder and smiled at the sight. JP—tall, dark, and six-plus feet of awesomeness—stood at the stove with a "Kiss the Cook" apron tied around his neck and the top of his designer slacks. The sleeves of his white shirt were rolled up to his elbows, his suit jacket and tie nowhere to be found, and the man was softly humming under his breath.

She zoomed in as he lifted a spoon from one of the pans to his mouth then sprinkled a couple spices into the mix. "You cooked dinner that first night, too, didn't you?"

Twinkling eyes turned in her direction, and a half-smile brightened his face. Her heart thumped. She loved that look. The viewers would, too.

"Of course I cooked for you. Why would I invite you for dinner and do anything else?" He narrowed his eyes a fraction. "Who did you think cooked?"

"I don't know." She hated to admit she'd at first assumed he'd hired a chef. "Cat?"

He laughed, his head thrown back and his white teeth gleaming, and she struggled to remember she needed to pull back from what they had. "Cat and the kids would never get home-cooked meals if it weren't for me. Her husband was the cook of the house."

"So, cooking for your family is a common occurrence? That's pretty cool. I wouldn't have expected it from someone like you."

"Why not?" He turned back to the pans. "Because I'm a man?"

She stepped farther into the room, watching him through the eyepiece all the while. "Because you're a Davenport."

He raised an eyebrow at that but didn't look her way. "You think we don't cook?"

"I think you don't need to cook." She zoomed in until only his face filled the screen and fell a little more in love. She pulled the view back out. "Doesn't your family employ a chef? Why isn't he cooking tonight?"

JP tasted the sauce one more time, then flipped the burner to low and faced her full-on. His strong jaw and wide frame made her think about what he looked like naked. He held his arms out to his sides. "This is me. I cook." He winked. "And I cook damn well."

Man, this was good stuff. He could certainly turn on the charm when he wanted to. "I can vouch for that. You definitely know how to make a mean steak." It was a good thing her words would be edited out. "Care to share who taught you?"

He chuckled. "What makes you think I didn't teach myself?"

"Well, yeah, I guess that could be the case. Is that what happened? You got tired of eating out all alone because poor you, you never have dates, so you taught yourself to cook?"

A wry smile curved his mouth, and she almost begged him to kiss her then and there.

"Not exactly." Without warning, he moved in her direction with a spoon held out to her. "Taste this."

She shifted the camera to the side and let him feed her. Their eyes connected as she closed her lips over the spoon, but she quickly forgot the look in his eyes when her taste buds picked up on the delight now in her mouth. "Mmm…" The moan slipped out on its own. She swallowed and gaped up at him. "That's amazing."

He used his thumb to wipe the corner of her lips then licked the spot off his thumb. "I know. Even better than the steak, right?"

"Amazingly, yes." She marveled at the fact he had such hidden talents. "Seriously, where did you learn this?"

He shrugged. "I hired Wolfgang to teach me."

"You went to classes with Wolfgang Puck, and no one spilled

the news on that? You're better at keeping the press out than I thought."

"Not quite." He went back to the stove and scooped up a taste of the first sauce. "This one is a traditional Italian, but with a secret ingredient or two."

She tasted it and almost begged him to marry her right then and there. This was a way of life she could get used to. She licked her lips before he got the thought to use his fingers again. "What do you mean, not quite?"

"I hired him to personally come to my home and teach me. Six months, one night a week, and I can now cook most anything as well as anyone in the city."

"Probably in the world." She edged closer to the stove and motioned to the first sauce she'd tasted, indicating she wanted more. "Seriously, this is amazing. If you weren't already capable of getting any woman you wanted, this is all it would take."

He slipped another bite into her mouth. "Is it working for you?"

Tension thickened the air, and she realized she now stood chest-to-chest with him, and she didn't want to move away. Yes, it was working. If she didn't have so many faults against her, she'd throw caution to the wind and say a silent prayer that he could somehow fall in love with her too, and that they could live happily ever after.

"Wait until you try the chocolate cake I made."

Oh boy. She gulped and looked around as if contemplating escape. He was very good at pulling her under his spell.

"It has dark chocolate shavings from Belgium and France. Only the best for you."

The sight of her camera sitting on the counter a few feet behind her reminded her she hadn't been filming the last few minutes. "Crap! I need to get you on camera, talking about learning to cook."

When she started to move away, JP captured her around the wrist. "Answer my question, first. Is it working on you?"

"You're seriously trying to woo me with your cooking?"

"I seriously am."

"I'm not even here for dinner."

He eyed her as if considering having her for a meal. "You'll eat."

"It won't work, you know. I can't be the woman you need by your side." But maybe she didn't believe that quite as much as she once had.

She stared up at him, begging with her eyes for him not to do as she wanted and kiss her, but he didn't listen. He lowered his mouth.

But before making contact, he changed course and touched a soft kiss to her cheek, then grazed his way over to her ear. A shiver shook her body. "I'm not giving up on us, Vega," he whispered.

"Ahem."

Vega froze at the sound of someone behind them. She turned to find Emma, Cat, and Cat's kids all watching the stove action from the door. Cat wore a look of cockiness. Emma did not.

"I'm so sorry," Vega hurried to explain. "I...uh...was sampling the...uh..."

"Sauces." JP's deep voice was tinged with laughter. "You were sampling the sauces. I was the one thinking of sampling other things."

Vega grabbed her camera while JP grumbled something about taking their elevator key away from them. He moved to the convection oven sunk into the wall and checked on something inside.

"I'm so sorry, Emma. Cat. I know that wasn't professional."

Emma crossed her arms over her chest and gave her son a look. "I very much doubt it was your doing, dear." She turned her gaze to Vega. "We just wanted to let you know we're here and that

Governor Chandler will be joining us a little later. You can go ahead with the interviews with Cat and the kids if you would like."

"Tyler will be tired soon," Cat joined in to explain. "You won't want him on camera after that."

"You're planning to get Tyler?" JP asked, turning sharply back toward them.

"Sure." Cat slid a hand over the shoulder of her youngest. "He loves his uncle, and he wants to talk about you for this."

"I don't think you should."

"Why not?"

Vega watched the ping-ponging action between brother and sister.

"We've talked about this before, Cat. Tyler shouldn't be exposed like that. We don't want people giving him a hard time."

"He has a mild case of dystonia, JP." To Vega, she explained, "It's a neurological disorder that, luckily for him, only affects movement in his right arm. That's all." She turned back to JP. "It's not the dark ages. There is nothing wrong with him."

"I didn't say there was."

Vega hadn't thought to lift the camera for this argument, and she wasn't about to now, but she would love to be catching JP's emotion on camera, if only for her private viewing pleasure later. He may try to pretend to be a cold, emotionless tyrant, but the man ran deep.

He faced Vega. "If you insist on recording Tyler, you must make sure nothing about his disorder is visible in the final result."

"Of course." She nodded. "If that's what you want. But I must say, I think Cat's right. Plus, I was hoping to get you and Tyler interacting together."

JP hardened his features to what she now thought of as his "public" version. "It's not up for discussion."

She silenced herself as Cat glared at her brother, her matching eyes shooting fire the same as JP's, but Cat was no match for him.

"Fine." She turned to Vega. "But he wants to be on camera, so we're getting him on camera."

"Absolutely." Vega glanced down at the boy who'd been watching the argument with interest and wondered why this seemed such a big deal for JP. Sure, he was a protective uncle, but this was the twenty-first century. Tyler barely had a disability, and making that public wouldn't do anything to harm him. Would it?

She looked back at JP and studied him. Or was the issue deeper than Tyler?

She'd tuck that thought away for another time. Right now, she had an interview to conduct.

VEGA KEPT one ear on the conversation going on in the hallway as she worked in the living room to get her lighting just right for the darker surroundings. During dinner, the sun had dropped, and the night sky now surrounded them, leaving the strategically placed lamps to cast an intimate glow around the room. It would have been better to film JP talking with the governor before eating, but JP had insisted they do it last.

Cat had disappeared to one of the guest rooms to gather up the now sleeping Tyler, and JP had followed to help. They now stood in the hallway having a heated, whispered conversation.

Vega glanced around to ensure she was still alone, then continued to eavesdrop. She wouldn't normally be so crass, but she'd heard Cat mention the announcement, and Vega couldn't help wanting to know what they were saying.

"Just because you are who you are, does not mean you have to do this. If taking this position isn't what you want, then tell them no."

"It's okay." JP's voice was low and sounded worn out. "This will be good. It'll make Mother happy."

"But what you've never understood is that she's happy as long as you're happy," Cat's whisper bordered on urgent. "Yes, you remind her of Dad, but she has to move on as much as you do."

"I miss him, Cat, but I've moved on from his death, just as you have."

"I'm not talking about you moving on from his death, and you know it." She sighed her frustration. "You need to follow your heart, JP, and don't worry about letting anyone down but yourself."

"I'm fulfilling my responsibility. I can do this. I will do this."

Two beats of silence passed, and Vega caught herself straining in the direction of the quiet. What was going on?

Finally, Cat spoke again, this time sounding leery and unsure. "I ran into Evan Martens earlier today and ended up having a short conversation with him. If you turned this down, I think it's something he'd be interested in."

"I'll accept just to keep that man from thinking he's beaten me," JP snapped, and Cat shushed him.

"All I'm saying is, you don't have to," she started again. "You can back out, and you won't be leaving Governor Chandler in the lurch. He'll still be left with a decent candidate."

"Chandler confirmed to me this week that Martens wasn't an option."

"Oh, then—"

Becca came running through the room looking for her mother, and the conversation in the hallway abruptly ceased.

Based on the snippet of conversation, Vega suspected Cat had sensed the same thing as Vega. Being senator was not what JP wanted at all.

Cat came into the room, one kid draped over her shoulder and the other with her small arms wrapped around her waist, and smiled warmly at Vega. "It was nice to have seen you again. And I have to say, I thought you might pull this off and convince him to do the interview, but I wouldn't have put money on it."

Vega blushed. "It's all thanks to you, I'm sure."

"Oh, I doubt that." Cat snickered. "I suspect you played hardball. That and the fact he doesn't seem to be able to say no to you."

Embarrassment flooded Vega, and she dipped her eyes. She didn't want anyone thinking JP had allowed her to do this interview purely so he could sleep with her, even though she'd asked him that very same thing at the time. "With this weekend's press conference coming up, I merely helped persuade him it would be good for his political career. I'm sure he had others tell him the same."

Cat shook her head and looked back and forth between Vega and JP. "I think you might be more into denial than he is."

Before Vega could ask what she meant, the others came into the room, Cat and the kids departed, and Vega went into action filming JP sitting with his mother and the governor, committing to doing what Vega was almost positive was the last thing he wanted.

He shook Governor Chandler's hand to seal the deal, and his mother beamed with pride.

"Jackson," Emma said as she reached out and hugged her son. "I am so happy for you. This is what you've always wanted."

The look of disgust that shot across JP's features caused Vega to jerk her head back from the camera. *Wow.*

"SEE ME TO THE DOOR, JACKSON."

His mother stood at the edge of the room, her purse over her forearm and her lips purposefully set, with clear intent of sharing some final words of wisdom before departing. She had her shoulder angled away from the governor, who practically hovered by her side, almost protectively.

JP almost laughed out loud. The man had it bad. He either

needed to get over his infatuation or make a move already. JP was tired of watching the warm-up.

He straightened from the bar he'd been leaning against while waiting rather impatiently for his home to clear of everyone but Vega. They were down to two. "What is it, Mother? Forget the way?"

She gave him the look, and he laughed. Her looks wouldn't work anymore. He'd just committed himself to her dream. That instantly negated any future looks from being able to keep him in check.

Moving across the room, he tossed a "Be right back" over his shoulder. Vega was repacking her equipment, and as soon as he got his mother out of his house, the two of them could finally share some secrets.

It was the moment he'd been waiting for. Now or never.

She was not leaving tonight without the two of them figuring out if they stood a chance in hell of making it work. He also couldn't imagine an answer of anything but yes.

They stepped into the foyer, and his mother blinked up at Douglas. "Would you be a dear and wait at the elevator for me?"

Geez, she really did have something she wanted to say. A sizzle of tension raced up the back of his neck. "What is it, Mother?"

She lowered her voice. "I wanted to talk about Vega."

Douglas quietly closed the door behind him while JP studied his mother. "What about her?"

She peeked around him as if making sure Vega hadn't followed them around the corner, then leaned in and whispered, "How serious are you about her? This is just a fling, right?"

His jaw clenched. She'd better not be about to stand there and suggest Vega was in any way not good enough for him. She may not be a debutante or come from money, but that didn't mean she couldn't fit in with the Davenports. Easily. He rolled his shoulders. "What does it matter?"

"I just...well, I wanted to talk to you about her. She's a sweet girl and all, but I think—"

"No."

She took a step back at his harsh tone. "No what?"

"No, we aren't going to stand here and have a discussion about Vega while she's twenty feet away in the other room."

"But there are things I need to tell you. You need to know—"

"No."

She harrumphed and planted each hand at her waist. "Now, Jackson, there's simply no need to be rude."

"Exactly. And talking about someone who's in the other room is rude." He took her by the elbow and turned her to the door. "You shouldn't keep the governor waiting, Mother."

Her feet dug into the rug for a brief second before apparently thinking better of it. She let him move her forward. "I'll be by your office first thing in the morning. There are things you don't know, Jackson. Things that could affect your plans."

"I know all I need to." And she had no idea just how big his plans were concerning Vega.

He opened the door and hustled her through before she could speak further. Edging his chin in Douglas' direction, he released her. "Please see her to her car."

JP said his goodbyes and closed the door, then went in search of Vega. It was time to come clean.

She stood by the piano, softly running her fingers over the ivories. "I had no idea you played."

"Most people don't." He grabbed a candy from a dish on the sofa table. The crinkling of the plastic was the only noise in the room as he trod over the rug to stand directly beside her. He held out the butterscotch in question.

"No, thank you." She fidgeted, picking up a lopsided bowl Becca had made for him in pottery class, then putting it back down, running her finger over the outline of a missing chunk from the lid of the piano, and just generally looking like she couldn't figure out what to do with her hands. Finally, she tucked them behind her. "So who knows you play?"

"As of right now?" He popped the candy in his mouth. "My mother, my sister, her kids. And you."

She glanced at him from beneath her lashes, her high heels—from the looks of them, a new pair—putting her even with his eyes. "That's not many people."

"Only the important ones." He stroked a path down the middle of her forehead and smoothed over a tiny crease. "Why the frown?"

A small shrug was all she managed. "Just confused about some things."

So was he.

"You look beautiful in my home. Did I mention that?"

"No," she whispered.

He tugged her hands from behind her and turned them over to study the palm of each. Finally, he lifted first one, then the other, and planted kisses on the inside of her wrists. She visibly shivered.

"Will you play something for me?" she asked.

"I'd love to."

He squeezed her hands together, then stepped back to allow her to escape. He then settled onto the stool and began to strum out a song that spoke of longing and hurts and love, all rolled into one.

His eyes closed as his fingers glided over the keys, and he imagined it was Vega's body he was playing instead of the piano. He couldn't figure out why she was the one, but he knew beyond a shadow of a doubt that he wanted her for his wife. And he did not want to blow that chance by moving too fast tonight.

When he finished, he opened his eyes and found her standing at the balcony doors, gazing out over the night sky.

"It's beautiful, isn't it?" he said.

She nodded but didn't look his way. "Incredibly."

"I often spend hours sitting here playing just so I can stare out over the city."

"That would be nice," she murmured.

He slipped his hands back to the keyboard and started again, this time pulling from memory one of Beethoven's more well-known works. He knew he was good, and he hoped like hell he was not only impressing her, but also showing her a little piece of himself through the music. This had been the one thing that had come easy for him.

Not because he knew how to read music. Reading music had been as confusing as everything else. But because he could play by ear. His mother had bought him this very piano when he'd turned ten, and he'd thought that meant she was going to pay attention to him again.

When he opened his eyes this time, Vega leaned against the opposite end of the piano, looking perplexed.

"What is it?"

"You're not playing to music. You must have a great memory."

His lips curved in a smirk. "I have a terrific memory." He'd had to, or he wouldn't have survived school.

Not wanting to get too serious yet, he began another song, this one a beautiful ballad that made him think of Vega and how she always seemed a fraction away from running back behind the curtain she used to shield herself with so protectively. As he played, she inched closer until she finally slid onto the seat beside him.

She kept a sliver of space between them, but his tension eased with her there.

When the song ended, her lips flattened, and she asked bluntly, "Who's the boy? If not yours, then whose? Your brother's?"

He strummed his fingers in a quick up-and-down arpeggio. "My father's."

Next, he ran over the lower octaves, producing a more sinister sound and ignoring her startled gasp.

When the music ceased, he felt her force a relaxed posture.

"Your father's?"

"Yep." His hands started moving again, but softly on the upper keys this time, so they could carry a conversation while he played. "He got a seventeen-year-old pregnant when he was running for president, then he got cancer and died."

Her eyes grew wide. She didn't look at him as if she thought he was lying but instead like she didn't know what to think.

"I met Lexi for the first time two weeks ago. And Daniel for the first time today." He pounded harder for three bars then eased off. "Pretty damn convenient; it was right after the rumor leaked that I would be announced the next senator."

Vega's hand lifted and rubbed at her temple, then dropped back to her lap with a thud. "So she's blackmailing you?"

"She's trying."

"Trying? And what? You said no, of course?" Her hand lifted again, this time fluttering around her neck. "Supporting a kid is one thing, but you can't let her blackmail you. Only...if you don't pay, she'll go to the media, won't she?" She looked at him, her eyes widening again. "Even if she doesn't, there's no way this won't eventually come out. You couldn't stop it if you wanted to."

She sucked in a harsh breath and reared back, then pinned a narrowed gaze on him. "Or is that why you took me today? Did you want me to expose him in the program to beat her to the punch?"

He lifted his hands abruptly, and the music stopped.

"Are you kidding me?" His voice was tight as he turned on the seat. "After everything that's happened this week, you can ask if *that* is the reason I took you to the school?"

CHAPTER TWENTY-SIX

*S*he'd made him furious. Vega reached out to put a hand on his, but at the look on his face she stopped.

"I'm sorry, I'm just..." She shook her head, unsure what to say. "Floored, I guess. I'm...trying to piece this together in my mind. Your father..."

"Yeah," he grumbled, turning back to the piano. "I'm trying to piece it together too."

She waited, but when he didn't continue, she pleaded. "I'm sorry, JP. I know you took me today to share a part of you few people get to see."

"No one gets to see." His tone was hard, the words spoken slowly.

She nodded, the intention clear. She was special to him, and he wanted to make sure she knew it. "I know," she whispered. "A part no one gets to see. You wanted to show me you care." She turned his head to her and nodded again. "I care, too."

She watched as the tension in his shoulders slowly eased, terrified she'd killed the moment but knowing she couldn't walk out tonight without finding out how this whole thing had come to be.

His father had sired a love child. This was the type of stuff she should be after if she really wanted the job, but the last thing she could do was run to the station with this news. Neither JP nor his half brother deserved that.

Finally, he put his fingers back on the keys and began to draw out a sad, lonely song.

"He's dyslexic." His words were flat. "She came to the office, demanding money. I refused. I won't be blackmailed, and especially not for something my father did.

"Then I find out Dad had already paid her over a million dollars before he died." The song built in volume then tapered back off. "Only, she's blown through most of it and wanted more. So she tells me about Daniel." He pounded on the keys. "And it's not his fault he needs help."

He closed his eyes and lost himself in the song for several minutes before suddenly jolting and turning to face her. He slipped one leg to the other side of the stool and straddled the worn cushion. "He needs a good school, good teachers, and a tutor for hours a day to even begin to maintain his classmates' level. Don't you see? I can't say no and let Daniel suffer."

His urgency took her by surprise. She knew he would do the right thing for the child, but the passion exuding from him was urgent, almost painful, and Vega was unsure of the best thing to say. She swallowed a deep breath. "Of course you can't."

"You don't get it, I can tell. But the thing is…"

She waited, slipping her hands over his as she did. "What is it? What aren't you telling me?"

His shoulders slumped then, and his face took on the insecurity of a small child. His eyes seemed to beg for understanding. "I was just like him," he ground out. "Diagnosed as severely dyslexic at the age of six. I know exactly what he's going through."

Shock kept her eyes from blinking and her mouth from producing saliva. JP was dyslexic?

"I'm sorry." He cupped her jaw. "I should have found a better way to spill that. But the thing is, there is no better way. I'm severely dyslexic. No one knows but my family and Beverly." He gave her a small smile. "I'm also aware it's not the most impressive thing to learn about someone. But I can't turn my back on Daniel. He's a Davenport. My brother." His voice cracked with the last word. "And even if I can't be there as a true brother, I have to support him any way I can."

His hand was still on her jaw, so she reached up to hold it in hers. "Not impressive? My God, the things you've accomplished are amazing. What you want to do for Daniel only makes you more beautiful in my eyes."

She smiled, hoping to coax him to do the same, but it didn't work.

"Lexi wants to keep him a secret, but she needs help." His lips twitched as if to smile but didn't quite make it. "I'll help any way I can, but I'm not sure it won't come out. Especially with me stepping into office." He looked off past her shoulder, and his voice changed to take on a faraway quality. "I'm also not sure if she wants to keep it quiet because she's ashamed of him, or if she really just doesn't want him to have to deal with the media frenzy the way the rest of us do."

"Why would she be ashamed of him? It's not his fault." And then she got it. JP had felt that way. Her heart pounded so hard she was sure he would hear it. If not, he had to feel the vibrations simply from touching her. "Is that how you felt?"

Blue eyes swiveled back to her, and she wanted to cry for what she saw.

"Oh, honey." She lunged forward and wrapped her arms around his neck. "How could you have ever felt that way? You didn't do anything wrong."

"No?" His laugh was hard and cold, but he locked his own arms around her. "Every day up until I was diagnosed, my mother spent hours with me. Playing games, reading. She called me her perfect little boy. I never asked why I was more perfect than my older brother, but at the time, I loved being doted on like that."

Vega almost couldn't stand to hear the decades-old pain pouring out of the man she loved but knew he had to get it out. She stroked his hair and pressed a kiss to the side of his face. "Tell me the rest," she whispered.

"The rest." He sighed. His arms tightened around her. "Fine. Around the same time they figured out what was wrong with me, we moved to DC. My dad's mom came with us. She became the one I spent all my free time with. She did my exercises with me, homeschooled me for a few years, then helped me with homework every night so I could go to school the next day and fake it long enough to come home and do it again. My mother spent most of her time with Dad. She hired Beverly as an assistant and got regular updates about me from her."

Pain ached throughout every part of Vega. There had to be more to it than what he was saying. She'd seen how Emma loved her son. How proud she was of him. "Maybe the timing was just a coincidence or something? Didn't she help your dad a lot with his political career?"

JP stiffened under her, then pushed out of her arms. His face wore no warmth. "Neither she nor my father ever spoke of my disability again. To this day."

Ouch.

Wow. She sat there with her arms empty, unsure where to put them, and could not imagine bearing that kind of pain alone at such a young age. She lifted her hand to touch him, but he pulled back, suddenly eyeing her as if she were the enemy.

She lowered her hand. "Is there more?"

At first he shook his head, then he looked away and blew out a breath. "It's just…I've never told anyone that."

"I know," she murmured. She could see that she meant that

334

much to him. Which made the fact she still had to walk away even harder. Yet she wouldn't be the one to cause him any additional pain, especially not after what she'd just learned. She wouldn't ask him to stand by her when her history could ruin him. Walking away was the right thing to do. But before she went, she had to know one thing more. "Can I ask you something?"

His laugh was sardonic. "Why would I keep anything from you at this point?"

"Are you taking office only because of your mother? Is this your attempt to win her approval after all this time?"

"Of course not." He stood and moved to the balcony.

She followed. She may not be able to be there for him in the future, but she would do anything she could before she left. "Then what is it about? Because politics isn't what you really want, is it?"

JP stood at the railing, his hands curled over the top of the wrought iron, his arms locked at the elbows. "Why would you think that?"

"I watch your face anytime it comes up. I saw it tonight as your mother hugged you and said you were finally getting what you always wanted. In fact, I'll have to edit that shot because no one in the world could look at it and believe this is what you want."

"I'm doing what I was born to do, Vega." He glanced over at her, his eyes asking her to support him. "I don't have a choice."

"You always have a choice."

She'd kicked off her shoes earlier and liked the height now separating them. Wanting to give him as much strength as she could, she slipped under his arm and put her back to the city. She lifted her face to his. "Quit making choices based on your mother, JP. Do what *you* want. What is it you would do if none of this other stuff was in the way?"

JP STUDIED HER, staring down into her eyes, and saw the same love he felt staring back at him. She really did get him. He used his thumb to caress her cheek, then above her eye, tracing one perfect brow. He loved touching her. "You mean other than spend the rest of my life with you?"

Her inhalation was short, but he didn't miss it. She might care for him, but she wasn't ready to discuss forever yet. *Damn.* Yet he couldn't stop now, not after he'd put it out there.

"I love you, Vega. Surely you know that. And yes, I want to spend the rest of my life with you. I'm sorry to put it out there so bluntly, but I had to tell you. It feels like I'm running out of time."

He could sense her desire to flee.

She nodded. "We are running out of time. Let's not ruin it by pushing for something we can't have. You have to trust me on this. I would be worse for you than Daniel's parentage coming out. I swear. If not..."

She shook her head and moved as if to step away from him, but he tightened his arms, trapping her to his chest. The tear glinting in her lashes broke his heart. "Tell me what you're afraid of, baby. We'll figure it out together."

The tear slipped loose and trekked down her cheek. She wiped it away with the back of her hand before he could do it for her. "I think I should go."

Her words lacerated his heart. She was going to run. And without understanding why, he knew this time would be forever. "Tell me you love me," he pleaded, hating himself for it at the same time the words clawed from his throat. "I know you do, I can see it. Tell me."

She bowed her head, her forehead landing against his chest, but she remained silent. *Dammit.* His chest rose and fell with his breaths. What had he done wrong?

Thoughts of not being good enough flitted through his mind, but he pushed them aside. He was a success, and he could take on anyone who wanted to challenge him. He couldn't be any better for her.

Only, she was still going to leave him.

With a soft moan, Vega pushed against him, and he dropped his arms.

"I need to use the restroom to clean up," she said. "And then I'm going to go."

He watched her hurry inside and fought the urge to chase her. He wanted to tie her down and force her to share with him. Force her to admit she couldn't just walk away unaffected.

But he wouldn't do that. He wouldn't push her again. He'd laid his heart on the line, and she'd said no thanks. He was finished begging.

He glanced at the corner of the piano that had the chunk missing and shook his head at the irony. He would never beg again.

Ten minutes later when Vega hadn't returned, JP could wait no longer. If she was leaving, he wanted her gone.

Stalking down the hall, he drew up short at the light leaking through his open bedroom door. With cautious steps, he moved to the doorway and peeked inside.

Vega sat on his bed, his old tackle box in her lap, digging through the trinkets he'd stored there so many years ago. As she poked her finger inside, moving items around, tears rolled down her cheeks.

It took everything he had not to go to her, but he couldn't do it anymore. If she wouldn't give him her heart, he had to hold on to his.

But he also couldn't walk away.

She pulled out a piece of paper, read it, then spread it out flat on the comforter. Next, she held up a matchbox car and smiled. The Jaguar was a replica of a car his father had once driven. In the fourth grade, JP had taken it to school for show-and-tell.

When she got to the tattered copy of *The Three Bears*, held together by the thread his mother had sown through the spine, she turned it over and over as if doing so would reveal all its secrets.

"She read that to me so often I could repeat it verbatim by the time I was four."

CHAPTER TWENTY-SEVEN

"Oh!" The book slipped from Vega's fingers at JP's words. She hadn't known he'd come to the bedroom. She glanced around then, trying to figure out how she'd gotten into his bedroom, before remembering she'd caught sight of the open chest as she'd returned from washing her face. She'd been unable to walk out of his life without seeing what items meant so much to him he'd kept them all these years.

She swiped at her cheeks and worked on a smile. "Who read it to you?"

"My mother." He remained in the doorway, looking relaxed, but Vega didn't miss the clutch his fingers had on the doorframe. "She read it to me every day."

"Did your grandmother teach you how to read the words once you started learning?"

He shifted and crossed his arms over his chest, resting one shoulder against the jamb. "No one has read that particular book since I was six."

Oh. She gulped. Another tear rolled over her cheek for the little boy he'd once been. Picking up the book again, she placed it on top of the paper listing the specifics of his diagnosis and reached back into the box. Pulling out a string, she held it up to him in question.

His smile was small but real. "I used to do a magic trick with that. There should be a knot in there to go along with it."

A bleep of laughter gurgled up her throat. She put the string, as well as the knot, on top of the book, and lifted out an envelope with colored pieces of paper tucked inside. She peeked in, then pulled them out without waiting to see if he minded. They were report cards from fourth and fifth grade. Straight As on every one.

"Wow," she murmured. "I wouldn't have expected that."

"I was a driven child." He shrugged. "And I think those teachers had me figured out. They made adjustments so I didn't have to read or write in class as much, and I took a lot of my tests orally."

"Sounds like you were in a good school."

"I guess."

She wondered if his mother had seen to that or if it had been purely accidental. Rarely are things quite so random.

Next was a slightly curved, worn piece of paper, folded the right size to slip into a young boy's back pocket. She wiggled her eyebrows at him. "I think I might have found a love letter."

He didn't respond.

Nervousness shook her fingers as she unfolded the yellowed paper. Written in a child's shaky hand, she read the words *Dear Santa* and glanced up at him. He stood by the bed now.

"I didn't know how to spell, and I still got some of the letters backwards, but Cat wrote it out for me first. I copied from hers. It took me three hours to get it just right."

Vega couldn't breathe. Something was in this letter that she didn't want to see. She looked down and read.

DEAR SANTA,

I have been as good as I can this year so I could get what I wanted for

Christmas. All I want is for you to please tell my mother I'm learning to read real good and it is okay to like me again.

Love,

Jackson Parker Davenport, Jr.

HER STOMACH REVOLTED, and she almost lost her dinner. Covering her mouth, she kept the food down but couldn't stop the stream of tears. They came fast and hard and dripped all over the paper before she could move it out of the way.

JP took it from her hand.

"I'm sorry." She blinked up at him. "I didn't mean to—"

"Not a problem." He ripped the paper into pieces and tossed the shreds in a nearby trash can, a muscle ticking at the back of his jaw with his movements. "I learned there was no Santa a couple weeks after I wrote it. I should have tossed it then."

"JP." She reached for him, but he pulled away. She deserved that, but she couldn't stand seeing his young hopes and dreams in this tiny box. "Do you want me to go?" she whispered. She felt like she shouldn't be seeing these things.

"Go. Stay. Whatever." He nudged his chin at her lap. "But you haven't seen the best part yet."

There was more? Her chest burned at the thought, but she couldn't bring herself to stand up and walk away. Instead, she reached inside and pulled out the only thing remaining. A shiny black piece of wood. She placed it in the palm of her hand and studied it.

Gripping it between two fingers, she held it up in front of her and eyed the misshapen sides, a memory tugging at her, but she couldn't figure out what it was. Finally, she looked up at hooded eyes and a face seemingly made of granite. "What is it?"

JP's jaw tensed before he took the piece from her and tucked it into his pocket. "It fits that gap in the piano."

He turned and left the room then, and she followed without thought. "That's it? You're not going to tell me more than that?"

"I've decided you should leave."

She stopped in the middle of the hall, refusing to budge. "I'm not leaving until you tell me about that piece of wood."

"Then I'll carry you out." He came toward her, and though she didn't think for a second he'd harm her, the anger emanating from him sent her scurrying backwards and straight into his room.

She hurried across the Oriental rug and out the balcony doors. Once there, she pivoted and locked her hands on her hips. "I'm not going anywhere, and you can't make me."

He laughed out loud. "Are you kidding me?"

With barely two strides, he made it to the balcony, tossed her over his shoulder, and was heading back through his penthouse.

Well, that didn't work.

Vega bounced off his backside as he stomped through the rooms, then studied their situation from an outsider's point of view. She'd just stomped her foot like a child, dared him to "make her leave," and he was now doing just that. Like some Neanderthal. And all because they were both shying away from feeling too much.

He stooped long enough to grab her camera and lighting in one hand. She snagged the strap of her purse at the same time. Then she took a deep breath and said a silent prayer that she was making the right decision.

"I had an affair with a married congressman."

JP froze. He'd stopped by the couch, and all she could see from her viewpoint were the rings left on the end table where he routinely set down a glass and his wide stance, frozen in midstep. "You what?"

She closed her eyes and repeated herself, then added, "I was twenty, oblivious to the evil ways people could behave. He said he was getting a divorce, and I believed every word he ever told me." A harsh laugh slipped out. "Until he turned his back on me."

He didn't move. "What happened?"

The weight of her head was suddenly too much to bear, and she let it hang free. Her purse dropped to the floor with a thud. "We saw each other when I was on shoots. He would show up, wine and dine me. Treat me more special than anyone ever had. The other models snickered behind my back, but I thought they were just jealous. Anyway, it wasn't like they wanted to spend free time with me, so why would they care if I was spending my time with him. But then, one of them decided to be my friend. Or so I thought. Next thing I knew, there was a sex video online of me and him, a very explicit video, and I find out that my *friend* had been the one to sneak into my hotel room to plant the camera. She sold it to the highest bidder, then Ted played it off like I was the one framing him."

Her head began to hurt from hanging upside down, but fear of him depositing her on the other side of the door kept her quiet.

"Are you talking about Ted Pritchard?"

God, he remembered. "Yes. I modeled under the name Reveka."

"From what little I remember, didn't others come forward to speak out against you? Saying..." He shook his head one time. "What was it? Something about you willing to do anything to marry a politician?"

"Yes."

He shifted her weight on his shoulder and dumped her equipment on the couch. His free hand came up to hold her at the back of her thigh, then he stooped and set her on her feet. She straightened to face him.

"Are you saying what they said is true, or not?" he asked.

"She was supposed to be my friend, JP. The only one who ever pretended to like me. After her tabloid windfall, I guess she decided that wasn't enough. The next thing I knew, practically

343

everyone I worked with took payoffs from Ted to run me in the ground. He was all about trying save his career and marriage and didn't have a concern in the world for what it might do to me."

JP's forehead crinkled from deep thought. "It didn't work, though, right? Didn't the jerk step down a short time later?"

She nodded. "Three weeks. And his wife ended up taking him for everything he had. But I lost everything, too." She crossed her arms over her chest and stared at the floor. "I thought I loved him. We had even talked about a future together. When this came out, he not only laughed at my pleas to stick beside me, he did everything he could to soil my reputation. I was done at that point. I could have posed in *Playboy*, probably could have gotten a joke of a reality show, but I was a laughingstock. All serious opportunities quit coming my way, and there was no way I'd ever get the chance to report on anything that mattered to people.

"Everywhere I went..." she continued, then cringed as the memories replayed inside. "It was horrible. All I wanted was to make a name for myself and be able to support my mother, and suddenly I was such an embarrassment she didn't even want me to come home. She eventually went back to Mexico because of the shame of walking down the street I grew up on. I changed my looks, making sure to never wear makeup or enhance my appearance in the slightest, and went to photojournalism school." She lifted her shoulders and let out a soft sigh as they settled back into place. "It wasn't exactly what I wanted, but it's the closest I could get."

JP's hands slid up her arms and cupped her shoulders. "Ted Pritchard was a bastard."

"It doesn't matter. He took me down with him, and all I ever asked from him was..." She brushed off his hands and walked away.

"Was what?"

"It doesn't matter."

"Was what, Vega? Don't stop now. What did he take from you?"

Tears once again filled her eyes and edged over her lashes. She touched the back of her hand to her cheek and kept her back to him. "I just wanted to be special. Have him love me. I was discovered and talked into modeling at sixteen, two months after my father died."

JP's body heat enveloped her from behind, but he didn't lay a hand on her. She closed her eyes and fought the urge to lean back and let his strength support her.

She sniffled. "I missed Dad so much. He and I used to do everything together. By the time the agent approached me, Mom and I were having such a hard time financially. We were having a hard time period. She missed Dad, I missed Dad. We couldn't figure out how to be there for each other. So I went into modeling to help pay the bills." A shiver racked her body. "I lived all over the world, alone, no friends, and all I wanted was someone to love me. Like my father used to."

She faced him, knowing she was a puffy-eyed mess. "Instead, I not only lost out on love, I lost who I was. I'm so tired of hiding, JP." She sniffled. "So very tired."

He held out his arms and she went willingly into them. They closed around her, and for the first time in years, everything felt right.

JP HELD Vega until her tears dried, stroking her back and generally doing anything he could think to soothe her. She'd been through a lot in her life, and he suddenly felt petty about his own troubles.

So what if his mother wasn't happy with him unless he was the perfect politician? He knew that deep down, she did love him. Probably. Plus, he had Cat, Becca, and Tyler. Even Beverly.

And Vega had no one. Not even her mother was close enough to be there when she needed her.

He couldn't figure out what to do about her. He peered down at the top of her head and wondered which way her breakdown would send her. It could make her run even faster, or it could shed some light on what they could have.

She mumbled into his chest, but he couldn't make out her words.

He pulled back and tilted her tear-soaked face to his. He stroked his fingers across her cheeks to brush aside the tears, then touched a soft kiss to the tip of her nose, savoring the salty taste. She'd needed to go through that. "What did you say?"

"That I love you."

The words were spoken almost as resignation, but they put a smile on his face he wouldn't have thought possible. "You love me?"

She frowned. "I said I did, didn't I?"

He squeezed her tight to his chest. "Damn, lady. If I'd know my hauling your ass out of here would spur your love, I'd have tried that much sooner."

She smacked at him and pushed back, but he didn't let her escape.

Fear shone bright from her water-logged eyes. "So what do we do now? You see why it can't work?" She dropped her head to his chest, resting her cheek against his pounding heart. "I can't put you in the position of having a politician-hungry, husband-stealing woman by your side. And..." Her shoulders sagged. "And honestly, I don't want to go through the public scrutiny again either. I just want to do something that makes me happy and go on about my life."

Panic exploded inside him. "And what about love? Don't you want that in your life?"

"I wrote love out of my life years ago."

"Yet it found you anyway."

His throat hurt as he watched her slim frame seem to shrink before his eyes. He dug his hand in his pocket and pulled out the chunk of piano she'd pulled from his box. He held it up between them. "When I was ten, my mother bought me that piano over there. Gran had been teaching me to play on an old upright by showing me videos of other people playing. I watched their fingers and could easily duplicate their actions. I also played at school. It took away some of the sting of knowing that with everything else, I wasn't as good as all the other kids.

"One day, the teacher sent home a note expressing how musically inclined I was. Beverly took the note to my mother, and she was thrilled. She'd heard me play at home, but I guess the teacher validated my talent."

"So she bought you a piano? That shows she cared, right?"

"And she bought stacks of sheet music. She and Dad wanted me to perform for an upcoming dinner they were throwing. She wanted me to play the music she'd picked out."

He could tell she saw where this was heading.

"Right. I couldn't read the music. It didn't make sense to me, and Gran didn't play herself. I suggested taking real lessons, but both Mom and Dad were against it. I guess they were worried someone would learn I wasn't perfect."

Vega pressed her palm over his heart. "What happened?"

He wrapped a hand over hers and replayed it in his head. "The night of the party came, and I still couldn't play the music. I begged Mom to let me play the other songs I knew, but that wasn't what Dad wanted. She said my father had people coming from his alma mater, and these were the songs they wanted to hear. She walked out of the room after telling me to just forget about it, and I swear it hurt worse than what felt like her desertion when I was initially diagnosed."

"You'd gotten your hopes up that you could please her with this, hadn't you?" Vega spoke softly.

He focused on her, thankful to have her in his life. "You're pretty smart, you know that?"

"Nah," she shook her head. "I can just see it in your eyes."

He gave her a wry smile, then tucked her back against his chest. He kissed the top of her head. "Yeah, I'd gotten my hopes up." He pulled in a deep breath. "I had convinced myself if I could do this one thing, she would be proud of me again. When she walked out, I went a little crazy. I found my brother's baseball bat and started wailing on the piano. I busted one leg and took that chunk out before Cat stopped me. She and I sat on the floor of that room for what seemed like hours, both of us crying because I wasn't good enough, and she didn't know how to help. She even offered to take piano lessons herself and come home to teach me." He chuckled. "But it was too late. I didn't want to take lessons anymore, and I didn't care if I ever pleased my mom again."

Vega's arms slid around his waist and held him tight. He squeezed his eyes shut because he knew as well as she that his hope had not died that day. But his young soul had definitely been shattered.

"My sister and I became much closer that afternoon. She even started helping me with homework every day."

"And the piano?" Vega remained tucked against his chest, enjoying the feel of his strong arms and knowing she was giving back some of the same comfort. "Clearly you started playing again."

"The leg got replaced, and by the time it was fixed, I realized that playing helped me more than being mad at my mother did. I eventually took lessons, but only years later after I had learned on my own how to make the sheet music make sense to me."

"And that piece in your hand? Why didn't it get put back into place?"

JP nuzzled the top of her head, and she had the thought she should probably get out of his arms. They'd shared too much not to have grown closer, but the same issues still sat like deadweight between them.

He laughed gently. "For some reason, they could never find that piece. Since it didn't affect how the piano sounded, it was left as is."

"But you found it?"

"I took it." One hand smoothed up her back to cup loosely around her neck. "I took it that night and locked it away with the promise to myself that I was finished begging for love. I put the box away, and it was never opened again." He pulled back and stared into her eyes, his blue orbs darkening. "Until tonight."

"Oh." She wet her lips, her gaze dipping to watch his tongue do the same. The air between them suddenly thickened and warmed, and she whispered, "We shouldn't."

"We should."

"But nothing's different. We can't be together."

He put his mouth to her temple and nuzzled his way to her ear. "We've got to be together. Don't you see? We're both so damned broken, we're the only ones who fit each other."

Her neck tilted to allow him better access. "But..."

She struggled to remember what she intended to say as his fingers tugged at her blouse and slipped underneath. He slid one hand up and palmed her breast, and she was lost. She had no idea how they could possibly make a relationship work, but for the first time, she wanted to believe they could.

Vega began working on the buttons down the front of his shirt and smiled at the gleam in his eyes. "We'll figure it out later?" she asked.

He growled. "We'll definitely figure it out later."

He closed his mouth over hers, and with a quick shift, her feet once again left the floor. Only this time, she wasn't tossed over his shoulders like a bag of potatoes.

She wrapped her arms around his neck and curved into him. "I think I like this position better than the last time you carried me."

The fingers beneath her lightly pinched her butt and sent her wiggling in his arms. "I liked the other way, too. It was everything I could do not to grab your ass when it was practically in my face."

"Right." She giggled. "You were so mad at me, I doubt my rear was even on your radar."

JP stared down at her, love shining from his eyes, and winked. "There hasn't been a day go by that your rear wasn't on my radar."

He entered his bedroom, the single lamp the only light glowing, save the twinkling city outside, and laid her gently in the middle of his big bed. He shucked his shoes, then crawled on top of the covers with her.

As she rolled to her side to face him, she reached up to trace her finger over his lips and couldn't contain the hope that bloomed wide inside her chest. She wanted this man. As a friend, a lover, but mostly as a husband. She wanted it so bad the depth of her desire terrified her.

"Love me, JP," she whispered.

He gave a single nod as he wrapped long arms around her and fitted her body to his. "Always."

CHAPTER TWENTY-EIGHT

"*I* want to start a program for kids."

Vega cracked open her eyes to the early-morning hue of JP's bedroom and squinted to focus. Red digits beside the bed said five o'clock. Their night had been better than she could have ever imagined, waking time and again to seek each other out, but they had yet to return to reality and discuss anything more substantial than what position they wanted to try next. Looked like JP was now ready to face facts.

She rolled to her back, forcing him to loosen his hold, and peered up at him in the gray dawn.

"A program?" A yawn escaped with the question.

"I'm sorry." He brushed hair off her forehead and replaced it with a kiss. "Did I wake you?"

"No." She stroked his rough jaw, enjoying the intimacy of the moment. "I was listening to you breathe."

His mouth curved. "I like that."

She stifled another yawn. "Sorry." She waved a hand in front of her face as if swatting it away. "I'm tired. Something kept me awake most of the night."

He nudged his nose to the side of her face, forcing her head to turn, then nipped at her earlobe. "You can sleep when we're old and our four kids are taking care of us."

Fear thundered through her as instantaneously as it had the first time he'd mentioned forever. She still couldn't figure out how they could make it work. Instead of addressing the subject of how many kids they may or may not have, she returned to his opening statement. "What kind of program?"

His gaze narrowed as if he knew what she was up to, but she also caught a tightness around his mouth. He didn't know how to deal with her past any more than she did. He snuggled against her side, one arm heavy over her waist, his cheek pressing to hers. "Something similar to what I'm doing at the Montessori school. Not your ordinary program designed to help kids figure out their best way of learning, but attention given to building within them a confidence they've never had. Hope. Show them there's nothing wrong with them just because they're different."

She liked the feel of the vibrations from his body as he lay against her and talked. "It sounds perfect. What's stopping you from doing it?"

He released a long, sad breath. "I don't want to just fund it and forget it. I want to be involved. Make sure it's being done right. I want to visit the schools and help train the counselors. I want to be a part of it."

"You want to make a difference," she whispered.

Several seconds passed before he answered. "Yes."

"Then I'll ask you again. What's stopping you?"

He rolled to his back and bent his arm across his forehead. "How can I do that *and* be a senator? *And* keep an eye on the company?"

"And not let it be known you've dealt with dyslexia yourself?"

She felt his gaze on her, but she didn't look his way. He had to figure out that he hadn't quite developed that confidence yet himself that he wanted so badly to instill others.

"I've overcome it." His voice was low.

"Then why keep hiding it?" She rolled to her side and faced him. "It still hurts you deep inside, but yes, you've overcome the obstacles."

"What would be the point of putting it out there now?"

"Because you can't move on from your past until you do. Do you realize you're doing the same thing to Tyler that your mother did to you?"

His jaw clenched. "Like hell I am."

"Then what's the problem with showing his issues on-screen? You're treating him like something is wrong with him by refusing to allow him to be fully seen in public."

"That's not..." He paused, then slammed his mouth into a straight line and glowered at her. His nostrils flared. "What about you? You're so busy hiding, you're afraid to even have a life."

"Why are you turning this on me? We were talking about you and what you want."

"Yet you're doing the same thing you accuse me of. Do you want to cower behind a camera the rest of your life?" His tone hurt, but she knew he was simply lashing out because she'd struck a nerve. "Why not step out there and grab what you want?"

"It's not the same thing. I brought mine on myself. You were born—"

"Bullshit. You may have been naive, but you didn't set out to trap a man into marrying you. And you certainly didn't bring any of this on yourself. The only thing you did wrong was run from it instead of face it head-on."

She sat up and pulled the sheet up with her. "What would facing it have gotten me? More offers of tawdry reality shows? More porn producers calling?"

He followed her up to the headboard. "It would have gotten you the ability to have a life."

"A life with you, you mean?"

The sun had begun peeking over the city, and a harsh slash chose that moment to streak across his face, highlighting his eyes as well as the pulse pounding in his temple. He looked at a spot beyond her, and the atmosphere in the room changed. "I can't figure out how to do it, Vega."

Her hand covered her mouth. He was talking about them. Though she knew it was the only choice, she wasn't ready for this.

"No matter how much I love you, and you love me." The pain in his voice hurt as much as her crushing heart. "I don't know how to make this work. You know you'll be in the spotlight every day if you're with me."

"I am aware of that."

"And I…" He glanced at her, then just as quickly looked away. "I can't be the one to do that to you again."

"Or to you?"

He blinked, refocused on her. "What?"

"You can't do it to you either, right? You can't put me out there and watch your political career get destroyed before it ever gets off the ground. You can't risk disappointing your mother. Again."

"If I could just figure out—"

"Don't worry about it." She swung her legs over the side of the bed to get up, but he grabbed her before she rose.

"No! I'm not saying to leave. Just…give me some time to figure out how to protect both of us. Please."

Her laugh was hollow. She glanced over her shoulder. "You're trying to figure out how to keep doing exactly what you just blasted me for. Hiding me in public. And on top of that, you're ignoring everything else that means so much to you."

His fingers clenched on her waist so tightly it hurt.

She gave him a sad smile. "You just convinced me of something."

"What's that?"

"I'm finished hiding. I may not be ready to announce exactly who I am and what I once did, but I'll no longer stick with a life I don't like." She stood from the bed, leaving the sheet and all her insecurities behind. "I won't be afraid anymore. I hope you figure out how to do the same before it's too late for you."

With her parting words, she scooped up her clothes and marched from the room. She didn't stop when he said her name, and by the time she reached the front door, she was fully dressed. She may love JP more than she'd ever thought possible, but she'd also discovered she loved herself more. She needed someone who could not only stand up for her, but for himself as well. Or she wanted no one at all.

She stepped out of the penthouse and pushed the elevator button. Her heart shattered when the doors silently slid open, then closed with her inside, without JP coming after her.

CHAPTER TWENTY-NINE

*V*ega shifted the car into Park and stared out into space, ignoring the hotel hovering to her left, as well as the crowd of photographers milling out in front. She could not believe she'd gone from such an emotional high to an all-consuming, heart-wrenching low within the span of a few hours. Yet her swollen eyes and emaciated heart were clear indicators that's exactly what had happened.

She scrubbed the heels of her hands over her eyes, then leaned her head on the steering wheel in exhaustion. She needed sleep. And a year's worth of healing.

After leaving the penthouse, she'd been unready to return to the hotel. Doing so would mean she had to pack and head home, because no, she wasn't sticking around for the press conference the following day. Someone else could cover that. So instead, she'd spent the last two hours driving around in a haze, making turn after turn, yet never getting anywhere. It felt strangely right, and in a funny way, that made sense. It was the same thing she'd spent the last few years of her life doing. Going around in circles, avoiding everything that could take her on a path out of there, and constantly seeing the same views passing by, time and time again.

She was done with it.

It was time to start over.

And that meant her time in Atlanta had come to an end.

A sob bubbled in her throat, but with no energy remaining to push it up and out, it sat there, lodged like her life had been for the last eight years.

She and JP were over.

Pain ripped through her chest, and she folded in on herself. This was so much worse than anything she'd gone through with Ted. But unlike then, there wasn't a thing in the world she could do about this one.

Last time, she should have stood up for herself and fought for the truth. If she had it to do over, she would. But the past was just that. All she could do was learn from her mistakes. That's why she wouldn't pretend with JP.

He couldn't hide her. It simply wasn't possible. Even if she was willing to continue living that life.

She straightened in her seat and turned off the ignition, blinking her eyes several times to clear the fog. No sense sitting around moping any longer. She had a new life to get to, and it was time to make it happen.

Hanging on to her false bravado, she climbed from the van and headed to the front door of her hotel. She may not be perfect, but people would have to learn to take her for who she was, or not take her at all.

Stepping inside, she was temporarily stunned by the bustle of activity going on. It was barely seven thirty in the morning, but businessmen and businesswomen hurried through the lobby as if the world would cease to exist if they didn't stick to their overly tight agendas.

She skirted one particularly well-dressed woman, admiring her Dolce & Gabbana shoes, and nearly ran smack into Greta Kirby.

"Vega!" Greta practically shrieked. "I'm so glad I found you."

Great. Vega stood rooted to the spot, taking in the woman's flashy outfit and wishing she could disappear off the face of the earth. Of course she'd run into someone like Greta when she had swollen eyes and probably looked like death warmed over. Mentally kicking herself for not having the forethought to grab her sunglasses from the car, she gave her smile all she had and pretended she didn't look such a mess. "Hello, Ms. Kirby. What are you doing here this morning? Were you looking for me?"

And then she remembered suggesting that maybe they could do a girls' day on Friday.

It was now Friday.

Oh, good grief. Entertaining Greta was the absolute last thing she wanted to be doing today. She had to find a way to politely extricate herself.

That's when she saw the man with her.

Greta had waved him over, and he now stood slightly behind her, a video camera propped on his shoulder. A microphone appeared out of nowhere to find Greta's hand.

Vega stared, wide-eyed, as her brain worked furiously to catch up.

"Is your thought that going after an unmarried politician is your ticket into the White House this time?" Greta's voiced took on a serious tone, then she thrust the microphone at Vega.

Oh, for the mother of all things holy. Vega's gaze bounced around the lobby, looking for the quickest escape route, as she finally caught on to what was going on. Greta Kirby had somehow become the one person, after all these years, to discover her identity.

"You're different today, boss."

JP raised his head and scowled at his assistant. He didn't feel like mindless chatter. And whether he was different or the same was none of her damn business. "Why are you suddenly calling me *boss*? What happened to *Mr. Davenport*?"

She shrugged. "You seem more real these days. Less 'procedures and policies and cold efficiency.' More human." She finger-quoted his mantra, which only pissed him off more.

"You know why I need procedures and policies, Bev. Give me a break." She'd been there as he'd gone through the years of struggling over making every single task in his life so literal. A dyslexic child couldn't help it; it was simply the way their brain was wired. But knowing that didn't make it any easier. To help matters now, he always insisted on structure and clear procedures. Otherwise simple tasks could lead to undue stress.

"I know, I'm sorry." She pursed her mouth and parked her hands on her hips. "But something is different. You look like a weight of some sort has been lifted from your shoulders, but at the same time, you seem sad and more detached than I've seen you in a while." She perched on the edge of one of his guest chairs. "Anything I can help you with?"

"I can take care of my business myself. But thanks." He added the thanks to hopefully take the sting out of his words. "Don't you have something else you could be doing? Go look at the tabloids or something, and make sure nothing new has shown up we need to deal with before my mother gets wind of it. She plans to stop by this morning."

The thought of his mother coming over to talk to him about Vega pissed him off even more. He didn't need her opinion.

Beverly didn't immediately leave, instead tilting her head one way and then the other, never taking her eyes off him as she did so. He waited as patiently as his crappy morning would allow, knowing her well enough to know she wouldn't leave until she was good and ready.

Finally, she nodded. "Yep, it's love."

"What?" he barked. Where had she pulled that one from? "What are you talking about?"

"You love Vega. It's clear as day." With those words, she stood, brushed her hands together, and sashayed back to her desk.

He followed, only realizing once he'd left his office that he'd had the perfect opportunity to slam the door and lock her out. Instead, he found himself trailing her, fuming like a raging bull. What did she know about who he did or did not love? And why should her guess make him so furious?

The last thought brought him up short. He knew why it bothered him. Because he knew he'd lost Vega at the very same moment he'd finally gotten her.

Beverly pulled her keyboard to her and began typing out a serious of strokes without paying one bit of attention to him. The celebrity website popped up on-screen, and since he had no desire to return to his office to be alone with his thoughts, he stood there watching her.

A headline caught his eye, and he reached down, stopping her arm in midmotion. "What is that last one?"

The headline read, "Eight years later, is her goal the same?"

A video clip was attached. "Show me that video."

Beverly shot him an irritated look but clicked on the link. A video began playing. Greta Kirby was on-screen, dolled up and looking as cheap as ever, and she stood in the lobby of a hotel. He quit breathing.

She went into her spiel about tracking down and finding one of America's most well-known home-wreckers. JP picked up Beverly's wastebasket and threw up his oatmeal.

The next several minutes were spent watching Greta shove a microphone in Vega's face, her eyes red as if she'd been crying, then chasing her through the lobby and into an elevator. Finally, Vega got to her room and slammed the door in Greta's face. Greta then turned to the camera and explained all the atrocities Vega had supposedly committed, as well as the fact she'd been seen leaving Jackson Davenport's penthouse at sunrise that morning.

"Is Vega Zaragoza, otherwise known as the ex-supermodel Reveka, after another politician? At least this time she didn't choose one who was already married. But the question remains, will she ruin his life like she did Ted Pritchard's?"

The video ended. Beverly gawked at the screen for several dead seconds before turning a worried gaze to his. "That's who she is?"

No sense hiding it. "Yes."

"But she…" Beverly glanced back at the computer as if it could right everything in her world, then she once again faced him. "But she's not like that at all. And I don't for a minute believe that Ted Pritchard was innocent in all that. I never did."

He nodded, unable to say anything. His biggest worry at the moment was Vega and what she was going through. He walked into his office and called her. The hotel was probably so surrounded with cameras she couldn't even stick her head out.

The phone rang on the other end until it finally dropped into her voicemail. He slammed his hand on his desk. *Dammit!*

Bringing up Google, he searched for the number of the hotel, but before he could call, his mother burst into his office.

"We have to get a statement to the press before this gets even more out of hand. Tell them it was only a fling and you never intended anything to be serious. That you didn't know who she was. That—"

"Stop," JP butted in. "Before I do anything, I've got to get Vega on the phone and make sure she's okay."

"Are you hearing me, JP? Now is the time for distance, not chasing after her. She may or may not be after you because of who you are, but we've got to make sure just knowing her doesn't do you any more damage. I've got my people working on a statement already."

"Mother," JP began. He stood and put both hands on his desk, palms down, and leaned into the wood. "First, I'm not releasing anything at the moment. Second, she is not after me because of who I am. There is no doubt about that. And third, before I do anything else, I'm going to find Vega and make sure she's okay."

His words seemed to register, and she crinkled her forehead. "But we've got to..." Her voice trailed off as she studied him, looking him up and down. "You care about her?"

He stared. She had always been all about *the job*, letting nothing stand in her way to get his father—and then him—where she thought they needed to be, so he was surprised with the fleeting hint that his feelings might actually come into play. He decided to go for broke. "I love her."

"Oh, my." His mother sucked in a huge breath and slowly lowered herself into a guest chair. "Well, that..." She looked puzzled. "What are you saying, Jackson? Love, as in, you want to stand by her on this?"

Frustration warred at him for the reality of his life and the things he'd had to give up because of it. "Love, Mother. As in, I want to marry her." He folded his hands into fists and lightly tapped his knuckles on the polished wood. "I just have no idea how to make that happen."

His mother scooted back in the seat and wove her fingers together in her lap. She was putting on her public face, and it pissed him off. "I'm sure we can come up with some way to fix this. I've been doing research on her myself—"

She looked up, guilt splashing across her face. "I was concerned with the amount of time you seemed to be spending with her, so I hired a private investigator. I'm sorry, Jackson." She hurried her words; she no doubt knew how much that one statement infuriated him. "It was something I felt I needed to do. But I have good news. I don't think she was after Pritchard the way they say she was."

"She wasn't."

"It's just," she continued, "she got mixed up with a man who was married. And, well, there is the sex tape. And people's perceptions. So what I think we should say—"

"First of all," he interrupted. He was taking charge here, not her. "We don't *say* anything that isn't completely positive and supportive of Vega. If you can't handle that, then keep your mouth —and your people's mouths—shut."

That got her attention.

"And second." He picked up the phone and dialed the hotel. "I need to make a phone call before we discuss anything further."

An attendant answered and let him know that Ms. Zaragoza had checked out of the hotel. The dial tone came next. The act of hanging up on him irritated him, but he knew it was the best course of action for both the hotel and Vega. She didn't need some overly chatty hotel personnel sharing her business with a reporter.

Out of other ideas, he grabbed the little-used remote from his desk drawer and pointed it at the television mounted on the far wall. He found a news station where he watched footage of Vega being hustled out to her car, bags and camera in hand. Hotel security did what they could to hold back the reporters but failed miserably.

He gritted his teeth at the thought of her being accosted and him not being there to help, and he fought the panic trying to take hold at the question of where she'd gone after she'd left. Probably —hopefully—she was heading back to Savannah, but he was terrified that she could also be heading to parts unknown with the intention of disappearing like she had the first time.

He jabbed the button to turn off the TV and punched out the number for Vega's cell. It went immediately to voicemail. He hung up without leaving a message.

"No luck?" His mother still sat in the chair, but he could see from the look in her eyes that she was tired of waiting. She thought statements needed to be made and reputations polished. He wasn't there yet.

He stalked to the window without answering and looked out over the city. Something else had been on his mind since he'd seen the video. If Greta could so quickly figure out who Vega was, he wondered how long it would take her to find Lexi and Daniel, and out them, too. She seemed to be a woman on a mission.

He turned from the window and crossed his arms over his chest, eyeing his mother in a fashion she had done to him over the years. "I need to tell you something about Dad that could potentially come out. If it does, it'll be even worse than Vega."

His mother's face turned white. Her gaze lowered to the hands in her lap, and her fingers tightened, fading in color to match her face. "What about your father?"

"Oh my God," he ground out. "You already know, don't you? Did she come to you too?" And then another thought hit him. "Or did you always know?"

She fidgeted in her seat, but when she spoke, she did so with the same confidence she normally portrayed. "What are you talking about, Jackson? What could I possibly have known?"

She was lying as plain as he was standing there with his heart ripped out of his chest.

"Dad got a girl pregnant before he died."

A muscle ticked in her jaw, but she didn't bat an eye.

"You do know." *Son of a bitch!* "Did you know he paid her off too?"

Her nose tilted in the air at an angle worthy of every Southern aristocrat who'd ever stepped foot in Georgia. "I know that he gave her some money, yes."

"And you didn't have a problem with it?"

"With what? The pregnancy or the money?"

Anger coursed through him. "Let's start with the pregnancy."

Her nose inched higher. "Of course I had a problem with it. It broke my heart when I found out."

"So the perfect marriage and decades-long love was a fake. Perfect. How many other siblings do I have out there?"

"None that I know of." Her jaw twitched again.

"And the money? Did you have a problem with that, or was it something else you could easily overlook?"

She suddenly lost her composure. The lines of her face drooped, and he was almost certain he caught a slight sigh. "It's not that I didn't have a problem with it, but sometimes..." She closed her eyes. "Sometimes things like that have to be done for the good of everyone."

For the good of everyone? Or for her? He was trying to decide if he wanted to ask that question when she opened her eyes and looked at him.

"I take it Lexi has been to see you? Can I ask why?" Emma said.

"She wants money."

She arched an eyebrow. "The extra million wasn't enough? You'd think the little tramp could spend it more wisely."

"She wasn't exactly mature enough to be handed that kind of money, and now her son, Daniel, needs special attention."

His mother stood and began pacing around the room. He watched her, intrigued by how the lack of control in the situation had gotten to her. Rarely did he see his mother struggle in this fashion, but right now, he would venture to guess she had no idea what to do next.

"I got him in the right school and lined up tutors for him," he said.

She stopped. "You paid her off, then?"

"No." He edged back to his desk and picked up his cell, unable to keep worry for Vega far from his mind. He'd hoped she would at least text to let him know she was okay. "I won't be blackmailed, and especially not for something my father did. But I also won't sit by and watch a kid go through what I experienced, and not at least try to give him help."

"What do you mean? What you experienced?"

He choked out a laugh. To this day she acted like he hadn't had anything wrong with him. "Dyslexia, Mom. Tests show he has as severe a case as I did."

"Oh, no." Her arms crossed, and she grabbed hold of both of her elbows. She finally looked concerned for something other than how to spin a story. "Poor kid."

"Poor kid?" he sneered. Not that he disagreed, but... "Where was this sympathy when I needed it?"

The question lingered in the air, pinning them both in place, JP wishing he could take it back, his mother looking like she wanted the same. But it was a question that had needed to be voiced for years. Where the hell had she been when he'd needed her?

No reason to stop the slitting open of old wounds now. He lowered himself into his chair and worked to soften his voice. "It's a question I want answered. Where were you after I was diagnosed, Mom? When I needed you there for me?"

"I made sure you got the help you needed."

"Really? Gran did all she could, and I'm thankful for her, but honestly, you don't think there might have been programs or teachers who would have known more what to do? Or that you being around as a mother might have made a kid feel like he hadn't done something wrong?"

Her shoulders stiffened, and the dark-green sheath she wore shifted to look like it was hanging off her bony shoulders. She'd literally aged before his eyes. "Your grandmother knew what to do. She had already been through it once." Her gaze met his. "With your father."

His jaw fell open. "Dad was dyslexic?"

She nodded. "It's hereditary."

"No shit." That explained both him and Daniel. But it still didn't explain her. "So you got Gran to come take care of me, and that gave you license to disappear from my life?"

"I did not disappear on you, Jackson. I saw you every day I was at home, and I made sure Beverly and your grandmother kept me updated on your progress. I couldn't help it that your father's career took off at the same time." Her eyes pleaded, but he wasn't sure if it was for forgiveness or merely understanding. "It's what we'd worked so hard on. I couldn't quit on him then."

The silence between them finished her thought. But quitting on her son *had* been acceptable. He laughed internally and scrubbed a hand over his jaw. Maybe that soul-touching love she and his father had always claimed had been true after all.

"I apologize for my obtuseness, Mother, but I still don't get it. I understand government and politics have always been important to you, and yes, I see that you wouldn't want to step aside just when Dad finally got a chance in Washington, but how was it that you could so easily push me aside? I simply do not get that."

Her pacing commenced again. This time with shorter and harder steps. He watched her cross the room three times before she stopped and thrust an accusing finger at him.

"I had already let your dad down so much in our marriage. To discover that I had…" She stopped and pulled in a deep breath before continuing. "That I had once again bore a son who might not grow up to be the man your father so wanted—"

Once again? What had been wrong with his older brother? He would return to that question in a moment. Right now, he needed another answered.

"A son that couldn't be the man my father wanted, Mother, or one that couldn't be the man *you* wanted?"

Her jaw clenched. "Both of us, okay? *Both.* We both wanted to maintain the Davenport name, and we were doing everything we could to make that happen. So when we discovered your..." She flapped her hand around in the air. "Issues."

"Dyslexia," he ground out. "Say it. I am dyslexic."

Her eyes shot fire. "Your dyslexia." Her hands tightened into fists, and she looked away. "When we discovered your dyslexia, we thought the best plan was to get you the same help he'd had and to focus that much harder on his career."

Something wasn't exactly adding up. She was explaining how they'd made all these decisions, and her anger made it clear she didn't appreciate having to discuss them, but he also sensed something else in her. He wanted to believe it was shame, or maybe sorrow for pushing her youngest child aside, but he wasn't that hopeful kid anymore. He rose from his seat. "Mom?"

Thirty seconds passed before she turned to him. "What?"

"What did you mean, you *once again* bore a son who might not grow up to be the man my father wanted? Does Bennett have dyslexia too?" There was a pretty big gap between his brother and himself, but he had a hard time believing Cat wouldn't have known, nor that she wouldn't have shared the fact with him as they'd gone through his own troubles.

All the blood once again seeped from his mother's face, and she sank to the spot on the couch where Lexi had sat when she'd first come to his office. "Your brother isn't your father's biological son."

Shock chilled his every nerve. "What?"

She nodded, then something happened he had never before seen. His mother began to cry. Silent tears rolled down her face. "Your father went away the month before we were to get married." Her lips pressed closed then released, and she let out a long, shaky breath. "He'd been out of the Army for years, but he'd been asked to help promote some new equipment they were putting into use. His family agreed it would be a good opportunity since he was just starting to dip his toe into politics.

"While he was gone, this older man I knew apparently saw it as his opportunity to make a move. Our families had been friends for years, had money as we did, traveled in the same circles. So my mother thought it sweet he would offer to keep me company while waiting on your father's return. But what she didn't know was that he had been after me for some time." She flicked her gaze up to him, then just as quickly back down. "Or that I was just as attracted to him."

She wet her lips and kept going. "So I attended a couple dinners, a dance or two, and all the while ignored his advances. I was an engaged woman, after all. But one night, we'd both had too much wine, and I let him talk me into a kiss." She closed her eyes, and more tears dripped out. "And I liked it. I convinced myself that being with him was okay. Just once, before I became a married woman. Only…"

She shook her head, and JP crossed the room to shove a wad of tissues in her hand.

"Thanks," she murmured but still didn't look his way. "At the last minute I changed my mind. I didn't want to be that woman."

Her words drifted out into the room, but no others came. He settled on the couch beside her, unable to watch her pouring out her emotions any longer without comforting her, and he put his arm around her shoulders. He then stiffened as he understood what she'd said. He continued his actions, forcing his palm to settle gently over her shoulder. "Are you saying you told him to stop?"

She nodded. Silently.

"And I take it he didn't?"

Negative shake of her head.

His stomach spasmed in on itself as if he'd been punched low in the gut. How many more shocks would he have to endure today for the people he loved? He put pressure on her shoulder, and she melted to his side.

"I'm sorry, Jackson." She sniffled. "I'm sorry I wasn't there for you, and I'm sorry for..." Her shoulders lifted in a jerky fashion, then sank. "I'm sorry for everything."

He had no idea what to say.

"I didn't find out I was pregnant until after your father and I were married. He did love me. So very much. And I loved him. But the pregnancy just about killed him. I never told him I was raped," she whispered.

Every part of him ached for her. "Why not?"

"Because it was partially my fault. I'd flirted back. I'd said yes."

"But then you said no."

"Yes, but things weren't the same then. No one would have believed me after they'd seen us dancing and laughing together that night. And if I'd admitted it and your father had gone after him, it would have ruined all of us. I wouldn't let that happen."

"So you pretended you had an affair while he was gone?"

"Yes."

"And what about Bennett's real father? He was okay with Dad raising him as his own?" He looked down at her, feeling guilty for the question he was about to ask, but understanding with his mom, it needed to be asked. "Or did you even tell him?"

She stalled by wiping her eyes with the wadded-up tissues. "He quit coming around the day after we...you know. But I did call him and tell him. Your father insisted on it. We didn't want him showing up someday to fight for custody if we were going to pretend your brother had been a honeymoon baby. Only, when I called, he laughed about the pregnancy. Offered the name of someone who could do an abortion and keep it quiet. I told him that wasn't an option, and he laughed again. Said good luck with that." She shook her head against his chest, and he hugged her tighter. "In the end, it was the outcome we'd hoped for, but it hurt to be treated so cruelly."

"Yes." He had to clear the lump from his throat before going on. "I can imagine." He couldn't think what else to say, but so many things had become clear. Why his dad never treated his brother the same as him and Cat. Why he got his father's name instead of his older brother. Why his brother so rarely came home. He sucked in a breath. "Does Bennett know he has a different father?"

She shook her head, and there was a long pause before she spoke again. "We never told him." Her voice sounded pinched. "But I wronged him too, Jackson. I'm the reason he never comes home. I couldn't make myself dote on him the way I wanted to because I was afraid it would hurt your father."

JP could not believe the secrets held so closely all these years. He felt like a fucking Boy Scout compared to the rest of them.

"I always felt so bad about what I'd done to your father, and then we had you, and I was determined to make sure I gave him the best son in the world. Only…"

He finished for her. "Only I wasn't good enough either."

Her tears had stopped, and she pulled away from him now to sit up on her own, her back ramrod straight. He could see her pulling her public persona back in place, and he finally got something he had missed all these years. His mother hadn't simply chosen public life over her children—that's just who she was. She thrived on that side of her life.

She got her face on and corrected him. "It wasn't that you weren't good enough, but we wanted so much for you when you grew up. We had to make sure you didn't get damaged in the public view early on, and we had to continue building the Davenport name so that when you reached the right age, our reputation would be there waiting for you."

He started laughing then and couldn't stop. His chortling did nothing to soothe his mother, who fumed and sniffed at his improperness. That only made him laugh harder. Finally, he got himself under control.

"Are you about finished, Jackson?"

He nodded, a smile growing on his face. "I'm just about finished."

"And what is it you find so funny?" She sniffed.

"You." He chuckled again. "You were so worried about maintaining 'the Davenport reputation,'" he said, finger-quoting as he did, "that you never saw anything for what it really was. You and Dad painted this lifelong love."

"We did love each other."

He raised an eyebrow. "Yet you had a child that wasn't his, and years later, he did the same to you."

"And I never blamed him for that. He'd lived with the pain of my desertion all those years. I couldn't walk away when he did the same."

"He got an underage girl pregnant, Mother. Not just an affair, but a *child*. And then he paid her off."

The quick movement of her head and lack of eye contact stirred something else in him. There was more here he had yet to figure out.

"I was disappointed in her age, yes, but..." She stalled, and sadness once again filled her features. "He was diagnosed with pancreatic cancer two weeks after he found out about the pregnancy. I couldn't bring it up to him then. I just had to deal with it."

"What do you mean bring it up? I'd assumed from what you said, you had both dealt with it when she first told him."

She shook her head. "I overheard them having a conversation one night. He didn't know I was in the campaign office. He thought they were the only ones there."

"So she told him, and what? Dad paid her off without sharing with you where all that money was going? He paid a million and a quarter. You don't ignore anything about our family. How did you not know that?"

The quick look away this time answered the missing piece of the puzzle. He shook his head, disgust souring his mood even more than he'd thought possible. "You gave her the second check, didn't you? The one million dollars."

"I had to."

He began to laugh again. "Right. To protect the family name."

Her jaw locked, and he could tell there was something even more that she didn't want to admit.

"Don't stop now, Mom. Might as well get every last bit of the dirt out. Tell me now before someone else digs it out for you."

She looked at him then, and a growing lack of comfort began swirling like an eddy in his stomach. He had no idea what might be coming, but he wanted distance from it. He stood and moved to the window to stare at the skyline he loved so much.

"The night she told him," she began, her voice flat, "he laughed at her. He told her to get an abortion and wrote her a check. Said it would cover her medical expenses, with a tidy sum left over to buy her something special for her troubles."

JP didn't speak. His father had been a complete ass.

"I couldn't believe it. He'd . . ." She paused and pressed her lips together before continuing. "He'd seen how much it had hurt *me* when that very same thing had happened. I knew the pain she was going through. I couldn't live with myself if I didn't try to help."

He pressed his fist to the window. "So you...what? Gave her enough money to make sure she felt better about the situation?"

She remained quiet for a full minute, then whispered, "I deserved that, but no." Her chin inched upward. "I went to her, asked if an abortion was what she really wanted. It wasn't. And I believed her. I could see this girl was in way over her head and had no one to turn to, so I made my offer clear. I didn't want to ever hear from her again; she could never reveal the father, but I would help her enough she'd never have to struggle as a single mother. I wrote her a check from the money on my family's side. Your father never knew anything about it, and I never told him I knew what he'd done."

And their lifelong love had continued.

He finally faced her, leaning his shoulders against the window and letting the heat from the sun soothe his nerves. Between all the secrets in his own family and worrying about Vega and what he could do to help her, he needed a fifth of whiskey, but he would take the warm sun.

"So, what now, Mom? She's back in our lives, and I won't turn my back on her son. You know it's all likely to come out eventually."

"Is she threatening to expose everything?"

"No," he said, anger lacing his tone. "She's not threatening anything. She just needs help. Which I'm giving her. But there are nosy reporters out there, looking for anything they can find." He paused to make sure she was listening. "And the boy looks exactly like me. Vega saw it within minutes of seeing us together."

She gasped. "Is Vega planning to expose him?"

"No." His control was slipping. "Believe it or not, she loves me, too. She's not going to do anything to hurt me, but she's not the only one out there looking at us either."

His mother nodded, and he could see her mind whirling to find the correct course of action. This was his mother in her prime. Give her a problem that needed to be "handled," and she thrived.

"I'll tell you what," he began. "You figure out whatever you want to do concerning Lexi and Daniel. I won't be a part of it."

"That's insane. It'll have to involve you. You're going to be the forefront of this family come tomorrow."

"Yeah, that's what I hear." Though he knew he wasn't. He didn't want this life of lies and cover-ups. He wanted Vega, and he wanted to make a difference. "But I'm actually not."

Her eyes grew round. "You're thinking of turning it down? But it's what you've—"

He shook his head. "It's what *you've* always wanted, not me. I've never wanted anything of the sort."

"Really?" She slowly rose from the couch. "But I thought…"

He raised his brows and waited. What could she possibly have thought?

"I thought you wanted to follow in your father's footsteps."

He began to laugh again, this time more relief than stress. "You've told me that for so long, I honestly had no idea what I did want. But I promise you this. I've got it figured out now."

"The announcement is tomorrow."

"I'm canceling it."

"Because of everything you've learned today?"

"Because it's not what I want."

"Okay," she said, almost to herself. He could see her mind working on how to spin this turn of events.

He studied her, beginning to understand his mother for the first time in his life. He didn't have to agree with everything she did, but he got that she made choices based on what she thought was the right thing for their family. And even for the illegitimate child that would never be a part of their family. He had to love her for that.

He softened his features to let her know that he forgave her as best he could, and he wondered how long it would take for her to reach the same conclusion he had already come to. He decided not to wait and see.

"Why don't you go for it, Mom?" He spoke gently. "You're the one who loves politics so much. Get Douglas to appoint you as Mitchell's replacement."

The idea pleased her, he could see. That made him happy. As long as she kept her nose out of his onslaught to win Vega back, all would eventually be okay between the two of them.

She stood a little straighter. "You think?"

He chuckled. "You can't tell me you haven't thought about it."

"Not seriously, no. I always assumed you wanted it. I'd planned to spend my time helping you."

"Well, think about it now." He pushed off the window, feeling happier than he had in years. "One thing, though."

"What's that?"

"You might have to keep holding him off for a few more years if he's going to put you in office."

Wide-eyed innocence marked her features, but guilt-laden heat colored her cheeks. "I don't know what you're talking about, Jackson. Douglas and I are nothing but friends."

"Sure, Mom. Keep saying it if that makes you feel better, but we both know he's sweet on you. And you're likely just as sweet on him." He crossed to his desk. He was oddly enjoying the moment with his mother, but he had plans to put into action. He needed to get busy.

She sniffed and moved to the door. "I can see you have things to do, so I'm going to step out now."

"Thanks, Mom." He picked up his phone, intending to try Vega one more time. "Before you go…"

She glanced back. "What?"

He hated to risk ruining the silent truce that seemed to have forged between them within the last few minutes, but he couldn't let her go without making sure she understood Vega's importance. "I'm going to figure out a way to get Vega back. Don't release any kind of statement that involves her at all. She and I will figure that out once I convince her she needs me in her life."

She nodded, pride shining his way. "Love is a wonderful thing, Jackson. Don't ever take it for granted."

"That I can promise."

Seconds after she departed, Beverly stuck her head in. "Anything I can do for you, boss?"

Her total support had been the one thing he'd always been able to count on in his life. Hers and Cat's. He suddenly knew what he had to do. He waved Beverly inside and began making plans.

CHAPTER THIRTY

*T*he final seconds of the video counted down, and the tension in Vega's shoulders lifted to the air. She leaned back in her chair, feeling smug. She'd done it. She'd made a really terrific piece.

She glanced over at Bob, wondering what his response would be. Both nerves and excitement had warred in her all night as she'd waited to show it to him. "Well?"

Her mentor scratched his jaw, his gaze lingering on the now empty screen, and slowly nodded. Finally, he faced her. "I knew you'd be good, hon, but this blows the cover off even what I thought. You're magic with knowing exactly what to show to draw emotion from the viewer while also keeping the scenery and background as interesting as what's going on in the forefront." He nodded his head in a steady pattern as pride edged up his features. "Simply terrific."

A smile exploded on her face. It was the first real one in the last twenty-four hours, and though a little stiff, it felt good. "Thanks."

Bob moved to stand in front of the screen, his body language saying that he was still in thought. They were in the station's viewing room, just the two of them, and his features suddenly turned to concern. The light of the projector went out as he faced her. "You doing okay?"

Ah, they were going to talk about "that." She shrugged, embarrassed to acknowledge to him who she was, and that she'd kept it from him all these years. "As well as can be expected."

Concern shone back at her, easing her discomfort, but just barely. "I honestly didn't know whether to expect you back here or not. Thought you might disappear, at least until this died down."

Her cheeks heated. She had considered the idea. Getting away from the hotel had been rough, but fury had stirred deeper than her need to hide. Also, she'd already decided, no one was going to run her off ever again. After all, she hadn't done anything wrong, now or then.

Other than falling in love.

She gritted her back teeth at the thought. No one had to know that JP had been anything more than a fling. She tried to reclaim the smile she'd had only moments before. "I had a job to finish. I wasn't raised to ditch out on a job, and especially not to someone who's been so good to me over the years."

Bob nodded. "You've grown since I met you."

She had, but she didn't know exactly what he meant. "I've learned a lot under you, Bob. And I thank you very much."

"I'm not talking about your skill. I'm talking about growing as a person." He cocked his head. "When I first met you, you wouldn't have come back yesterday. Especially not after everything had been put back out there like that."

He was most likely right. Hell, who was she kidding, he was totally right. From the botched exit of the hotel to the resurgence of the sex tape, she would've ducked her head like an ostrich and hit the road, not coming up for weeks.

Instead, she'd phoned her lawyer, requested he once again get the videos taken down, then she'd stiffened her back as if completely in the right and ignored every single question thrown her way. What was she doing with JP? Had she already gotten an engagement ring? Why had she set out to ruin Ted? What had his wife ever done to her? Would she really have gone so far as to kill his wife?

She'd headed to Savannah, knowing it would be a madhouse trying to enter the station, but what she'd worried about most—aside from wondering if JP had seen the video and what he thought of her now—was what Bob would think of her. She'd been sick over the thought of his shame.

The occasional snicker had reached her ears as she'd entered, but Bob had been nothing but supportive. The fact that she hadn't gone home—first editing her story, then sleeping on a cot because she couldn't stomach the thought of stepping outside—hadn't gone unnoticed by her friend.

She nodded. "You're right. I wouldn't have been able to stand tall and deal with all this eight years ago. It was still too raw."

"And you felt you'd done something wrong."

A burning ache gnawed at the base of her throat. "Yeah, I was pretty sure I'd done something wrong."

He returned to the seat beside her. "And now?"

"Now?" She lowered her head to the cushion and stared at the rectangular panels of the ceiling. "Now, I still feel bad for being a part of something that hurt his wife so terribly, but I didn't do anything wrong. All I did was believe in love."

He patted her knee, and she took comfort in the touch. He probably would have come to Atlanta and rescued her himself if she hadn't had the courage to push through the crowds.

"I have something to admit," he spoke quietly. She raised her head, the room suddenly sizzling with electricity.

She repeatedly clicked the pen in her hand, the ink cartridge pushing in and out. "What's that?"

His gaze found a spot on the opposite wall. "I've always known who you are."

"What?" Her eyes bugged, and her breathing became heavy.

He nodded, facing her with chagrin. "I'm sorry. I should have told you a long time ago. It just wasn't something that I could easily bring up in conversation."

Shock held her to the seat. "But...how? I changed my hair, my looks. I made myself as plain as I could possibly get."

She glanced down at the clothes she wore today, one of the outfits she'd bought in Atlanta. She was tired of hiding behind plainness.

Bob laughed softly, then shrugged, a bit of a smug smile on his face. "I didn't win all those awards on my wall for nothing, kid. I sensed something was weighing pretty heavy on you and went in search of the answer. Of course, I was blown away to realize who I'd just hired, but that didn't change my opinion of you."

She was almost afraid to ask. "And what was that opinion?"

She'd definitely been a different person when she'd first graduated from school and landed the job here.

He reached over and patted her knee once more. "I thought I'd just hired someone who would one day become one of the best. I could see my drive in you, and I wanted to do everything I could to help you get there."

Pride swelled in her at his words, and before she could ask, he gave a nod. "And yes, you've lived up to all my expectations."

Love grew inside her. She would definitely miss this man, no matter where she ended up. "I can't go back to Atlanta today, Bob." She looked over at him. "Can you send Darrin to cover the press conference?"

"He's already on his way. I can't say he was upset about the fact."

She chuckled, a soft, exhausted sound. "I'm sure that's an understatement."

They sat in comfortable silence for a few moments before Vega looked over at her boss. "I appreciate you putting in a good word for me in Atlanta."

"But?"

He knew her so well. "But I don't want to be a videographer anymore."

"No?"

She shook her head. "No. At least not a regular news photographer. There are stories I want to tell, yes, but stories that touch people's hearts. And I want to be the one in front of the camera when I report on them. It's what I've always wanted."

Bob reached one long arm over and wrapped it around her shoulders. He squeezed her to his side so hard she thought the metal arm of the seat might crack one of her ribs. "That-a-girl."

Rightness filled her. She rested her cheek on his shoulder and breathed out a long breath.

"I'm going to do absolutely everything I can to get a position reporting on exactly the kind of stories I believe in."

He pointed a finger at the screen. "You show them what you just showed me, my dear, and you'll get a chance anywhere you want it."

"You think?" Pride took hold inside her and ballooned in size.

"Not a doubt in the world."

She sat up and eyed him, wanting to make sure he wasn't just saying what she wanted to hear. "Even with my past? And everyone talking about me again?"

"Even then. But for your sake, I think you need to come clean. Clear the air about it all."

Her brow scrunched together. "What do you mean?"

"I mean, tell your story. Ted Pritchard may be out of your life and out of the picture, but his lies still haunt you. They cripple you to the point that you continue to worry you did something wrong." He shook his head. "It's time to quit hiding, Vega.

Completely. Stand up, fight back, and go take everything you want."

His speech resonated within her. Both because she thought he might be right, but also because without even asking, he believed in her. He trusted that Ted had been at fault without asking for her explanation.

Maybe it *was* time to take what she wanted. But the thing was, she also wanted JP.

Sadness feathered over her heart. He'd called several times the day before, but she hadn't wanted to talk. With the combination of realizing he wouldn't be standing up to his mother, and Greta accosting her in the hotel lobby, Vega hadn't been able to stomach the thought of dealing with one more thing. She'd needed escape. So she'd taken it.

But since returning to Savannah, she'd been thinking about JP. She missed him. A lot. Was she really ready to give him up without a fight? And if she wasn't, that meant she'd have to risk being in the daily glare of the tabloids.

She had no idea if she could even convince him to take the chance on her.

All kinds of footage had floated around since Greta had outed her. She might be too much trouble in his eyes. After all, it wasn't like he'd called even once today.

Vega sighed and pushed her maudlin thoughts to the back of her mind. She pressed her palms down on the armrests, propelling herself up. "Thanks, Bob. I think you might be right."

He winked. "Want me to set you up to make a statement?"

"Oh, no." She shook her head. "We're doing better than that. I want a press conference. First though, I have makeup and hair to do, along with new shoes to buy. If I'm going to announce to the world I did nothing wrong and have no reason to hide, then I'm going to come back in my own way."

A laugh echoed through the small room as Bob rose and patted her on the back. "That's my girl. I'm proud of you."

She straightened with pride. She was back, and no one would push her down again.

And if that meant living the rest of her life without JP because he couldn't handle being by *her* side...well, she'd eventually get over him. But she would be glad to have known him.

CHAPTER THIRTY-ONE

*V*ega tipped up the bottle of water and drained it, her throat parched with nerves before ever taking a step outside to the waiting crowd. She glanced at the clock on the wall. Five minutes.

She wiggled her fingers at her side, trying to calm the anxiety, but nothing was working. This was going to be brutal. And she'd set this up herself, so she had no one to blame. She turned to Bob.

"You can do it," he soothed.

"I'm not sure," she groaned. She wanted to chew on her nails—a habit she'd broken years ago as a teenager—but the sight of the French-tipped acrylics reminded her she was different today. She was herself again.

She glanced in the glass door of the darkened office to her right and studied her reflection. A little curvier than she'd once been, her skin not quite as youthful, but all in all, she still had it. And though the makeup wasn't so heavy to totally change her appearance, she absolutely hadn't lost her touch.

She fingered a curl draped over her shoulder. There was a good chance if the crowd didn't know it was her who would be coming out that door, they would have never guessed it to be the same woman who'd quietly been capturing the news around the city for the last few years.

"You know they're going to bring up Davenport's canceled press conference, right?" Bob asked.

"I would expect nothing less." She took a fresh bottle of water from a colleague and rolled it between her hands. "Any word yet on what happened?"

"None. Darrin stuck around to see if he could find out, but so far, all is silent from the governor's office."

She pressed the bottle to her throat, hoping its refrigerated temperature would calm her nerves. No such luck.

"I was counting on the news of that announcement to over-shadow this one."

Bob laughed. "No such luck, kid. I took a peek outside. There's a crowd here."

"Freaking slow news day," she mumbled.

They both smiled at each other, enjoying the moment before things could go either really good, or really bad, then Bob broke eye contact. "There's...uh...something I should probably tell you."

"Are you kidding me? What?" Geez, what now?

"Davenport called earlier."

"Here?" That hadn't been what she'd expected to hear. She studied him, trying to figure out if she wanted to know why. Curiosity won. "What did he want?"

"To make sure you were here and not...gone."

So he'd worried she'd taken a hike. She wondered if that meant he wanted to see her. Could she have anything to do with the canceled press conference? Anything good? She'd been shocked not to hear a word from his family's publicist yesterday or today, releasing any sort of statement about their relationship. Everything had been strangely quiet.

She nodded, unsure what the movement meant, but unable to think of anything to say.

Bob tapped his watch. "It's go time. You okay?"

A surprising calmness settled over her. "I'm ready."

Bob stepped in front of her and exited the building, moving toward the small podium he'd had erected at the edge of Oglethorpe Square. A small gathering of colleagues patted her on the shoulder in encouragement as she followed him out the door.

Security guards lined the walk across the street, and she held her head high and proud as she crossed.

Once in front of everyone, she scanned out over the gathered crowd and wished with all her might she wasn't up there alone. The old feeling of being one against the world returned and saddened her. She knew nothing had really changed yet, but then, everything had.

She would no longer let past lies hold her down. Instead, she'd now go after each and every single thing she wanted. Including JP.

When she finished here, she'd go after JP to convince him he couldn't live without her, even if he did one day want to be president. She might bring a little tarnish to his name, but she would spend the remainder of her days doing nothing but polishing it.

Darkness surrounded the outer edges of the square, but the space immediately in front of her was lit so brightly she could barely make out any faces. Might as well get this over with.

She leaned forward and pulled the microphone to her.

JP EDGED around a crowd of people, a baseball cap low on his head and his gaze on the ground, hoping no one recognized him before he wanted them to. He wanted to do this on his own terms—and the way it would make the biggest impression on Vega.

He might have only one chance to win her, so it had to be perfect.

Well, that wasn't true. If he didn't make her see reason tonight, he wouldn't stop until he did get her. But for her sake, he wanted it to be perfect tonight.

Another question about her past relationship was lobbed up through the crowd, and the sound of Vega's voice soothed him. He'd refused to watch the sex video that had apparently made the rounds over the internet, and hearing her talk about another man seriously irritated. Not just because she'd been in that relationship —though knowing the man had touched her in those ways fed JP's urge to hunt him up and take him out—but because she'd been treated so poorly. She hadn't deserved that, and she didn't deserve to have to be up there defending herself now, either.

He hated that he'd gotten here late. The plan had been to find her beforehand and be onstage with her from moment one, whether she wanted him to or not. Traffic on the drive from Atlanta had dictated he go to plan B.

"James Lewis, *Savannah Chronicle*, Ms. Zaragoza. If what you say is true, why did you disappear instead of explaining all this back then? It makes it look like you're trying to sail in on your notoriety now, without having to deal with all the consequences in the heat of the moment."

JP caught a glimpse of Vega as he continued to jockey for a position in the dead center of the crowd, and he stopped in his tracks. She looked amazing. Hair flowing in long curls, eyes shining and sexy hot, and oh my God, those lips. She had a deep crimson painted on her gloriously wide mouth, and he suddenly wanted to punch every man in the crowd, because he knew what they were all thinking.

Picking his jaw up, he pulled his gaze from the black-and-white dress clinging to her every curve and ducked his head, continuing quickly through the crowd.

"As I stated before, Mr. Lewis," she began. "I was twenty. Everyone was calling me a home-wrecker, suggesting I might go so far as to physically harm Mr. Pritchard's then-wife, and everywhere I looked, my supposed friends were taking money to lie about me. Your daughter, sir, how old is she?"

"Nineteen," Mr. Lewis said, his voice remaining strong and sure of himself.

"Can you imagine, Mr. Lewis, your daughter innocently falling for the wrong man, having every last secret about her life as well as her body and sexual preferences graphically shown for the whole world to see, and then telling her to step out in front of everyone... all these same people who are accusing her, who already have their minds made up...and tell them they were just wrong. That no, she can't prove it, but they'd just have to take her word for it?"

"I would encourage her to do exactly that, actually. Hiding does nothing but indicate guilt, and I teach my children to stand with pride, no matter what."

"And would you plan to be there standing by her side, Mr. Lewis, as she faced them?"

"Absolutely. She knows she has my support."

"Say you're dead. What then?"

Pause. "Then her mother would be there for her."

JP found a spot he liked and faced the front, waiting to see how this was going to play out.

"What if her mother couldn't be there? Or her sister, or her brother, or any other family member, or anyone in the whole entire world who she'd ever thought was a friend? None of them are able to stand there and give her support, sir, and most of them have already publicly called her a liar, anyway."

Mr. Lewis apparently stood to JP's left as half the crowd turned that direction.

"Then I would hope she..." He paused. "She would..."

"I'll tell you what she would do. She would stand there, all alone, nineteen years old, and be ripped to shreds by people often more interested in creating a headline than reporting the facts. When she finished and walked away, she'd be so broken she wouldn't be able to face anyone with any sort of pride again, for a very long time. Yet she'd continue to wonder, as she'd been doing every single moment since the 'news' had broken, how she'd come to be such a bad person as to do all those things everyone said. Only, before she spoke, she'd only have read their words in the news. Afterward, they'd have said them to her face.

"Where would she go then, Mr. Lewis? What would she do? My guess, she'd run and hide, exactly as I did, only in this instance she wouldn't have even a shred of pride left to cling to. She'd have had all those people telling her, to her face, just how pathetic and evil she really was. And no matter what she wanted to believe...she would believe them."

A hush fell over the crowd, and JP fought the urge to clap. That was the woman he loved up on stage, standing up for herself. He couldn't have been more proud.

"What do you say to reports that you went after JP Davenport with the same intention as you did Ted Pritchard? That you wanted to trap him into marrying you?" This question came from JP's right. He swiveled his head and caught the red hair of a reporter he recognized from Atlanta. A woman he'd refused to sleep with no matter how many attempts she'd made. She'd always struck him as particularly devious.

"I'm not sure what you're asking, ma'am. Are you asking if I got involved with Mr. Davenport for the same reason I dated Mr. Pritchard, or are you asking if I set out to somehow trap Mr. Davenport? Because those are two completely different things. And if your question is the second one, I'd like additional information on how, exactly, you're proposing that anything I did could have 'trapped' Mr. Davenport."

He loved that she was finished shirking from people and obstacles. If he wasn't careful, she'd be the one seeking office in a few years, and he'd be left riding her coattails.

"I'll rephrase my question." The reporter pasted on an evil grin. "Governor Chandler canceled a press conference earlier this evening. One intending to announce Mr. Davenport as the newest Georgia senator. Rumor is, Mr. Davenport won't be taking office anytime soon. Do you believe you ruined his career, as you did Mr. Pritchard's?"

Pride sharpened the line of Vega's jaw, and though he wanted very much to hear her put the reporter in her place, this was the moment he'd been waiting for.

"I'd like to take this one, if I may." He removed his ball cap and spoke loud enough to be heard, even though he carried no microphone.

Vega stilled at the podium as everyone in the crowd shuffled to get an eye on who had spoken. She held a hand over her brow to shield the light and peered into the crowd.

"Sir?" she asked. "Could you use a microphone, please? I'm having trouble hearing you."

One was thrust in his hands.

Soft gasps punctuated the evening as others recognized him, and everyone around him began to step back as if they'd come into contact with either a man of great respect, deserving of a polite distance, or a man with a highly communicable disease. He honestly wasn't sure which way they were feeling.

Lifting the microphone, he stared into the eyes of the woman he loved, knowing she couldn't see his in return, but wanting her to feel them, all the same. "To the question of—"

Her indrawn breath echoed over the speakers, and he smiled. There was zero doubt she knew who spoke to her.

"Did you ruin my career. I'd like to answer that, if I may."

The square was dead silent.

She nodded. "Please."

The fingers gripping the side of the podium began to twitch. He hated that he'd made her nervous, but it couldn't be helped.

He took several steps forward, the crowd shifting with him, opening before him and closing the gap behind him as he moved. "The simple answer is no."

He swung his gaze to the redheaded reporter. "Would you like more of an explanation than that, Ms. Keen?"

She jerked to attention as if shocked to find him focused on her. "Please, Mr. Davenport. I'm sure everyone would love to hear the explanation."

"Including me," Vega said.

When he turned back to her, it pleased him to see her hand stilled and the spark back in her eyes. He loved her more with every passing minute. "It would be my pleasure. By the way, has anyone mentioned how amazing you look tonight?"

From her quick downcast eyes, he guessed they hadn't.

"That's what I thought," he said into the microphone, his voice low, but it felt as if he were by her side, speaking directly to her. He continued to move closer. "You are beautiful, Vega. Every man here is jealous of me right now."

A smile touched her lips. "That wouldn't be unusual. Men often wish they were you. A Davenport, able to have any woman he wanted, all that money, the power."

"A beautiful woman I love?"

Her eyes widened in shock, then she glanced nervously around at the still-silent crowd, and he started laughing.

"That's right, baby. I just announced to everyone here—and on the live feeds from their cameras—that I love you." He took the two remaining steps until he stood at the base of the stage, directly in front of her. "And that's why the answer about whether you ruined my career is an unequivocal no. You made my career, not ruined it."

A line formed between her brows. "I don't understand."

"Can I come up?" He nodded to the stairs leading up to the risers.

"Please."

With a spring in his step, he leaped onstage and moved to stand beside her. She turned to him.

"Without you," he continued over the speakers, "I would have never seen what had been right before me all along. I wouldn't have accepted that politics is *not* what I want, but rather, something else even more important."

The deep brown of her eyes darkened. "And what would that be?"

"We can't hear you!" someone yelled from the crowd.

Vega blushed and seemed to remember they stood before everyone, having what she had to know was a highly important, and personal, conversation. She pulled the microphone from its base and brought it to her lips. "I asked what that would be."

A collective *aah* went through the crowd, and she once again turned to him, an I-can't-believe-this-is-happening smile on her beautiful face.

"I'm not going into politics. I'm starting a new program instead. Just like I told you I wanted to do."

Vega stared at the man she'd dared to hope would show up tonight, unable to believe what he was currently doing in the middle of live, national television. By now, stations across the country, and probably some outside the country, would have tuned into what was going on here.

She wondered just how far he was willing to go. "Would you like to tell me about it?"

"I would." He nodded. "But first, I need someone to come up here and help me."

Who? She glanced around, trying to figure out what he meant, when she spotted Cat off the side of the stage, Tyler at her side with his hand in hers. JP met them halfway and picked Tyler up in his arms. He then returned to center stage. She couldn't keep her love from bursting wide-open in her chest and showing across her face.

"Hi, Tyler," she spoke, the words echoing over the silence.

JP held the microphone up to Tyler.

"Hi." He ducked his head in embarrassment.

"Are you going to help your uncle tonight?"

He nodded. JP whispered in his ear, and Tyler reached for the microphone. He grasped it with both hands, and his right arm began to twitch. "I'm helping Uncle P tell 'bout his program."

And they were apparently going to do that by letting everyone see the dystonia that affected the movement in Tyler's right arm. Vega remained silent as JP introduced Tyler and turned to the crowd to explain the program he had already put into motion, as well as the dyslexia he himself had suffered with all his life. He couldn't have done anything more to impress her than what he was doing right now.

"So, no," he wrapped up. "Vega did not ruin my career. She merely helped me see there were far more important paths I needed to be following."

He winked at her, and she quickly brushed tears from her eyes. At least these were tears of happiness.

"I have one more thing I need to point out tonight," he said to the crowd.

Turning away from her, he motioned toward Cat, and Vega saw Becca now standing by her side. She carried a very large, rectangular box in her hands as she made her way to JP.

"Everyone, this is Becca."

The crowd responded in unison, "Hi, Becca."

"Becca is going to help me with something for Vega."

The child stepped around her uncle and held out the box, and Vega burst out laughing. It was imported chocolates.

"You brought me chocolates?"

"I'm trying to butter you up," JP rumbled. "And they weren't easy to get overnighted, so I deserve lots of points for them."

The crowd laughed, then immediately fell silent. Clearly, they were as interested as she to see where this might go next. She took the box from Becca and leaned down to kiss the girl on the cheek. "Thank you, sweetheart," she murmured.

"Hey," JP complained. "I'm the one who paid to get those here. Why didn't I get that kiss?"

Vega grinned. "Becca's cuter."

JP acted as if he'd been stabbed in the heart, and Tyler cackled out with laughter as any child would. Then Vega saw both Cat and Emma step up on the stage behind JP, and she looked around. What was going on?

He stared into her eyes, the moment quickly going from light-hearted to intense. "I apologize for ambushing your press conference. I know this wasn't how you intended it to go, but from what I heard, you explained the past quite succinctly, and that should be good enough to move on."

She couldn't disagree. She nodded.

"And I want to say, to you and everyone here, there couldn't be a better person in this crowd than you. You're sweet and moral, worried about others before yourself, and when given a choice, you always do the right thing. My family agrees with me, and that's why they're here. They wanted to show you that you have their full support."

He paused, then set Tyler down and reached for her hand. "*We* have their full support."

The next instant, JP was on one knee, a ring box in his hand, and smiling up at her. Vega looked wildly around at everyone on the stage, caught Bob's wink and Emma and Cat's supporting smiles, then finally redirected her attention back to the man she loved. The man currently kneeling before her, and many, many others. She gulped.

"Before I ask this question, know that if you say no to me, if you break my heart...here before this very large crowd, *and* my family..." He shook his head with sadness, as if a very bad thing had happened. "Well...everyone will feel so sorry for me. They'll likely shower me with gifts and attention..."

Several ladies from the crowd let out a *whoop* as if they would gladly shower him with attention.

"See what I mean?" One side of his mouth lifted, one dimple shining. She loved that smile. "They're already lining up to make me feel better."

"Stand up," she whispered. Still into the microphone.

He lifted an eyebrow.

"I want the man I love to ask me to marry him on his feet. So when he's done, I can kiss him in a way that'll leave no woman out there with any doubt that I'll be the last one he'll kiss."

The half-smile grew to a full-blown one, and he rose, seemingly towering over her even though she had on very nice, and very high, brand-new Louboutins.

"How is it I always feel so small next to you?"

He squeezed her hand and stepped right into her space. "It's the power of my protection. I won't ever let anyone hurt you. Ever again."

She smiled. "For as long as we both shall live?"

He gave a gentle nod, then flipped open the jeweler's box and the aquamarine ring she'd admired on their trip to the islands glinted up at her. It was as breathtaking as the moment.

"For as long as we both shall live," he murmured. "Will you, Vega..." He lifted the back of her hand to his mouth and kissed it. "...the love of my life, do me—"

"And his family," Cat, Emma, and both kids chimed in. Love glowed from JP's eyes.

"...the greatest honor of being my wife? Of being by my side for the rest of our days on this earth...and probably even some after."

Before she could answer, he cupped her jaw. "I love you, baby. I can't stand the thought of not having you in my life."

Nor could she. She broke eye contact and looked from one Davenport to the next, so proud to know that they would all be a part of her new family. Love overflowed at the realization of just how totally JP got her. He'd known she'd question how his family would feel about this, so he'd shown her before she could ask. She couldn't be happier.

Leaning forward, she put her face in front of his, brought the microphone to her mouth, and whispered yes before forgetting about every single person watching them and giving him that kiss she'd promised.

EPILOGUE

*V*ega lifted her hand in front of her face and studied her ring. She still couldn't believe he'd bought it for her when they'd been in Anguilla.

"You like it, right?" JP snaked an arm across her bare stomach, his breath ruffling the hair at her nape.

They were lying in his bed, balcony doors thrown wide, watching the sun set and the city lights come to life. It was one week after her press conference. One week they'd been all but hidden from the world—both in Mexico visiting her mother, then back to his place, where they hadn't stepped foot outside for the last two days. Most of the hours had been spent right there, in his bed.

She turned her head to capture his lips with hers, then pulled back and smiled. "You couldn't have gotten me an engagement ring I would love more. But how did you know to get this one?"

"You mean other than the drool rolling off your chin as you eyed it in the store?" His light chuckle warmed her from the inside out. She loved his voice, but his laugh caused her heart to bloom.

"I did not drool." She sniffed. "I merely admired it. I also never told you why I liked it so much."

"I assumed it was because it matched my eyes." His mouth curved into the smile of the power-hungry playboy she'd first met. The one who'd never met a woman he couldn't have. "You were totally crazy about me already, so clearly you'd want a reminder."

"A reminder? As in when you were gone?" The thought brought her upright in bed, the sheet dropping to the mattress. When his hand reached up to her naked breasts, she slapped it away. "Did you buy this ring intending to give it to me when you dumped me?"

The look on his face was utter horror, then his earlier chuckle returned and quickly turned to a full-on laugh. He flung himself back on the bed, laughter rolling from him.

"You did, didn't you?" She punched him in the gut, making him grunt. "You total pig, you got it to use as a parting gift!"

"I didn't," he said, grabbing her hands to keep her from hitting him again. "I swear."

"Then explain it. There's no way you knew you wanted to propose to me then."

When she tried to pull her arm free, he tugged, yanking her across him so that she lay draped over his chest. He clamped one hand over the back of her head and pulled her mouth to his, kissing her in the way she loved. Long, deep, and hard.

After they were both out of breath, she lifted her head and gazed down at him. "Tell me why you bought it."

It didn't matter at that point whether he'd bought it to wish her well in a life without him or not, but something about the gleam in his eyes made her want to know. Had he somehow known while they'd been on the island that he wanted more from her?

JP kissed her on the forehead, then shifted them both so they were once again sitting up. He propped himself on the headboard and settled her in close next to him. He then reached into the drawer at the side of his bed and pulled out a flat, narrow box. It looked suspiciously like it held either a necklace or a bracelet.

"I wanted to save this for our wedding day, but at this point I'm thinking I shouldn't wait."

She took it in her hands. "Why not?"

"Because I want to make sure you believe me when I say that I bought that ring only after knowing I wanted you in my life."

The lid lifted easily, and she peeked in. The bracelet matching her ring lay nestled inside, as gorgeous as the afternoon she'd first seen it. "I don't understand."

He lifted the piece off its cushion and gently snapped it around her wrist. "You were wearing this in the store, and you had this look in your eyes that said you wanted it badly."

"I did." She wiggled her fingers in the air between them. "Actually, I wanted this ring, but only because it reminded me of the one my father once gave me. I'd lost it years ago."

"Ah." He nodded. "That explains the look. Anyway, I wasn't kidding when I said that day that I've been known to buy women jewelry when I say goodbye to them." His cheeks now wore a hint of pink. "It tends to appease them when I remind them that I really don't want anything more serious."

"So…what are you saying?" She was confused.

He slipped a finger between the bracelet and the inside of her wrist and rolled the jewels across his knuckle. "While you were trying on clothes for dinner, I called the store and made arrangements to have this delivered to the plane. It was beautiful, and it did remind me of my eyes. *I* wanted to make sure you always had something that would remind you of me, whether we went any further than dinner or not."

Things were becoming clear now. "So you did buy me a bauble that day, just not the ring?" It seemed like the action should make her feel cheap, but for some reason it didn't.

He ducked his head in embarrassment. "I did. But I knew what we had was different, even then. I wanted you in a way I'd never wanted a woman, yet I had no idea if you would even allow me to kiss you again, much less ask for more. It was driving me insane."

"Luckily I came to my senses." She reached up and gave him a quick peck. "But I don't understand about the ring. When did you get it?"

The color of his eyes darkened, taking on the exact hue of the center stone. "The next day."

She sucked in a quick breath. "As a token of what we'd shared that weekend?"

"No." He shook his head. "Not as a token. At least, not of anything in the past. I knew then that I had to have more of you. I hadn't figure out how to make that happen, or even how much I wanted, but all I could picture was you wearing this ring. I wanted you to be mine, Vega. I wanted to give you the world."

She couldn't believe he'd cared for her that much in such a short amount of time. But then, they'd met and fallen in love in less than a week.

She recalled the first time they'd made love . . . the way he'd stared into her eyes and bared his soul. He'd been giving her the deepest part of him that day, and she was so glad she'd allowed herself to take it.

He squeezed her to his chest. "I love you, Vega. However it came to be, we were definitely meant to be together."

"I agree." She snuggled in, loving every minute in his arms. "I love you too." She reached across him to grab the remote from the bedside table and pointed it at the television on the wall. "The press conference will be starting soon. You think your mom's really okay with us not being there?"

Since the media circus surrounding them hadn't yet died down, they'd elected not to attend the announcement, thereby not risking the moment being taken away from his mother.

He nodded. "I talked to her earlier today. She's thrilled we've done so much hiding this last week. She's never been one for the kind of media coverage we've been pulling in lately."

Vega sighed. "I know. I feel bad about that."

"Nothing you can do about it, babe. It was her stirring up a private investigator that got Greta on your trail to begin with."

Greta apparently had had more than one iron in the fire, all with the same goal. She'd wanted to be in the limelight. If she couldn't do that by catching someone at the center of attention, she'd been willing to settle for plan B. She'd been sleeping with the PI on the hopes of riding the fast track to hot information when it came, and it had finally paid off.

"I'm still not sure you should blame all of that on your mom. I modeled with Greta one time, years ago. I'm thinking she might have already been onto me."

"Maybe." He gave her a quick kiss and turned to the TV. "However it happened, I'm over it. We're both living the lives we want now. I'm willing to let it go because I have you."

She grinned, loving the man he was. "Me too."

The news station tuned into the group congregated at the governor's mansion. Governor Chandler and Emma both stood in the middle of the wide porch, with Cat, Becca, and Tyler all on one side.

"I feel like we should be there," she whispered.

"Shh. We're on our honeymoon. We should be exactly where we are."

"We are not on our honeymoon. We aren't even married yet."

"We will be soon. And since we likely won't get to take a proper honeymoon due to your new job, I'm calling this week our honeymoon." He turned to her, mischief playing in his eyes. "Did I forget to mention that? I also plan to get you pregnant before the week is over. We have four kids to work on, you know."

He'd brought up four kids more than once now, and though she acted every time as if it would be punishment, she honestly couldn't think of anything she wanted more. Other than her upcoming children's father.

"You planning to travel with me to take care of the baby in nine months? You know I want to get my new career going."

With the contacts she'd made over the year, and a bit of help from Bob, she'd secured a freelance job doing exactly what she wanted—special interest stories—and the best part was that JP did plan to travel with her at times. He wanted to be active with the start-up of his new program. Where their schedules worked, he would be right there by her side.

"I guess if that's what I have to do, then that's what I'll do."

"With your company, my job, your program, kids . . . you sure we're ready for all this?"

His arm bunched around her, holding her tight and close. "I'm ready for everything, sweetheart. As long as you're by my side."

Governor Chandler's voice got their attention and they turned back to the screen, JP rising wordlessly from the bed to stand several feet from the picture as if he were there himself. She did feel bad that they had to miss the announcement.

"I'd like to thank everyone for coming out tonight," the governor began.

In the span of a few minutes, Emma was instituted as the next Georgia senator and had brought Becca, Tyler, and Cat up to the podium to stand with her as she made a short speech.

The two children were suddenly bringing in as much media time as the rest of them, but she supposed they might as well get used to it. Seemed you couldn't be a part of the Davenports without having your share of attention.

Wanting her fiancé's attention to return to *her*, and knowing they had the press conference recording in the other room for later viewing, Vega pointed the remote at the wall and the picture went black.

"Hey," JP said, reaching for the remote and snapping the television back on. "I was still watching that."

"Yeah?"

She slid low and stretched out on the bed beneath her. She then trailed her fingers over her abdomen. "I'm pretty sure you want to get back in here with me instead."

His gaze caught on her fingers, then crawled up to her eyes. "What are you doing?"

"Trying to seduce you back to our bed."

He glanced at the remote, then briefly back to the TV. "I was..."

She brought her other hand to her mouth and he grew quiet. She licked her fingertip and rolled it over the tip of her breast, beading the nipple between her fingers. "I've got something I want to show you."

JP glanced once more at the screen, but she could tell from his glazed expression that he was no longer thinking about Emma or Cat—or any person other than her.

"You've got a good point," he said. In slow motion, he turned to her, snapped off the press conference . . . and then he dove head-first under the covers.

ACKNOWLEDGMENTS

As with most books, this one did not happen alone. I wrote it alone, yes. Many, many hours alone. Yet it didn't come together without the help of many friends. Without all of you, this book could never be what it is today.

I'd like to thank Chuck Henry and Robert Dillingham first of all, for the speed plotting session at Calypso Café. Many changes happened from the initial plot to the final one, but without you, this book would not have happened at all. You guys are the best. Thank you.

To David Lynn for spending a wonderful lunch with me answering all my questions about dyslexia, and even the ones I didn't think to ask. Thanks to you I was able to figure out just who JP is.

And of course, to my wonderful brainstorming group: Trish Milburn, Lara Hansen, and Gretchen Stull. Not only did you help steer me in the right path along the way, but you gave me the press conference scene. For that alone, I bow down to your excellence. This book could not have ended any other way, and I simply couldn't have gotten there without you.

Additional people who helped are all the writers who joined us during the first annual Ruby-Slippered Sisterhood's Winter Writing Festival. Not only were you guys excellent when I needed a quick idea or just pure motivation to keep going, but I finished this book with you. It is my greatest pleasure that this is my debut novel, as I had so many friends writing with me along the way.

To Susan Carlisle. I absolutely could not have gotten the edits turned around so fast without you and your family's cabin. Thank you so much for bringing me into the group!

And last, to my wonderful agent and editor. To Jill Marsal for taking a chance on me and finding the perfect home for this book. And to Kelli Martin for loving JP and Vega as much as I do and helping me make this book the best it can be. You made the publishing experience a true pleasure. I could not have seen this dream realized without either of you and am so glad to have you both in my corner.

ABOUT THE AUTHOR

Photography by Amelia Moore

As a child, Kim Law cultivated a love for chocolate, anything purple, and creative writing. She penned her debut work, "The Gigantic Talking Raisin," in the sixth grade and got hooked on the delights of creating stories. Before settling into the writing life, however, she earned a college degree in mathematics, then worked as a computer programmer while raising her son. Now she's pursuing her lifelong dream of writing romance novels—none of which include talking raisins.

A native of Kentucky, Kim now resides in Middle Tennessee. You can visit Kim at www.KimLaw.com.

Sign up for Kim's newsletter at:
www.kimlaw.com/newsletter-sign-up

To know when Kim's next book releases, follow her at any
of the following:

- facebook.com/kimlawauthor
- tiktok.com/@kimlawauthor
- instagram.com/kimlawauthor
- bookbub.com/authors/kim-law
- goodreads.com/kimlaw
- amazon.com/Kim-Law/e/B008Y5AAVM

Made in the USA
Columbia, SC
21 September 2023

23163942R10252